D1094116

Second
Wife

Acknowledgment is gratefully made to Norma Millay Ellis for her permission to quote from the poem "My Heart, Being Hungry" by Edna St. Vincent Millay. (*Collected Poems,* Harper & Brothers, copyright 1923-1951 by Edna St. Vincent Millay and Norma Millay Ellis.)

Second Wife

Lewis Meyer

PRENTICE-HALL, INC.
Englewood Cliffs, N.J.

For Natasha

You picked up this book on the sheerest whim.
Did the title catch your eye? or the color of the dust
jacket? or perhaps you know a second wife?
You told the bookseller you were just browsing
and she nodded at you and went on working with her
papers.

Ask her about it. (Her name must be Hazel Watts.
That's the name of the store and she acts like the
owner.) Maybe she'll level with you.

"This one any good? I don't mean good and
literary—I mean good. Good reading. You know."

Hazel puts down her paper work, walks toward
you as she would to an old friend (you are no longer
a promiscuous browser—you've shown interest), smiles
big and says," . . .

1

JOHN LONG slept naked in the bedroom of his eighteenth floor apartment. His light blonde hair was matted in clumps of damp curls, and he lay at a crazy angle, with his face nestled close to the open window.

His wife, Ann, lying by his side, was neither awake enough to be aware of her indelicate, spread-eagle position nor asleep enough to be oblivious to the hair that clung to her neck and the discomfort of her sticky gown. She opened her eyes and saw his long back stretching toward the window, his neck and shoulders glistening with sweat, droplets of it rolling lazily down the small of his back to the bare rump. Her eyes closed quickly as she rehearsed her "good morning" words to him. "You're crazy, John Long—just plain crazy to reject the coolness of an air-conditioned apartment which you pay for to sleep with the bedroom window open in July." She opened her eyes again. How could he sleep so soundly with the morning sun full on his face?

A lukewarm breeze from the East River came into the bedroom, but it was not enough for two. If we're this warm up here, she thought, it must be murderous below. July in the city. Hot. Streets and sidewalks stoking the furnace of Manhattan to a slow broil. Make-up streaks. Perspiration glues and heads aching. The yeast of life baking sour-tasting bread. No wonder so many turn tail and run from it, to Maine, the Vineyard, Deal, Grossinger's, or Fire Island. They take to the lakes, cavort at resorts, tramp to camps as the city's volcanic dust settles in their silent and deserted apartments.

Her just-awake voice asked hopefully, "Hey, are you up?" But John slept on. She thought, I wonder how many women have seen him like this—naked and asleep? His mother . . . probably

2

some wild oat when he was in college . . . and Madge. *Change the subject.*

Why did they stay put on summer weekends while most of their neighbors were fleeing to cooler places (where, according to the brochures, you sleep under blankets)? Because they actually enjoyed the small-town feel of Manhattan in July. They had more fun behaving as if they were summer visitors to the big city than the actual visitors did. Last night had been the kind of Saturday-on-the-town that Ann wouldn't trade for a dozen weekends away. Dinner at Leone's with too much cheese to whittle on, too much antipasto, veal scaloppini, wine, and too much crying violin. Typically tourist, and they'd loved it; then a play she'd waited weeks to see because John had been on the road and she'd wanted him to see it with her.

On the road. I remember Mama. "What does he do for a *living?*" her mother had asked, long-distance, almost before Ann could announce the name of the man she was to marry. Then: "Sells books on the *road?* You mean you're marrying a *traveling salesman?*"

She'd said, "Oh, he's a whiz at other things, too. He sells books on the road but most of the time he's in the New York office. He's young, handsome, and very important to his firm already."

"Ann, dear. Are you *sure* you're not glorifying him? After all, if he *travels* and if he *sells things* on the road he's a traveling salesman, isn't he?" And that hadn't been the first time Ann had used the operator's, "Your three minutes are up," as an excuse to get rid of Mother. Try to explain to Mother that in the book business a salesman is not a salesman; he's a traveler. Try to explain John's special setup with Laverty and Clarke.

Did John sleep naked in Nashville and Memphis? He always packed pajamas to take with him on his trips, but it hadn't occurred to her to ask him until this moment as she studied him breathing quietly here beside her. She had an absurd desire to place her index finger on the nape of his neck and trail it slowly down his moist back, but John was ticklish and that would wake him. It gave her pleasure to watch him sleep. There's no bed like home, he invariably said after every trip. He liked returning to his own bed, his own refrigerator, his own closet where clothes got to know

3

their hangers and he especially liked his own bureau, which didn't shriek, Stop! Have You Forgotten Anything? Toward the end of every trip, fall and spring, he grew restless for this apartment which he called The Estate, and now that he was home again the heat didn't faze him because he was where he liked to be.

The Estate was one corner of one floor of a twenty-four story apartment house that had barely been completed when Ann moved into it seven years ago while John was still in Korea. Mother had volunteered that she didn't like it, but Mother couldn't understand why anyone would pay for a terrace in Manhattan. Mother didn't understand why her husband had left his money outright to their daughters while tying hers up in a monthly income. But Mother didn't really like anything. Ann showed the apartment to her before the building was completed and she had complained, "One bedroom. You could have another bedroom if it weren't for that silly terrace." But Ann thought the floor plan perfect.

To the left of the foyer, as you entered, was the kitchen. Straight ahead was a large living room and to its left their bedroom, a hall, and the bath. Commonplace enough, except for the terrace you reached through the French doors of the living room. The window of the bedroom looked onto that indented patch of earth and green, a tiny, rectangular Eden on the eighteenth floor—a postage-stamp garden, John liked to say, big enough both ways to lie down in if you drew in your legs. Mother had fortunately gone to live in California before Ann moved in, leaving housewarmings exclusively to Ann and John. The first one on the night he got home from Korea, was unofficial. The second, official housewarming was a few weeks later after they were married. The Estate. That's what he'd called it the minute he saw the terrace. It had been his idea to plant petunias there the first spring—foolish little flowers that bloomed robustly, unaware of such a thing as an afternoon sun.

Again. "Are you awake?"

No answer.

She opened her eyes and wiped the perspiration from her temples, automatically looked at the clock, then stifled the reflex to punch the alarm button before it began to chatter. She hadn't set the alarm last night; this morning was for sleeping. Her friend, Bess Frankel, would drive by in her new Jaguar at noon and the

4

three of them woud go out into the country to eat. John would like that.

At the thought of food Ann closed her eyes again. It was too hot for coffee—too hot even to move. So she resumed her study of John's body. Her eyes went slowly up his long legs, then lingered a few seconds before moving on. She felt within herself the familiar response and squirmed sensuously. She wanted him again this morning. She wasn't afraid of wanting him. Still, how nearly insatiable was she? *Oh-dear-God—not like Madge!*

She turned her mind to Monday thoughts. Often, between awakening and the ringing of the alarm, she blocked out openings for radio spots. She had a gift for words and she turned out twice as much work as Irene, the other continuity writer, in half the time. She never had to reach for an attention-getting twist to a message for lawn mowers or air-conditioners. She liked being a radio writer. It was more of a challenge than TV, where the picture says it better.

She pushed the damp hair out of her eyes and indulged in her favorite wish-fulfillment dream of short hair—really short. Her hair was long enough now to wear up over her ears, but in her dream she told herself, "Cut it off—all of it except just enough to run a comb through." She never said this awake because John insisted, "I fell in love with your ears before I fell in love with you. Men like to see women's ears. Show a man a tiny ear under a piled-high upsweep and you've got him going." He liked hair on top and ears that showed so that's what she gave him. Could any woman in her right mind do less to hold a man?

She asked again, softly, "John, are you awake?"

There was still no answer, but she knew he'd heard her. "If you're awake, and just lying there like a dummy, give me a signal. *Grunt.*"

He grunted and she laughed.

"Don't act so put upon. I'm hot, too. And at least you're stripped. I'm stuck fast to this so-called summer-weight gown." She arranged her gown full length and tried to fan her knees by picking it up and dropping it rapidly, running on, "Where does wearing a nightgown get a girl, anyhow? I'd be cooler without it and be just as modest for all the audience I've got. The man, the

5

light of whose life I fancy myself, has his rear end in my face, his chin on the sill and his nose in the garden. He begrudges his loved one her fair share of the breeze."

John opened his eyes long enough to groan, "*What* breeze? So help me Hannah, tonight we close this window and the air-conditioning stays on," and signed off again.

Ann loved him like this, relaxed and easy. "I'll remind you of that at bedtime when you insist on opening the window because it's not healthy to sleep in air-conditioning."

"Well, it really isn't, you know."

She sighed. "You're really hopeless—but I guess I like you anyway. And now I know you're awake, there's something I want to say. You might call it an announcement, even a revelation."

"Shut up," John said into his pillow. "Fan my body, mop my brow, go to the bathroom for me—but don't start revealing things this early in the morning."

She danced her fingertips up and down his back. "You may not like what I announce," she said, punctuating her words with her tapping, "but I'm still going to announce it. I am going to write a novel."

"Oh, come *on*," he said. "Not you, too."

"Me, too."

"I get it everywhere I go—at the office, on the street, at parties—everyone's got a book he wants to write. Besides, it takes time."

"I've got time. I'm always on top of my work at the station, I've got a good typewriter and a quiet office and the nights are terrible when you're out of town. I get tired of gossiping evenings away with Bess, and I don't enjoy going places without you—so why should I *not* write a book?"

He yawned again. "And this, too, shall pass. You'll get over it. Maybe you're bored. Ten years of marriage and you're bored with me."

"Recheck your vital statistics, dear. We've been married barely seven years—in the eyes of the law, that is. And I'm *not* bored with you!"

"Oh, *that*," he said. "Well, anyhow we stirred up one helluva lot of dust those first three years. Agreed?"

She nodded. "It was just as much fun the first three. In fact,

6

I always felt as married to you while you were in Korea as I do right now. Remember the first year?"

He closed his eyes. *Remember? Oh . . . remember!*

He'd still been married to Madge then. He and Ann had spent one whole terrible, wonderful year dodging people, finding out-of-the-way places, avoiding mutual friends. The art of cheating. But not really cheating, he told himself, because his wife was a slut and you can't cheat on a slut. Still, when a man's married and he goes out with another woman the word is cheating, and he learns the cheater's game. The cheater must find a neutral place—not nice enough to attract his friends, not bad enough to be depressing. Huge places are out. Too much chance for the long arm of co-incidence. Small places where "everybody goes" are out, too, because atmosphere attracts the right people, who are the wrong people when you are cheating. The cheater's hideaway has to have some drawback to discourage his friends from choosing it. A jarring decor, soggy frozen French fries, too much clatter. And you have to be really in love to cheat for long in the back booth of that dreary Food Shoppe on Forty-Fourth, or in the Chinese place with the neon sign that says CHOW MEIN 75¢.

Remember the first year?

The fountain girl at Schrafft's, the hostess at Ye Food Shoppe, the Chinese boy at the CHOW MEIN 75¢ place knew that Ann and John were lovers as well as they knew that iced tea was a dime extra. Cheaters find allies in their secret spots and these allies protect them. You can't fool a hotel chambermaid by mussing up a bed that hasn't been slept in and you can't fool a waiter, either. Not when he sees you and your love together, day after day. These people know, and do not disapprove.

The art of cheating. There is a way to walk into a restaurant. Togetherness in reverse, with him three or four steps ahead of her. He puts his hand over his face to remove his hat, only he doesn't complete the gesture until he's cased the place. This feint conceals his features for the split second necessary for his experienced cheater-eyes to scrutinize the diners in the room. It is more than just good vision and timing. There is a third factor—an urgent something akin to the will to survive—that enables a man to do it well.

7

Once, he'd been careless. (You never hear about the cheaters who aren't careless!) He'd taken Ann to Luchow's for lunch and spotted Bill Haley of Fortune House the minute he walked in. Bill was intently buttering his bread, his head bent down, when John turned and almost knocked Ann off her feet, brushing past her toward the ancient swinging doors as he whispered: "Food Shoppe!" And without even knowing who John was avoiding Ann went to the ladies' room, waited a moment, then walked out of the restaurant and took a cab to join him in the back booth of the Food Shoppe.

"Sorry, sweet. I saw Bill Haley in there. He's a book traveler and he sells Madge at Troxell's."

"You don't have to explain," Ann said, touching his hand. Still, she'd been depressed for a few days afterward. "When we're married," she used to say, "and we walk into a place, I don't care if it's the Automat or Chambord, I'm going to stand up and scream, 'Here we are, folks! Ann and John! We love each other and we've come here to eat! Any objections?'" Meanwhile, they had to play their edgy game. The cheater must be cautious and patient; and until he can quit the game he must pay the price. John Long was an expert on the high cost of cheating.

Ann had thought he'd dozed off. Now she shook him gently and said, "You still haven't said you approve—about the book, I mean."

"I approve," he said, "but you're too young for it. You'll have to live a little more."

"*Young* for it? I'm thirty-three. Look at those eighteen- and nineteen-year-olds who're writing."

"Writing? You mean scribbling. When an otherwise healthy female announces before breakfast that she's going to write a novel, she's either getting over a love affair or getting ready for hormone shots."

She started to roll over and hit him, but thought better of it, knowing if she touched him now he would grab her, and she'd let him grab her and—not now. She wanted to know more about his reaction to her book, so she said, helplessly, "You're *mean!*"

He turned to her smiling and reached out his hand. She let it stay where he placed it. As they lay quietly together for a moment

8

John thought, perhaps Ann *could* write a book. She was original and tenacious and she knew how to string words together, but some people go haywire when they try to write books. Even original, tenacious people. There wasn't an author on his spring list who had Ann's way with words, but that of course was damning with faint praise. He'd never seen so many duds on any list: a superficial war experience report, a novel about a drug addict called, of all things, *The Fixers,* two books on space travel—stuff like that. His mind flashed an instant, vivid image of Hazel Watts, his best account in Dallas. Hazel had refused to order more than the merest representation of any title on his list. Personal contact with booksellers was vital to anyone who wanted an honest grasp of the publishing business. His twice-a-year selling trips to cities from Miami to San Antonio told him what readers wanted. Keeping his accounts in the field while working in the home office gave him an advantage, salary-wise, and prestige-wise, too. Some day he'd take Ann with him on the road. Let her meet the girls. He wondered if she'd like Hazel Watts as much as he did—and Doodles Lee in Memphis and all the others. By golly, he'd be proud to show off Ann to all of them.

Suddenly he had a pinched feeling that made him sweat more freely. He saw himself standing in Hazel Watts' Personal Book Shop in Dallas pointing to a novel in his advance catalog and saying, "Here's something you're going to love. It's got everything: action, sex, good writing. Take my word for it and buy fifty." Hazel would say, *"Fifty?* Of a first novel? Who's the author?" And he'd say, "Ann Long." Hazel wouldn't get the connection right off and she'd ask, "Relative of yours?" and he'd say, "My wife. I've told you about Ann." Hazel would assure him that she wanted to do what she could for Ann's book, but *fifty copies.* No telling what Hazel would say . . .

"Honey," John wheedled, "you could do me an awful big favor."

"What?"

"Bring me some ice-cold orange juice. Ice-cold."

"That's easy."

She kissed him, got out of bed and pulled her damp gown away from her skin. The moment she opened the bedroom door and stepped into the hall she wondered why she hadn't acted sooner.

9

"Turn on the air-conditioning," she called to John. The bathroom seemed icy cold by contrast to the bedroom. When she got to the kitchen she stood for a few seconds in front of the open refrigerator. The beginning of a radio spot went through her mind: "Have you ever tried to keep cool by standing in front of an open refrigerator? Well, here's an easier way. *Tastier*, too. Just pour . . ."

She poured John a tall tumbler full of orange juice, a smaller glass for herself, put the bottle back into the refrigerator, and picked up the Sunday *Times* from the hall before she carried the glasses back to the bedroom, leaving the door to the hall ajar. John had opened the vent and closed the window and the bedroom was already almost pleasant. He forgot wanting orange juice when he saw the *Times*. He flipped through the folded paper until he found the sports section, pulled it out and started reading scores. She almost chose Theater but took Books instead, turning the pages quickly to see what was reviewed; then John saw her fold the magazine section to the crossword puzzle and he grabbed the paper, saying firmly, "Oh, no you don't! If you start working a puzzle now you won't be good for a damn thing the rest of the morning."

"Really?" Ann smiled, "I haven't the faintest idea what you mean, understanding precisely what he meant. Then, to change the subject, "Drink your orange juice, you certainly wanted it bad enough. And now, what is your pleasure next, my lord? Should I peel you a grape? You command and I obey, but not forever, I warn you. Some day this worm will turn. Your ever-lovin' will grab the cool side of this bed and you will go for a form of refreshment that will not be orange juice. It will be Napoleon brandy because I will be the author of a best-seller entering its nine hundred and ninety-eight thousandth copy."

"Take off that nightgown, Jane Austen. Here come the photographers and the press."

"Shut up," Ann said, pulling her gown down as far as it would go, "and be decent enough to pull that sheet over part of yourself."

"What part?"

"*That* part."

"Go to hell," he said, turning on his side with his face to the window and his shoulder bathed in the single shaft of sunlight

10

that cut into the room. "Thanks for the orange juice, dear—but go to hell, anyway."

Slowly, John rolled over until he faced her. He wanted terribly to kiss her and he did, and then each of them wanted more.

If he heard the telephone, it made no impression on him.

"The telephone," Ann said after the third ring.

"The hell with it!"

"That's five times," she murmured. "Bess always counts ten and hangs up—and when she hangs up this morning there goes our drive to the country in her new car."

He got up from the bed and walked self-consciously to the telephone. She smiled as she watched him. Can I put *this* into a book and make it real? she thought, this wonderful feeling I have for him right now?

"Swell, Bess, swell," John said. "We'll be ready in an hour." He looked at Ann, and, feeling just as he had felt ten years ago when he first saw her in the advertising office of Troxell Brothers, he said, "Uh, better make that an hour and a half, Bess. OK? Goodbye."

He stood by the phone for a second and smiled across to his wife. He looked taller than he was, because now he was wholly male and wholly alive. As he made his way across the room to her, Ann forgot to make a mental note on a good way to end her first chapter.

As they breezed along the Merritt Parkway, Bess in the rear seat leaned forward and said to John, "I know I'm not the Jaguar type but it *does* something for me. Mama and Papa say I'm crazy for not getting another Oldsmobile."

"I like the way it handles," John answered, "and the thrill it gives you." Then, because he wanted Bess to continue carrying the conversational ball, he asked a question she'd be sure to answer. "What does *he* think of it? You know who I mean. Dr. What's-His-Name . . . ?"

"Dr. Darnell," Bess answered. Dr. Darnell was Bess's psychiatrist. "Dr. Darnell says I've done the right thing in buying a sports car. I think it pleases him when I make any decision that's unpopular with my family. I'll bet Dr. Darnell would say there's a

11

psychological reason why so many people are buying small cars. Have you ever watched the faces of drivers of Fiats and Volkswagens? They have such *secure* expressions."

Ann, in the bucket seat next to John, detected the merest sort of smile on his face, mostly around the corners of his eyes, as Bess talked on. He was amused at Bess's obvious dependence on Dr. Darnell for explaining her emotions and motivations, while she was a thoroughly independent girl in other respects. He'd heard her expound on Dr. Darnell-inspired theories before. As soon as Bess used the word "secure," John was certain that "womb" would not be far behind.

"I think Dr. Darnell would say the compactness of these cars serves as a sublimated return to the womb. Most people's basic sense of insecurity subconsciously drives them to return to the womb. When I get inside my Jaguar I do feel more secure than I ever did in the Olds. How does it make you feel?"

He suppressed a laugh. "The thought of returning to the womb cramps my style a little. Does Dr. Darnell drive a small, *secure* car?"

"No," Bess replied almost apologetically, "Dr. Darnell drives a Mercedes Benz."

There was nothing wrong with Bess Frankel that being an orphan wouldn't cure. It was one of John's favorite subjects when he and Ann were alone. "How an otherwise intelligent person—and Bess *is* intelligent—can let stupid parents gum up her life is more than I can understand. No wonder she thinks she needs a psychiatrist."

"There's a lot of my mother in Bess's parents," Ann reminded him.

"Yes, but you stood up to your mother."

She'd had her sister Birdie to thank for that. Birdie married Abe Zelkin and moved to California. Mother's reaction was typical. "*Zelkin!* Couldn't he *change* it? Other Jews do." She mellowed considerably when Abe Zelkin suggested a fantastic monthly allowance for her, and descended on California where she could watch over Birdie and keep her from being too happy.

12

"Mother got out of my hair," Ann said. "Bess's parents are in her's morning, noon and night."

"Poor little rich girl."

"Exactly. They give her too much to spend—and yet make her so dependent on them it's almost impossible for her to break away. They've always resented our friendship. They think I'm a dangerous influence. They're positive it was I who got her to go into analysis."

"Was it?"

"Not really. Dr. Darnell was Bess's own idea. She took a lot of psychology courses in college and she reads a lot on the subject. She's smart enough to see that something's wrong. When she asked me what I thought about her going to a psychiatrist I did tell her I thought she'd made a wise decision, but it was her idea."

Ann remembered something now that Bess had once said. "My parents are the kind of rich people who love to say, with tears in their eyes, that money isn't everything." How right Bess had been. The Frankels reeked of money. Their enormous duplex on Park Avenue; their cars and servants; their endless spending, where it showed. They endowed their children with too much of everything. Bess had always been overstuffed, overdressed, overindulged, overpossessed. When she was 23, she'd fallen in love with a boy who was not Jewish. Her mother got shingles; her father developed a heart condition; even her brother turned on her. So Bess surrendered her gentile sweetheart, went with her parents on a grueling trip around the world, and began to compound her resentments. Since her brother's marriage (strictly kosher), Bess had received her parents' undivided smothering. She was thirty-two-years-old now, yet she was still their baby girl. They had the power of convincing her, as so many parents can, that she would be lost without them.

Ann and Bess had been "best friends" in the truest sense since their freshman year at Barnard. While they came from totally different backgrounds they had much in common. To begin with, each was at Barnard in defiance of her family (Ann's mother had chosen a state university in the Midwest, the Frankels had insisted on Brandeis) and Ann had discovered in Bess a naively honest, utterly loyal person who had never really had a friend. Ann's

13

mother resented the friendship because Bess was Jewish; the Frankels tried to discourage the friendship because Ann wasn't. Later, when Bess's romance was skewered by her parents, Ann—who hardly knew the boy since she was too busy falling in love with John at the time—received most of the blame.

Back in those days John and Ann saw their share of friends and attended their share of parties, but they preferred being alone with each other. Often it was John's idea to call Bess to spend the evening with them and he'd say, "Bess is family. She's like my sister. Darn it, it's too bad I feel so brotherly toward her. I might (with your permission, of course!) give her a little of what she needs!" John had said a dozen times that most of Bess's problems could be solved by a red-hot love affair, with or without the love. That would beat those prescriptions of hers all to pieces. But to Ann, Bess's problem wasn't that easily solved. She saw in Bess Frankel buried depths which, if exposed could make her an exciting person. Bess was more than just comfortable to be with; she was attractive. She wore her hair in a French roll to make herself feel more secure, and she looked immaculate (but never chic) in expensive tailored clothes. With judicious Metrecal-ing, she could be downright striking. But in order to make the real break from the Frankels' influence—to rid herself of the Old Maid tag they'd pinned on her—Bess needed help. Dr. Darnell had his work cut out for him.

2

THE trouble with Sunday is Monday morning. The alarm caught Ann asleep. Any other morning she beat it to the draw. Today, with John privileged to sleep late, she had overslept. He started at the sound, rolled over on his back and went to sleep again. Ann care-

14

fully pulled the sheet over him, thinking, it's cooler today than yesterday, thank heavens.

She felt good, and that was the proper way to begin the day after Sunday. Yesterday had been wonderful. As she stepped into the shower, she promised herself that she would put plenty of oomph in her commercials if the Jaguar people ever bought spots on the station. She even composed a few phrases just for the fun of it.

Ann decided to have coffee in the office building luncheonette rather than rattle dishes while John slept. A half-day's grace from work was a rare and precious thing for him, and this was his way of enjoying it. Before closing the door of the apartment she sent him a kiss across the room, and went out, thinking, anyone can throw a kiss when she knows it'll be caught, but to toss it with all one's skill at a sleeping husband, that's pure, foolish love.

Love? she thought. And what is love in July in New York? It's when a girl takes a crowded Second Avenue bus to Forty-Second Street, walks those long crosstown blocks toward Fifth in the morning traffic, passes the luncheonette where she almost forgets to go in for coffee, gets off the elevator at WOOZ, and ends up at her desk without ever really having left Apartment 18-C. That's love —and I love him and hope he is still sound asleep.

The nicest thing about her work—about radio in general and WOOZ in particular—was her boss, Harry Shell. "Don't call me boss," Harry reminded her constantly. "Boss is a dirty word to me. I've had too many."

"But you *are* my—"

"No!" Harry'd say. "Not boss. I'm just not the boss type. To begin with, I've a happy home life and the average boss gripes all day about that. My Hope likes you, but a boss's wife would be jealous as hell because you're pretty even in the morning. Besides, you've got money of your own, you don't have to work, and I'm always overspent and will probably touch you for twenty-five bucks before payday. Also, you're smarter than I am." Before Ann could protest he'd add emphatically, "Yes you are, and you know it."

Harry Shell was a radio veteran, meaning that he'd been through a kind of electronic hell. He'd talk your arm off if you'd listen, and sometimes even if you didn't. His slight, frail, frayed-around-the-

15

edges look and his pale eyes might make a stranger think Harry was wishy-washy, but he wasn't. Harry was tough. Any man who could survive four sets of station-owners and twice that many policy changes had to be. Harry had been everything—errand boy, salesman, bookkeeper, traffic manager, announcer, public relations head, station manager and program director—though not necessarily in that order. "I have really been dead for years," Harry would say, "ever since we gave up the network . . . Why, I remember when we were Winchell's New York outlet on his Sunday night show. And *everybody* used to listen to Winchell—and Burns and Allen, and Kate Smith, and Edgar Bergen. How they used to fight for tickets to those radio shows! Hell—I remember when Lux Radio Theatre had a bigger following than *any*thing TV's got to offer. *TV—!*" Harry would snort when he said it. "Why, TV'll never be what radio was. Just ask somebody who remembers when the whole nation went crazy trying to guess Miss Hush, and flipped when she turned out to be Clara Bow!"

Ann knew the whole story by heart. How Harry died again and again every time the station changed its face—from all-classical to all-jazz to radio-preachers to rock-'n-roll around the clock. "Oh, God!" Harry would moan, running his hand through his thinning hair. "I still wake up screaming when I dream about rock-'n-roll! That was the worst. Absolutely the worst."

But now radio, after its knockdown by television, was definitely coming back and Harry had been among the first to know. But it would never be the way it was. It was streamlined now, almost to the point of automation. At night, one man served as announcer, engineer, music librarian, programmer, and telephone answerer. A few years ago Harry would have said this couldn't be done, but now, with radio's recovery from its nervous breakdown, Harry Shell's patience and tough stamina were paying off. He was slowly changing the colorless record-commercial-spot-news-on-the-hour format to variety programming, the way it used to be: sports events, news commentaries, music shows built around themes, personality interviews. The last Hooper ratings were excellent. And WOOZ was being referred to as King of the Independents.

Ann treasured a sharp and clear image of Harry Shell. It had nothing to do with his yakking about old times, nor his pummeling

16

by and his fierce defiance of TV. It was a memory of something that had happened last spring when Harry'd reinstated high-school day on the station.

One of the students who was dabbling at dee-jaying cornered Harry between records and ad-libbed earnestly, "What is your philosophy of life, Mr. Shell?" Ann, hearing the question on the monitor in her office, stopped dead to listen to Harry's answer. To his credit, he hadn't hesitated. The student, and listeners in five boroughs, had heard Harry say, "My philosophy of life can be summed up in just six words." He paused only long enough for the housewife, the driver of the car, the teen-ager, the hospital patient to switch over from half-hearing to actual listening, and then he spoke those six words: "When in doubt, play *Deep Purple*."

That was Harry Shell, bless his heart. He was Ann's boss—and a good one.

But despite radio's metamorphosis, the spot announcements, its life blood, were pretty much the same as they used to be and you had to have the knack for them. They still had to be original and ear-catching. A new trend in commercials had begun with the great crash campaigns known as saturations: sixty or more spots every day for the same sponsor, repeated over and over, for impact. Sometimes agencies sent over copy that could be used over the air without major editing; sometimes the spots came to the station already transcribed or taped; but most of the commercials had to be written on the premises, and that was where Ann and her assistant, Irene, came in: they were WOOZ's continuity department.

"Annie, dear," Harry began this morning.

That was his pet name for her. She liked it when he called her Annie, but when he started the day with it, and tacked on the dear, it meant that something had gone wrong and the boss needed help.

He was saying, "We begin this summer day with—to coin a phrase—a problem. Old Jonesy at Troxell's is unhappy with our sport shirt commercials having heard an announcer stumble through one while he was driving to work this morning. So I told him our super-duper Troxell graduate would doctor them up immediately—and that means you can start ten minutes ago."

Ann had heard the announcer gumshoeing through the booby-

17

trap of "short sleeved sports shirts" and had expected a complaint. "Why *can't* we teach Irene to write copy that's speakable?" Harry asked.

"Irene's all right," Ann said firmly. "She just vibrates better to storm windows than to sport shirts. I'll do them over for you—if you promise not to say anything to Irene about it."

Harry sighed. "That's payola, but I promise. Get busy and give 'em the magic touch and I'll call Jonesy and tell him to listen."

Ann darted through the phrases of copy like a shuttle through a loom.

"Have you ever tried to keep cool by standing in front of an open refrigerator?" No flight of fancy, however slight, is wasted when you write for a living. "Well, here's an easier way—if you're a man who likes to *look* cool as well as *feel* cool. Troxell Brothers has a special sale of sport shirts today and tomorrow. Special summer weaves, many white-on-white patterns, and *all* with cool, cool short sleeves! The price? *It's* cool, too. Only—"

The mind, Ann thought, is like a PBX switchboard, honeycombed with holes which form connections for the taking and sending of messages when you plug into them. Only on my board one connection is plugged into a line that sends words about sport shirts whizzing through my fingers onto the paper in this typewriter.

Each time she typed the name Troxell Brothers she set up another connection—one which had nothing to do with sport shirts. It was a memory circuit that recalled a tiny scissors-and-paste office in the advertising department of Troxell Brothers where John Long had kissed her neck every time he leaned over to point out a copy change.

Another line plugged into a conversation a long time ago.

"Are you crying because of something I've said, Ann?"

"No, darling. I'm crying because I'm still my mother's daughter, damn it all. All Mother'd see about you and me is that you have a wife and I'm sleeping with you and that makes me a wicked woman."

"Are you sorry?"

"Only that I'm my mother's daughter. I'm deliriously happy to be your lover or mistress or paramour—or whatever Mother'd call me."

18

"You're my wife, Ann. You're the only wife I've got. Madge and I haven't got a marriage. It never was one—even before I caught on to her sleeping around. Everything about her, every move Madge made was Sex. She even had a sexy voice. It was lust on my part—"

"And on her's?"

"I don't know. I never could figure out why she married me. She was trying to prove something, I think, but I never knew what. When we're married, Ann, you'll be the only wife I've ever had."

"I love you, John."

"Ahhhh, that's the way I like to hear my girl talk."

Sport shirts . . . Troxell's . . . John . . . Lust . . . Madge . . . There was a place on the switchboard where Ann's mind could plug in Madge's number, but she avoided it. She sometimes made the contact and actually pressed the ring button, but she quickly broke the connection. The operator in Ann's brain would ask, Why don't you talk to her? What are you afraid of? And then John's words would reappear like a light on the board, "It was just lust on my part." Was it only lust that had kept him married to Madge in spite of her infidelities? Ann wanted to believe that, but she couldn't help wondering what else besides lust had made him stick.

The spots were finished now and Harry was already fitting them into the day's spot schedule. Ann sat quietly at her desk. The operator in her mind had pulled out all the plugs on the switchboard—except the one to Madge's number. That one kept blinking and blinking. And suddenly she knew she must do something. She must go to Troxell Brothers today and see Madge. She remembered that Bess Frankel had an appointment with her doctor at three. She'd ask Bess to meet her at two.

"Have you lost your mind?" Bess asked incredulously when Ann suggested that they meet in Troxell's book department.

"No. There comes a time in every second wife's life when she wants to confront the first wife—even for a minute."

"You're a plain damned fool, Ann. Why don't you let well enough alone?"

"Will you or won't you meet me in the book department of Troxell Brothers at two o'clock?"

19

"Oh, hell. I'll be there."

Ann left the sizzling sidewalk for the revolving door that whirled her into the cool, high-ceilinged maelstrom of Troxell's. She felt like a criminal returning to the scene of the crime.

Ten years ago she'd come here every day, but not through this door. Then she'd entered from Forty-fourth Street before the store was open, and taken the express elevator past all the selling floors to nine where the executives had their large offices and the advertising department their tiny cubicles. Here she spent her days writing ad copy, being in love with John—and despising Madge Long, manager of the Troxell book department and John's wife.

Still shocked by the transition from hot to cold, Ann picked her way through the noisy, confused street floor. She felt an unpleasant nostalgia as the elevator ascended fitfully, its operator droning the wonders of each floor. When she heard the girl chant, "Seh-vun: children's wear-luggage-gift-wrapping-ladies'-lounge-restrooms-and-books!" she stepped out and looked around for her victim.

The book department still sprawled over most of the far end of seven, merging into the ladies'-lounge-rest-rooms. A planning engineer undoubtedly designed this juxtaposition. All the rest-room traffic had to thread its way through tables stacked with books to reach its journey's end. Madge called this impulse buying and for years she had made questionable jokes about her department's location. She actually arranged the books psychologically. "I make them go through inspiration and self-help on their way in; then, children's books on their way out." Ann used to smile when John told things like that about Madge. Once she'd said, "She's really clever, John. She knows how to give people a good time." "You can say that again, Sis," he'd answered grimly. "Madge sure knows how to give people a good time."

Ann paused a moment to steady herself. She stood near a table stacked high with boys' jeans and stroked the rough-textured, dark blue material with her fingertips.

A salesgirl, poised to pounce the minute a customer vacillated, asked, "May I help you, please?" Ann answered mechanically, "No, no. I'm just looking," and remembered there'd been a time when she shared the disdain all department store employees had

20

for customers who murmur, "No, thank you, I'm just looking." Looking for what, how, where? And now she was intoning the gibberish herself, "I'm just looking."

Looking, yes. Looking for Madge—who didn't have a chance this time.

Ann knew what Madge looked like. Soon after she and John had fallen in love she became obsessed with the desire to hear Madge's voice. John had called it a sexy voice and she wanted to know what a sexy voice sounded like. One day she decided to find out; she wore a hat to work and went to the book department during her lunch hour. She recognized Madge, from John's description, talking to a man and squeezing his arm. Really squeezing it hard. Ann thought the gesture vulgar and, in that first glimpse, sized Madge up as common. She could not understand what John had seen in this stringy, plain-looking girl with the shiny too-long nose and the coarse too-loud voice. He'd always insisted that Madge had married him, but he couldn't get off that easily because he had married her, too.

And then as Ann browsed among the books, she heard Madge talking and laughing. She altered her first impression as she sensed a certain magnetism, a charm which could be explained only in terms of being near the woman—seeing her, hearing her, feeling her personality.

After the man had gone Madge walked over to Ann, smiling at her, and it was a good smile. "Any particular book you'd like to see?"

Ann had felt cheap. Instead of gloating, she was ashamed of her unfair advantage. Without quite knowing why, she'd asked Madge, "Do you have a copy of *The Big Fisherman?*" The name came to her suddenly because everyone was reading it then.

"Why, yes. Right here," Madge had said, finding the book. And then, so effortlessly that surely it was a sudden impulse, she picked up another book from a nearby stack and showed it to Ann. "Have you seen this one?" Ann shook her head. "I recommend it highly. It's called *Light from Many Lamps* and it's a wonderful collection of famous inspirational quotations. Not sticky—really worthwhile. I keep a copy on my bedside table and read it often."

"I'll take them both."

21

"Cash or charge?" Madge had asked.

"Cash," Ann had said, not wanting Madge to know that she worked in the store. "Cash."

Now here she was again . . . on the seventh floor . . . ten years later. Only now the stakes weren't so high. John belonged to her. No squatter's rights. She had a legal claim on him.

She wanted to turn back and if she hadn't told Bess she'd meet her in the book department she certainly would turn back. Instead, she walked slowly through the department, glanced at the Modern Library books, lingered over the cookbooks, and she had just reached the "new fiction" table when a voice said, "May I help you, please?"

Without looking up she knew that it wasn't Madge's voice. There was no urgency in it, no—face it, nothing sexy. Ann looked up at a short, thick girl with horn rims that covered half her face, professionally pleasant, asking, "Did you have any special book in mind?"

"Uh . . . no. I'm—," She'd be damned if she'd say she was just looking, "I'm waiting to meet a friend. Uh, I don't get up here as often as I used to, but I remember there was a Miss—uh—the tall girl. I *believe* she was the manager." (*Oh-dear-God-please-don't-let-her-say*, "She's in her office. I'll go get her!")

"You mean Madge King? She's not here any more. She left the store right after T. Harold—" The girl caught herself, quickly, "after the store manager died."

"Left the store?"

"Yes. She's been gone more than a year now . . . That's a good book. Have you read it?"

Ann's hand rested on *Hawaii*. She had read it, but she said, "No, I haven't read it and I've been meaning to. I'll take it."

"Cash or charge?"

History repeated itself. "Cash."

Ann took her change, saw Bess coming, and rushed to meet her.

"We can go now," she said to Bess. "Mission accomplished."

"But I thought I'd go to the rest-room while I was here," Bess protested.

"Go later, Bess. *Please.* I want to get out of this store. I feel—dirty."

22

They were seated in Schrafft's before Bess asked, "Well?" "She doesn't work there any more. She's gone." "Serves you right." "I bought a book, though. *Hawaii.*" "You've read that." "Yes. I still don't know why I bought it. Guilt, maybe. Or relief. I never thought Madge would leave the store. Maybe she had to."

"I shouldn't wonder," Bess agreed. "I'm sure everybody in Troxell's knew what was going on between her and that store executive." She started to speak, thought better of it, then decided to go ahead. "Ann, I want to say something—personal. But I don't want to hurt you."

Ann looked up from the fruit plate she had ordered but somehow couldn't eat. "What could you possibly say that would hurt me, Bess?"

"Well . . . I've been thinking about your compulsion to come to Troxell's to see your husband's first wife. Compulsions can be dangerous things. Why *today*—after all this time? There must be a reason, and, well, I just wish you'd talk with Dr. Darnell."

Ann smiled. "D'ya mean I should be psychoanalzyed? I haven't the money, for one thing."

"No. But I think it would help you just to talk to him a few times. And I know he'd see you if I asked him to. You see, I don't want you—" Bess stopped, not knowing how to finish.

"You don't want me doing goofy things like this every day?" Ann reached out her hand to her friend. She was glad it had stopped shaking. "I think I'm all right. Now that it's over, I'm glad it happened. But I'll make you a promise. If I keep on acting oddbod you can book me with Darnell. Meanwhile, I've got to get back to the station. I'll call you tonight when I get home."

"How can you work?" Bess asked with concern. "You've not eaten a thing." She looked guiltily at her own plate where an eclair had been. "Mama says I gain weight because I eat from nervousness." Ann thought to herself that when it came to dieting Bess was like the sinner who tries to reform but enjoys the lapses.

Bess looked at her watch. "It's almost time for my appointment. Honestly—he could help you, Ann."

23

Ann got up from the table and, with a graceful motion of her free hand, arranged the pleats in her skirt. Its fullness accentuated her slender waistline. "A good psychiatrist can help anybody," she said.

"Sure you're not mad at me for suggesting it?"

"Of course not!"

They walked toward the cashier. Ann looked up to see the hostess charging at her. "You left your package, madam."

"Oh, thank you," she said, taking the copy of *Hawaii*.

She looked hopefully at Bess, who was holding the door open.

"No, thanks," Bess said. "I lent you my copy six months ago. Remember?"

3

ANN ran her index finger along the shiny black keys of the typewriter. Her red fingernail journeyed from row to row, idling back and forth, stroking the letters. From these lifeless, metal keys she hoped to make a book of living people. She counted the keys. Forty-two, including the fractions and the asterisk. How many times must she touch each one to produce a novel? How many h's, for example, does a person need for a book? How many j's? How many y's? These cool, black keys were old friends. Every day she touched them hundreds of times as she wrote spot announcements. Only that wasn't called writing. Where spots were concerned, you knocked, pounded, and sweated them out. But a book you wrote. She felt the keys in a new way—as though for the first time; much as a blind person runs his fingertips across the features of someone he meets and wants to remember. Whatever she wrote—good or bad—would come from these smooth, elliptical letters. This morn-

24

ing her fingers had flown over this typewriter as she proclaimed the wonders of sport shirts with cool, short sleeves. There was never this hesitation when she attacked commercial copy. Fifty and one hundred word spots were a cinch for her. Harry Shell called her the best writer in radio. But what of fifty to one hundred thousand words? The same letters, the same keys, the same ribbon and paper—suddenly she was an amateur instead of a professional.

Some people spent weeks, months, even years, writing books. Why? For money and fame? Yes. But there was another incentive: a need to examine one's values by setting them on paper. The paper in the machine was her own Dr. Darnell, listening to the words from the keyboard, sifting the important from the unimportant.

Ann reached over and touched the paper. A writer had to touch the people he wrote about to make them talk and act like real people instead of he-saids and she-saids. And the writer had to touch the reader, too. Not hundreds nor thousands of hypothetical readers, but a single real reader who was, in a way, a projection of the writer.

She wanted to be honest when she dealt with the emotions and habits of people. Take sex. She wanted to write about it the way it really was. Either the hero or the heroine would have to be equipped for the moment of intimacy. If, in his urgency, her hero whispered, "Honey, did you remember to—?" he would be no different from other men who whisper the question. And in that inevitable moment when immediacy causes both to forget, Ann would tell the simple truth there, too. If the boy and girl weren't married when it happened, she'd be able to describe their anxiety accurately. You had to know about the finger-crossing, the weeping, the praying, too, until all was clear again. If, indeed, the all-clear blessedly materialized.

Ann had forgotten twice. Only the first time it wasn't a forgetting. It was a recklessness which couldn't be explained rationally but was comprehensible to anyone who had experienced it. She and John had worked late on one of those eternal Troxell promotions (a Golden Harvest sale this one was called). In the taxi he'd held her hand but hadn't tried to kiss her. "Look at the Troxell moon!" he'd said, pointing to a full moon not unlike the

25

one that illuminated the bargains in the Golden Harvest section. As she leaned over to look at the moon she got a too-good look at him. He wore no hat and his hair needed combing. He was tired and sad. If she had let herself look any longer she would have kissed him. She turned away. Trying to repress her desire was like fighting a feeling of vertigo. The October night had a chill in it that her light jacket wasn't equal to, but she dared not move closer to him. Twice, *twice* she'd gone to bed with him within a week. She'd sworn to herself a dozen times it mustn't happen again tonight. There had to be a brake to slow things down, to get their relationship on a less physical plane. *Not tonight.* Not because he had concealed anything from her, nor lied to her. He hadn't. They had discussed Madge at length and it was obvious to Ann that John's wife was using her marriage to him as a front for her promiscuity. Ann knew it was a question of time before they divorced, and not too much time, either. But where did that leave her? Was she just another rebound in a world of rebounds? Or, worse, was she rationalizing her own promiscuity? It would be easier to take a stand if she didn't ache all over for wanting him.

"I love you, Ann," he said quietly.

She didn't answer because she couldn't without giving herself away.

As the cab pulled up in front of her apartment house she said to him, "Don't get out. You're tired." Then lied with effort, "I'm tired, too."

"No," he answered, paying the driver. "I want to say goodnight."

They stood on the sidewalk. The night air was warmer than the cab had been. He still held her hand tightly.

"You shouldn't come up," she said.

"No—"

"I've fallen in love with you, too."

"I know it."

"So you really shouldn't come up. It's got to be right, or it won't be any good. Do you know what I mean?"

"I know. I know. It's only a matter of control. Give me a try. *Please.*"

Another surrender? She'd lost the battle of the taxicab, and the battle of the sidewalk. The apartment would be her last stand.

26

Mechanically, she opened a window, turned on lamps, fixed him a drink. Should she fix herself one? She knew she needed all her reserves and shouldn't run the risk of even a faint glow. Then, remembering what he'd said about it only being a matter of control, she let herself have one.

"*Look,*" she said to him. "I'm not fighting you off, nor playing hard to get. I keep thinking what Madge would say about me if she knew. She'd make it sound good and rotten."

They had a second drink. He kept looking at her and then looking away. He was trying as hard as she was. "You'd better go," she said, finally. There was no place to retreat. The ammunition was gone. She knew, as he held her in his arms to kiss her good-night that this battle, too, was lost. Never did a soldier care less. Foolish, foolish girl and boy. It was she who should have whispered to him at that moment about . . . But she hadn't. It might have saved those days of worry, despair, self-recrimination that preceded the immense relief of learning that she—both of them—had been lucky that night.

The other time it was her fault. She had simply forgotten and she had become pregnant. She knew she was pregnant every minute of the day: dizziness, nausea, flashes and flushes. But she was trapped. John was at the army camp, waiting to leave for Korea. Madge had filed for a divorce but it had not yet been granted. What in the hell could he do about it even if she told him?

A girl's best friend is not her mother when the girl is Ann. Mother would have—well, never mind what Mother would have said. She was in California with Birdie, thank God. So Ann's best friend had to be her best friend, Bess.

"*Look, Bess. I'm in a fix. I'm pregnant. About two months. I've got to have an abortion and I don't know what to do. I thought maybe you'd know a doctor.*"

How kind, how downright efficient Bess had been. Theirs was a friendship which did not include exchanges about each other's love life. Yet, when asked to help, Bess was neither shyly curious nor embarrassingly protective. "I know a doctor," was all she said. Bess was a walking directory of doctors. Her family indulged itself in the fanciest forms of hypochondria. Bess knew the perfect

27

doctor for every ailment, including Ann's. Bess made the appointment, went with Ann to the doctor's office, then moved into Ann's apartment and cared for her until she was all right.

And all this despair because the real-life heroine forgot to prepare and the hero forgot to whisper. It happens every day.

That is reality, Ann thought. To ignore it is to be unfair to life, to the reader, to yourself. Yet when she wrote it for people to read she knew she'd be criticized. She could hear Mother saying, "Can't you leave something to a person's imagination?" Mother would call it trashy. She would never be able to convince her mother that it wasn't trash when it was true—that it wasn't trash when it hurt this much to put it down on paper.

She stared at the blank sheet of paper in her typewriter. She studied the lacquered nails of her fingers poised upon the keys. Her mind had been writing but her fingers obstinately refused to cooperate. She had spent half an hour thinking about the kind of book she *didn't* want to write and had produced nothing. She sympathized momentarily with writers of unrealities. They might perform unfeelingly—but at least they got the job done. They had something to show for their concentration, if only a stringing together of words. As yet she had nothing to show; no beginning, not even a single mark upon the paper. *Why?*

There was a reason and she thought she knew what it was. It had nothing to do with John's indifference to the idea of a book. John was a gentle person who knew the heartbreaks of a book even after it was written. He didn't want her to be a disillusioned novelist. No, the real reason came from within herself. Some censor there opposed the theme of the book she needed to write. This unspoken opposition was similar to a patient's fighting his analyst in the beginning of their relationship. Bess had told her about the first long stretches of awkward silence during which she was unable to say a single word however much she had wanted to. Ann had a similar block now. But she had an inner compulsion to break through this block and get things out. It was part of the same drive that had taken her to Troxell Brothers that afternoon to see a woman she had avoided for ten years. She was tormented by questions that needed answers—questions about a first wife. How much of a husband does the first wife own? How much of

28

a mark does she leave on him without his knowing it? Ann never worried about whether or not John loved her. She knew that he did. His love was honest with nothing held back. But she did wonder how much of John was all hers to love—and how much still belonged to the woman who had him first. His likes and dislikes in food, his choice of clothes, his preference in perfumes—was Madge still a part of all that without his being aware of it? Ann was ashamed to acknowledge that she sometimes wondered at the very moment of the love act how much of his most intimate, impulsive giving of himself had been learned from Madge? How much of a first wife's love does a husband wear even as he tells the tale against her?

This was what bothered Ann as wife, as author. This was what she wanted to write and to this minute couldn't begin to get on paper.

She closed her eyes and said a short, fervent prayer. When she opened them her mind was ready to speak, her fingers ready to receive.

She began to fill the page.

4

As he headed for the sales meeting John Long thought about books. For every book there was an author, for every author an editor. The editor sweated the manuscript through from acceptance to final revision and became a kind of father image to the writer. Put all editors together, add an editor-in-chief, and you get Editorial. He thought about the other end of the business. For every sale there's a bookseller; for every bookseller, a sales department where decisions are made as to size of printing, amount of promotion and

29

getting the book into stores. Put together all the people involved in this end of the business and you get Sales . . .

Since Editorial and Sales give each other a headache, the periodic sales conference in which the editors brief the sellers on the coming list is hell on wheels. The sales conference is despised by all who attend it, John thought—yet it is tolerated as a necessary ordeal of publishing out of which the new titles achieve their identities before they are brought into the world.

John felt schizophrenic as he walked along. The part of him that worked with authors as editor was sympathetic to Editorial; the part that lived with orders and percentages and returns liked Sales. I'm a schizoid, he thought, as he stood at the curb waiting for the traffic light to show WALK. Since he traveled for the company too, and since most travelers are at odds with both Editorial and Sales, he was probably a trischzoid.

He was the tallest person in the cluster of men and women poised in a common captivity of DO NOT WALK for fifteen seconds, and in his new tan featherweight suit he had a fresh, loved look. As he waited he glanced at the street sign that read Park Avenue South and he thought, It's not Park Avenue Anything. It's just like what it used to be, Fourth Avenue.

A perspiring man with a soot smudged collar decided that he could WAIT no longer and elbowed past John as he started to cross, leaving a scuff on John's shoe. The man didn't look back. A woman in a black sheer dress that clung to her shoulders as though it had been hosed there ran awkwardly toward a bus that closed its door in her face. She didn't like it and barked her disapproval at the bus's exhaust smoke. John smiled to himself. The sign said Park Avenue South but this street still had Fourth Avenue manners.

John stepped into the lobby of 424 Park Avenue South and the sudden transition from hot to cold made him giddy. Air-conditioning felt good, but it was—he groped for a word—*unnatural*. That was what he'd tell Ann next time she asked him why he balked at sleeping in the stuff. He could take unnatural temperatures at work, but when he went to bed he wanted nature on his side. He exchanged hellos with the starter, stepped into an elevator and got off on the eighteenth floor.

30

The foyer of Laverty and Clarke could have inspired a dust jacket for a novel on the publishing business. The walls were waist high in blonde wood, then pale blue canvas to the ceiling. Glass display cases housed the newest Laverty and Clarke publications. John saw a copy of *The Fixers* and shuddered.

In the center of the room was an oversized semi-circular desk with a highly varnished blonde wood finish. It acted both as window-dressing and barricade for the highly varnished blonde who sat behind it. Her name was Jackie and she was expert at handling the wrong people in precisely the right way. Jackie read every Laverty and Clarke book that had the promise of sex in it. She had a free-wheeling way that men liked, and John knew that he was her chiefest crush because she made no secret about what he did to her viscera whenever he walked into the office. Almost every day—half-playfully, half-seriously—she warned him that she would break down his resistance eventually. But John liked Jackie in spite of her eager-beaverishness. She seemed almost desperate for affection. He supposed her flirtations satisfied some basic need. Anyway, he felt compassionate toward her. Thorg Thorgeson had told him that Jackie's seventeen-year-old daughter was married and had a baby. Thorg collected vital statistics like that and John supposed it was true, but he never let Jackie know that he knew she was a grandmother.

"Whom do you wish to—oh, it's *you*, Mr. Long."

"Where's the meeting?" John asked trying to keep the conversation on an even keel.

"In Mr. Laverty's office. Plenty of time. Mr. Clarke's at his hunting lodge in Maine. Calls in every hour on the hour . . . You look sharp in that suit."

John smiled. "Jackie, you're incorrigible. If an author put you in a book his editor would make him delete you because you're unbelievable."

"*Me* in a book. You're *kidding*." She crossed her legs too obviously.

"See you later, Jackie. The meeting's ready to begin."

The men were seated around a ten-foot rectangular table talking in low tones in the same pseudo-relaxed way an audience waits

31

for a lecture to begin. John quickly took in the seating arrangement. Cecil Laverty at the head; Ransom, the editor-in-chief, at the foot. The travelers, Wilson, the publicity director, and Boal, the advertising manager, occupied chairs on either side of the long table. The chair to Laverty's left was empty and John slid into it, marveling at his good luck. Usually, this was the first seat taken because it was known to be Laverty's blind spot.

Cecil Laverty rose to his feet. He resembled Mr. Toad of *The Wind in the Willows,* with none of Toad's charm. Cecil reminded John of a weak sovereign who inherited the throne only because he had been the eldest son. It didn't matter if he was an ass to boot. Cecil was the end of the line of three generations of Laverty publishers. His father, Cecil Laverty, Sr., aware of his son's ineptitude, had hung onto the helm and the checkbook until 1940 when he was ninety-three.

Laverty and Company, as it originally had been called, was founded by Cecil's grandfather, Cyrus Laverty, in 1856. Cyrus Laverty's goal was to publish good books in larger quantities than they had ever been published before and he had succeeded. His son, Cecil, carried on the publishing tradition, with considerably more stress on the "larger quantities" than on the "good." He neglected his father's Library of Classics while developing a stable of fiction writers whose books sold in the hundreds of thousands. During sixty years as head of the firm Cecil Laverty, Sr., sired a long string of successful best-sellers. In an off moment he had sired Junior.

With such sound beginnings how could the line poop out this way? John heard some people blame the old man for hogging the spotlight twenty years too long and vetoing any decisions of Junior's which displeased him. When John learned that Cecil's mother had been a writer of juveniles in which birds and flowers talked to each other, he saw in Cecil the operation of the natural law. Anyway, from the moment Cecil, Jr., took over the firm's management it was plainly headed for the proverbial shirtsleeves in the proverbial third generation. He alienated authors who had made fortunes and reputations with Laverty and Company. He lost his father's best editors and his most valued travelers. Whereas father had preferred to be out-of-print than out-on-a-limb, Cecil

32

became King of the Remainders. Alongside him on the roller-coaster was his beloved wife, Dora, who had a penchant for thinking up titles to books she would never read.

It was Billy Clarke who produced the oxygen Laverty and Company needed in its moment of extremity. Billy had inherited vast sums from his family's soap business and had gone on to make even more money. He knew nothing about publishing but was intrigued with the idea of being a publisher. He'd stepped in in 1945, acquired seventy-five per cent of the Laverty stock at a price that must have made old Cyrus kick against his coffin, and began a subtle campaign to wean Cecil, Jr., of all authority while keeping him in great good spirits. Dynamic, sensible, tireless, and with just enough understanding of writers to master them, Billy Clarke pumped new life into the sagging company. Although he was still in his mid-forties, Clarke's gentle, devoted leadership had made him a genial father to writers and to most of the people who worked for him. This admiration, however, was not shared by the trade in general and other publishers disliked him for his piracy. Snagging big names was a game with him; he won more often than he lost and a story was making the rounds that the President of Fortune House, after one too many at the Algonquin Bar, proclaimed that Billy Clarke could pull Houghton away from Mifflin and Little away from Brown after a two weeks visit with them at his blankety-blank hunting lodge in Maine.

John studied Cecil Laverty. He wore the expression of a man who had wandered into this office accidently while searching for the Men's Room. His too-tight dark blue double-breasted suit bunched up under his pot. His wife constantly talked about how much weight he must lose, so he never let his tailor fit him properly. He wore a hand-painted necktie, a large diamond tie-pin and two pairs of glasses. He did not wear both pairs simultaneously but he almost did. The constant switching kept him and everyone around him in a state of nervous exhaustion. He wore one pair of glasses for near, the other for far but he never had on the pair he needed when he needed it.

John settled back into his chair and slid his long legs under the table. He nodded, "Hi, Thorg" to Ted Thorgeson, the West Coast representative, and waited for Laverty to take off his near-

33

sighteds, put on his far-sighteds and call the meeting to order.

"Where's Evans?" Laverty bellowed.

"Here," Bob Evans, the New England man, said from Cecil's right blind spot.

"Oh." Cecil faltered as he changed to his near-sighteds.

"Gentlemen," he began, and there was contempt in the way he said the word, conveying his opinion that any resemblance between book people and gentlemen was coincidental, "Mr. Clarke is out of the city, so we shall proceed without him."

John detected a cutting edge in Laverty's use of the prefix "Mr." Cecil addressed his editors, travelers, publicity people and authors as Long, Ransom, Thorgeson, Evans—never by their given names or nicknames, never even by "you," and he had a way of pronouncing a name that made the pronouncee bristle. For example, when he said "Evans," he added a singing intonation at the end of the word which reminded John of the tone a schoolteacher might use confronting a pupil caught writing naughty words on the blackboard.

John had a favorite daydream that occurred and reoccurred at these conferences, and in it he took arms against this impossible man, jumping to his feet in the midst of the meeting, shouting, "Laverty!" (Not "Mr. Laverty!") Sometimes he snapped it and sometimes he made a sing-song at the end of it: "Lavertyyyyyyyyyy! You fat-headed old twerp, shut your trap and sit down!" It was a frighteningly vivid dream and it gave him a great deal of pleasure every time he dreamed it. Some day . . .

"Gentlemen," Laverty repeated. "The honeymoon is over."

Oh my gosh, John thought, the same speech he made for the spring list.

"I repeat: the honeymoon is over. The reader is getting tougher and tougher to please. He has to be won anew with every book we publish and that means that all of us have to be on our toes!"

John tried to shift his legs realizing his own toes were asleep. Why did furniture makers design their tables and chairs for the median man? Laverty was droning on.

"This meeting between the men who edit and the men who sell is the high spot of our fall and winter planning. I have tried repeatedly to schedule these sales meetings for three days instead of

34

one. You can't do justice to all these books in one day. I can name a dozen publishers who have three-day meetings. But Cl—Mr. Clarke says, 'Hit the high spots in one day,' so we'll just have to do the best we can. Ransom will speak for the editors who have done a damned fine job in getting these books in shape. Now it's up to the rest of you to sell them."

When he said "the rest of you" he aimed his index finger straight at Jerry Trigg, the Chicago man, and Jerry, who obviously wasn't sure whether Mr. Laverty was wearing his nears or fars didn't seem to know whether he was being pointed to or at.

"And let me add, gentlemen, that the current Laverty and Clarke list is one of the best—if not *the* best—in the history of the firm."

John wiggled his toes to wake them up. This was what Cecil had said last time; the spring list had been one of the worst if not *the* worst in the history of the firm. John remembered Hazel Watt's wry-faced reception of the titles he'd shown her on his last trip to Dallas.

"Your sales of *The Fixers* was spotty," Laverty was saying. "Thorgeson, what's the matter with *The Fixers* on the Coast? And Long—where's Long?"

"Right here, Mr. Laverty."

Laverty changed to his near-sighteds. "Long, you haven't sold *The Fixers* in the South the way it ought to be sold. Why, that's dope-fiend country! Did you *read* it, Long?"

"Yes, Mr. Laverty."

"Didn't you think it was a great book, Long?"

If he should say what he really thought about the book Cecil would have a stroke. John glanced at the men around the table and saw that the air-conditioning and the smoke, plus Mr. Laverty, had already lulled them into a stupor.

Shut your mouth and sit down, you fat headed old twerp . . .

"I expect to get reorders on my next trip," John said aloud. "After the booksellers read it they'll sell it."

Cecil scowled now as though he'd been cheated, but John's answer was quibble-proof. Cecil made a mental note to watch this fellow Long. *Used to be just a traveler. Clarke's given him too much responsibility—and too much salary. He's Clarke's man, all right!*

35

"I don't want to steal Ransom's thunder," Laverty continued, "but I can't help saying that *Milk in the Sky,* our big fall novel, is sure to make the best-seller list. You've all read this book by now— I *hope.* It was ready last spring but we thought we had a book club bite and moved it to fall. Bill Holt of Everybody's Book Club practically promised me they'd take the book and then the son-of-a-bitch backed out. Well, he'll be sorry! This morning at breakfast my wife said to me, 'Cecil,' she said, '*Milk in the Sky* is as big as all outdoors!' And that's exactly what it is, gentlemen: as big as all outdoors!"

John knew better. *Milk in the Sky* was a 650-page pastoral novel about a dairy farm and the book simply hadn't come off. John had waded through it when it was first submitted and had voted against publishing it but Laverty and Ransom had made an issue of the thing and Billy Clarke had let them have their way. The man from the book club had probably reneged after reading the first chapter. Cecil's father never would have published it. Good fertilizer would sell—but *Milk in the Sky* wasn't even good fertilizer. Billy Clarke had tried to read it and had given up—and come to think of it, Billy Clarke hadn't liked *The Fixers,* either, so one fine day Ransom might be applying for an editor's job someplace else. It occurred to John now that Billy Clarke might have avoided this conference because of the weak L and C list.

"Since the honeymoon is over, gentlemen, I'm reminding you to get the lead out of your pants and visit more booksellers. Don't just contact the large accounts. See the college outlets, the denominational book stores, the small dealers. We've got books for everybody."

This too will pass, John droned inside.

"You've got to believe in what you're selling, gentlemen. And you've got to see people."

This was the place, John knew, for the Six Rules of Salesmanship, and sure enough, he heard now:

"The six rules of salesmanship are: see people, see people, see people, see people, and see people."

That's only five. Can't you count past one set of fingers?

"The minute you stop seeing people you stop working for me!"

36

Laverty pounded his point home with his fist, barely missed his far-sighteds, and then said, "I don't have to hire anybody!"

John sat up straight as though Mr. Laverty had slapped him instead of the table. *"I don't have to hire anybody!"* How many years ago had John heard those very words—and not from Cecil Laverty, either. It took a real effort for him to pull himself out of the past and into this close room.

"There's just one thing else, gentlemen. You aren't scouting for talent the way you should."

John looked up.

"You've got to keep your eyes and ears open for promising authors right under your noses. Everywhere you go you must find out who's writing a book and if it sounds good get your hands on that manuscript so that Laverty and Clarke can see it first!"

Right under his nose. Well, Ann might conceivably be a promising author, but it'd look funny for me to be promoting my own wife's book. *Well, wouldn't it?*

"And now, gentlemen, Ransom will sketch for you the high spots of our fall list."

Ransom was frail. His expensive suit was nondescript. He wore a do-it-yourself bow tie with ends a shade too long. He cleared his throat and began his recital in a thin voice. "As Mr. Laverty has told you already, *Milk in the Sky* is our big book this year. . . ." John concentrated on what Ransom had to say, hoping against hope for a miracle, but the list only looked grimmer as Ransom described each title in detail. Another war experiences book (this one by a WAC captain), a novel that Ransom was describing as "really not a novel at all; more of a fantasy based on real-life adventures—sort of a cross between Robert Nathan and *Born Free*"; a non-fiction blast at Jim-Crowism which wouldn't sell worth a damn; a few run-of-the-mill juveniles; a cookbook which John had found and edited entitled *The Put-the-Guests-to-Work Cookbook.* . . . .

The lunch break came and went. Publicity told what it planned to do. Advertising told what it planned not to do. John remembered other meetings when there had been real hassling—with the travelers taking the headquarter boys apart. But this list could inspire nothing but pained silence and a kind of omnipresent ennui.

37

John looked through the clouds of smoke at Bob Evans who was allergic to tobacco and had turned a pale green. He always got violently sick at a sales meeting. John and Bob were the only two men in the room who didn't smoke, but it wasn't a matter of allergy with John. He just didn't like it. He'd rather drum his fingers on the underside of the table than use them for cigarette business. Poor Bob. Thorg was laying a real smokescreen with his cigar; Jerry Trigg pulled on his pipe; Ransom was chain-smoking cigarettes. The room was oppressive with smoke.

"We've tried to give you the best list we know how," Ransom chirped as he turned the meeting back to Laverty.

"And *now*, gentlemen!" Laverty was waving the near-sighteds in one hand and the far-sighteds in the other. This gesture always presaged Something Big.

"Get set for something big! I've saved the best for the last. How would you like a Christmas present—right now?"

Nobody tried to answer. When Laverty wore no glasses at all it was smart to fly blind with him.

"In early spring—maybe February—Laverty and Clarke will have the honor of presenting Harold Albert's latest and greatest book."

This *was* something big. Harold Albert, whose first two books had sold a half-million copies apiece under the Fortune House aegis, was a big name for sure-fire sales. He had resigned from the State Department in protest to the handling of the U-2 spy plane incident. He had begun his book then and had been quietly writing it all this time. Although Harold Albert was the acknowledged leader of the get-tough-with-Russia school, both liberals and conservatives bought his books and any Albert book was sure to rate front page reviews in the *Times* and *Herald Tribune* book sections.

"Albert is with Billy Clarke right now, up in Maine. Mr. Clarke called me on the phone last night to say that the book's almost ready. And the *title*, gentlemen, the title of Harold Albert's greatest work is a stroke of genius. My wife—with all due modesty—thought up the title all by herself one evening when Harold Albert was at our place for dinner."

Oh-oh! John recalled that Dora Laverty, with all due modesty, had coined the title *Milk in the Sky*.

38

"The name of Harold Albert's new book, gentlemen, is going to be—*I Want an Enduring Peace.*"

Thorg Thorgeson reared back so suddenly that he spilled cigar ashes all over the table. He opened his mouth to say something by way of protest but no words came. Jerry Trigg clamped down on his pipe with such feeling his lips went white. Bob Evans looked so green John was sure he'd never make it to the end.

"*I Want an Enduring Peace!*" Mr. Laverty repeated the words stentoriously, waving hands and lenses in great arcs to the rhythm of their sound.

The fuzzy lethargy of the room was changing to a raucous nightmare, and once more Laverty said it. "*I Want an Enduring Peace.*"

The words, coming from a bulbous, tight-coated, frog-faced nincompoop like Cecil Laverty sounded indecent.

"Every man, woman and child in America will want an enduring peace if you get behind this book and sell it the way it deserves to be sold!" Laverty shouted. His face was red, his handfuls of glasses trembled uncontrollably. "And gentlemen, just to start the ball rolling, I want you . . . every one of you . . . to repeat that title after me at the top of your lungs. *All* of you—Thorgeson, Long, Evans, Trigg, Wilson, Boal, Ransom—*everybody!* Let's shake the building with the sound of a book that will make publishing history. Gentlemen, repeat after me—I WANT AN ENDURING PEACE!"

"I WANT AN ENDURING PEACE!"

John shouted it with the others—and despite the noise, he was certain he could hear Hazel Watts shrieking her derision all the way from Dallas, Texas.

The two drinks John had with Thorg failed to brighten the depressed mood the conference had left him in, so as soon as he got home he fixed himself another drink and lay down on the couch to wait for Ann. The room was almost dark when she came in. He got up, walked over to her and kissed her.

"You're 'way ahead of me," she said. "How many have you had?"

"Only three. You look wrung out."

"I am. Don't put the light on yet," she said, pulling her dress

39

over her head. "Let me take a shower first. Then hand me something cold and good so I can start catching up with you."

In a few minutes she was sipping the drink John had fixed her and reading a letter from her sister. "Birdie sends her love."

"Good old Birdie," John said. "And how's your dear mother?"

Ann read on, laughing, "Birdie says Mother keeps dreaming I'm going to have a baby."

"Hmm. I wonder if your mother expects time-and-a-half for heckling people while she's asleep."

"Wonder why she keeps dreaming *that?*"

"Elementary. She wants a little Aryan grandchild and she's convinced Birdie's and Abe's kids are half-castes."

"Poor Mother," Ann said. Then she corrected herself. "I don't know *why* I say Poor Mother. She thinks of me as Poor Ann. . . . How was the conference?"

"Awful. Billy Clarke wasn't there, and Laverty was his usual nauseous self. Clarke's up in Maine with—guess who? Harold Albert."

"I thought Harold Albert was a Fortune House author."

"He was. But Clarke's got his new book for L and C. It's coming out the first of the year."

"That ought to pep you up."

"It does. Except Laverty has put the kiss of death on it already. Mrs. Laverty has christened it with the title to end all titles."

"What?"

"*I Want an Enduring Peace.*"

"You're joking!"

"I wish I were."

They laughed and the good feeling was there between them. She had her hair piled high and was wearing only a white cotton robe with no buttons. There was just a cord to tie it loosely around her waist.

"What kept you so long this evening?" John asked.

"Surprise—I started the book at the office today," she answered. "Once I got the first words out I couldn't hold it back. I'm well into what, for better or worse, is chapter one."

John remembered what Laverty had said about talent under the nose. "Did you bring it home with you?"

40

"No. Why?"

"I—well, I thought you'd like me to read it to give you moral support."

She held her glass against her forehead to feel the cold against her skin. "I'm glad you said that. I want you on my side as I write this thing. But save the moral support and give it to me in one big bundle when I write The End. I'll need it more then."

"I'll save it."

"What you think about it means more to me than what anyone else thinks," Ann said slowly. "But I want you to read it through from beginning to end. It isn't fair to you or the book to shove it at you piecemeal. You'd try to be objective—but you'd give me the benefit of the doubt."

"Ann, will you do me a favor?"

"Since when do you have to *ask* for a favor?"

"Submit your book someplace else. Not to Laverty and Clarke. I mean, well, I mean one of the boys with another house could give it a better break in presenting it. Bill Haley, for instance. He could sell it—and he likes you. Or maybe Scribner's. Or the Harper man. I don't want to throw cold water on this project but it would look funny for me to be promoting my own wife's novel. You can see that."

"Anything you say," Ann answered. "You know those angles better than I do."

She said this evenly and lightly but she was disappointed. Was he trying to discourage her? No. Not really. He was just being honest. He was a good enough salesman to know what he couldn't sell and that was being smart. Besides, wouldn't it be better to do it on her own? Anyway, maybe he wouldn't like what she wrote. He might want to see himself in the book, and her, and remember things he wanted to forget.

He read her mind. "Ann, what's this book going to be about? You aren't going to do anything crazy—I mean like opening up any healed wounds? All those starry-eyed yokels on publishers' lists who pop up with first novels that Tell All. Hell, they make me sick. All they do is hurt people—themselves mostly—and nobody makes any money. We print 3000 copies and sell a third of 'em mostly to the author's friends and enemies who get a kick out of

41

seeing him stripped, with every wrinkle, every mole, every roll of fat showing. He makes a few hundred dollars for a year's work— and loses his self-respect. Is that what you're going to be, my girl? An author with a capital A, who talks to much about things that are nobody else's business, and ends up on a page of remainders?"

"Ouch!" Ann said. She gulped a good part of her drink before continuing. "My novel is hardly started and already you've practically got it remaindered!" She had heard him talk a lot about those isles of lost ships—the remainder houses. Remainders were books nobody—not even the author's friends and enemies—wanted. So the publisher lumped them off to a remainder house for a quarter or sometimes a dime apiece and the remainder house tried to sell them at 60¢, sometimes 30¢. Everybody knew at least one hoped-for great-American-novel that ended up in a drug store under a sign: YOUR CHOICE, 39¢ . . . ANY THREE FOR ONE DOLLAR! John always spoke of a book's being remaindered as he would speak of a friend who had died; the Marboro Book Shop ads in the *Times* made him think of obituaries so she wanted to change this mood, now.

She said, "Just be patient with me while I'm writing it. That's all I ask. Be patient."

He was quiet for a moment. He had a curiously uneasy feeling about this book of hers. He said now, "You know, all these writing teachers and successful authors are always telling the neophytes, 'Write about what you know.' The hell with that. I'm sick of people sitting down with malice aforethought to write about what they know. What the hell *do* they know? A lot of boredom and trouble and very little fun, which is what everybody knows, and wants to get away from when he reads a book. But the neophytes are going to write about what they know if it kills 'em, and they're dead sure that what *they* know is vastly different from what the reader knows. *Their* adultery was more beautiful than anyone else's; *their* abortion hurt more; their childhood bedwettings were more significant; their marriage more doomed. The 'awful thing' that happened on the way home from sixth grade; the first night with the brute who wasn't gentle; the valley of the shadow when baby came early; these are the things they know, by gosh—and just

42

try to stop them from writing them! And the *depression!* Nobody went through the hell they did—and the war! Books and books and books are being ground out right this minute because some G.I. heard you're supposed to write about what you know. Result? Blood, sweat, and an extra carbon. *Don't* write about what you know, I say. Write about what you don't know. If you love me, my darling, you'll write about what you don't know. Oh, hell, get me down from this soap-box. When do you expect to have it ready?"

Ann smiled. "D'y'mean when will I be ready for Dr. Darnell and my nervous breakdown? Well, it may be fatal, but I've set up a time-table. This is July, and by Thanksgiving I hope to have it out of my system."

John whistled. "Why so soon? Five months isn't much time for writing a book—especially when you've got a regular job."

"Not when my husband's away part of the time," Ann said. "Every lonely wife should write a book that never ends. Like Penelope's shroud, she should work on it every day until her husband returns. And every night, too."

"Those damned lonely nights," John said in a voice that was almost as soft and faraway as hers. "Do you ever wonder if I—? I mean, do you wonder about what I do with those nights when I'm gone?"

"Should I wonder?" Ann asked. The private feeling was spreading over her again and it made her throat tighten, then it raced downward. She squirmed without meaning to. It was like a drug taking effect.

"You don't have to wonder," John said. "I'm the only traveling man in America who's both oversexed and monogamous. Not many people would believe that, but I think you do. Which reminds me. Why doesn't your heroine excuse herself for a moment while her hero puts out the light and takes off his shorts? At least, when the nights get lonely again, we can get some small consolation from remembering an extra matinée played on the spur of the moment between cocktails and dinner."

"My heroine doesn't have to excuse herself," Ann said. "My heroine is a smart cookie."

"Ann—" he began. And that was all he could say. "Ann—" He

43

held her terribly close, as though he were storing away this physical impression for a future time. He was intensely aware of everything about her: her breathing, the smell of her skin, the way her hand stroked the back of his neck as he kissed her. *Make it last, make it last. Keep this moment alive.*

All the midsummer irritabilities were gone. Cecil Laverty's inanities didn't matter any more.

"*I want an enduring peace,*" he said confidentially.

"Who doesn't?" she giggled.

The rest was whispers.

Complain to Hazel Watts that the novel she sold you starts slow and she'll answer that a novel's gotta start slow. If it starts fast it will run itself out at the eight-pole.

"Isn't too slow, is it?" she asks warily. "Keep going. You'll like Ann. She's a nice girl. And John Long's no gray flannel image. He's for real. Madge? She may be an image now but she'll soon be flesh and blood. Bess is lively enough, but her Dr. Darnell is tired. A tired psychiatrist whose couch is busy.

"The publishing bit is accurate. Publishers like to think of themselves as horn-rimmed, high-minded, guest-panelist-type patricians. They are just like other businessmen, aimed at a definite goal. Some call the goal one thing, some another. Why not call it an enduring peace?

"It moves faster now. The first four chapters are like a pie crust. A good crust has to have enough body to cradle the pie. If the dough's too thick the reader gives up. If it's too flakey the crust crumbles and you've got cobbler.

"Stay with it, kid."

5

"I DON'T have to hire anybody!" It was T. Harold Barnes who had said that. The words seemed unnecessary, because the store manager of the large Troxell Brothers operation should be entitled to hire or not hire anyone who applied for a job in his store.

John had heard that the best way to overcome uneasiness and to make an impression on an executive was to mentally undress him—take off his shoes and socks, for instance; one was less likely to be awed by an interviewer who was barefoot. But T. Harold Barnes was the exception that proved the rule. He remained the same, with or without shoes. Although he hadn't budged from his chair when Madge and John entered the office, he obviously was not tall. His bald head had a high sheen to it, almost a waxed-and-polished look. He had a thin line of hair that rimmed his ears and encircled the back of his head and John wondered fleetingly if such a man had to pay the full price for haircuts. He wore glasses with thick lenses, had a round face and one of those congenitally red noses. John made a mental note to tell Madge that T. Harold Barnes would make a perfect Santa Claus—right down to his little round belly. His clothes were in quiet, good taste—a pin-stripe blue suit that had a tailored-to-order look, a Countess Mara necktie, and gold cuff links set with diamonds. "I don't have to hire *any*body!" There was something about the uncomfortable way that T. Harold Barnes looked at Madge while addressing his remark to John that presaged his ultimate capitulation.

"I didn't say you *had* to hire Jack," Madge countered. "It's your store and you're the boss, but if I like him enough to marry him I want you to like him enough to give him a job!"

There was unconcealed admiration for Madge in the way T. Harold Barnes listened when she spoke. But he wasn't going to

46

give her her way without a token show of resistance. "I can't see what being a husband has to do with being an advertising man. It's a possibility, however, that your Mr. . . . Mr. . . ."

John's name got stuck in his throat and he almost didn't make it. "Long," John managed to say.

"Mr. Long may have the qualifications to be both a husband and an advertising man."

Madge beamed.

"Take my wife, for instance. I married her, but she'd be the last person I'd recommend that you hire in your book department!"

Madge exploded with laughter, as though she had just heard the funniest joke in years. John uncrossed his legs, then nervously recrossed them in the other direction. Everything about him felt wrong at that moment. His necktie was choking him, his shoes needed a shine and too much of his shirt cuffs protruded from his jacket. As a matter of fact, the whole job interview was cockeyed. Instead of Madge wheedling Mr. Barnes, he ought to be telling the man his qualifications and trying to look impressive. Madge sat on the edge of her chair with her elbows on Mr. Barnes' desk, leaning forward as she talked to him.

"Isn't he *cute?*" she said happily.

Mr. Barnes, who had been leaning back in his swivel chair, sat up and looked at John as though he was trying to detect the qualities that made Madge think him cute.

"Tell him, Jack," she said. "Tell Mr. Barnes why you are qualified to work in the ad department."

John compared himself to a standing rib roast forced upon a vegetarian. "Well, sir," he began, "I'm very interested in advertising. I was art editor of our college humor magazine at Syracuse, and since my graduation two years ago I've had newspaper experience on the *Syracuse Post Standard*. I learned to do layouts and write ad copy there."

John had the feeling that Mr. Barnes wasn't listening. He was peering down the front of Madge's blouse and wiping off the sweat that was collecting on his bald spot.

"Have you ever done any layouts, Mr.—?" Mr. Barnes had forgotten John's name again.

Before John could reach for the ball, Madge grabbed it and

47

rushed through the line. "Look, Mr. Barnes," she said, half belligerently, "it all boils down to one thing. Either you like Jack's personality or you don't. A store this big can always use one more ad man and you can hire him right now if you want to—you could, even if he didn't have sense enough to come in out of the rain—which he *has*."

Mr. Barnes knew when he was licked. Or had he known all along? He smiled at John now for the first time and said, "You're hired, young man." Then he looked at Madge in a friendly way and said, almost sardonically, "I hope he's half as good as you say he is."

For a second John thought Madge was going to bend over and kiss Mr. Barnes' bald head. She didn't though. She stood up, came close to John, who was already standing, and laid her head against his shoulder. He looked at Mr. Barnes over the top of her blonde head, and then realized Madge had slipped out of her shoes and was leaning against him in her stocking feet. In contrast to her relaxed composure he was considerably flustered and he had actually begun to blush.

"It's your lucky day," Madge said to Mr. Barnes. "May 31st, 1947. This is the day you made a wise decision in hiring Jack Long."

"And when is *your* lucky day?" Mr. Barnes asked in a voice which was, if anything, overcongratulatory.

"This afternoon at four o'clock," Madge said. John hoped that she wouldn't invite T. Harold Barnes to the wedding. Enough was enough. "May 31st, 1947 is my lucky day, too!" Madge went on. "Keep your eye on my book department while I'm gone next week. Bride or no bride, the manager has to beat last year's figures!"

T. Harold Barnes laughed, got out of his chair, shook John's hand, patted Madge on the shoulder, touched her breast as though by accident, and gave the couple his blessing. The next thing John knew he and Madge were out of Mr. Barnes' office and walking down the long hall.

"Happy?" Madge asked.

"And how! But he never did say how much I'm going to make or when I'm to begin."

"That part's easy. The important thing is you got the job."

48

"You razzle-dazzled him into it. He didn't really want to hire me."

"But he *did*," Madge said triumphantly. "And he'd jolly well *better* after my giving the ten best years of my life to his book department. I'm going to drop down now and tell the girls good-bye. I'll meet you at the apartment in an hour." The apartment was her apartment and he'd been living there for a month. "Okay?"

"Okay!" he said, from down deep, his hands doing outrageous things to her in the dark hall. Relief and desire coincided in him and he showed his excitement.

"Kiss me," he commanded, and Madge put her arms around him, increasing his agitation. She kissed him hard on the mouth and then he pushed her against the wall and put his whole body against hers.

She had to squirm out of his embrace. "Not here," she said. "Mr. Barnes wouldn't approve!"

She ran on down the hall toward the elevator, leaving him alone with his confusion.

Madge King was what is known in department store circles as a go-getter, a hard worker, a sales-force pusher, a quota-beater, a bonus-winner. T. Harold Barnes had pounded his polished desk more than once at buyers' meetings and exclaimed, "If we want to get something done *right* around here all we've got to do is appoint Madge King to the committee! It's an inspiration the way that girl gets results!"

It was rumored here and there in the store that Madge King was an inspiration to T. Harold Barnes in other ways, but, like so much department store gossip, no one could put a finger on anything concrete. Department stores are rumor factories where the tiniest indiscretion is distorted into the worst of sins. A sense of easily outraged moral righteousness is everywhere, compensating in part for the low salary scale. The cosmetics buyer pats the new girl in perfumes on the rear. Mary, the Arden girl, sees him. Three minutes later, Helen, in Rubenstein, Cora, in Monteil, and Kitty, in Charles-of-the-Ritz, know about the pat in its most intimate detail. The faintest wisp of smoke becomes a flaming inferno quicker than the sound of "May-I-help-you-please?" But even the most vicious

49

rumor bearers had to admit that T. Harold Barnes was right in praising Madge's abilities. Whether it was a Red Cross Drive or a campaign for volunteers to help put over Troxell's Summer Kiddies Camp, when Madge King got behind the project, it went over.

Look what she'd done for Troxell's book department. Ten years ago, as an inexperienced kid of twenty, she'd started as a salesperson in the book department. Two years later the manager of that department had sent an ultimatum to old John Troxell that either he have Madge King fired or get himself a new manager. Troxell referred the matter to T. Harold Barnes who called Madge in for a talk. After weighing all the evidence (or almost all) Mr. Barnes decided that a new manager was in order. Madge became, at twenty-two, the youngest buyer in the history of Troxell Brothers. That was in 1939. In the eight years that followed, Troxell's book department underwent a metamorphosis from a rundown rental bookery located in a corner of the mezzanine to its formidable seventh floor location where it did one of the biggest book-department volumes in New York. The Troxell Brothers Book Club, with eleven thousand members, was the result of one of Madge's brainstorms. Shunning the solid best-sellers, Madge offered her club members publishers' overstock of missed best-sellers at bargain prices. In the brochure about each month's books (there were always three to choose from—and special inducements to the members who took all three) Madge wrote an editorial entitled "Why You'll Like These Books" and signed it John Troxell, Executive Director of the Troxell Brothers Book Club. John Troxell loved that. Not every president of a large store can wear a halo of literacy, month after month, year after year.

Then, there was Madge's original Rent-a-book-and-buy-it plan. If a customer liked a rental book enough to buy a stock copy, he was excused from paying a rental fee no matter how long the book had been checked out.

Autograph parties, full-page-ad remainder sales, and her famous double-decker sale table which she constantly filled with enticing goodies made Troxell's a live and respected book center. She had a way with those who worked for her, too. They gave her absolute loyalty and a do-or-die devotion which she repaid by standing by

50

them and taking their side in the issues which constantly arose in the store. She ran what amounted to a subtle training course for employees, repeating over and over her maxims for selling books. "Most people do not buy books to improve their minds," she'd say. "They buy books to impress themselves or other people. Always act impressed yourselves to make them feel good." Selling books was a game with Madge. She could make a customer feel bookish and brilliant whether he asked for *The Collected Poems of Edgar Guest* or *The Magic Mountain.* She could spot potential victims who glanced briefly at certain titles as they hurried toward the rest rooms. Then, on their way out, Madge, who would just happen to be standing by the book that took their attention, pounced on them, and more times than not made the sale.

And she knew how to buy as well as how to sell. The travelers who called on her respected her judgment, even when she refused to go for their leaders. A salesman wouldn't get to first base with Madge on a novel like *The Fixers* or *Milk in the Sky.* But when she liked a book she got behind it and pushed it. The books she believed in she sold in enormous quantities, never giving a hang about best-seller lists. She never let personal feelings toward a traveler color her judgment or influence the quantity of a title she purchased. And she made it a strict rule never to talk books in bed.

To some people Madge King was dynamic, a genius in her field; to others she was overly aggressive, pushy; to others she was an opportunist who would stop at nothing to get what she wanted. She was something of all these things yet not wholly any of them. She was best described as Madge King—a tall, plain-faced, straw-haired girl with amazing breasts, some freckles, and few inhibitions.

Thirteen years is a long time to remember a party, but it was quite a party. It started off as "a couple of drinks for the bride and groom" and ended in a miasmic, drunken trauma. Some book travelers threw it in Madge's honor at the Plaza Hotel and it began at five in the afternoon, right after the ceremony. It was John's first experience with book travelers. He'd heard Madge refer to them so many times as bums, bastards and black-hearted liars he was astounded to learn that they were nearly all personable fellows, easy to know and like. They accepted him without any over-politeness,

51

and if any of them thought it strange for Madge to have picked a husband who was only twenty-three, nobody mentioned it. In fact, John felt immediately at home with these men who knew Madge so well and therefore had a lot in common with him. As he got drunker and drunker he kept telling Madge what a swell thing it was of them to do all this for her and him. "It's just as swell for them," Madge shrugged. "It's nothing out of their pockets. We're drinking up expense accounts because I'm a good customer. It gives them an excuse to ditch their wives and get stinking on their own. Book travelers! They won't buy you a cup of coffee out of their own pockets, but they'll drown you in champagne cocktails when someone else is footing the bill!" However, despite the names she called them and the way she rode them, John saw immediately that she loved these travelers and that they seemed attached to her in more than just a business way.

Bill Haley was there, and Arthur Diehl, and Karl Thompson, and Allen What's-His-Name who was killed in a car wreck a couple of years later and also the Morrow and Macmillan and Doubleday boys and—there must have been at least ten of them. But finally the party narrowed down to John and Madge and Karl Thompson. All the others had kissed the bride, figured expenses, and gone their various ways. Karl was over at the bar giving his Sunday pitch to a cigarette girl. Madge watched him with interest.

"He'll never make her," she said to John. "His approach is too highbrow. Bill Haley could make her but Karl doesn't know how. I'll bet he's talking literature to her, and that poor girl couldn't read anything more difficult than her daily astrology in the newspaper."

"Shhhhhhh," John shushed, "you're talkin' too loud. People are listening."

"Oh, the hell with people," Madge said loudly. "I don't give a damn about people tonight. Only 'bout you, Jack. You're all the people I care about tonight. Kiss me, Jack."

He kissed her.

"Where's Bill?" she asked suddenly.

"Bill who?"

"Haley. Did that big bum leave without even kissing me good luck?"

"He kissed you. He kissed you three times."

52

"He owes me ten bucks. Don't let me forget he owes me ten bucks. Swell guy, Bill. If he was single I'd married him but Bill seems to like 'em rich. Anyhoo, he still owes me ten bucks!"

How many champagne cocktails had John had? Ten? Twelve? He tried to think back if he'd eaten any lunch that day but couldn't remember. He'd never been this drunk before. It was a great effort for him to get his words out in any sensible order. He had to send them slowly and in single file or they tripped over each other and got entangled. Madge was doing better than he was. Maybe she'd had fewer cocktails. But her voice was terribly loud in this sedate room.

"Watcha thinkin', Jack?" she asked.

"I'm thinkin' how come Bill owes you ten dollars?"

"He bet me you wouldn't marry me."

John used this remark as a provocation for getting drunk-mad. "Why'n hell did he say a thing like that? He didn't know me from Adam."

The waiter brought two more champagne cocktails to the table. Karl Thompson had sent them and John looked up in time to see Karl wave as he left the room—alone. John waved back at the empty doorway.

Madge raised her glass and clicked it against his, spilling part of her drink onto the already damp tablecloth stippled with cigarette butts, ashes, wadded paper cocktail napkins, torn straws and similar debris.

"I'm gonna be real original," she said. "Here's to us!"

"He didn't know me from Adam!" John said again. "Why'd he bet I wouldn't marry you?"

"Oh, for Pete's sake, you still harpin' on that?"

"You damned tootin' I'm harpin' on it."

"Bill knew 'bout you from me. I told him all about you. I told him about your beautiful blonde hair, your cleft chin, n' your blue eyes. Blue, blue, blue." Madge's voice trailed away. She forgot to continue.

"What else'd you tell 'im 'bout me?"

"I told him how everybody else calls you John but how I call you Jack, 'cause John allus reminds me uv where you go when you have-ta. I told him you were the first man I ever wanted

53

t'marry and I said by God I was gonna marry you an' he bet me ten bucks I'd never make it."

John was muddled. The room had begun to spin slowly in a counter-clockwise direction. Easy does it, he told himself. Pull yourself together, take a deep breath, get on the beam, boy. Remember who you are.

I'm John Long, three months out of Syracuse, New York. Check. Yesterday at this time I had no job, no wife. Check. As of this minute I have a job, a wife and half a champagne cocktail. Double check. And how'd it all happen? Wait a minute. Don't tell me. I got the job because Mr. Barnes didn't have to hire anybody, and I got the cocktail because that waiter brought it to me and I got the wife because Madge won a ten dollar bet. No—that's not right! The room was spinning faster now. He made a mental note not to take another sip because he must not get sick —tonight. Check, check, check.

"Honey," Madge said. "Let's go home and go to bed."

He forgot his mental note, gulped the rest of his cocktail, dribbled some of it down his chin. "Soon . . . soon. First let me ask you a queshun."

"Shoot."

"Why'd you bet the ten bucks in the firs' place? Why'd you pick me? I'm nobody. I'm nothin'. You're brilliant. You're wunnerful."

Madge cupped her chin in her hands and grinned in a half comic, half pensive way. "Wait 'til I catch up with you and I'll tell you all about it." She paused long enough to drink from her cocktail, and must have thought she really did drink, but the truth was that she didn't move from her chin-in-hands position. "It was really simple, Jack. Very simple. You walked into the book department an' I studied the shoulders. I love your shoulders. I knew there'd be muscles and I love muscles. You smiled at me. It was a sweet smile—kinda sweet and sexy, an' I said to myself, got to have him!"

"You thought all that about me?"

"I thought all that."

"That why I ast you for a date?"

"Why. I made you."

54

The room was spinning violently now.

"Let's go," he said.

Madge got up. She was having a little trouble with her reflexes, but she made it, mumbling, "Come on, Jack. We got to begin catchin' up on our readin'!"

There's an aphorism about the human male which Dr. Kinsey missed but which most men think about from time to time. It says: a man can get mighty far behind with his sex life, but can get caught up in a helluva hurry. John thought about it many times in the years that followed.

In retrospect, there was no doubt in John's mind why he had married Madge King. He was not only far behind in his sex life; he hadn't ever really got started good. He'd made a few sporadic conquests back in Syracuse—hit-and-miss affairs of no meaning which had left him, if anything, more unfulfilled than he was before. When he'd met Madge in her book department he felt something friendly and outgoing about her that made him forget his discouragement and homesickness—a sort of electric current that dissipated his innate shyness and made him want to rub up against her.

She wasn't a beautiful woman, not even pretty, but she invited a second look. She was tall and wore her yellow hair in a short, careless bob which she kept brushed back of her ears. She wore no makeup except a thin line of lipstick that made her complexion seem overwhite. That first day she'd had on a solid color, tight dress with a low V-neckline and one of the first things John noticed about her were the magnificently developed breasts, with the rest of her all-in-a-line. He'd stared at her breasts that first day as he chatted with her in the book department and she must have known he was staring at them. They made him very excited. Very.

On their first date she'd told him that she was thirty and he'd felt infinitely younger than his age—inept, ineffectual and unequal to her. But the electric feeling was there and that took up the slack.

At the end of their first date he had stood at her door, shaken her hand, and said goodnight. She'd said, "You're a funny duck." So, the second date he hadn't shaken her hand. He had just walked inside, shut the door, and stayed.

55

In the very beginning he'd been skeptical about Madge's choosing him for a lover, since he had so much to learn on the subject. He was repressed, inhibited, not confident about procedures.

Much later, at a time when he had actually come to dread sharing the same bed with her, he tried to remind himself that she had picked him with a purpose in mind—that she went about selecting a lover as she selected an employee in her book department. She had a preference for green and inexperienced help. It was easier to teach them her way of doing things than it was to unteach what someone else had taught them. All that she asked was a willingness to learn. John was green enough, heaven knew, but he was exceedingly willing and had learned a frightening amount in a short time. He likened himself to an appliance which a housewife selects with the idea of trying it out in her home. If it works she keeps it, if it doesn't she sends it back. Obviously, he'd worked out fine.

Had he ever loved Madge? He had asked himself that question many times and he thought the answer was yes because love is a state of mind. He'd loved her if he thought he loved her and there was a time when he thought that. If it wasn't love it was the next thing to it, and that was close enough. So, yes. Thirteen years ago he had loved Madge. Five years later he hated her, or anyway, thought he hated her, and once again that was close enough. Love and hate. People bandied the words about with appalling authority and looseness. I love you can mean anything from "Thanks for the dinner and show" to "I shall but love thee better after death." I hate you can range from "You didn't invite me to your party" to "I killed him and I'm not sorry." So with all these gradations why pin a person down about love and hate? Psychologists say the two emotions are blood brothers. So as long as he hated Madge there must have been some part of the love left alive. It had been only after their divorce, in these years since he had married Ann and discovered how being in love and being happy could coexist, that he'd lost his hate completely and substituted pity when he thought of Madge. It takes a while to reinterpret hatred and learn that what you really feel now is sympathy—sympathy for yourself as well as the person you once hated. Instead of saying he had loved and

56

hated her, it might be more accurate to say he had once had illusions about her and had now become disillusioned.

Whatever it was, it felt good then and the electric current was generated so fast his battery was constantly being overcharged.

"Where do you live, Jack?" She asked the question idly that first night he'd stayed.

"In the Village. It's cheap and it's awful and I'm there as little as possible. Just a place to get my mail."

"Get your mail here."

"Huh?"

"Move your toothbrush here. It's nice to have a man around the place. Hand me a cigarette."

He reached for the pack of cigarettes on the bedside table and gave her one. She sat up in bed, smoking, saying nothing, just looking at him.

"Penny for your thoughts," she said, finally.

"If I move in here I'll want you to marry me, Madge. I come from proper people. We believe in matrimony."

"D'y'mean . . . ?" She had started to say something flippant and vulgar, but turned, leaned on an elbow, looked at him steadily and asked almost incredulously, "You aren't really proposing are you, Jack? I mean do you actually want to make an honest woman of me?"

It was obvious that what he had said touched her deeply. He saw her hand tremble as she took a drag on her cigarette. Hadn't she ever in her life had a proposal? Half-mockingly, but part seriously, he got out of bed, sank to one knee, took her hand, and said, "Madge, I'm not properly dressed for the occasion, but at least I'm in the proper position to ask you to be my wife."

She closed her eyes a moment and then rubbed each one quickly with the back of her hand. "Get back in bed, Jack," she said softly. "You'll catch cold."

John had fit into Madge's home routine, or rather, she'd made a place for him. She ran her house with the same precision that she ran her book department. She paid her maid more than maids usually earned, but she expected more work and got it. There were set days for window-washing, for waxing, for cleaning blinds,

57

just as there were regular days at the store for taking inventory, checking stock, and filling special orders.

In the beginning she ran John the way she ran her house and store—competently and efficiently. Because she liked him best in sports jackets and slacks, he wore them, and she made him throw away his bow ties and his shirts with button sleeves and give up his boxer type underwear for Jockey shorts. And because he was still so far behind and hadn't begun to catch up, he called all this love and maybe it was. When Madge had got him the job in Troxell's advertising department his cup of contentment ran over. Was it sex alone that had brought them together, held them together and made him think that he was in love? No. Sex wasn't all. Because, for one thing, there was her laugh. He loved to hear her laugh and she laughed a lot at first, a very personal sort of laugh, overloud, overlong, but intimate. Madge was a woman who could really laugh.

And it took a while before he'd first become aware that Madge was no ordinary woman where sex was concerned. He'd been too intent on satisfying his own keen sexual appetite to observe that she was infinitely hungrier. A lot of men, he knew—particularly when they're young—toy with the idea of meeting a nymphomaniac who's both attractive to be around and attracted to them. Few men ever realized this dream. They married girls slightly more or less sexed than the so-called norm and went through life wondering, occasionally, what it would have been like with the nymphomaniac who never materialized. But John Long not only met and lived with a girl who was a classic Aphrodite-type; he had married her. His initial ecstasy combined passion, lechery and lust; then amazement set in; then alarm; then, finally, despair. Madge was indefatigable, unquenchable, more than excessively libidinal. She taught him how to make love her way and she brought books home from the store which he studied with an eye on lengthening his staying power.

He became adept at lovemaking—almost a master—but he was never able to satisfy Madge. She was capable of a fortissimo abandon bordering on depravity that went on and on for minutes—hours, even—until he was totally wrung out. When he lay there spent, immobile, she tried arousing him again by strange, fey ways that

58

sometimes worked wonders. He felt the first stab of pity the night he awakened after what he considered a Herculean performance to hear her crying. He had withheld his climax for more than an hour, and had, he believed ridden her into a state of complete satiation. Now there was this crying, soft and private.

"What's the matter, honey?" he asked.

"Can't you guess?" she whispered. "I want more."

"My God, Madge! How many times—?" He had lost count of her orgasms.

She sobbed. "It's the way I'm made. It's all wrong, Jack—but what in the hell can I do about it?" She was crying harder now and he felt genuinely sorry for her.

"Let me get you a glass of milk," he said.

"No, thanks," she answered. "Milk won't get the job done."

"But, Madge, I *can't* any more tonight. I just by God *can't!*"

"Go to sleep, Jack," she said and kissed him lightly. "Go to sleep. I'll see you in the morning."

And he knew what she meant by that.

Hers was a terrible illness without a cure. He sometimes had a feeling that if she could ever be completely satisfied—by him, or by someone better than he—or maybe by a half dozen men, her animalistic craving might leave her and she would become a relaxed woman for the first time. But of course, that never happened.

The breakup of a marriage can be compared to falling plaster in a room exposed to water from above. There is the faintest line of a crack at first, barely discernible, then a crack for sure and then an area that loosens and begins to sag. The final bit of stress brings it all down in a confusion of noise, dust, and breakage. The infinitesimal cracks in the ceiling of his marriage to Madge had started within six months.

Little things like neckties . . .

"Why do you buy those stupid bow ties?"

"Because I like them. Because four-in-hands get in my way when I lean over an ad layout."

"They make you look like a kid."

"Maybe I am a kid."

"You sure act like one."

59

"Shut up!"

Little things—like asking her for lunch and always getting a turn-down.

"I can't make it, Jack. I'm sorry."

"You mean you won't make it. You've got a full hour coming to you for lunch but you can't ever make it—with me."

"Don't be impossible. You know how I hate to leave the department for more than a few minutes. I've got to be here. A book store's not like an ad department. Nobody knows what's under these tables but me . . ."

"You'd say yes if I were a salesman."

"That's business. I have to do things with the salesmen."

"I'll bet you do!"

Little things like, "Why don't we ever have anybody over to visit?"

"I never know when I'll have to work at night in the store. Ask some of your friends over."

"I did . . . and they wanted to know where my wife was. Let's set a night for next week and have some travelers over. How about Bill Haley? We owe him a dinner. Please. Let's set the time right now."

Madge shook her head. "Bill's not in town. He's on his fall trip. We'll have a party soon. I promise. Be patient with me, Jack—and don't be lonely."

"I won't be."

But he was lonely. During the day it was all right. He spent his lunch hours alone exploring the city. Sometimes he'd take a bus or a subway to eat his meal in a part of Manhattan he'd never seen before. He window-shopped and listened to people and went in book stores and sat on park benches. He still wasn't accustomed to the size of New York but he was learning it a little bit at a time, discovering something new every day, and as he became better acquainted with the metropolis he seemed to feel more sure of himself.

In the apartment alone at night it was different. Madge always had dozens of new books to read, but he would find his mind leaving the page to wonder where she really was tonight. Sometimes she'd come in very late. Two and three days might go by without

60

his seeing her except in bed and in the morning when they dressed for work. The apartment was not his home at all. It was hers, and he still felt just moved-in. He could leave tomorrow and this apartment wouldn't know it: he was just an attachable fixture in the bedroom, which she used as matter-of-factly as she used the plumbing.

As the second year pressed the third the cracks in the ceiling grew more perceptible. He saw that he couldn't go on living like this forever, but he kept telling himself he couldn't quit her simply because she was sexually obsessed. Hers was an illness and he should make her consult a doctor, but he couldn't climb the high wall she kept around her libido. She refused to discuss doctors. Only once, in all their marriage, did she speak of an operation she had had years before, mentioning it casually when he brought up the subject of contraceptives. "Nothing can happen . . . I've had an operation," she'd said. And he wondered if that operation had anything to do with her insatiability.

Then the ceiling began to sag under a final pressure, for he learned by accident about Madge and T. Harold Barnes. He was in a booth in the men's room on the ninth floor and the two men who came in, thinking they were alone, continued their conversation.

"I don't think Long has the faintest idea about his wife and Barnes."

"Well, you know what they say about a husband. Always the last to know!"

Then they saw the feet in the closed booth and said nothing more.

After that, he became an eavesdropper, a pussyfooter, a spy. Merely by walking down the hall from the advertising rooms it was possible to ascertain that T. Harold Barnes was not in his office and John would then go to the book department to find that Madge was also missing. Sometimes she'd be gone most of the afternoon and that was strange behavior for a girl who couldn't take a full hour for lunch for having to watch the business. He disbelieved her stories about working nights in the department now, and he didn't, in fact, believe anything she said any more.

His attitude changed toward his own work, too. He'd been

61

happy in the advertising department, pleased with what he thought was progress; now he wondered how much of his success was the result of a fast play from Madge to T. Harold Barnes. He became wildly furious when he thought of all the things that hadn't been said that day in Barnes' office when Barnes had hired him. What fun Madge must have been having then at his expense.

Over a paragraph of copy or a partially filled-in layout he couldn't keep himself from imagining Madge in bed with Barnes— old fifty-ish, pot-bellied, glisteningly bald Barnes, groping his way to the bed after leaving his glasses on a dresser. The mental picture of this man who, God knew, was unromantic enough completely dressed, stripped and in bed with Madge made John Long sick at his stomach.

So it was only a question of how long before the weakened ceiling buckled and fell, and when it did happen he knew there would be casualties—Madge, T. Harold Barnes, himself—who would suffer injuries that would never heal. He hated himself for sneaking around spying on his wife, but he knew that he couldn't stop doing it until he caught her red-handed.

And so the strain between him and Madge grew worse daily. He had never thought a time would come when he would turn down offered sex, but he found it increasingly difficult in those days to cooperate when she wanted him. Madge was stunned by this, for in place of the heavenly violence she needed she sensed his distaste for her, and more than once he frightened himself and humiliated her by being unable to perform, try as she did to arouse him. She could have accepted accusations, insolence, physical abuse, she simply could not accept impotence. An impotent man was worse than a dead one to a woman like Madge.

"What's the matter with you lately, Jack?"

"Nothing's the matter with me."

"Like hell it isn't. You're all right in your job, aren't you? You're making what you think you're worth, aren't you?"

If he said no would she rush out and fix it up for him with Barnes?

"I'm happy enough in the god-damned job," he told her.

"Then what's the matter? Is it me? What have I done?"

"It's . . ." He couldn't say it. "It's just that we never see each

62

other any more, Madge. We're in different worlds, and we don't have anything to talk about."

"You want to *talk?* All right, let's talk. What shall we talk about? Your work at the store?"

"The hell with my work at the store."

"That isn't the way you acted when I got the job for you."

More fighting words. He knew how she'd got him the job.

"Haven't I ever thanked you? Well, thanks."

"Kiss my ass," she said.

Eventually, toward the very last, he lost some of his antagonism and felt pity for her. He did not argue with her; just kept still, and waited to see what would happen. He wondered why she didn't kick him out, but he guessed that she needed their marriage for a front of respectability and he drifted on, restless, desperately unhappy.

He had been in this mood the morning T. Harold Barnes called him into his office and introduced him to a slight, intelligent-looking girl with shiny black hair worn up high so that her ears showed.

"Long," Barnes said, "this young lady is Miss Ann Austin. She's going to work here as a copywriter and I want you to be nice to her and show her the ropes."

That had been Ann. And he had shown her the ropes.

6

ANN straightened up from her slumped-over position. She worked her head up and down and from side to side in a slow, circular motion to relieve the tautness at the back of her neck. She tried to massage away the soreness that resulted from keeping her eyes

63

focused so sharply on the paper in her typewriter. She opened and shut the fingers on each hand, stretching them as far apart as she could.

Her watch showed almost midnight, so she had been writing without a letup since before seven. She rubbed her eyes with the backs of her wrists and thought dully, Mustn't rub the eyes; it's not good for them. But it felt good and she kept on until she saw bright oranges and greens and geometric patterns dancing like shooting stars.

On the floor at her feet was a pile of paper where she'd dropped the finished pages one by one. She pulled the last sheet from the roller, added it face down to the completed pages and gathered the stack together. Another chapter.

She should not have worked this late. All afternoon and all evening was too much, she kept telling herself, and yet she had done it every day for three weeks since John had left for the South, right after Labor Day.

He was so much more than a traveler now. In the sales office he was a kind of liaison man between the editorial and the commercial ends of the firm. Billy Clarke had entrusted him with scouting for manuscripts; he had served as editor on several of these books, and at least two authors he'd discovered were valuable L and C properties. With him away Ann had intensified her efforts on the book, working in her office past midnight.

She knew she looked terrible, but she had to get it over with and the sooner the better. Then she could rest and forget it. She had been getting home at night around one, telling herself that since she didn't have to awaken until eight she could count on seven hours' sleep. But often at two, three, four, even, she found herself lying wide awake—her mind racing, her brain unable to relax for fear of forgetting some new piece of plot it had invented. She would jump out of bed at all hours, turn on the light and write down a thought lest it vanish before morning. All the people she created by day came to visit her at night and refused to go home at a decent hour.

Also, of late, when she lay in bed unable to sleep, a new and disturbing feeling came over her. Not the worry that she wouldn't get the book written but the uneasy knowledge that she was writing

64

herself into trouble. She felt ashamed and disgusted with herself —like an informer obliged by a compulsion stronger than himself to tell all he knows, yet one who hates himself for betraying secrets. Was this what John had meant when he warned her against writing about what she knew? She wasn't sure she *knew* these people she put on paper. They were real enough, all right, but they were unpredictable, moving about as they saw fit, ignoring her directions. She felt she was, at best, a reporter, describing what they did but unaware of their motivations. She wished that she could control them, mould them, embroider them with imaginative stimuli and responses, but they, instead, seemed to conspire to make her book her enemy.

When she'd begun to write her story it had flowed with an ease and naturalness that delighted her, her people themselves telling her what they must say. There were three main characters: Jerry, her hero, Mona, his first wife, and his second wife, Norma. *Jerry. Mona.* When she saw the characters' names on paper now cold sweat popped out of her and she remembered a thing John had said at least eight years ago when he'd registered them in at that hotel in Omaha. They'd both been working in the advertising department of Troxell's at the time and John was still married to Madge. Just barely, yet still married and he'd talked her into taking what he called an "illicit weekend" in Omaha before he went into the army.

"Why Omaha?" she asked.

"*Because it's the last place in the world anyone would look for either of us if we never returned!*"

They'd flown to Omaha and stayed in that rococo hotel with the oversized rooms, registered as Mr. and Mrs. Jerome Langston and John had whispered in her ear as they were going up in the elevator to their room, "*A criminal always uses his real initials when he's faking a name.*"

Their diet those three days had consisted mostly of champagne and it was the first time they had been together without having to practice constant deceptions. No back booths for those three days and no passing each other without speaking. In Omaha they ate in the hotel dining room, went to a movie, drank vast quantities of champagne and loved prodigiously. It was a carefree shore-leave

65

and a welcome vacation from being circumspect—except at breakfast when John was ultra-proper. He made the room service man wait until Ann had shut the bathroom door behind her.

"Why?" she asked over her breakfast roll the second morning. "I look innocent in my robe, don't I? We're registered as man and wife. Yet the minute the waiter raps on the door you hustle me out of sight. Why?" He'd pinked ostensibly around the neck and ears, and she'd cried, "Why, you're blushing! I've caught you in a habit from your dark past. You make 'em all go and hide!" And she'd said, "All right, you win for now, but I warn you, my darling: when Mrs. J.L. stands for Mrs. John Long I'm not budging. In fact, I intend to specialize in staring waiters down."

And, if the good citizens of Omaha thought it strange that a tall man and a not-so-tall girl should be holding each other up on the Omaha National Bank corner at high noon on a Saturday in May, no word of complaint was heard. Maybe such things happened all the time in Omaha when it served as a neutral corner for lovers on the lam. Anyway, Mr. and Mrs. J.L. had been deliriously happy, moon-eyed, champagne drunk and careless. Oh God, how careless! Ann's face flushed when she thought of it . . .

Jerry and Mona—John and Madge! Some part of Ann's subconscious had played a deliberate trick on her. It hadn't seemed important, but now she wished for other names. It was too late. They existed. She couldn't change their names any more than she could change the names of real people. Her book was more than half done, and she knew her people as well as she knew Bess or Birdie or Abe.

Don't write about what you know. Well, her story was set against a backdrop of radio. She had worked at WOOZ long enough to know the picture of day-to-day broadcasting, and she'd heard Harry Shell's vivid and picturesque stories of the golden days of radio so many times she felt a part of them. Other than a book of people with problems, she was writing a novel about an industry whose dazzling ups and depressing downs were a vivid part of the American scene and she had drawn upon the people she worked with in making her characters: Harry, of course; her assistant, Irene; the receptionist, announcers, engineers, time sales-

66

men. Yet no person in the book was a portrait from life. They were all a blend of reality with make-believe.

She had meant her book to show the integrity of a marriage from the viewpoint of the second wife, but something strange and uncontrollable began to happen early in the writing. An inexplicable affinity began to grow between her and the character of the first wife. No, not an affinity—an *attraction* which softened her pre-existing concept of the first wife, and in place of the revealing white light of the early chapters, shadows appeared now which hid and protected the character's blemishes. An odd, unaccountable empathy for this girl, Mona, began to seep between the lines and color the story. Ann explored her beginnings and found a basis for her unfaithfulness in a tragic childhood. She found that Mona needed Jerry's love desperately even when she least deserved it.

All sorts of things, in fact, were creeping in to change her book and the people in it—compulsive things she could not control, but which, instead, threatened to control her. A subtle picture of marriage and remarriage was emerging, different from her original concept. Although the rules of writing precluded seeking sympathy for a character who broke the moral law this first wife was becoming a sympathetic character. And why was Norma, wife number two, jealous of her? Is every second wife jealous of the first? Or, if jealousy is too harsh a word, curious? Everything was going wrong with her people. Instead of Jerry's being the victim of his wife's unfaithfulness, there was a feeling (which Ann could not control) that he was less a husband than Mona deserved. Ann's fascination with this first wife was running away with her imagination and wrecking her plans for the love story of a second wife.

Was the character she created really *Madge?* Ann wearily ran her hand across her forehead. How many times had she asked herself that question during these weeks? How *could* Mona be Madge? She hadn't known Madge except through hearsay, had spoken to her only once.

"Do you have a copy of The Big Fisherman?"

John had told her what he thought she had a right to know: about Madge's sexual excesses, about T. Harold Barnes, and such behavior revolted her, made her despise Madge. Yet this book character, Mona, did the same things or worse and Ann found

67

her appealing. At one point Ann had written the question: Who is to blame when a marriage breaks up and a husband remarries? but she x'ed it out. Don't ask that!

As for Norma, the second wife, Ann knew this girl by heart. She brought Jerry tenderness and contentment instead of embarrassment and shame. She was deeply in love with him and surely right for him—but the incredible truth remained that this girl, with whom Ann wanted her readers to identify, grew weaker as the book gained momentum, while Mona, the girl to be rejected, grew stronger. More than once Ann tore a page from the typewriter, ripped it into small pieces and threw it into the wastebasket, only to have the next page make this same point more deeply.

She told herself that when the time came to write of the second wife's abortion the values would right themselves. Norma's sacrifice because of Mona, who even then was sleeping with other men, would put right and wrong into their proper places. Then the right girl would win the reader's sympathy for keeps.

But although she tried with all her skill to express Norma's grief at having to stop the baby, she still could not win the battle against Mona. The bad girl, for all her weaknesses, was more convincing, more—*say* it!—*human* than the intended heroine. There was no doubt now as to who was troubling the triangle of Jerry, Mona, and Norma. It was Norma's own shadow, the shadow of the second wife, interfering with the marriage. Ann kept protesting: this isn't *true*—but as the story stood it seemed true enough. She remembered John's earlier reaction: *"You aren't going to do anything crazy—I mean like opening up any healed wounds?"* This book was a sharpened knife, all right, that kept the old wound bleeding and that was the reason she had to finish it as quickly as possible—before it finished her.

The telephone rang, startling her so much she trembled as she said hello.

"Atlanta, Georgia, calling Mrs. John Long."

"This is she."

"Hello, Ann?" John's voice sounded excited and concerned. "What in the world are you doing at the office? It's past midnight."

"I was just fixing to leave. I've been working on the—thing."

"You sound bushed. Do you feel all right?"

68

"I'm fine. The telephone scared me, that's all."

"I keep thinking about you. The beetle-brains in the accounting office want to know why all these calls are on my expense account. Damn it, Ann, I *miss* you!"

"I miss you, too." Her voice sounded far away, even to herself. She was groggy and sick with fatigue.

"Ann, you're killing yourself. I usually call earlier. Do you work this late every night?"

"No," she lied.

"Why don't you ask for a week off and fly down here? I'll be in New Orleans Friday. We can have fun."

"I can't, dear. Irene's on her vacation, so I've got to stay here."

She was glad to hear his voice and she didn't want him to stop talking—yet it was all she could do to speak half-way intelligently. It was like being in a dream and wanting to talk and not having the power to utter a sound.

"How's the trip?" she asked.

"Terrible. It's still hot down here. Indian Summer they call it. Business is off, too. Nobody's buying. Now, listen, Ann: promise me you'll go right home and get some sleep."

"I promise. I'll be out of here in five minutes."

"I love you, Ann."

"I know it, darling. And I love to hear you say it. I'll write you a long letter tomorrow and send it to New Orleans . . . to the Roosevelt?"

"Yes, the Roosevelt."

"Oh, swell. I'll write. Goodbye."

"Goodbye."

She put the telephone back into its cradle, feeling that she had been unscintillating but she was pleased that he called. It was as if he'd been looking over her shoulder as she typed and guessed that at that moment she needed reassurance. She clipped together what she had written tonight to add to the finished part of her manuscript at home, remembering she had read once that Hemingway advised writers to begin a bit of the next chapter before calling it a day. She smiled sardonically and decided that even Hemingway would have quit when he was this depleted.

She stood up and tried to press the wrinkles out of her skirt with

69

the palm of her hand and noticed that it fit sloppily. I ought to eat more, she thought. I ought to eat something now. She decided to go to the Automat across from Grand Central and have a sandwich before she went home, but that would take a half hour more. She looked at her watch again. Oh well, what difference did it make? She would not go to sleep anyway. She could promise herself to go home, all right, but she couldn't promise herself to sleep.

Mrs. Snyder, who cleaned the office at night, was just finishing the hall when Ann rang for the elevator. A woman of sixty or so, she looked at Ann with bright blue eyes and smiled wistfully. When Ann worked late like this, Mrs. Snyder always cleaned all the other offices and the hall, then came back to Ann's office last so as not to disturb her.

"You really worked late tonight, Miss." Her soft, drawling voice gave the listener the impression that she'd had her full share of sadness.

"Ann. Call me Ann, Mrs. Snyder. I—I'm doing some extra work," she explained, without knowing why she felt impelled to say anything at all. Perhaps Mrs. Snyder saw the truth with those wise, blue eyes. Perhaps Mrs. Snyder had a novel of her own—a novel that was better, mainly because she knew better than to let it be put down on paper.

"Good night, Mrs. Snyder," Ann said as the elevator arrived.

"Good night, Ann."

After she had eaten, she felt better. When she got home it was after one and she took a hot bath and got into bed, but she didn't sleep. She kept thinking how stupid she must have sounded talking with John, and then she wondered how she had been able to write in such a daze. Evidently the book was one thing, her own feelings another.

She wondered how it would read. She could show it now. There was enough of it finished for a reader to brand it good, bad, or indifferent, and she tried to think of people she could show it to without feeling like a fool. She thought of Bess, but Bess wasn't the kind of friend (thank God!) who would be objective. Perhaps being a friend and being a critic were antipathetic. With Bess it was hear-see-speak-no-evil where someone she loved was concerned.

Who, then? Suddenly she remembered Bill Haley. She was

70

going to submit it to his company and Bill was smart. His advice on a manuscript would be worth listening to—but perhaps he was on the road now. She would find out first thing in the morning.

She got up and drank a glass of water. It was almost two and she knew that she wouldn't sleep for a long time.

She went to the telephone and dialed long distance.

"I'd like to speak to Mr. John Long, please. In Atlanta, Georgia. He stays at the Atlanta Biltmore Hotel. Try to get it through right away, will you?"

She heard the Atlanta operator, then the hotel switchboard operator. She heard the ring in John's room, and then another ring. He was asleep and she shouldn't have awakened him.

"Hello."

"Hello. John? I'm sorry to wake you up, but I wanted to talk to you again."

"What time is it?" He was still not quite awake.

"Almost two. I was in bed and lonesome for you and I couldn't sleep, so I decided to call you back."

"Glad you did. I'm worried about you."

"Don't worry, *please*. I'm all right. Honest I am. Tomorrow afternoon I'm not going to do a darned thing. I'll work like hell on my radio copy in the morning and then I'll take it easy."

"That sounds more like it. Get into mischief; it'll do you good."

"I may do that! . . . Describe yourself to me, darling."

"Huh?"

"Tell me what you're wearing. I'm wearing the blue nightgown you like. What are you wearing?"

"My striped pajamas. The red-and white ones—just the bottoms." Tall as he was, he loved stripes. In his pajamas he could wear what he pleased.

"And are you on your side of the bed?"

"Natch."

"Move over to my side, dear."

"Okay. I'm moved. Is that better?"

"Oh, that's fine. Now I can go to sleep because I know where you are. Goodnight, darling."

"Goodnight, Ann."

71

She felt infinitely relieved, as though she'd just learned that someone she loved who had been very ill was much improved. Well, she had been ill—tired and ill—and now she was better. She set the alarm for eight, turned out the light, and lay down. She bolted the door of her brain against Mona, Jerry and Norma, closed her eyes and thought of John.

Long John Long in his red-and-white striped pajamas.

She laid her hand on his side of the bed and fell asleep.

7

BILL HALEY slept with the sun in his eyes. In his sleep he had moved toward the window where he lay peacefully on his back, breathing deeply, his face washed with the morning sunlight. His mouth, which was usually grinning when he was awake, was drooped dejectedly in sleep and his red hair, tufted and plastered, gave him the look of the man in the Vitalis ad before he learned about Vitalis. His was a round face, full of mounds and vales with no sharp peaks and when he was awake it had a sweet, pretty-boyishness to it. Only sleep unfrocked him and endowed him with an expression of flatulence.

Bill Haley was the kind of fellow people liked from a distance. He seemed too sure of himself to invite closeness and an offer of friendship is usually extended to someone who looks as though he needs a friend. As is the case wtih many men, however, Bill's self-sufficiency was merely a drawn curtain that concealed more than the average amount of loneliness and frustration. Whatever you thought about Bill Haley had to be analyzed from which side of the curtain you looked at him. He would make a remark like, "My business is selling books, and if I can't sell 'em standing up

72

I'll sell 'em lying down," and be branded a self-styled lady-killer, a self-centered blow-off, and a self-inflated salesman.

But Ann knew the other, the gentle, generous side of his nature. He had stuck his neck out once to do a favor for John when doing it could have cost him plenty in many ways. He had bumped into John by accident and learned that he'd just returned from Korea and was at loose ends. He didn't seem to be hurting for money but it was apparent he needed to find an outlet for his abilities. When Bill found out that Laverty and Clarke had an opening for a traveler in the Southwest he went to Billy Clarke, gave John a terrific buildup, then literally forced him to apply. Clarke had found in John Long a man tuned to his own wave length, immediately hired him as a traveler and kept piling on additional responsibilities in the home office until John was an important part of the L and C operation.

When Bill Haley first took the southern territory for Fortune House in 1945 he was permitted to keep three New York accounts which he had been servicing for the company and Troxell Brothers was one of them. He'd every right to expect violent repercussions from Madge who would want to know why in hell he was going out of his way to help Jack when he was supposed to be her friend, for Bill sensed a definite hangover of bitterness from the divorce. But strangely Madge never mentioned it to him—although she'd known it was he who got Jack the job.

Bill had been with Fortune House twenty-four years now, beginning in 1938 after his graduation from Cornell and including a hitch in the navy during World War II. He'd come from a wealthy family in Columbus, Ohio, where he'd owned the best bike on the block when he was a kid and the fanciest convertible in Columbus when he was a senior in high school. Because his family had money, he couldn't qualify for an athletic scholarship at Cornell where scholarships were awarded on the basis of need, so he paid his own way while playing football like a pro. The thing he wanted most—in fact, the only thing he ever really wanted—was to be All American. Then, from the moment *Collier's Magazine* nominated him All American Fullback in his senior year, ambition became his short suit. Some men work a lifetime to achieve a goal, but Bill Haley didn't have any goal left. He was lucky; he had

73

made it, and that was one reason he was so popular at Fortune House. He'd made it plain from the beginning that he was happy just being a traveler and wasn't bucking for anybody's job in the sales office.

Although he'd been married twice Bill still had the temperament of a bachelor-playboy. He had served a ten-year apprenticeship in Cafe Downtown and repeated the process at Cafe Uptown. He liked expensive women mainly because of a crazy notion that a woman who demands a lot does so because she's been used to a lot. His two wives had had money of their own but the only advantage he claimed from that was the not inconsiderable privilege of foregoing alimony. If Bill Haley had one cardinal fault it was an ants-in-the-pants inability to stay put in the same place more than three months. He liked his job with Fortune House mainly because he could pack his suitcase and light out on a selling trip at a moment which usually coincided with his wife's getting on his nerves.

The telephone woke him up and on the third ring he opened his eyes, blinked at the sun, groaned and rolled over. It took him two more rings to crawl to the other side of the huge bed and reach the receiver.

"Hello." It was a parched, forlorn greeting.

"Hello. Bill . . . Bill?"

"This is Bill."

"This is Ann." She still wasn't sure whether he was asleep or awake.

"Ann who?" Bill Haley, awake, would have had more finesse.

"Ann Long . . . Remember? Or don't I count?"

"Oh, sure, Ann. You woke me up."

"I'm sorry, Bill. I wasn't sure you'd even be in town. I just wanted to talk to you before I went to work this morning. You can go back to sleep when I'm through."

"I don't want to go back to sleep. I've been asleep since five yesterday afternoon when I passed out. Now I just want to die."

"Bill Haley! You have no business getting that drunk in the middle of the week!"

74

"I do, too." He was waking up. "Do you want to marry me, Ann?" His voice was still raspy and blurred.

"Thanks for the compliment, but I have a real nice husband. Remember? Friend of yours. And if I'm not mistaken, you have a very—."

"You mean *had* a very—"

"Bill! No!"

"Yes. Divorce was final yesterday. In Reno. That's why I purged myself with alcohol. She was noble, though. Gave me the apartment . . . Marry me, dear?"

"Don't be crazy. Besides, even as a joke you shouldn't say that to the first person you talk to the minute you're free."

She laughed. "Seriously, I wanted you to do me a favor today. No, not marry me. I wanted—if you've a hangover, I'm not even going to ask."

"Go on and ask. I haven't a thing planned and I'm bound to get better because I couldn't feel worse."

"I'll come there."

"Come *here? Now?*"

"Oh, *Bill!* The world's not going to come to an end if I see you in your pajamas. I'll stay exactly three minutes and have the cab wait. What's your address?"

He gave it to her, explaining, "The front door will be open. Walk in. Go straight ahead for three miles, turn to the right at the gold statue, then left at the twin blackamoors. A half mile farther down the road is the bedroom. I'll be there."

Bill's facetiousness had a kernel of truth, Ann found. The Sutton Place apartment building consisted of nine and ten room ultra-ultra cooperative apartments and it had been generous of his ex to give it to Bill, Ann thought, as the elevator man (with only the suggestion of a raised eyebrow at such a lovely passenger so early in the morning) pressed the automatic button, let the door open (automatically) and pointed (automatically) to Bill's apartment. If the eyebrow went higher at the open door, Ann didn't look back. She walked inside, careful to leave the door ajar, wandered through rooms and halls, turned at the gold statue and again at the blackamoors, walked into what turned out to be the master bedroom and saw the master.

75

Bill Haley had put on a robe, but he was back in bed, leaning against a small knoll of pillows. The bed was not only enormous, it was circular, making its occupant look rolier and polier than he really was.

"This *place*," Ann said. "It's—."

"Big," Bill finished it for her. "It'll be easy to sell. Hilda's lawyer wants it, for one, and I'm going to throw in this bed. Isn't it cute?" He frowned. "I feel ousy-lay." He crawled several feet across the bed to a table where he poured himself a glass of water and took some pills. Then, settling back again he asked, "Where's Jack?"

Whenever she heard anyone call John Jack she had to think for a second before she knew who was meant. Bill was the only person she ever saw who still called him that.

"He's on the road. I thought you'd be, too."

"Nope. I'm not leaving till early next week because we're having what's playfully known as a sales conference this week. I'm on sick leave today. Food poisoning." He grimaced. "In a way it's true. Hilda was a terrible cook."

Ann remembered the cab downstairs. "Bill—." She faltered and tried again. "Bill, I've got a novel half finished and I need your opinion of it. I've got it here in this box. Can you look it over today?"

"A novel? My God, Ann!"

Ann frowned, then said, "Why are all book travelers allergic to novels and novel writers? Go on, *tell* me."

"Maybe it's because allergies are supposed to spring from constant contact with what you work with."

"Well, allergic or not, here it is," she said. "You can read it today and have dinner with me tonight. Cold cuts and potato salad—."

Bill greened. "*Please!* Do not mention food at a time like this! All I ever want the rest of my life is something sour and cold—by the gallon." He moaned. "I've tried for years to get you in my bedroom and what happens? Cold cuts and potato salad!"

Ann laughed. "You know very well we settled that once and for all a long time ago." She had been one of the few who had ever resisted the Haley make and he had practically worshipped the unattainable ever since. "Well, what do you say?"

76

"It's a deal. What's the book about?"

She placed it on the foot of the incredible bed. "You'll see. Come tonight around seven-thirty and I'll have somebody for you. Somebody special."

She said goodbye to him, turned, and left the bedroom before he could attempt any gallantry. She closed the front door this time, gave the imperturbable elevator man a Mona Lisa smile and headed for her cab.

Bill Haley fell back into bed and put his hand on his stomach to quiet the butterflies. I wonder why she picked me, he thought. If the book's any good Jack would latch onto it, wouldn't he?

Or did Ann simply want to know what he thought of it?

His thinking came to an abrupt end as the picture of a plate of cold cuts with potato salad flashed into his mind. He barely made it to the bathroom in time.

Ann felt wonderful. Today was a vacation day from the novel by official decree, so she'd worn a new silk print with a matching sweater and even a little hat with white wings which John said made her look like an angel. Bill was too hung-over to notice it. When she got to the radio station she dove into a spot campaign one of the salesmen had sold to a tire dealer. Two treads are better than one was the theme, and Ann began thinking of attention-getting ways to open the pitch . . . Two *somethings* are better than one! was the right opening provided she had the proper "some-things." She thought of, "Two pairs of nylons are better than one!" but discarded it because nylon stockings are feminine somethings while nylon tires call for a masculine appeal. "Two steaks are better than one!" Better. "Two World Series seats are better than one!" Okay . . . Then she fit them together and wrote: "True or false: Two steaks are better than one? *True.* True or false: Two World Series tickets are better than one? *True.* True or false: Two treads are better than one? *True*—because two treads on a tire mean *double* protection and . . ."

She went at her work without the usual coffee break and talk. Each day she got her copy out of the way as early as possible, which meant saying no even to Harry when he asked, "Coffee,

77

Ann?" Come to think of it, Harry hadn't been around for several days.

Be patient one more day, dear Harry. Tomorrow I'll invite you for coffee and tell you what's been eating your Annie all these weeks. She thought of Bill Haley, maybe at this moment reading what she had written, and said mentally to Harry, *I'll tell you all about it—either way.*

"Two wives are better than one," she almost wrote as Mona and Norma stared back at her from their hiding places inside the typewriter. She pounded the keys harder than usual as if to drive them out of sight. Today she was not allowing herself to think of anything more disturbing than tire treads. Now that Bill had her manuscript there was a truce in her war with the people in it. She felt like calling John again but if she did he'd know for sure she was crazy. She'd write him a letter as bright and bubbly as she felt this morning. She wouldn't mention Bill Haley, though. Better get his reaction first.

Earlier she had called Charlene, her hairdresser, and wangled a three o'clock appointment. It took some fast talking but she'd succeeded. Years before, Ann had given Charlene tickets to a radio quiz show on which Charlene had won a washing machine. She'd kept it in her living room at first and made a kind of shrine of it, so Ann thought now, smiling, that so long as the machine held up Charlene would always work her in.

The last minute copy didn't floor her as it sometimes did. Her desk was soon clean and she had only one more call to make before she could leave.

"Ann! You haven't called in a week!" Bess Frankel wasn't as patient as Harry.

"There's a reason," Ann said, "which I'll tell you later. Can you make dinner tonight at the apartment? Bill Haley's coming over. Come early and we'll catch up."

"Who's Bill Haley?" Ann smiled at Bess's effort to sound casual. Bess was relating Ann's absence to something concrete—like a man.

"Bill is part of the reason—but not what you think. I'll tell you everything. Can you come?"

"I'll be there early," Bess promised, and Ann felt curiously relieved. Even though Bill Haley knew where he stood with Ann,

78

it was still good insurance to have a third party present when he called.

She looked at her watch. Two-thirty. She grabbed her purse and gloves, stamped her letter, had a sandwich at the building luncheonette, and made Charlene's with thirty seconds to spare.

If Bill likes my book . . . *if* I continue writing it, I'll try to explain what a hairdresser's salon means to a tired woman, Ann thought as she relaxed under the drier. Most men thought of beauty parlors as places of shrill confusion where women read movie magazines and gossiped *ad nauseam,* but Ann knew better. She found Charlene's a place where she could know a kind of serenity usually associated with a church or a museum. The quiet, efficient shampoo girl, the manicurist who said little, Charlene, herself all worked with a kind of easy rhythm that belied tension. Ann did some of her best thinking here. She couldn't express it without sounding silly, but perhaps she could tell on paper how Charlene's gave her a feeling of inner calm. She was glad to be here now, even with her anxious feeling about Bill's verdict, excited and frightened. If he didn't like it—*really* like it—what? Only she could answer and she found the answer here at Charlene's restful salon. If Bill didn't like her book—. She still had three hours of her vacation and she'd not trouble her good mood until she had to.

Bess Frankel hadn't shut the door before she blurted out, "Tell me; who's Bill Haley?"

"He's a book traveler. Like John. Only Bill's on the road most of the time. Matter of fact, Bill got John his job. You've never met Bill because—well, we don't see a lot of him because he belongs to the past. He's lots of fun but he still sees the—Troxell people. He's coming over tonight to tell me his opinion of something."

"Something in the past?" Bess asked.

"Only indirectly. I've been concealing something from you, Bess, for almost three months. No. Not a love affair. I'm writing a novel."

"A novel?" Bess said. And then she repeated it. "A *novel?*"

"Yes. And I couldn't say anything about it to you or anyone until I was far enough along with it to be sure I could do it."

79

"What's it about?" Bess asked impulsively. "Am I in it? Is Dr. Darnell in it?"

"It's about . . . the right kind of wife and the wrong kind of wife," Ann answered and as she said it she thought again how perverse the people are that you write about; how sometimes, if a writer doesn't watch her step, the right kind becomes the wrong kind and the wrong kind becomes the right kind. "Don't worry. You'll see it as soon as it's finished." *If I finish it.* "I told John about it and he suggested Bill's company as a possible publisher, so I asked Bill to look at what I've written so far and tell me what he thinks. A smart traveler knows as much about what people will read and buy as a smart editor."

Bess was obviously surprised and relieved. "A book. And I was trying to think of everything else."

"You aren't mad at me for not telling you earlier?"

"No," Bess said. "I understand." And then, with childlike eagerness, "I can't wait to read it."

"I asked Bill over tonight to get his opinion of it. I want you to see that he and I have a minute or two to ourselves somewhere during the evening so that he can let me have it straight. But only a minute or two."

"Why did you ask me tonight?" Bess said in her open way. "I'm glad you did, but don't you want to be alone with him for the criticism?"

Ann shot her a woman-to-woman look which made the next words unnecessary. "You don't know Bill Haley!"

"Where's the blonde?" Bill demanded as Ann let him in. "I hope your friend's a blonde." Then, before Ann could say a word he rushed on with what really was on his mind, "It's wonderful, Ann. *Wonderful.*"

She took the cardboard box containing the manuscript from him but remained planted to the spot unable to speak or move. Bess heard what Bill said, saw Ann's surprise, and decided to introduce herself. "I'm Bess Frankel," she said holding out her hand to Bill, "and I'm sorry I'm a brunette."

Bill examined her as though he were paying for his look by the ounce. "You'll do! I'm Bill Haley. I like brunettes, too!"

80

"You seem to have hypnotized one." Bess snapped her fingers to dispel Ann's trance. "Wake up! *Ann!*"

"I'm sorry," Ann said. "Bill shocked me."

"I'll fix the drinks while you're getting unshocked," Bess said. "I'm supposed to disappear anyway. I'll give you two three minutes, alone."

Ann looked at Bill. She wanted to ask him if he'd lost his hangover, to tell him how well John was doing. Instead she looked foolishly at the typewriter paper box that held her book and said almost pleadingly, "You wouldn't want to say it again, would you?"

He walked over to her. "It *is* wonderful, Ann and I'll tell you frankly: I wasn't prepared to like it. I was prepared to hate it and I sure as hell never dreamed I'd *love* it. You're a born writer. If you keep it going the way the book is now, you've got a best-seller. I know."

She felt dizzy, nauseous, flushed—the way she had felt those mornings after John had gone away and she'd known she was pregnant. There really was something to the simile about "giving birth" to a book, she thought; she sat down and closed her eyes.

"What's the matter?" Bill asked.

"Nothing. And everything. It's just that I'm overwhelmed. Can't you see?"

"I read it objectively," Bill continued, earnestly. "I forgot that I knew the person who wrote it; but over and over in my mind I kept saying, she knows how to write, she knows how to write. And by 'she' I meant whoever might be the writer. It just so happened 'she' was you. What does Jack think of it?"

"He hasn't read it. He's going to wait 'til it's finished."

"Oh."

The way Bill said "oh" made Ann take the offensive. "It was John's own idea that I submit it to your company."

"Why?"

"Well, he thinks you could sell his wife's book better than he could. And he has a point—provided Fortune House wants it."

"Fortune House will want it. I say this even before I know how it's going to end, because I can tell a natural when I see one. By the way, how *is* it going to end?"

81

"I wish to God I knew," Ann said as Bess came in with the drinks.

"It's so *simple*," Bess volunteered, flushing with pride at Bill's repeated compliments. "I just squeeze one lemon for each double jigger of gin, put in some powdered sugar and fill the blender up to the brim with crushed ice. Then I turn on the juice and these come out!"

"Delicious!" Bill said for the fourth time. "Cold, frosty, and—delicious!"

"You sound like one of Ann's radio commercials," Bess answered as she salvaged enough of the meltings to fill Bill's glass one more time. "There's no secret to making them. Just add too much lemon and not enough sugar and you've got it."

Ann felt high—incredibly high. Bill and Bess had done the talking while she'd sat in a pool of disbelief. Had Bill said that he liked her book just to be kind? No, she decided; he would have been polite but not so effusive. But why?

"Either come out of it, Ann," Bill said, "or take us up to Wuthering Heights with you."

Ann laughed and got up from her chair. "I'm hungry," she said, "and I'll bet you're both starved, too. Dinner is served!"

Bill looked at the buffet table and saw a platter of cold sliced chicken, deviled eggs, artichoke hearts and tossed salad, with accoutrements of pickled peaches, olives, cranberry jelly, and hot rolls. He looked at Ann and said, "I *knew* you wouldn't serve cold cuts and potato salad." Then he turned to Bess and gave her his most devastating grin. It was his All American grin which he summoned whenever he wanted to make a fast conquest. His chubby face was a relief map of hills and valleys as he smiled at her. Bess speared a large piece of white meat and put it on Bill's plate and her hand shook like the cranberry jelly.

Bess insisted on clearing the table and stacking the dishes in the kitchen so Ann and Bill could discuss the book further.

"I'll call you the minute I get back to New York from the trip, Ann. You'll hear from me while I'm away. I'm excited about *our* book."

82

"Don't pressure me," Ann said. "I'm pressuring myself too much as it is."

Bill nodded. "You're right. Ordinarily I'd say take your time, but there's a reason for pressure. Let me put it this way: could you possibly have the final draft ready by Thanksgiving?"

Ann remembered her timetable. Bill was reading her mind.

"I could, but—"

"The Fortune House Prize Novel Contest closes on Thanksgiving day."

"Oh come on, Bill. It's not a prize novel."

"Why not?" Bill asked seriously. "Last year's winner was terrible. And the year before the entries were all so poor the judges didn't award the prize to anyone! Your book—hey, what are you going to call it?"

"The Heart Being Hungry," Ann said. "And don't ask me what it means. I'll tell you later. You were saying, 'Your book—' "

Bill didn't answer. He was thinking of Ann's title, sampling it with his mind's taste buds. "I'll have to think about that title," he said. "But then, the title's not important at this stage. The book's the thing, and you've got a book going! Maybe you won't win nor even come close, but it's worth shooting for—an outright twenty thousand dollar cash award—not chargeable against royalties."

"Bill! Don't be ridiculous! I've written it too quickly. I've—."

Bill interrupted. "The people you write about are alive."

"The first wife—Mona?" Ann asked against her will. "Is she alive?"

"She sure as hell is," Bill said with feeling.

Bess came into the room with her hat and gloves and Ann suddenly saw her in a new light. How really pretty she looked. Her figure at last was trim. After years of promises Bess had done it at last. There was a new sureness in her walk. Her brown eyes, with their inordinately long lashes, looked larger and more appealing now that her face was thinner. Lately, Bess reminded Ann of an ugly duckling who has just looked into a mirror to discover that she's a swan—and the mirror had been Dr. Darnell.

Ann went with them to Bess's car that was parked down the block from Ann's building.

83

"I'm not sure I ought to let you drive Bill home," Ann said. "The night is very starry, the moon is full and Bill Haley is a bachelor again."

"Now, *Ann*," he protested innocently.

"Promise you won't get fresh with Bess!" Ann said, jokingly and not jokingly.

"Oh," Bess said, "I can take care of myself."

The last thing Ann saw as Bess gunned the Jaguar was Bill Haley's wink.

She walked slowly back into the building to the empty apartment, still a little high—partly from the drinks, but mostly from Bill's words which she kept hearing after the car was out of sight. "*It's wonderful . . . Wonderful!*" And then she thought of John and what he'd say, and she sobered up.

8

BESS FRANKEL sat in Dr. Darnell's expensively undecorated office. The room had been engineered (office decorators prefer that term) by a firm which specialized in specialists. Where red furniture or carpets might be *de rigeur* for M.D.s or dentists, psychiatrists balk at anything colorful or, as the decorators put it, challenging. The analyst's office must be attractive without attracting, comfortable but not comforting. Dr. Darnell had had many conferences with the head of the decorating firm who had tried hard to appear business-like when his client explained that the office should "give the non-appearance and non-feeling of the womb."

Bess sat in a neutral colored leather barrel chair directly across the desk from her doctor. When she had first begun her therapy she'd fully expected to be told to lie down on the off-tan, off-beige

84

leather couch, but Dr. Darnell had said nothing and so she sat in this chair. She wondered vaguely at the moment if a patient in treatment graduated to the couch as the analysis progressed, but now that all these months had gone by she felt reasonably sure that the only one who used the couch, which gave the appearance of being used, was Dr. Darnell himself.

The heavy neutral drapes were always drawn, although Bess often wished they were pulled back to let in some daylight. She thought that today it was just as well that they were closed because the windows were being peppered by hard pellets of rain. To a woman trapped in psychoanalysis, this wet day of greenish-gray light was a formidable depressant, and even though the drapes shut out the sight and sound of the rain, the dreariness of the day seemed to trickle into the room. The first few days of November had all been cold and wet. The warm September and the bright, crisp October were now merely memories.

Bess noted silently that on rainy days Dr. Darnell's black hair developed a distinct wave, making him look younger and much more human than usual. The wall behind her was cream-colored and empty except for a large framed picture of Sigmund Freud. The other walls were panelled in mahogany from floor to ceiling. The carpeting was a solid non-color, which blended into but did not complement the neutral couch, the barrel chair and the executive's swivel chair Dr. Darnell sat in, wearing his solid brown, no-second-look suit, his beige-tan-no-color shirt, his uncolored dark four-in-hand necktie. There were two plain chairs against the wall to Bess's left, both of which she used occasionally. Once or twice she'd sat on the couch and sometimes she stood. Dr. Darnell had never told her where not to sit—except once. That was the day she'd sat in his swivel-chair. For some inexplicable reason she'd been wanting to sit in that chair for a long time and finally, when he met her at the door she went straight for his chair and tried to look casual as she rotated soundlessly in it. Sitting there she had experienced a kind of excitement. Then he walked to her side and said quietly, "This is my chair," and she'd given it up.

Once, when Dr. Darnell had swiveled around to open the cabinet under the window-sill, she'd caught sight of a pipe rack filled with an assortment of pipes, but Dr. Darnell did not smoke

85

during the interviews. It was a pity, Bess thought: on this gloomy day he should be wearing a red smoking jacket with matching red leather slippers and be puffing away on some rich, appley tobacco mixture.

Five days a week, Bess Frankel came to this office and faced Dr. Darnell or—when she preferred not to face him—the drawn, no-color drapes. As he spoke and listened, and took an occasional note, she studied him. She knew the way his left eye twitched when he was intensely interested in the procedure of the interview, just how much of a smile it took to show the dimple in his right cheek, and how much more of a smile would make his dimple deteriorate into a crease in his long, pale face. She wondered if the mole on his left cheek gave him much trouble when he shaved. She knew to the tooth where the three gold crowns were (one upper-right, one lower-middle, one far-right-lower-back) and loved to watch the light dance on them. She was in awe of his deep-set, bush-browed brown eyes that saw right through her when she told either little white lies about herself, or giant, black ones. Whenever she held back any information she carefully evaded those eyes. Looking at Dr. Darnell must be like looking at God, she thought; it took the same kind of honesty. At the start of her analysis she had said once, "Am I going to fall in love with you?" and he hadn't answered her, but he had smiled, first to the dimple, then to the crease. During the months that followed Bess wondered whether she was in love with Dr. Darnell or not. If it was love, it was a different kind of love than that of a child for a parent. Bess couldn't even imagine saying to her father what she said to Dr. Darnell every day.

Alexander Darnell was forty-seven and acknowledged to be one of the best analysts in New York. Even at fifty dollars a visit, five visits a week, ad infinitum, he was booked solid with a waiting list. He had studied in Europe as well as America, had been psychoanalyzed twice (Freudian school in Switzerland, Jung school in New York), had written two books on the psychoanalytic theory of neurosis, and had presented papers at medical meetings all over the world. Dr. Darnell had once been known as a psychiatrist's psychiatrist (and a good bit of his supplementary income still came from his serving as control for other doctors in analysis). Now he

86

was more and more referred to within the profession as a society doctor.

It hadn't always been mahogany panels and supple leather. He'd known lean times in the beginning years, first as an institution staff doctor, then as a practitioner who owed everybody from the telephone company to the diaper service.

His wife, Alice, was responsible for his changed status.

Alice had her troubles in those early years. With the birth of her second baby following closely on that of the first and the absence of her husband from home twelve to sixteen hours a day, she couldn't be blamed for wanting such creature comforts as two servants, a Cadillac convertible and a swimming pool. He had long ago promised never to blame her, *ever*. What he had made of his life and work was his own doing. It was important to him that Alice, who had been so wretched during those early years, had become happier since he achieved the sixty thousand dollar a year bracket, with all the byproducts of success, including weekends off.

He became a doctor to the rich almost accidently. Furious at a patient who told him she was going to try him for a while and then try another psychiatrist for a while and choose between the two, he quoted her a price-per-visit of fifty dollars. She stunned him by agreeing to the fee without a quibble. He discovered then that a fifty dollar fifty-minute hour was no more difficult to perform than a fifteen dollar hour-and-a-half.

When the misgivings first began he was always away from his office. He'd meet an old colleague who appeared happier and better adjusted despite a smaller income, or someone would make the inevitable remark about rich neurotics and their richer doctors, or he'd visit outpatient clinics where hundreds of people needed the kind of help he was giving to so few. Usually, when he had returned to his thickly carpeted office-retreat, his misgivings vanished and he felt contented again—the kind of contentment a gourmet feels when he eats a second helping of some irresistible dish. In the last three or four years, however, his doubts followed him into the five-hundred dollar beige leather swivel chair. Today, for instance, all during his consultation with Mrs. Lipschultz who preceded Bess Frankel he could not rid himself of a truth all psycho-

87

analysts must accept: that no analysis can rise above the optimum potential of what is being analyzed. An old doctor in Switzerland had expressed it bluntly many years before, "Analyze *dreck* and you get *dreck!*" Mrs. Lipschultz was a blowsy, rich, mean, stupid, rich, overbearing, baby-voiced, whining, rich woman who was an uncomfortable example of what the old man had meant by *dreck*. She was also a symbol of the life he had chosen.

He looked at Bess. Here, at least, was better material. Miss Frankel was rich, all right, but she was deeply troubled, and her analysis, which would be of immense help to her, was also proving an immense satisfaction to him.

"I'm glad you're telling me these things now, Miss Frankel," he said. "They'd come out eventually and your concealing them for almost two months has only made it more difficult."

Bess concentrated on his mole. "I feel better now that I've told you. Now you can tell me: why did I give in to him the very first time we met?"

"We're going to try to find the answer," Dr. Darnell said objectively. "Right now it might be interesting to know why you suppressed all mention of this Bill Haley for almost two months."

Bess pulled at her handkerchief. "I just couldn't tell you. I wanted to, but I couldn't. I won't pretend he took me by surprise. Ann practically drew me a picture of what to expect. Before Bill arrived that day she told me he had just had his second divorce. She described his apartment—even that big circular bed where I . . . where we . . ."

She saw Dr. Darnell make a note ("big circular bed") and wondered what he'd written. She knew he expected her to do the talking. He never assumed the initiative when she wanted him to and his impersonality was like a wall. She was surprised when he asked, "Do you like Ann?"

"Why, sure. I like her very much. She's not only brilliant, but she's kind. She and John are my best friends. We're all three honest with each other, and yet—"

"Yet—?"

"Well . . . I haven't told Ann about Bill and me. Don't get the idea Ann's a prude. She isn't. In fact, I think she and John both would approve, so I don't know why I haven't told her."

88

Dr. Darnell looked at her, listening, not overtly leading.

Bess went on: "Maybe I wanted to punish myself for giving in to Bill so easily. Not telling you nor Ann is a way of doing that, isn't it?" She was trying to rationalize, but she gave up. "I don't *know* why I didn't tell you. We'd had a grand evening, the three of us. Bill had been nice to me, but that was all. We drove around for a while, then when I took him to his apartment he asked me up—"

"Up—"

"And I went. I knew exactly what would happen. But I was motivated by some kind of need and it was more like my seducing him than the other way around. I suppose my guilt feeling came from this." Bess occasionally found herself using psychological terms like "motivated" and "guilt feeling" and she wondered if the doctor resented or approved. He did not comment. Instead, he placed his gold pencil on the palm of his right hand and rolled it back and forth, studying it as he spoke. "Could it be that Haley had a need similar to your own? Did you like him from the moment you met him?"

Bess wished that he'd stop rolling the pencil. "Well . . . it started when he got into my car. Until then I couldn't say I was especially attracted to him, but at that moment I *wanted* him to make love to me. He didn't really have to talk me into it." She wished that Dr. Darnell would open the drapes. The murky day and spattering rain would be a welcome distraction. "What I'm actually trying to say is that I was ashamed that he got the impression I was a pushover."

Dr. Darnell stopped rolling the pencil and used it to write the word "pushover."

"You said he called you the next day."

"Yes. And look what happened. The same thing all over again."

"Do you love him, Miss Frankel?"

"I don't know. I've told you before that men aren't usually intersted in me that way."

"This one certainly is."

"Yes. And it flatters me . . . and makes me feel ashamed at the same time. Bill is a book traveler. He represents Fortune House in the southern cities. He was leaving town soon, so we

89

saw each other every night before he left." She paused. "And every night—it was the same."

"Same?"

"Yes. We always ended up in the same way . . . in that circular bed. Then he went away for almost seven weeks and I told myself that what had happened was madness. I swore it was all over—the madness, I mean—then he came home last Thursday and—"

"The same?"

"The same. And Saturday and Sunday. Then, on Sunday I told him I didn't want to see him for a while, but it wasn't easy to say. I didn't answer the telephone Monday or yesterday, even though I knew it was Bill. He has tickets for a football game this Saturday and expects me to go with him."

"Does he ever talk about himself?"

"He didn't at first. But now he's told me about the break-up of both his marriages. He's very fair—doesn't put all the blame on them. Says he feels like a heel—but he's *not* a heel. He's kind and sweet and when he talks that way I feel sorry for him. I told him about you."

"Me?"

"Yes. You could do him a lot of good. But he won't come to you. It's not the money, either. His parents are wealthy."

Dr. Darnell looked sharply at Bess and she knew she had caught him thinking, "He can't afford me," instead of, "He doesn't need me."

She kept pulling at her handkerchief as though her fingers were stuck to it and she was trying to pry them loose; then suddenly she looked straight at the bushy eyebrows and said, "*Am* I a push-over, Dr. Darnell?"

"No."

"Then why am I so easy for Bill?"

"What do *you* think is the answer?"

"I'd like to think I represent something he's looking for. I'm so tired of Mama and Papa giving me everything I want and think-ing of me as Good Old Bess. And maybe—just maybe—Bill thinks I'm a—a desirable woman." She felt embarrassed, and suddenly said, "I'm going to put a stop to it!" too loudly for the quiet, rich room. "I know there's only trouble ahead if I keep on with it. I

90

can't expect him to have marriage in mind. How *could* I, so soon after his second divorce?"

Instead of answering her question, Dr. Darnell stayed behind his wall and waited for her to continue.

"It would be wonderful if he were genuinely in love with me," Bess said softly, half to herself. "It's too much to hope for, though. I'm sure Bill Haley's never really been in love so how could it be that for the first time in his life he would be in love . . . with *me?*"

"Now you're saying what you are really thinking, and we are getting somewhere," Dr. Darnell said, reassuringly. "What you're really thinking is the important thing." His left eye twitched.

Of late, his private thoughts sallied over the desk, circled the barrel chair, and then boomeranged to hit him hard in the vicinity of the occipital lobe. *What you are really thinking.* His own mental health had been sour for some time. He was fixating on non-medical objects entirely too much and engaging in an unreasonable amount of sexual fantasy. His office thoughts and bedroom thoughts had become oddly juxtaposed. While he should be listening to his patients strive for total recall he dwelt on the most puerile forms of sexual wish-fulfillment—with himself as both active participant and voyeur, at one and the same time. Then, in moments of intimacy with Alice, he found himself over-eager and too quick. Alice complained so much about this prematureness that he had taken to thinking over patient problems while engaged in the love act. This had diminished his own enjoyment—but it had lengthened his staying power and done wonders for Alice's morale. *What you are really thinking.* He knew that it would not take an expert diagnostician to know that something was eating at Dr. Alexander Darnell, and it was a relief to be thinking professional thoughts again during this interview with Miss Frankel. A development had occurred in her life which could—if understood— help her immeasurably. Otherwise, it would set her back, and this was a challenge to him not only as a psychiatrist, but as a doctor and as a man. He liked using all of his powers with a patient. The preceding hour with Mrs. Lipschultz had been filled with resentment against his own patient—who always paid promptly— and sexual perigrinations which frightened him. Lately, he had seriously considered putting himself back into analysis; now, diag-

91

nosing Miss Frankel's problem, he was almost his own self again and he felt better. After all, another fling at analysis would cut his yearly income in half; and Alice wouldn't like that.

He looked at Bess Frankel who was obviously distraught when she should be happier than she had been in years. He could not originate opinions for her and he couldn't chastise nor wheedle her. So he just leaned forward, cocked his head slightly, and looked at her expectantly, knowing from experience how she would react.

Bess Frankel knew, too. She disliked Dr. Darnell when he looked at her this way, calmly waiting for her to keep talking, because she sometimes got excited and talked too much. She could feel her throat tighten and a tear beginning in her right eye. She knew she was going to cry and she didn't want to. She spoke rapidly: "One minute I want to call the whole thing off and the next minute I want to go to the football game with him . . . Columbia plays Cornell, his old school. He used to play football there and he was All American. He—" Dr. Darnell was close enough now for her to slap his face right on that precious mole! He was so . . . so *smug*. And what did *he* know about sex? She'd love to slap him and pull out a fistful of his black, wavy hair and run out of this room clutching it triumphantly in her hand.

"He may not even call me again," she went on. "I'm not at all sure he'll call. But if he *does*—" The tear left her eye and perched on the side of her nose. It was a small tear, with a larger one already forming. "I'm going to tell him that he makes me *feel* like a pushover and I'm *not* one." She was crying now. "Oh, I know *just* how it'll end. I'll go to the football game with him . . . and we'll end up in that damned circular bed!"

Bess wanted to stop now, but she couldn't. Like the raindrops falling on the windows behind the drapes, her tears came steadily. She blew her nose and dabbed at her eyes with the mutilated handkerchief.

Dr. Alexander Darnell wrote down something with the gold pencil, then, settling into the contours of his chair, he turned very slowly away.

92

9

ANN LONG would remember this year—the year of her novel—as the year without an October and October had always been her favorite month. In other years, with John away on his fall selling trip, she had taken Fifth Avenue buses for long Sunday rides. The city's buildings looked whiter than usual in the October sunshine, the skies were bluer, and the people seemed less harassed. And she used to spend October days, too, in the postage-stamp garden, sharing John's pride in the clusters of yellow pompom chrysanthemums that grew there on the eighteen floors above the street. No matter how thin-necked his flowers turned out, John always planted more, nourishing them from sacks of ersatz sunshine. But this year she was only vaguely conscious of the little garden, and if the leaves of trees in Central Park had colored and fallen she had not seen them. Her October color scheme was black type on white paper and the autumn smells she used to love were traded in this October for the stale, after hours closeness of an office building.

She ached everywhere. The pages of her book hurt like blisters and the people she wrote about were hostile and recalcitrant. They continued to behave as they damned well pleased and she asked herself in despair if writing a book got the best of everyone in this way. She didn't live for herself at all. She lived for *the page,* and as she walked down a street she was a human sponge, soaking up everything she saw and heard and felt, observing minutely now what she used to take for granted. Take yesterday—in a routine bus ride, she'd found herself studying the driver closely and intently, thinking he was a sensitive bus driver. As soon as two or three passengers entered his bus and dropped their fares into the coin box he turned the little handle on the box and removed the change and placed it in his change container. He did not wait until ten

93

or fifteen riders had deposited their fares, for that would have been too easy. He couldn't wait even for five: he had to take the nickels and dimes two at a time and never more than three. This kept him busy—and surely made him nervous—but that was the way this man had to do his job. She knew, because she had this same kind of edginess. She didn't trust herself to remember anything so, like the bus driver, she couldn't accumulate too much at a time, even of thoughts. She wrote everything on a slip of paper the moment it happened so that she wouldn't forget: something Irene had said to her boy friend and then repeated to Ann; the telephone call Marta had taken from the drunken listener; the bloop the new announcer made on the first spot she'd written for him. She scribbled all these things down, shoved them into her purse or pocket and then emptied them into her top desk drawer that had become a cauldron for the preparation of this mulligan stew that was her book.

Her fingers were stiff tonight as she worked on the last few pages —stiff from inner tension. The triangle she had so skillfully designed had got away from her and she knew it. The wicked wife, the handsome husband, the understanding sweetheart—none of them performed as ordered. The wicked wife was no longer wicked, and Ann used her interpretations of psychiatry to endow Mona with a new personality. The understanding sweetheart had changed, too—and when *her* turn came to be the wife, she stopped being understanding. Only the handsome husband remained the same—just as impressionable as he had been in the beginning, and just as likeable. He was the apex of the isosceles triangle that still looked the same from his corner; yet the poles at the base had been switched. The other woman had become the wife and the wife had become the other woman.

Bill Haley had asked how her book was going to end, and Ann knew now. It was not the ending she had originally planned nor hoped for. She didn't like the ending, and God only knew what John would think of it—but that was the way it had worked out and she was as helpless to change it as she was to keep from writing it.

Who was the real author of *The Heart Being Hungry?* Certainly not Ann Long, she thought. None of these characters had paid

94

any attention to her. The book was ghost-written, surely, by another Ann Long who existed within her own subconscious. And the characters—encouraged by the ghost-Ann—had first defied and then defeated her.

She finished the book on Veterans' Day and the occasion was appropriate even though she thought the old name, Armistice Day, would have been even more appropriate. The battle of the book was over but the battle of John's reaction to it was yet to be fought. And she would not let herself think about that until the armistice was over.

When John first saw her he was stunned. "Ann!" he said, and could say no more. He took her in his arms and held her for a long time and, unable to control herself, she began to cry.

"You're not touching that damned book again!" Suddenly his initial alarm turned to fury. "Can't you *see* yourself? Can't you see how you *look?*"

He was berating her, but she knew that this was his way of telling her that he loved her and wanted her well and beautiful.

"You *hear* me, Ann? No more *book!*"

She stopped crying. She felt relieved, calmed and at the same time provoked with herself for letting go like that and indulging in self-pity.

"There is no more book to write," she said, sniffling. "It's finished. All written—and most of it re-written."

"My God! Really?"

"Yes. It's no professional secretarial job and it should be retyped, but I'm submitting it just as it is. Bill wants it at Fortune House before Thanksgiving."

"Bill? Bill *Haley?* What does he think of it?"

"He—likes it. That is, he thinks it will sell."

"Come here," John said. He led her by the hand to the full-length mirror in their dressing room. "Look at that girl. Do you know her?"

"I never saw her before," Ann said. "Puny little deal, isn't she?"

"Be careful. You are speaking of the woman I love."

"Then why don't you give her a square meal?"

"I mean to. I'm taking her away from it all as soon as she's strong

95

enough to pack. So what you see now, madam, is *before*. Soon I shall lead you to this same spot and show you this girl *after*."

Ann took a step closer to the mirror. "Look at her," she said, pointing at her reflection. "Husbands shouldn't let wives write books. When a healthy female announces she's going to write a novel she's either getting over a love affair or getting ready for hormone shots—remember?"

"Yes." He smiled, then took her in his arms again. "We were in bed at the time. *Remember?*"

She didn't answer this because she didn't need to. Everything was suddenly all right. He was home again, and she was no longer alone with the book.

John bought airplane tickets and made reservations in Florida for the week after Thanksgiving. Ann kept protesting that she didn't want to go anywhere but he assumed the role of tyrant, over-poweringly assertive, in a no-compromise, boss-of-the-family way. He informed her that she was going to Florida with him if he had to gag her, tie her arms and legs and carry her onto the plane by force.

"But, John—"

"You haven't had your vacation yet, have you?"

"No."

"Everyone at the radio station back from theirs?"

"Yes, but—"

"Will WOOZ go off the air if Ann Long deprives it of her services for seven whole days?"

"Don't be silly, no. But still . . ."

"Shut up!" he said and that was all there was to it.

But she had a kind of uneasy misgiving about a trip. Now that her book was finished she felt an odd attachment to it, and though it was a ridiculous simile, going away made her feel like a mother abandoning a new-born baby in a public place. *The Heart Being Hungry* would be in safe hands—yet she felt as though she were leaving it before it was properly weaned.

On November 23rd, a week before Thanksgiving Day, she took the book to the offices of Fortune House and left it with the person whose name Bill Haley had given her. Haley had offered to sub-

96

mit the novel for her, but she had insisted on taking it herself. Bill had been enormously enthusiastic when he finished reading it, but Ann felt that perhaps the powers-that-be at his publishing house might charge up some of his enthusiasm to a personal enthusiasm for the author. Where a woman was involved, Bill Haley's opinions didn't cut much ice with neutral observers.

She had not forgotten her promise to Bess. Three days before taking the book to Fortune House Ann had given her the manuscript to read, waiting until then because she wanted to do nothing that might upset Bess who seemed to be in a highly nervous phase of her analysis. When Bess returned the book Ann had expected an outburst of exuberance, but Bess, instead, had told her simply and quietly that she loved it. Then she'd started to cry and wept intermittently for a half hour.

"Ye gods," Ann had said, trying to carry it off lightly, "If it has such a depressing effect on *you* I hate to think what it will do to the readers of Fortune House."

"But it isn't depressing," Bess sniffled. "It's just so damned *real!*"

Bess could have called it any of a thousand things, but her saying the book was real gratified Ann. If Bess thought it was real, it must be. She had tried to write a real book and been afraid she had got lost in the web of unreality that brainwashes the mind of every fiction writer. Suddenly a wave of understanding went from Ann to Bess—for now that she was free of her book she wanted Bess to be free of Dr. Darnell's psychoanalysis. Bess had never looked so beautiful, she thought, nor so lost. Obviously, hers had been a longer torture. She said, "How much longer, Bess? When will Dr. Darnell let you go?"

Bess shook her head. "I don't know. He says it will be the first of the year at least. Mama says she's going to sue him for ruining my personality—but he's helping me. He's—I don't know how to say it—but he does for me exactly what your book did when I read it. He fills me with a sense of what's real, what's worth living for, and he makes me cry. If it weren't for him I'd have lost my mind these last months. Because, you see, something's happened that—"

Bess stopped.

"No. I'm sorry," she said. "I think I'd better stick to Dr. Darnell

97

for my confessing. Otherwise, I'll have to confess to him that I confessed to you and that will only double the agony."

Ann wanted to do something for Bess to make things easier for her but she didn't know how to begin. "I understand," she said, not understanding at all. "And I love you for saying my book is real. Now I'm not afraid of anything."

But she was afraid. Bill and Bess were merely sparring partners. Now she had to climb into the ring to meet John, the champion. And the way he reacted to her book would be infinitely more important than the reactions of editors and friends. A publisher could say yes or no, and if it were no nothing would be hurt but her pride, but John Long might say more than yes or no. He might want to know *why*—and she could not answer that question. The pride she'd felt when Bill and Bess praised her story changed to anxiety when she thought of John. It was the same anxiety she had felt when she found that her creations became stronger than she was. The thought of John's reaction made her wish that she had never finished *The Heart Being Hungry*. Now, more than anything in this world, she wanted to renege on her promise to let him read it, and she found herself thinking of ways to put him off. If it were published before he saw it, some of the sting would surely be taken away; if it were rejected, she might have an excuse to say, "It isn't good enough to sell; therefore, it isn't good enough for you to read." But still she didn't quite know how to keep it from him—all she knew was that until he read it her troubles were not over.

He had said, the day before they left for St. Augustine, "Don't forget to pack the copy of your book. While you're soaking up the sunshine I'll soak up my wife's brilliance." Then he'd improvised his reminder to the old tune and sung, "Pack up your carbon in your old kit bag and smile, smile, smile."

"I thought we were going on a vacation," Ann parried. "What book man wants to read a book on his vacation?"

"This one," John said. "What have I got to lose? If it's great I can tell everyone I married a genius. If it's punk I can be kind and sweet to you in a nauseating sort of way—and if it's good enough to be published yet not good enough to sell, I can laugh

98

at Bill Haley sweating over low advance orders and breaking his neck to avoid seeing you." He laughed. "Give him fits if that happens. Give him fits!"

Ann felt as a person who lives on the coast must feel when the weather bureau warns that a hurricane is headed for that spot. What is there to do but hope that it will spend itself while you wait for it? She packed the carbon of her book in her old kit bag and smiled, smiled, smiled—in the face of what she dreaded and feared might be disaster.

"But why St. Augustine?" she asked as John waved the tickets under her nose triumphantly. "Why not Miami?"

"Miami's too exciting," he told her in a therapeutic voice. "You need peace and quiet—and those two words describe St. Augustine. This is a mercy mission, not a fun frolic." Then, with a kind of boyish pride he added, "You'll love the spot I've picked out for us, honey. Billy Clarke got us guest memberships at the St. Augustine Beach Club. Wait till you see it."

He was so genuinely excited that she was glad she'd let him do all the arranging. "But what if it rains?" she said. "Should I bring along a sun lamp, just in case?"

"If it rains," he said solemnly, "I personally shall sue the St. Augustine Chamber of Commerce."

It did not rain and the weather was perfect from the day they arrived: a high of eighty degrees during the day, in the sixties at night. They learned that it had rained a great deal the week before—that there'd been a storm, too. While the natives were polite enough to them, more than one intimated discreetly that it was a trifle early for perfect weather—as well as winter visitors—and three or four weeks from then would have been much nicer for both. Ann got the feeling that November visitors invaded the privacy rights of the St. Augustinians and she almost felt like a guest who makes the mistake of appearing for a dinner a full hour ahead of the time specified in the invitation. But she was so entranced with the balmy weather, the tropical look of the place and the blue water that this feeling of too-early intrusion disappeared almost immediately.

"Rich but not gaudy," John said as he showed her through their

99

cabana that was more like an elegant summer house. "And please note the front yard," he said, pointing to the ocean, "which doesn't have to be mowed."

Ann was impressed. "Is this the bridal suite?"

"Honeymoon Cabana they call it. Ain't that cute? And all the comforts of home."

She walked delightedly from the combination living room-bedroom with its large-paned casement windows facing the beach to the sea-green tiled bathroom on to the tiny kitchenette complete with refrigerator, stove and dishes. "How much is this costing per day?" she asked and then added quickly, "No. Don't tell me. I don't want to know!"

"Cost is no object," John said pointing to the telephone. "And when you want food you don't go to the kitchen. You just go to this phone and lift the receiver. The mess boys wear white starched jackets and bring you anything you wish, here or on the beach."

"Anything?" Ann said, over-innocently.

"Anything within reason in a starched jacket," he said, giving her a look that said she was already getting better.

"Which reminds me," Ann said confidentially, "I don't have to run and hide any more when room service knocks. Why, I can just stay put and stare the man down!"

"Ouch!" he said, remembering Omaha. And then, "Your attention, please. I feel a speech coming on."

Ann faced him quickly, and sank down before him in mock obeisance, her full skirt billowing around her on the carpet. He intoned, "This picture postcard paradise with our own private ocean, these red tiled roofs, this lush green shrubbery, these palm trees, that fine white sand—it's all part of a celebration, Madame."

"Of what?" she asked. "My book?"

"Heck, no. Who wants to celebrate something that wrecks his wife's health. It's a celebration of that day on Olympus, or wherever the gods're hanging out this century, when Venus and Zeus decreed that Ann Austin and John Long should meet and merge."

"I'll buy that," Ann said with conviction. "Good old Venus and Zeus."

100

"And I don't care what they call this cabana. It's not a second honeymoon," he said with feeling.

"Why not?"

"Because," and he spoke softly now because he really meant what he was about to say. "Because, my darling, I never want to stop celebrating our first."

They spent the first days resting, swimming and sightseeing. They invented stories about the people who lived in the old Spanish mansions that lined the narrow streets. They visited America's "oldest house," ("*John Long, you have an evil mind!*") and toured the Fountain of Youth Gardens where Ponce de Leon once drank the water of immortal life. Ann's brunette coloring took to the sun easily and she tanned quickly, but John who always insisted that he blistered when he took his hat off to let the flag go by was sun-shy to the point of keeping under cover by day and showing himself *sans* canopy only at night. So, Ann lay on the beach in the sun-shine, coaxing her tan in stages, while John stayed fair and unper-turbed under a huge beach umbrella.

After breakfast on the fourth morning he asked for the book. Ann, who had wishfully hoped he would forget it, almost felt let down when he brought it up. She remembered a colloquialism an English professor at Barnard had once used about a "treed possum." She'd asked him to explain what the expression meant and he'd gone into detail about the way men in the South go possum-hunting at night with hound dogs. He'd gone possum-hunting himself, and recalled vividly the dogs howling at the base of a giant cottonwood tree in whose branches a possum was trapped. He described the nervous despair of the little animal, its eyes glazed to blindness by the flashlights of the men who kept poking at it with sticks trying to make it fall from its precarious perch into a waiting gunny sack. Ann recalled the phrase because now, in her fright and hopelessness, she felt like a treed possum as she handed John the box that contained her book.

He kissed her, pulled up a straight chair to the table in the middle of the room, and sat down with his back to the windows and water. She went down to the beach for a swim.

That was at nine o'clock in the morning.

101

At noon she came back to the cabana, ordered sandwiches and iced tea and tried to decide from studying his expression what his early reaction to the book was, but he was a thousand miles away as he let the pages flutter to the floor face down after he had read them. She tried to eat her sandwich and couldn't, then remembered how determined John was that she should regain her lost weight and forced it down.

She placed his plate on the table, saying, "Here's your lunch, honey. I've promised to spend the afternoon on the beach with that Mrs. Terrell from Chicago," but he didn't hear her. She walked outside into the sunlight and wished herself any place in the world except here in paradise.

In a city people can be neighbors for years yet never know each other's last names. At a resort, however, bosom friendships are born in a matter of minutes, and confidences exchanged which never should be told. Mrs. Harvey Terrell, who had taken a cloying shine to Ann the moment they met, managed to bob up like the proverbial bad penny whenever she found Ann and John together. Ann had contrived to avoid being alone with her until today, but now she figured that any sort of companion was better than spending this afternoon by herself. She found Mrs. Terrell and said hello as she slipped off her terry cloth robe and stretched out on the sand.

Mrs. Terrell wasted no time in getting down to intimacies. There was something about this woman that Ann instinctively distrusted. She had a kind of possessiveness that absorbed part of everything she touched and made it over to suit her own self.

It developed that this was the day Mrs. Terrell had chosen to tell Ann why she was at the Beach Club alone.

"I guess you've wondered where my husband is, my dear," she began.

Oh no, Ann thought, I don't want any of this. I'm not a compulsive looker and listener any more—my book's written, my stories are all told; I don't give a damn where your husband is.

Mrs. Terrell continued, "Your own husband is so attractive. Blonde, tall men just *have* something. You two are so well matched, you'd never guess how desperately unhappy and lost two people

102

can be when they are as poorly mated as Mr. Terrell and I. To begin with, you see, Mr. Terrell was all of fifteen years older than I when he married me . . ."

Ann couldn't help noticing that Mrs. Terrell said "when he married me" instead of "when we were married." She also observed that Mrs. Terrell had a habit of hurriedly slurring together the last few words of each sentence as though she were afraid she would forget them before they all got out.

Ann looked at the water washing the white sand with a slow, loving motion. She figured that John was as far as the first marriage by now. He had finished the parts about Jerry's early life and he was just getting into Mona's natural appeal to him—the magnetic appeal that her weakness held for his need.

"Use some of this sun oil, honey. It'll make your tan deeper." Mrs. Terrell's voice pulled Ann back to the sand and her story. "Oh, what a letdown it is for a woman when she discovers she's overrated the man she took for better or worse." Mrs. Terrell sighed. "I tell you, when I first learned that Harvey was . . . uh . . . not a well man, I could have killed myself."

Ann thought of the table John was leaning over as he read. Now he would be reading about Mona and Jerry at the radio station together; about the night they worked on election returns; the first time Jerry slept with her.

"Harvey was the victim of strange spells. He would get very moody. Once he came into the bathroom where I was in the tub and just stood there for the *longest* time staring at me. I knew he was thinking he hadn't the strength to drown me—and wishing he did have."

Ann tried to think about Bess and Dr. Darnell, about her sister Birdie, about her mother—anything but this.

". . . My life with Harvey Terrell has been a hell on earth from the day the doctor told him the truth. He gives me everything I want in a material sense but he has never touched me since he learned what was wrong with him."

As Mrs. Terrell droned on Ann rolled into the shade of the beach umbrella and lay on her stomach, resting her head on her folded arms. Had John come to the part about Norma yet? Would he like this name, Norma, for the second wife? Suddenly Ann

103

realized that she'd missed some of Mrs. Terrell's narrative. She was talking about an Alfred somebody and Ann tried to listen long enough for Mrs. Terrell to disclose inadvertently Alfred's identity. It didn't take more than a moment for Ann to pick up the thread. Alfred was the Terrell chauffeur who had apparently taken over where Harvey left off.

Why do people tell such things, Ann wondered. *Why?* Why do they force their most private, secret thoughts onto others who aren't remotely interested? Mrs. Terrell obviously had told her story many times before. Ann would have had her own tongue cut out before she'd tell a stranger a single detail she knew about John's marriage to Madge. But how about a *reader*—a thousand readers—ten thousand readers? Even if the names and places were changed, wasn't writing a story a kind of *telling?*

". . . any woman in my position would have done the same . . . I could face my maker with Alfred at my side . . ."

Ann must have dozed off. She had lost track of time. Mrs. Terrell was saying, "Are you listening, dear?"

"Uh huh," Ann said, not changing her position from head-on-arms, face to the sand. "I'm listening but I really don't feel very well. My lunch didn't sit right." That was no lie. The sandwich still stayed a lump near her throat.

"Oh, that's a shame," Mrs. Terrell said. "Maybe you've had too much sun. You've taken it awfully quickly, you know."

Ann knew she hadn't had too much sun, but she said, "That must be it. I do feel funny. I hate to go in, too, because you haven't finished your story."

"I can finish it some other time, my dear," Mrs. Terrell said, and Ann thought, Over my dead body!

She rolled over, sat up, brushed the sand from her arms and body, then stood up. She really did feel ill but it wasn't the sun and it wasn't anything she'd eaten.

She told Mrs. Terrell she was going to the drugstore in the Club to get something for her stomach and they said goodbye.

The drugstore was small and air conditioned to the point of deep freeze. Ann went to the fountain and ordered an Alka Seltzer. It was the first time she had ever taken one. She'd heard it adver-

104

tised and praised so soothingly and so often that she, as a writer of soothing copy about products she never sampled, was automatically opposed to trying it. She never in her life expected herself to order an Alka Seltzer to alleviate any ache or pain she might have and yet when the man asked what she wanted she said, "An Alka Seltzer, please."

She stayed in the drugstore a long time. She bought a magazine and read half of it thoughtlessly as she kept on thinking of John and the book. How far was he now? Had he reached the part where Mona consulted the psychiatrist for help? Perhaps he had stopped reading. He surely wouldn't, yet the thought occurred to her again and she found herself almost convinced that he *had* stopped, put the book back into its box and gone for a swim. She started to leave the drugstore and was almost out the door when the clerk caught up with her. "You forgot your magazine, Miss."

"Thanks," Ann said. "Could you tell me what time it is?"

"Yes, ma'am. It's five-thirty."

"Oh. Thanks. I'm—I'm late."

She started for the cabana.

When she walked inside she found John still at the table, reading. He had not touched his lunch and she could tell from the few pages left on the table and the pile of paper on the floor that he was almost finished. There couldn't be over fifteen or twenty pages left. She felt sick and dizzy as she went into the small kitchen to get the bottle of Scotch they'd bought yesterday. The bottle wasn't there and when she looked around the room she saw it on the floor near John's feet—almost empty. Then, for the first time, she noticed the glass in front of him. She didn't know whether or not to go over to the bottle and pour herself a drink. If she did this would she be disclosing her too desperate need for it?

She decided against it and fixed herself some ice water instead. John said nothing. The room was as quiet and dead as yesterday. She sat down and opened the magazine she had bought. She tried to think of Mrs. Terrell and shook her away. Five pages left to read—no more than five. He knew now that Norma had lost her battle to hold Jerry; that Mona had won him back; that strength and weakness had confused themselves in the three-cornered love.

105

Ann walked over to the windows behind John. She looked out at the ocean for a while, then turned in time to see him flip the last page onto its face and lean back in his chair.

What should she say? Should she say, "Well—?" or "What's the verdict?" or, the thing she'd said to Bill Haley, "Mona—Mona —is she alive?"

She said, "Why didn't you eat your lunch, John?"

He reached for the bottle with a reflex-like gesture, poured a triple Scotch into his glass, left the bottle on the table, and asked, "Want a drink?"

They were the strangest-sounding words she had ever heard him speak.

"Sure." she said. "Why not?" She felt numb.

He poured a drink and handed it to her. She poured some of the ice water in her glass into it and took a long gulp. It tasted good.

John tried to stand up and couldn't make it. She saw that his shirt was sticking to his back and that his trousers were stained with perspiration. He fell back into the chair twice before he finally succeeded in getting out of it. His face wore a puzzled look, as though he were surprised to find himself drunk when he didn't remember taking a single drink.

He finished the whiskey in his glass and walked into the bathroom.

She knew now that she had a problem on her hands. Not the book, nor his reaction to it, but John himself, because she had never seen him like this. He seemed to be another person. He had traded all his softness, his tenderness for an obvious surliness that was foreign to him.

When he came out of the bathroom he perched on a wicker table and just sat and looked at her. For one fleeting second Ann thought of Mrs. Terrell in the bathtub with Harvey staring at her there. There was something of that same murderous urge in John's look.

He walked over and picked up the bottle.

"Don't you think you've had enough . . . on an empty stomach?" She tried to say it as casually, as kindly as she could.

"Ann!" he said, more to himself than to her. His voice had more

106

of a ring of self-rebuke than offense at anything said or done to him, and he turned around slowly and looked at her. His shoulders sagged; he looked baggy and wilted, and she thought he was going to cry.

"Ann, do you be*lieve* that?" he asked quietly, pointing to the manuscript on the floor.

"You mean . . . you mean what I've written? Why, it's just a *book*, honey. Just a *story*."

"Yes, but do you believe it?"

"Of course not. I tell you it's just a . . . a novel. I didn't know that—"

She didn't finish because John wasn't listening. He had sat down in the chair by the table with his back to her and he still hadn't touched his last drink. He was drunk enough to laugh, to cry, pass out, do anything.

"Why don't you lie down?" she asked. "We'll talk about it tomorrow."

He said dully, "You do believe it, don't you? You believe that I ran out on her. That I'm as selfish as he is—that I'm like him . . . I thought you hated her. You *said* you hated her."

Ann's hand was trembling so much she had to put her glass on the windowsill.

"You think she's got something you haven't got. You think I still love her. I love *you*, Ann. God damn it, I love *you*."

She knew that he was drunk and that the time was wrong, but she had to say it. "I know that, John. We love each other—and I don't think she has anything I haven't. It's a story. I just couldn't *help* writing it, I tell you."

"It's not a story any other way," he said, dead-voiced. "I'm like him every other way. He's me and I'm him. Maybe you're right. Maybe I don't know me."

"John . . ."

"Why didn't you call her Madge?" He was crying now. *"Why didn't you call her Madge?"*

Ann was too scared to be angry. She didn't know what to say, where to go, what to do. She just stood there and watched him cry.

In a few minutes he got up and said almost soberly, "I'm sorry, Ann. I'm drunk. Forget it. I—I'm going to be sick."

107

He stumbled into the bathroom and shut the door. She could hear him retching, retching. She wanted to go in there, to put a cold cloth to his forehead, to wash his face and neck with an ice-cold towel. She knew how much he hated being sick where she could hear him. She was fully aware of the sensitive, shy, private something in his nature that wouldn't want her in, yet she wanted to open the bathroom door and try to help him.

Instead, she stood where she was by the window, too stunned to notice that the room was now totally dark.

You have now passed what Hazel Watts calls the point-of-no-return. It has nothing to do with your having to keep on reading this book to the end just as an airplane pilot must fly ahead because it's too late to turn back. Hazel has in mind a specific page after which you are forbidden to read if you expect to return the book to her shop for credit.

"Sure I let customers return books they don't like," she admits, "But I have to have rules! When a customer tells me he can't get past the first chapter I never argue with him; when he says he tried fifty or even a hundred pages and given up I still take it back. But when he keeps on reading after passing a major intersection there's no backing up. For example, one page into Part II and he's bought the book, like it or not."

Ponder that well. Just one more page and you've passed the point-of-no-return. You've got to decide right now. Hazel has a heart of gold but she can be tough when she has to be.

10

"WHEN I die," Harry Shell said to Ann with simulated feeling, "I hope it's in May or June. It'll be just my luck, though, to die in late December—after I've had to listen to *White Christmas* twenty times a day for a whole month."

Ann studied Harry. He looked more peaked than he usually did at this hectic season of hastily scheduled commercials, abrupt program changes, continuous personnel crises. Christmas, that once-a-year nightmare for those who buy and those who sell, took its heaviest toll from the conduit between the two, those who write the advertising. Special copy had to be prepared in a hurry to get rid of stocks of buyers' booboos, invariably referred to as "perfect last minute gifts!" Victims of their self-induced euphoria, sponsors insisted that commercials should exude good will toward men while at the same time selling musical powder boxes at $6.98. December meant sixteen hours a day for Harry Shell, and at least ten for Ann, Irene, and the staff. The normal madness of WOOZ changed to high hysterics from the day after Thanksgiving to Twelfth Night.

"When I die," Harry repeated tiredly, plaintively, but Ann interrupted him, "Don't die before Christmas Eve, Harry. John and I are having a party and we want you and Ruth there—alive."

"Well, that's an incentive to live 'til Christmas," Harry said solemnly. "Thanks, Annie."

"Don't thank me. I thank you for being such a peach while I was sweating out the book, *and* for helping with my work when I went to Florida, *and—*"

Now Harry interrupted. "Change the subject. It's getting gooey in here. Let's talk about the K.C.S.S. Remember the K.C.S.S.?"

Of course she remembered. Every Christmas Harry got wound up on the subject of the K.C.S.S.

110

"The Keep Christmas Simple Society!" she said, "And our purpose is to—"

Harry pretended to look around the room for alien ears; then satisfied that he and Ann were alone, he proclaimed, "To combat the shekelized institution December 25th has become through the machinations and greed of merchants and ad media!"

"Hear, hear!" She approved loudly. And then she asked, "When are you going to stop talking about the K.C.S.S. and really launch it?"

"Next year," Harry promised enthusiastically. "Next year for sure." It had been next year every year since he'd first started talking about it. "Remember the motto?" he asked, and then began it himself, "Can cards! Eliminate egg-nog!"

Ann continued, "Peace on Earth instead of Pride in Gift-Wrap!"

"You get a gold star!" Harry said. "You and I are the charter members. Some day there'll be millions of us pledged to can cards, eliminate egg-nog and abolish duty gift exchanges. We'll devote ourselves to the simple meanings of Christmas, like presents for the poor and visits to friends on Christmas Day. Next year, for sure, we'll start recruiting."

"Meanwhile," Ann said, smiling, "*this* year there's a gift exchange at my party and the two charter members of the K.C.S.S. are exchanging gifts with each other. Three dollar limit. Okay?"

Harry nodded. "Okay . . . *this* year."

"It's going to be a nice party," Ann said. "There'll be you and Ruth, Irene, Bess Frankel, a book traveler named Bill Haley, and another book traveler named Thorg Thorgeson. I'm inviting the same number of boys and girls but nobody's going to be paired off. The others will come alone and choose their partners after they get there. Oh yes! Ruth's to buy a gift for Thorg. How does it sound?"

Harry took her hand. "All of a sudden I don't want to die, *ever,*" he said gently and then winced as he heard *White Christmas* begin its ten millionth play on the disc jockey's turntable.

Well, Ann thought, if December was a radio man's poison, it was a book man's meat. Book travelers loaf in December. They've already sold their wares and there's nothing to do but wait. The

111

travelers' December headaches come in January when they have to listen to the booksellers' complain about the titles that have been oversold to them. (Book buyers never over-buy; book travelers always over-sell.) She remembered when John, too, loafed through the month, but his changed status in the company kept him busy from nine to five. Helping set up the annual December sales conference was his responsibility. So if it was purposeful on his part that she saw very little of him this December, it wasn't obvious. It just so happened that they were never equally awake, never equally hungry, never equally tired, and, this year, never equally sober.

When she and John had returned from Florida, Bess could hardly wait to get her aside to learn John's reaction to the novel. "Do you think reading it had any effect on him?" Bess had asked. "Does he seem *changed* any?"

Ann had been tempted to say, "He says less and he drinks more," but instead she said, "Don't be silly."

The truth was a subtle thing, hard to define. Of course he seemed changed—and yet, he was careful to pretend that things were as before. The morning after he had read her book he apologized for getting drunk and making a scene. When in all honesty Ann offered to recall and destroy the manuscript he wouldn't hear of it. "It's swell writing," he had said. That's the word he used—"swell." He was almost formal when he wished her "all the luck in the world." And that was that, period. Their social life, their conversations, their lovemaking were the same— maybe—but *The Heart Being Hungry* was taboo.

She did feel a certain relief about his giving her book the silent treatment. At least there were no more scenes because of it. But to a woman who had never before known an out-of-bounds subject with her husband there was a keen disappointment she could not put into words. The old closeness was there—*except*. He was as thoughtful as ever, insisting that she eat properly, get enough rest, regain her strength but the book was a sleeping dog that both let lie.

She was increasingly over-careful about what she said to him. She couldn't manage to sound casual about a trivial request like "Try to get home early today, dear" and so she didn't say it. After all, how many times had he waited for her while she worked extra

112

hours on the book? He came home tight almost every day now. Instead of coming straight home from the office he'd meet Thorg Thorgeson or Bob Evans at a bar and have a few with them and though he seldom got loaded, he always got tipsy. When he observed how late it was he was sincerely sorry.

"You aren't mad, are you?" he'd ask, taking her into his arms.

"I'm not mad," she'd answer, trying not to be.

She told herself that she didn't want to make John over. She wanted him to be himself, to be happy. In short, she loved him. Yet if she could have had one Christmas wish, and only one, it would have been that John be a shade less sweet, less thoughtful, less considerate—and less drunk.

Still, she felt a pleasant excitement in planning for the party. She wanted it to be extra nice, partly because it was a private celebration of the end of her writing chore, but mostly because she was sentimental about Christmas Eve. She planned it very carefully, right down to the decorations, favors, refreshments. She even decided on a bowl of egg-nog, knowing that Harry, with his battle cry of Eliminate Egg-Nog would tease her about it. Well, he'd have to check his K.C.S.S. precepts at the door for this party, and anyway, she was sure that in his heart Harry loved Christmas as much as she did. It was the prostitution of its observance on the couch of commercialism that infuriated him so much. Besides, Bess and Irene loved egg-nog, and, well, maybe John might drink egg-nog, instead.

Ann had finished her shopping two days before the party. Early last week she had mailed gifts to California and she was determined to get everything done early so that she wouldn't be frazzled the night of the party. Her word-happy brain formed the beginning of a sponsorless commercial. "All presents—and accounted for!" She'd written her last spot, left the station, and started home. As she threaded her way through the clogged sidewalks she looked up and saw the snow falling, then looked down and saw the slush in the streets. For two days it had snowed intermittently, but snow in Manhattan isn't like snow any place else. The streets are dark brown ruts of slush which the buses and taxis splatter democratically on the rich, poor, old, young, careful and

113

unheeding. The Christmas sounds struck her as protests against what Christmas did to shoppers. The bells clanging at contribution kettles, the car horns tooting at stalled traffic, the loud-speakers outside stores blaring Christmas carols, all blended into a cacophony of noise that Ann was happy to shut out behind her as she closed her front door and stood for a few seconds savoring the blessed quiet of their apartment. She glanced down at a large Chinese bowl on a commode near the door. It was filled to overflowing with opened and unopened Christmas cards.

John called to her from the bedroom. "Ann? Be there in a minute. I'm just about dressed for the party. Don't light the Christmas tree 'til I get there!"

He was giving the final tug to his four-in-hand tie as he entered the living room; he had a scrubbed look about him in his fresh white shirt and without a suit-coat he seemed even taller than he was. He took her in his arms and kissed her in a way which said that he liked what he was doing.

"Whew!" she said, as he released her slowly. "Better make that variety one-to-a-customer!" She smelled the combination of Scotch whiskey and her cologne which John stole from her atomizer on dress-up occasions.

"Did you see that crop of cards?" he asked, pointing in the direction of the bowl. "Who in the hell is Hilda Terrell? Postmark's somewhere near Chicago. If her card cost a penny it cost five bucks. Everything on it but mink trim."

"Don't you remember?" she began, and then shuddered at the memory of Mrs. Harvey Terrell and that awful day. "She's . . . Oh, it doesn't matter. I want to see the tree."

John led the way across the room, placed her in front of the tree and got on his knees to plug in the tree lights. "Close your eyes!" he ordered, then, "Open!" She opened her eyes, blinked, then opened them wider, seeing the tree brightened up into a mass of tiny blue lights. She behaved exactly as a child does when surprised and pleased at the same time.

"It's beautiful," she whispered, "and the tinsel star still looks heavenly after all these years!" She'd had the same tinsel star on the Christmas tree since she was a young girl.

John had arranged the presents around the base of the tree—

114

gifts from Ann to John and from John to Ann, gifts from their families and friends. They would open these on Christmas morning, just as they always did.

"It's snowing again," Ann said. "It's going to be a white Christmas in spite of the disc jockeys!"

"Speaking of a white Christmas, come with me," John said. Motioning for her to follow him to the French doors which opened onto their tiny garden spot on the terrace, he bent over hastily to plug in another cord, then stood up and pointed outside to a much smaller tree, also with blue lights.

"It's darling!" Ann said, and clapped her hands, forgetting she was no longer a child. "How did you think of it?"

"Beats me," he said. "I was looking outside this morning and thinking how nice it would be to have our own pine tree growing here on the Estate and before I knew it I'd bought the tree, lights and extension cord—and lugged them up eighteen floors on the freight elevator."

Ann saw the snowflakes sticking to the little tree's branches. In a few hours it would itself be a perfect Christmas card and she was still enraptured as she said, "It's all the lovelier because it will be shared only by those who come within our house. Thank you, my darling."

Neither of them spoke for a moment as Ann's words stayed alive in the room. Then John shattered the spell, saying, "How about a couple of drinks to quiet our nerves before the big show starts?"

Ann frowned. "Isn't it too early to begin? We'll have plenty to drink tonight. I'm going to set up a cafeteria bar in the kitchen with everything from beer to bourbon to brandy—to egg nog!"

"Oh *no*. Not *egg nog*." he said, with a pained look. "That's for the sweet-n'-sticky set."

"Oh, *yes*. *Egg nog*," she mimicked. "Egg nog *goes* with Christmas Eve. In fact, I'll have one right now."

"You can have egg nog," he said, heading for the kitchen. "I'll take one of those b's . . . B as in Black and White."

He had one, and another. After his third Ann said, "It's time to eat something, honey. They'll start coming around eight and we'll have our buffet much later in the evening, so I'll fix you and me a bowl of soup and a sandwich to tide us over."

115

"I'm not hungry," he said.

"John." She said the word pleadingly, like a mother begging her little boy to do something he doesn't want to do.

"Oh, all right," he said, and sat down at the table.

"Am I the first?" Thorg Thorgeson asked as Ann opened the door. Thorg was as big and burly as a professional footballer. His cheeks were red from the cold and he wore no hat.

Ann laughed. "The first is always the best because now the party can start. Let me have your coat, Thorg. What, no hat? John's over there by the tree."

No sooner had Thorg and John shaken hands than John was leading the way to the bar but even as she made a move to intercept them she heard the door bell ring, and went to welcome Harry and Ruth. Irene was next, then Bess, with Bill Haley so close behind her that Ann had scarcely shut the door before the bell rang again.

John insisted on having a Merry Christmas drink with each of them.

"John's the perfect host," Harry told Ann and she merely smiled at him as she thought, I hope he doesn't fall flat on his perfect face.

As soon as the exchange presents had been deposited at the foot of the tree Ann took her guests to the French doors and showed them the little outdoors tree, glowing away in the snow.

"It was John's idea," she said proudly. "He thought it up all by himself."

"Grew it all by himself, too," John said with a peculiar, rising inflection that meant he was well on his way to being looped.

Earlier, Ann had placed a stack of Hawaiian records on the hi-fi turntable and started them playing low; then she walked over to Harry and placed a lei around his neck.

"Happy fiftieth state," she said solemnly.

"Merry pineapple," he answered, "and Happy Fourth-of-July."

Ann noticed that Bill and Bess were already sitting close together on the couch, talking earnestly about something. Thorg and Irene were dancing to the slow Hawaiian music. John had

116

called Harry and Ruth into the kitchen, insisting they have another drink.

When Bess went to get Bill a fresh drink Ann walked over to the couch and sat down by him.

He said, softly, "Hello, Ann. Thanks for asking me. Christmas Eve can be the lonesomest night in the year when you're by yourself."

"I'm glad you're here," she said. And then, "Bill . . . there's something I want to ask you."

"About the book?"

"No. The book's finished. It's going to have to sink or swim on its own. It's . . . about John. He's . . . well . . . drinking quite a bit lately, and—"

Bill looked at her and then looked at the tree as he asked, "He read your book yet?"

"Of course."

"Did he like it?"

"He said he thought it was swell. Why?"

"Nothing." Bill studied the tree. "I only asked."

"You think the book has something to do with his drinking so much."

Finally, he looked at her. "Yes. Don't you?"

Now it was her turn to study the blue lights of the tree until they blurred her gaze. "I don't know," she said, almost whispering. "I just wondered if—as a favor to an old friend—you could maybe say something to him to slow him down a bit. He likes you, Bill, and he might listen to you. He's—I can't put my finger on it—he seems to be sort of forcing himself—even the *drinking*."

"I'll try, Ann," Bill said, "but Jack knows how hard I hit the bottle myself and he's never climbed me about *my* drinking, so I don't see how I—oh hell, yes. I'll try. I promise I will."

Bess came back, handed Bill his drink and said, "Let's open the presents."

Everyone crowded around the tree now and found his gift. Bill Haley opened his first and it was a book.

"For the book traveler who has everything!" Bess said, laughing.

Bill opened the book and read the autograph: "To Bill, this first copy of the big non-fiction best-seller of the year, *I Want an Endur-*

117

ing Peace. Merry Piracy to Fortune House from Laverty and Clarke. John."

Bill exploded. "Now, that's hitting below the belt and on Christmas Eve, too!" The others laughed and he smiled, but with reservations, Ann thought, as he said, "Okay, Pirate! You guys stole our big author, but just you wait—"

Ann knew he was going to say "until Laverty and Clarke discovers what we stole from *you*" so she caught his eye in time and shook her head violently. Harry saw her do it and said instantly, "Ooo, Look what *I* got!"

He displayed three phonograph records and read their titles: *"Santa Claus is Coming to Town, Winter Wonderland,* and—" he flinched, *"White Christmas!* Listen to what the note says: 'Upon receipt and examination, kindly break into a thousand pieces and oblige. Ann.' "

Harry obliged, lovingly breaking each record over his knee. Then he placed the pieces in their gift box and stomped on them.

"Never had so much fun in my life!" he exulted. "Beats the thrill of my first sled!"

Irene's gift to Ruth was a pint of whiskey with a label pasted onto it that read: "DIRECTIONS: One spoonful of giggle water to be administered to your husband at breakfast so he'll be giggly instead of grouchy when he comes to work." Thorg was next and Ruth had given him cuff links with bulls on them.

"Your birth sign," she announced, "Taurus the bull! I had one heck of a time finding out the birthday of a man I'd never met, but a nice switchboard girl named Jackie at Laverty and Clarke found out and called me!"

Bess had given John a leather picture-frame in a case he could travel with, knowing he'd want one for the photograph Ann was giving him for Christmas. She had slipped into the frame a snapshot of her Jaguar with John at the wheel.

Thorg gave Irene a charm for her charm bracelet. Ann had made the suggestion when she gave him Irene's name. Harry's gift to Ann was a fountain pen with an extra carton of ink cartridges. When she read his note. "Autograph the first one to me!" she knew she would cry if she didn't do something quickly, so she

118

ran over to Ruth and said, "Your husband is an angel and I love him!"

Bess was the last to open her gift. Ann had given her name to Bill Haley because he knew her and could better select something clever. Whatever Bill had bought was packed in a large dress-box, exquisitely gift-wrapped, and Ann thought, a typical Bill gag. Then Bess unwrapped the box, lifted the lid, dug into the layers of tissue paper, and held up a breathtakingly beautiful purple velvet robe.

Irene whistled. "Wow! Henri Bendel. Somebody got a bargain if he stayed within the three-dollar limit on that!"

Ann looked at Bill who was busy counting the bubbles in his drink, and Bess was so flustered that she ran into the bedroom.

Ann followed her. "It's lovely, Bess, but I don't know what possessed Bill. I told him to keep the gift funny and inexpensive. This robe's not funny and it must have cost a fortune."

Bess held the robe up to her and all that she could say was, "He —he shouldn't have done it." She slipped the purple, simply designed robe with its softly draped bosom and flaring skirt on over her dress and said again, stroking the velvet, "He shouldn't have done it. Y'see, Ann—" She started to cry. "Bill and I—we—"

She didn't get to finish because John stuck his head into the room now and yelled, "Let's eat, kids. We're starved!"

Ann made a mental note to call Bess first thing in the morning about that unfinished sentence. Then she started making coffee and getting the food ready while Ruth and Irene helped. Bess was still in the bedroom and Bill had gone in to talk to her, but Ann couldn't think about them now. She was simply, wholly grateful that John knew enough to realize he was hungry.

When he ate he would sober up a notch—she hoped.

They had supper at two tables that John set up in the living room. Thorg and Irene were at the table with John and Ann, Harry and Ruth with Bill and Bess. After they had finished eating they all sat for a long time and talked, then finally, Irene said, "Before we break up, let's all sing something."

"Like *Santa Claus Is Coming to Town?*" Harry said. "Over my dead body!"

119

"No. A Christmas carol," Irene insisted. "Let's sing *Silent Night.*"

Ann put out all the lights except those on the Christmas tree in the living room and those on the tree on the terrace.

"All we need is a roaring fire in the fireplace," she said.

"Why didn't you tell me?" Bill said. "I'd have brought you a roaring fireplace for a Christmas present."

Irene said, "Quiet, everybody. Here's the pitch. Thorg's going to carry the bass. All right, now . . ."

Silent night, holy night
All is calm, all is bright

The first words of the simple carol gave these victims of the twentieth century distortion of Christmas a mellow feeling for the original dignity of this night.

Round yon virgin, mother and child

The telephone rang.

Harry Shell, sitting nearest the phone, answered it, then pointed at John who got up and motioned for the others to keep on singing.

John carried the phone as far as the cord would stretch until he was almost in the hall which led to the bedroom.

He said, "Hello. Hello. Who's calling? . . . *Who?* . . . Oh."

Holy infant, so tender and mild

Ann kept singing the carol, but she was listening to John.

"Well, thanks and the same to you," John said. "We're . . . uh . . . having a little Christmas party. Singing *Silent Night.* Hear it?"

Irene started the chorus again.

"It's darned swell of you to call. How's the weather out there? Really? It's snowing here. Yeah. White Christmas. Mmmmmmm-hm. I'll bet you do."

Ann dabbed at the sweat that had suddenly beaded on her upper lip. She glanced at Bill Haley and saw that he, too, was listening to John instead of to the music—and watching her.

Sleep in heavenly peace
Sleep in heavenly peace.

"Goodbye. Thanks for calling. Goodbye."

Harry Shell flipped on the light switch.

"We've got to go," he said. "It's after midnight."

120

Thorg went for his and Irene's coats.

Bill and Bess were the last to leave, calling back over their shoulders,

"Merry Christmas!"

"Merry Christmas!"

When everyone had gone, Ann walked over to John and kissed him tenderly. She said, "I've repeated it so many times tonight, but this time it's for you, especially. Merry Christmas, my darling. Merry Christmas—with love from Ann."

He held her to him.

"Merry Christmas," he whispered. "It was a lovely party, darling."

He helped her with the dishes before they went to the bedroom.

Ann was taking off one of her stockings when she asked, "Who was the call from?"

He looked at her absently. "Call?"

"Yes. The call that came for you when we were singing *Silent Night*."

"Oh," he made a casual gesture, "just a friend of mine I haven't seen in years. Had too much to drink, I guess, and called me long distance to wish me Merry Christmas."

She held her stocking in her hand and looked at it for a long moment without seeing it. This was the first time John had ever lied to her when she knew for sure he was lying.

She looked outside and saw from the bedroom window the pristine little tree on the terrace, its blue lights shining on the snow. It was somehow a symbol of something continuing too long.

"You'd better turn off the lights on the outside tree," she said.

"Oh, yes. I'd forgotten." He seemed relieved to have something to do.

It made Ann sad as she watched the little tree grow dark.

121

11

HAZEL WATTS pulled at the girdle that was pinching her and wondered for the ten thousandth time why she'd ventured into the bittersweet world of bookselling. She was only forty-four years old and on the buxom side: big bosomed, broad beamed. Her skin had once been olive, now it was oily. Her eyes, once blue, were a kind of watery gray. Her high cheekbones still had a youthful rubbed-apple shine to them. Her hair stayed as black as the devil's heart because she kept it scrupulously dyed. (Hazel had made up her mind to continue dyeing it until she was fifty. Then, on her fiftieth birthday, she'd emerge with all the fanfare of a signed, limited edition, wearing her own silvery crown. Until then, she'd fight nature with woman's trusted weapon, the smudge pot.) In contrast to her large frame, her hands were almost dainty. She used them gracefully and unselfconsciously, although more than one customer complimented her on them.

She'd been called Czarina of American Booksellers and she looked it as she stood near the cash register of her Personal Book Shop surveying her domain which measured 30 feet by 60 feet and faced one of the most heavily trafficked streets in Dallas. This little kingdom was bounded by a motion picture theatre on one side and a five-and-dime on the other.

If all employers are despots, Hazel was at least a benevolent one, bestowing upon her three subjects a kind of heart-of-gold mothering. In return, they gave her a serflike loyalty bordering on adoration. She looked at them now. Mabel was selling a Bible, starting properly with the more expensive ones and working down as necessary; Betty was selling a librarian a large order of children's books; Billy was changing a display in the show-window.

Hazel loved Mabel and Betty as she did her own daughter.

They came to work for her because they liked books; they stayed because they liked Hazel. Billy had started while he was still in high school—unpacking boxes, runing errands, making deliveries. Then he came in afternoons after his classes at S.M.U. and joined the sales staff. When he quit college he asked Hazel if he could work full time. As happy as she was to have him (God knows, good help was too hard to get to wonder why it was there) she still questioned the fate which had led such a nice kid into the book business.

She hadn't been much older than Billy when she opened Hazel Watts' Personal Book Shop in 1939 with a legacy of $5,000 which her father had left her. Her first location had been in the partitioned half of a flower shop on a Dallas side street. Ten years ago she had moved to her present store which fronted a busy downtown street and was close to the Baker and Adolphus hotels. *Publishers' Weekly* ran a full page spread on the new store with a picture of Hazel standing between two baskets of gladioli. Mabel was in the picture, too, but Betty hadn't started working for her yet.

There were larger book outlets in Dallas, but none had Hazel's devoted following. When authors barnstormed through the city on autographing tours, and when local writers had books published, hers was the store they selected as their headquarters, even though some of the department stores' book sections had more room and ran larger ads. Hazel had been called everything from the bookseller's bookseller to a Texas institution (she loved that one!) and somehow they all fit. Even those who frowned at her frankness and impulsive tongue found it impossible not to respect her.

Twenty-two years. She lined the lean times up against the fat ones, the heartbreaks against the successes. Five years ago she was able to afford the luxury of dropping her rental department, but there had been a time when the rental books kept her alive. She remembered spending most of her day on the telephone calling, calling customers to keep the rental copies circulating. *"Hello, Gloria? This is Hazel. Hazel Watts. There's a new Frances Parkinson Keyes in and I've got it reserved for you. This one's a sort of mystery. Yes, plenty of good description. No, the heroine's not spoiled rotten as the last one was. Yes, she's a fine Southern girl. If you want my opinion, I think it's the best thing she's written yet.*

123

Have I read *it? Of* course *I have! You'll* love *it. Same rates: three days for a dime, and a nickel-a-day thereafter."* How many times had she gone through that routine? How many lies had she told, how much exuberance had she feigned for a dime—and a nickel-a-day thereafter?

The last few years had been good ones. Television, instead of destroying the desire to read, was helping the sale of books. Where she used to buy ten copies of a celebrity's autobiography she now bought fifty or more when she learned that the celebrity would be pushing his own book on TV. Viewers who hadn't read anything in a binding since Mother Goose came into the shop and asked for specific titles.

The good times had come none too soon. Hazel's daughter, Angel, was a sophomore at Wellesley and it cost like the devil to keep her there. Hazel had plans for Angel. Angel was pretty and as smart as a whip and some easterner with plenty of money would marry her and support her in a style her mother had not been accustomed to. God forbid that Angel should end up in a book store!

When it came to men, Hazel had one inflexible rule: don't trust them. She respected some of them, liked many of them, even loved one now and then, but she had trusted no man from the day her husband walked out on her shortly after Angel was born. "Ran" was a better word, perhaps, because he'd run away with the woman in the flower shop on the other side of the partition. Hazel had asked her to keep an eye on things while she went out for a sandwich at noon. The woman had kept her eye on things, all right. She'd swiped him, and he'd swiped all he could lay his hands on that could possibly be converted into legal tender.

Hazel sighed.

She spent a great deal of her musing-time cataloging the evils of bookselling. Surely no business in the world made less money and demanded more of your life. She had read somewhere that there were two thousand fewer bookstores in America in 1961 than there were twenty years ago. "A vanishing profession," the author of the article had called the book business. And no wonder! Mrs. James Sandgrove, who owned cotton, cattle *and* oil, had just telephoned to ask when *The Agony and the Ecstasy* would be available in a

124

paperback. Hazel had told her, "It'll be at least a year. It hasn't been out three months," and Mrs. Sandgrove had answered, "I'll wait."

Reluctantly, Hazel had made her peace with the paperback revolution and had installed a large paperback department which Billy kept up-to-the-minute. It hadn't hurt business, either. Hundreds of youngsters who could not afford regular editions came into the store to buy classics and reference books in paper at a few cents each. Booklovers on a budget never had it so good.

And the publishers themselves! Hazel was a dedicated crusader against those publishers who circularized vast mailing lists of her customers and ran full page advertisements with coupons to clip and mail in. She had addressed the convention of the American Booksellers Association on this subject and had pulled no punches. "The publisher slaps us in the face and we booksellers just stand there and take it! He sells us books, then tries to sell the same books to our customers—and I say the time has come for booksellers to fight back! If the wholesalers want to be retailers, too, let us stop selling books and start selling shoes!" She got her picture in *Publishers' Weekly* (that was when they'd coined that darned fool "Czarina of American Booksellers" title) but her talk hadn't done much good.

Hardly a day went by that someone didn't stroll in, look at the clean and inviting book displays in the store, and say, "Some day I'm going to get myself a little bookstore and catch up with my reading." Hah! Hazel thought. Hah! Hah! *Hah!* A bookseller was so busy opening boxes, checking invoices, lifting books from table to table, replacing back stock, and pulling returns that she was too tired to read a book. It also made Hazel boil when customers mentioned browsing (Oh, how they licked their chops over that word "browse"!) in "charming little bookstalls where the dust was an inch thick over everything." She kept her Personal Book Shop as clean as she kept her own home, The three girls (Billy had no aptitude for it) dusted and straightened the same books on the same tables every day. They dusted the standard stock on a so-many-shelves-per-day basis. Hazel had learned that the only way to know off-hand if you had a certain book in the store was to become intimate with it through a dust cloth. Then there were

125

the plants. Betty was called Queen of the May, because the healthy green plants all over the place were hers to water, wax and watch over.

But the hard work was only part of it. A bookseller differed from any other kind of tradesman in that customers expected him to be an authority on every subject under the sun, including outer space. He must have, or know where to get, (immediately) books on everything from tatting to skin diving to cooking-for-fifty to the rhythm method of birth control to yoga to psychoanalysis to weaning a baby to falconry to vintage cars to the positions in intercourse to extrasensory perception to *ad infinitum*. Because he sells books on these subjects many people feel that he knows all that is in them; therefore, they confide in him their most personal problems and innermost needs, expecting him to supply the answers.

Hazel paid better wages than did the other Dallas booksellers; still, her three trusted helpers could have made more money in other jobs. Mabel, Betty and Billy knew this. But they resembled coal miners the way they recognized the disadvantages of their vocation, grumbled a good deal of the time, yet hadn't the slightest intention of getting out of it. But, Hazel reasoned, how could she pay them what they were really worth? Her mark-up was forty per cent and out of that she had to pay rent, salaries, advertising, utilities, postage and wear-and-tear. Many of her customers actually thought the book business was a consignment business—pay only for what you sell, but Hazel knew better. She had experienced too many tenth of the month stomach pains and tension headaches from writing checks on a bank balance which didn't exist. Somehow the intake managed to balance the outgo, but there were times when her banker had to be indulgent.

Hazel moved from where she was standing so Mabel could ring up the Bible sale. The customer, after receiving her change, didn't seem to want to go. She described the store with a sweeping gesture and chirruped in a Billie Burke voice, "Don't you just *love* books? If I worked here I'd want to read them *all!*" Billy and Betty exchanged irreverent glances behind her back and Mabel kept her eyes on the register because she knew she'd giggle if she looked at them.

"Mabel," Hazel called from the door of the stock room, "do you

126

feel like coming back here and tackling these returns with me?" Mabel smiled a quick goodbye to the lover-of-books and winked her thanks to Hazel for rescuing her.

"Imagine wanting to read them *all*," Mabel whispered, looking at the stacks of books waiting to be returned to the publishers for credit because nobody had shown the slightest interest in them.

Mabel was an attractive girl in her early thirties—fair, with large, brown eyes and a perfect complexion. Her long, blonde hair was worn in a bun under her right ear and her quiet voice and delicate coloring gave her a cuddly-as-a-kitten softness. Although she had a good figure she wore a perennial middy and skirt that was neither in style nor out of style, but style-less. This unchanging uniform gave people the impression that Mabel herself never changed. During the sack dress's abortive reign, Mabel was actually in the vanguard of the fashion parade, but afterward her costume seemed more hopelessly outmoded than ever.

Hazel loved Mabel and knew that Mabel would never leave her. She'd be here until the place caved in—or until Hazel did. Mabel was constant in many things but mostly in her affection for Bill Haley. She'd always been crazy about Bill Haley and she waited patiently for him between his trips to Dallas. Mabel would have been the first to admit that she had as much chance of snagging Bill Haley as she had of trading in her middy for a sarong. But, still, there was that outside chance that he might fall in love with her. That was all she needed to keep her constant.

"I'd rather be shot than make returns," Hazel said stoically. "Honestly, it's better to put them on the sale table than fight it out with a returns department in New York. You have to apply at the proper time for permission, lose the postage both ways and often forfeit a big handling fee. Why-oh-why did I get fast-talked into buying these duds?"

Mabel smiled. Hazel said the same thing every six months. "Do you want me to start packing these?" she asked, pointing to a triple stack of *Milk in the Skys* in the corner.

"I'm afraid it's too soon," Mabel answered. "Laverty and Clarke won't give me permission to return them until July unless Johnny Long gives me an okay to shoot them back for credit now. How many are there?"

127

"I'll bet he will," Mabel said, beginning her expert count. "Sixty-eight."

Hazel studied the *Milk in the Sky*s as though hypnotized. "I bought a hundred last fall and we haven't sold half of them. Sixty-eight $5.00 books paid for—and as dead as doornails. Think of the Bibles we have to sell to take up the slack!"

"I'd like to see that customer who wants to read them all tackle *Milk in the Sky*," Mabel said.

"Me, too!" Hazel agreed, turning away. "A novel which needs a hard sell is a dead duck if it doesn't move during the Christmas rush. That's the one time of year when people will buy anything. Here it is the end of January and we haven't sold a *Milk in the Sky* for two weeks."

Betty called to Mabel for help in the front of the store and Hazel motioned for her to go. Standing alone, surrounded by returns, Hazel thought of the men who sold her these books. There were so many of them: from Harper, Macmillan, Prentice-Hall, Laverty and Clarke, Doubleday, Platt and Munk, Fortune House, Houghton Mifflin, Viking, Little Brown—that was only the beginning of a long list of book publishers with men on the road, each man with his own spring, fall and winter catalogs, his own leather brief case, his own bottle in his own hotel room. Some of the men on the road represented three, four, as many as ten smaller firms. These were the old commission men who were paid a percentage of their sales. Many of them earned more money than the men in the New York office did. In recent years most companies had gravitated toward younger men, on a salary-plus-expense basis. Book traveling was losing a lot of its glamour, she thought. One of the largest publishing firms of all was sending around kids in their early twenties to sell books to her, kids who sold books the way they'd sell paint, and who knew more about paint than they knew about books.

And Hazel Watts liked them all. She griped, cussed them out, complained about them—and liked them. Damn it, she thought, there isn't a finer bunch of gals in America than bookstore gals—and there isn't a grander bunch of guys than book travelers. Even when they're heels, even when they overload me, even when they get drunk and make passes, they're still okay.

128

She saw another customer walk in and went to help her. The woman asked Hazel, politely, "Pardon me, do you happen to have a copy of *The Milky Way*? I'm not positive about the title, and I don't remember the author's name, but it's rather new."

"I wonder if you could mean *Milk in the Sky*?" Hazel asked, crossing her fingers.

"Maybe that's it. It's about a dairy farm. My cousin met the author and said he's a really big person."

Hazel controlled the urge to hurry, walked to the stacks of copies ready for return, and picked one up.

"Is it really good?" the woman asked confidentially as Hazel put the book in a sack.

"I don't know," Hazel said absent-mindedly. "I haven't had time to read it yet."

The customer looked disappointed, and not a little shocked. Surely, a bookseller who is really on her toes reads *everything!*

"But," Hazel said quickly, affecting a look of burning intensity, "I certainly *intend* reading it—and *soon!*"

That always did it.

12

"PARDON me, do you happen to have fifty copies of *Milk in the Sky*?"

Hazel wheeled around.

"Why, John Long, you *devil*. I thought you were a browser." Then she remembered his question and glared at him. "I have exactly sixty-seven copies of that lousy book, you stinker. How about special permission to return them now? Should I gift-wrap them?"

John laughed. "Send 'em back any time—and tell L and C I said it was okay." He walked around the store quickly, yet paused here

129

and there as though to say hello to an old friend, then he came back to Hazel and took her hand affectionately in his. "Well, Hazel, how goes it?"

She smiled at him. "Can't complain. Why don't you send a postcard, like all the other travelers, announcing your arrival? A girl might want to fix herself up a little."

"Am I like all the others? I thought I was sorta special around here."

Her cheeks turned a deeper red. "You know you are," and her voice softened a shade. "I hear all the time how you're going up and up at L and C and what will we do when you don't pop in any more? You're no ordinary drummer, Johnny, and big shots don't travel the same territory forever." She looked closely at him, not liking what she saw. He must have been working too hard. Aloud, she asked, "When did you blow into Dallas?"

"Flew in last night and started work early this morning. I've sold five accounts today. Saved the best for the last. Meaning you, you old bat."

A closer look made Hazel wonder if he'd been sick. He was so much thinner. "Bill Haley's in town," she said.

"I know. I saw him at the hotel this morning. He wants me to fly to New Orleans with him tomorrow, so that's why I'm killing myself to sell Dallas in one day."

"Well, if your list is no better than it was the last trip, it's not worth the wear-and-tear on you. *Milk in the Sky*, indeed." Hazel pinched the end of her nose as she said it.

"I've got one corker, Hazel. The new Harold Albert. *I Want an Enduring Peace*. I told you about it last fall and you said you'd wait. It's coming next month."

Hazel smiled. "That *title*. If I didn't know you better, Johnny, I'd swear it was a proposition. Come into the office and we'll get it over with."

"The proposition?"

"The order, you fool."

They sat down in Hazel's tiny office and cleared off a small segment of her desk that was littered with *New York Times Book Reviews*, book pages from the Dallas papers, publicity letters, special orders and other important trivia.

130

"How's Angel?" John asked.

"Swell."

"She still hasn't called us in New York."

"She hasn't been there yet. She'll call when she gets there. How's your wife?"

"Oh—fine."

"Glad to hear it." Something wrong there, Hazel thought, seeing that his hand was shaking and his forehead was covered with sweat.

She asked casually, "You feeling all right, Johnny? Too hot in here? You don't have to sell me now if you're tired, you know. Put me down for seventy-five Harold Alberts and let me buy the others from the catalog and send the order to you."

"I'm okay," John said. "Never felt better." But he didn't look at her when he said it.

Hazel spoke again. "Don't try to kid me, Johnny. There's something bothering you."

"Bothering me?" he said, busying himself with his brief case.

"Yes, I can tell. Is it love trouble?"

John almost never talked private business to the book girls. They were all likable, but most of them couldn't solve their own problems, so why trouble them with his? Hazel Watts was different, though. He could talk to her. But not now.

"No love trouble," he said. "Nope. I'm an old-fashioned character who's in love with his wife, Haze."

She didn't want to pry, but she couldn't stand to see him like this. Almost shyly she reached out her pretty hand to cover his. "Then what's wrong? I don't like to see you unhappy."

"God damn it," he said flatly, "I'm *not* unhappy."

She took her hand away. "Pardon me!"

He shifted in his chair. "Sorry, Hazel . . . I'm sorry."

"You're just tired, Johnny. Let's start ordering."

They were almost finished when the telephone rang. Hazel answered it, said briskly, "Sounds good to me, what time?" and then, "We'll be there."

She looked at John. "That was Bill. He wants to know if I'll buy Fortune House in his room at the hotel and he says he'll take Mabel and me to dinner afterwards."

"How's Mabel?" John asked.

131

He knew about Mabel's feeling for Bill and he accepted the thing matter-of-factly.

Hazel shrugged. "Same as ever. Mabel's a wonderful girl and why she should be content just to have Bill Haley come through three times a year is more than I can understand, but then it's her life." She could tell now that John had relaxed somewhat so she said, "Still don't want to tell me, Johnny?"

John was glad that she'd brought it up again. He wanted to confide in her—if not the problem itself, at least the truth that he had one. He'd worked under tremendous pressure all day, selling over eight hundred Harold Alberts in Dallas. That was an excellent advance sale, even for a sure best-seller, so just let Cecil Laverty dare say anything about the returns on *Milk in the Sky.*

He tilted his chair now and stretched his long legs out straight, resting his feet on a stack of invoices on the far corner of the desk. Hazel, watching him, loved his honest informality. She knew that John Long would not unbend like this in any other store.

"Hazel," he said, gazing first at the ceiling and then meeting her eyes squarely, "I have a sneaking suspicion that all hell's going to break loose soon, and on my neck. I don't want to say any more now because maybe it won't happen but I feel it comin' on, just the same."

"Okie-dokie," Hazel said. "Don't you tell me if you don't think you oughtta." She put her hand on his cheek. "Only—if it does happen, Johnny—you come on down here. You know you can always count on old Hazel."

"Thanks, Hazel."

She stood up. "And make it a hundred Harold Alberts," she said over her shoulder as she went to tell Mabel that Bill Haley was expecting them for dinner.

John was lying on the bed in Bill's hotel room, his tie and shoes off, his shirt open at the collar. Mabel, in an overstuffed chair she had pulled over to the bed, was talking with John while Bill finished selling Hazel at the writing desk.

"All right, but damn you, Haley," Hazel said, pinching Bill in the ribs, "if I get twenty *Mississippi River Stories* instead of the ten I'm ordering I'll send every last one of 'em back *pronto!* Johnny lets

132

me off easy but *you* pin my shoulders to the mat and then double my orders!"

"Why, Hazel! You don't *trust* me." Bill turned on his most waggish grin.

"I do *not*. You oversold me something awful last fall. I must have been doped."

"I *couldn't* have," Bill said laughing. He put his arm around her. "Why, Hazel, I *love* you."

"You go to hell," Hazel said, but her hand trembled a little as she put the order book down on the desk. Bill was a sweet boy, a sweet boy. Mabel had a point, after all.

"Fix me a drink, Haley," John said.

Bill exchanged looks with Hazel. They both knew that John was drunk and they both hated seeing him this way because they also knew he wasn't getting any kicks out of it.

"Sure you want another, Jack?" Bill asked. "You've been slugging yourself."

John nodded solemnly. "Positive, my boy."

"How come?" Hazel whispered to Bill.

"Ahhh, he's got what is known as a *problem*," Bill whispered back.

"Anything to do with the book business?"

Bill started to say no, then reconsidered and said, "Well, let's say if it *weren't* for the book business he wouldn't have his problem." He fixed the drink.

When Bill and Mabel and Hazel came back to the room after dinner John was asleep. He had taken off his shirt and trousers and habit had put him to bed.

"He'll be hungry when he wakes up," Mabel said.

"Or thirsty," Bill answered wryly. "Jack doesn't pass out—he just sleeps long enough for the liquid to stop running over the dam. Then he wakes up and pours in another dipperful."

"Lord! Can't you say something to him about it?" Hazel asked. "You're his friend, Bill."

"Who do you think I am, Haze? Mr. Keeley of the Cure?" Bill snapped at her with exasperation. "You're the second person to ask

133

me to reform the guy and my A.A. friends tell me *I've* got a drinking problem."

Hazel squeezed his arm.

"Don't take it personal, chum. I just feel sorry for Johnny."

Bill scowled. "I do, too, but I've got a feeling things're going to get worse before they get better with him. I'm going to tackle his drinking problem tomorrow—but I sure as hell can't do anything about his other problems."

"Well," Hazel said, picking up her purse, "I hope he gets whatever's eating him out of his system. I like him, Bill." She looked at her watch. "I've got to go home, now. Ain't so young as I used to be before they brought me out in a paperback. Have to have my eight-hour sleep. Thanks a lot for the dinner, Bill."

Bill walked to the door with her. He said, "Good night, sweetheart. If I increase an order of yours, kick me in the you-know-what."

She smiled. "With *pleasure* . . . and remember! Ten *Mississippi River Stories! No more.*"

She looked back at Mabel. "Good night, Mabel."

That was what she always said when Bill Haley was in town.

Bill got John to his own room, undressed him again, and put him to bed. When he came back to his room, he found Mabel in a pair of his pajamas. She had rolled up the sleeves and trouser-legs and, strangely enough, looked very womanly in them. She had mixed two drinks.

He kissed her on the cheek.

She raised an eyebrow. "Is that all?"

"Hell," Bill said, "I look at you and feel like a heel. You're too nice a girl to fool around with a bum like me. Three, four visits a year, and that's all there is to it."

"You never heard me call you a heel or a bum, did you?" Mabel said. She was looking at him closely, thinking, He's finally found her, the right one. *Oh God! Please don't let him change it tonight. I know he doesn't love me the way he does her, but Please God, let him take this drink and get undressed—this one last time.*

He looked at her. She was a sweet kid; no, not a kid any more, maybe, but damned sweet. Quiet, good, clean and he knew that she

134

never looked at another traveler. What could you say to a girl like this at a time like this without hurting her? He said, "Look, Mabel—"

The telephone rang.

"Hello. Who? Yes, Ann. This is Bill."

"What's the matter with John?" Ann's voice had an edge of worry. "I called his room and got no answer. I thought maybe he was with you."

"He—he—"

"I can't hear you."

"He's asleep."

"Don't lie to me, Bill. Tell me the truth."

"He passed out."

"Oh."

"Not *exactly* passed out—just had a couple too many. He sold six accounts today and got awfully tired. Then he had too many too quick."

"Bill, take care of him."

There it was again.

"I will," Bill said. "He's going to New Orleans with me tomorrow. I'll talk a little sense into his head. I promise. Any word about the book?"

"Not yet."

"I've got my fingers crossed."

"Thanks, Bill. It's John I'm worried about now, not the book. Wait a minute. Someone wants to talk to you."

"Someone? Hello? Oh, hello, Bess."

"I'm spending the night with Ann," Bess said. "How are you, Bill?"

Hearing Bess's voice now, after being away from her, he got a strange sensation in his stomach.

"Fine," he said. "How are you?" He didn't add *dear*, but he didn't need to. It was there anyway.

Mabel took a sip of her drink and walked over to the radio. She turned it on just loud enough not to hear what Bill was saying.

"Me, too," he said. "That goes double for me. Tell Dr. Darnell I send love and kisses."

135

Mabel looked at Bill and saw that his ears had taken on a pink tinge.

"Well, goodbye. Goodbye." He put down the telephone. He was in love with Bess and he knew that she was in love with him. But here he was in his hotel room in Dallas with one of the sweetest girls he'd ever known. He would not hurt Mabel for anything in this world.

He took off his shirt and necktie. He had hoped against hope that Mabel would be unable to sleep with him this trip—wished it harder than he'd ever wished the other way around. This was the last time he would come through Dallas without knowing for sure about Bess and being able to tell everybody about her. He could pave the way next time by writing Mabel first and explaining, and she'd understand. It might be one hell of an epitaph but it was the truth: this girl was the understanding kind. He was sure she wouldn't be here if she thought he was in love with someone else, but the hell of it was she *was here*. He could not tell her about Bess Frankel now. He could not be that callous. Mabel was quiet, but she took things hard.

He took off his trousers and hung them up and when he walked back from the closet he saw his pajamas on the bed. Mabel was in the bathroom.

"Hey," he called, "what goes?"

"I think I'd better go home tonight, Bill."

He walked into the bathroom just as she was putting on lipstick. She was trying hard to keep from crying.

He put his hands on her shoulders from behind and looked at her in the glass. "I've never lied to you, Mabel."

"I know that."

"I've always loved being with you, Mabel."

"I hope so."

He could not do this. He could not be that mean. Softly, persuasively, he said, "If I asked you one favor, Mabel, would you say yes? Even if it was something you didn't really want to do?"

She looked up at him and the tears were running down her face. "What, Bill?"

"Stay tonight. Please—stay tonight." He took her by the hand

136

and led her into the room. "Please, Mabel. Please. I *want* you to stay tonight."

He turned off the light and walked over to her.

She threw her arms around him and kissed him passionately.

The two travelers started for the Dallas airport at eight o'clock on a dismal January morning of rain, which gradually settled down to a fine chilly mist. Large isolated globs of water splattered the hood and windshield of the cab and they said little to each other. John felt that he looked as gray as the day and he hadn't had breakfast. Bill had had a cup of coffee in the room with Mabel.

It was still soupy outside as they boarded the plane. They were hardly off the ground before the stewardess asked if they wished breakfast and Bill answered yes for both of them. He said, "Eat, Jack. After you eat something you'll feel better."

The breakfasts looked appetizing so John tried a couple of experimental bites and they stayed down. He ate everything on his plate and drank two cups of coffee.

Bill thought of his promise to Ann. He had told her twice that he would speak to Jack about the bottle, but each time he'd had misgivings. Ann shouldn't have asked it.

He said, "Jack, d'y mind if I say something that's none of my damned business?"

John closed the magazine he'd been leafing through. "Shoot."

Bill squirmed for a minute then took the plunge. "Where does this concentrated drinking get you? You missed a nice dinner last night. Hazel was at her best and you really should have come along."

"Hazel understands," John said. "We *like* each other."

"I know. But frankly, Jack, drinking like a fish doesn't—well, it just doesn't become you. It's too obvious you don't like whiskey that much."

John looked at the rain running down the plane window. He studied the drops as they started high, traveled down a few inches, then made abrupt turns and continued on until they dissipated themselves on the wet glass. Watching rain always had the same hypnotic effect on him that staring at a wood fire did.

"I don't want to harp on it," Bill said. "You'll snap out of it—but

137

it's going to be rough if you don't take it a little easier—starting now."

"Habit-forming, huh?"

Bill nodded vigorously.

They were sparring, and each of them knew it. The first body blow would be dealt when Bill asked or John told the why of this thing.

Bill went on, "I remember once before when you got plastered, but you were different then because you were having a good time. It was the night you married Madge. Boy, were you fumigated. Remember?"

Thirteen years ago, but John remembered the suit that he'd worn —the necktie, too—blue with a diagonal stripe. And the suit Madge had been married in: beige with a straight skirt, and a corsage of three camellias. Karl Thompson had just kept sending champagne cocktails to their table.

"Whatever happened to Karl Thompson?" he asked Bill.

"I dunno," Bill said. "Haven't thought about him in years."

John leaned his head back against the seat. There wasn't enough room because his legs were too long. That's what Madge used to call him—Long John Long. Now that Bill had brought it up, he couldn't tear his thoughts away from that wedding night party at the Plaza. He looked at Bill and wondered what he was thinking about.

He said, "Hey, why didn't you ever tell me Madge had quit Troxell's?"

"I didn't think you'd be interested."

"When did she pull out?"

"About a year ago. She asked me if I thought she was making a smart move. I said I did and it was no lie. Madge ought to have left Troxell's a long time before she did. She should have left as soon as old Barnes died, because after that the whole store started gunning for her."

John was silent so long that Bill thought the subject was closed. Then John said, "I didn't know Barnes had died."

"Should I have told you that, too?"

"No."

138

It was raining harder now and there was a constant splatter of drops.

Bill said, "Jack, as long as I'm asking personal questions, that was Madge on the phone Christmas Eve, wasn't it?"

"Yeah."

"Drunk?"

"I don't think so, no. She said she just decided to call and say Merry Christmas and no hard feelings. Where is she working out there?"

"She was at Barber's in San Francisco for six months. Then she wrote me a note saying she'd been offered the management of a leased department in one of the big stores in L.A. and I never heard from her after that. Where'd she call from?"

"Los Angeles."

"Guess she got the job."

"Has she ever married again?" John asked casually.

"Sure. I thought you knew. She married a newspaperman. Big fellow. They got a divorce after a couple of months. I only met him once—he didn't have much to say."

"This sounds crazy," John said, "but I always had the feeling that some day T. Harold Barnes would leave his wife and family and marry Madge."

"I didn't."

"Well, I know he didn't have to. But I always had the feeling he would. It's hard to explain but even though he knew she used him shamelessly to get what she wanted at the store, he really thought a lot of her."

Neither of the men said anything for a few moments. John Long's eyes were closed and Bill wondered if he was dozing or silently continuing their conversation. While he hadn't made any startling progress toward curbing Jack's drinking, at least the guy had opened up a little and begun to talk about the past. Bill saw him open his eyes and sit up, flip the pages of the magazine, lose interest, and close it again.

He tried again. "It's none of my business, Jack, but since we were on the subject, how in the hell did you ever get Madge to agree to a divorce? I'd have sworn she wouldn't let go of you so easily."

139

John winced. Bill was asking him to rehash dirty business and that was something he never liked to do. Still, maybe this was what he needed to get it out of his system. Maybe he'd feel better if he told it to somebody. The gloomy day, the confidential rapport, the desolate flight—all made talking easy. And, after all, what was so secret about something that had happened so long ago? Bill Haley wasn't a gossip, because if he had kept still about Madge's whereabouts he could keep still about anything. Bill was garrulous, but he always knew what not to say.

"I'd never talk about this if I'd had a couple of drinks," John began.

Bill nodded. "I know. It's sober conversation."

"There's not a lot to tell. Madge didn't know how much I wanted a divorce. She just knew I was unhappy. Believe me, Bill, it was hell there the last year or two."

"I'll bet."

"I knew she wasn't working nights as she claimed. One night, in particular, I had a hunch she was with Barnes, so I went to the store, told the night watchman I had to work on some ad copy, went up to the advertising floor and saw a light on in Barnes's office. Then I heard Madge laugh—and that made me insane. I didn't love her; I think I had nothing but contempt for her by then. I knew darned good and well what she was doing with other men behind my back, but it was coming face to face with it like that that made me wild. I swear I was crazy. I knew that laugh of hers so well— and I knew what made her laugh like that. I tried Barnes's door and it was locked; then, without stopping to think, I grabbed the typewriter on Barnes's secretary's desk. It was the first thing I saw that had the weight and body I needed and I threw it through the glass part of Barnes's door. The glass shattered and made one helluva racket. Then I saw them there on the couch. They were—. I'd never seen other people—. I reached through the broken glass and unlocked the door not giving a damn whether I got cut or hurt or anything. Barnes was still on the couch and I'll never forget the look on his face. Madge had jumped up and run over to me—in her slip and with no shoes on—and I remember thinking, crazily, how much shorter she looked in her stocking feet. She grabbed hold of me. I think she thought I was going to kill Barnes. I could have

140

killed him as easy as not, except that he looked so old and sad there. Madge was crying, too—and I'd only seen her cry once before.

"Well, it was easy after that. We agreed to disagree, as they say. If she'd known about Ann and me I think she'd have fought the divorce, but of course she didn't know."

"Thank God!" Bill Haley said.

John saw that the rain had stopped and the sun was actually poking its way through the clouds.

"It's all over now," he said, "and strange as it seems, I want Madge to be happy. I really do. I hope she's happy. She just couldn't help herself, Bill. For her, wanting men was like a craving for drink, and when she got that way she *had* to have it. It didn't have anything to do with love. She was . . . primitive."

Bill Haley suddenly thought about Mabel last night. There was something primitive about Mabel, too, only nobody knew that but himself—and, maybe, now nobody else would ever know it.

John went on talking. "Madge wasn't *normal*. She had to have it from everybody she met." He paused, as though weighing whether or not to say something, then added, "I used to wonder about Madge and you."

"Jesus Christ, Jack," Bill said, as the plane's wheels touched the runway. And then he said it again, "*Jesus Christ!*"

13

I *can't go on like this,* Ann thought, and then held herself in contempt for thinking it. She was annoyed whenever she heard people say, "I can't go on like this," or read the line in a book. Of course you went on, and to complain about the hands fate dealt you was weak self-indulgence. But even so as she went over the night she had

141

just spent, with its call to Bill, its report of John passed out in a Dallas hotel room, its tense wide-awakeness, she repeated the sentiment, I can *not* go on like this.

"You look awful," she said aloud to her face in the mirror, and then wondered if talking to herself was a sign of off-balance. She'd ask Bess to find out what Dr. Darnell thought about carrying on conversations with oneself. She walked into the kitchen and saw her last night's ups and down strung along the counters. Before going to bed she had tidied and put things away as she always did, but there was the glass she'd drunk milk from after the first sleepless hour; there were the Sanka jar, the spoon and the cup and saucer from her next visit and finally, the saucepan and Ovaltine she'd turned to in desperation just before dawn.

"Lonely people *do*," she said aloud. Lonely people talked to themselves. With some people, loneliness was hard to prescribe for, but in her case there was a simple antidote—John.

She had devised a cure for her ailment before she finished dressing: if John was agreeable, she would join him tonight in New Orleans. A few months ago he had phoned her late at night and begged her to come and be with him. She had been drunk with fatigue then from writing. Now he was drunk and it was her turn to beg. She was sure Harry Shell would agree to her taking a few days off. Just thinking of being with John made her feel less lonely.

As soon as she reached the radio station she called Laverty and Clarke to find out where John was staying in New Orleans and talked with someone in sales who promised to call her back in an hour. He would supply her with the names of a couple of accounts John would be seeing, in case she missed him at the hotel. Then she reserved a seat on a three o'clock plane from Idlewild. She was so absorbed in her plans that she didn't see Marta enter her office and when the girl spoke Ann started involuntarily.

"Oh, I scared you. I'm sorry," Marta said. "Maybe I should have rung your phone but I thought I'd better tell you about him first before sending him in."

"It's me," Ann said reassuringly. "I'm jumpy today. Send *who* in?"

"This man who wants to see you. His name's White."

142

"*White?*" Ann frowned. "What does he look like?"

"He doesn't look like anybody from an agency. "I'm sure he isn't in radio. He's more the college-professor type."

"I don't know anyone named White," Ann said. Her instant reaction was to blame her mother. Mother was always telling visitors to look up her daughter when they got to New York. "*She's in radio. Station WOOZ. Just think of being woozy and you won't have to write it down.*" It was discouraging how many really had dropped in. Usually she invited the strangers to lunch and sometimes they accepted. Many of them were under the impression that people who work in radio get free seats to Broadway plays just for the asking. "College-professor type," that sounded like Mother, all right.

Ann sighed. "He couldn't come at a worse time for me. Do me a favor, Marta, and ask Harry to come in here five minutes from now. Let him know I need rescuing again."

She and Harry had played this rescue game before. At the appointed time, Harry always burst into her office with some make-believe assignment that had to be done immediately and he loved using his imagination on the non-existent sponsor involved. Once it had been the Hilton Hotel chain, and last time, when Mother's little friend from Pasadena was settling down, the New York Central Railroad. Ann didn't take the time to freshen her lipstick or run a comb through her hair as Marta left her office. Mr. White would have to take her as she was, circles under the eyes, hair disheveled, troubled look.

Almost immediately the man was standing in front of her and she noted that Marta's description was accurate enough: he was about sixty years old, tall, quite erect, with more than a suggestion of bay window. He wore a reddish-brown tweed suit that looked as though it had come from Scotland with him in it and, to complete the college-professor picture, large, brown-rimmed spectacles.

He carefully placed his overcoat and hat on a chair before straightening up, and asked, formally, "Ann Long? *Miss* Long?"

"Mrs. Long."

"I'm Stuart White, Vice-President of Fortune House, Publishers."

Ann swallowed. "Sit down, Mr. White."

143

"I prefer standing for the present, if you don't mind, but I think you'd better remain seated." He paused for his effect, obviously enjoying himself. "I have here a check from Fortune House to Ann Long for her novel, *The Heart Being Hungry.*"

He handed it to her.

Ann stared at the slip of paper. "You mean they've *bought* my book?"

"Yes, we have bought your book and at a very good price."

She tried to smile. She felt both happy and confused and she stared at the check in her hand without seeing it at all.

White spoke again. "If you'll look closely, Mrs. Long, you'll observe that the check is drawn in the amount of twenty thousand dollars."

Ann looked at it, started to speak, couldn't.

"You are the winner of the Fortune House Prize Novel Contest," he continued. "Usually the winner is notified by mail, but since you are only ten minutes away from my office I thought it would be ever so much more personal to hand you the check myself. Your book was the unanimous choice of the judges."

Instead of grateful thanks, all that she could give him was a blank look.

"Tomorrow there's to be a conference with the people from Royal Pictures in Hollywood. They are definitely interested, and we think we can get a $100,000 down payment—with an escalator clause, of course. You get all the movie money except 10 per cent, y'know. If you wish to bring your own agent to the conference you're welcome to do so. If not, I'll continue to act for you without charge."

Ann said suddenly, coming to life, "Not tomorrow, Mr. White. I just made my reservation. I'm going to New Orleans today to join my husband." This announcement was so obviously unanticipated by Mr. White that she added, lamely, "He'll be delighted with the news about the book."

Mr. White sat down. "You don't understand, Mrs. Long," he said, plainly with controlled impatience. "Time is of the essence. We want to meet an early May publication date, the editors want to talk to you about a few minor changes and the publicity department has to work out some angles with you. You can't leave

144

New York at a time like this." He looked at her. "Is your husband ill?"

"No. He's not ill." But he *is*, she thought.

"Then you *can* postpone leaving?"

"I *can*, but—"

"Good. Mrs. Long, you've no idea—" He stopped, and tried again. "Do you *know* what you are? You're big business now. Other than the movie rights there's the book club. One of the judges of the contest is on the board of a book club, and from a phone call we received from him this morning there's a good chance they may substitute *The Heart Being Hungry* for their May selection."

Ann stared at White. In her daydreams of this moment she was always equal to the occasion, always brilliant in her responses. Now she sat dumbly in her chair trying to absorb all this he was saying about movie rights and a book club and bringing her own agent. She was not herself today, but he couldn't be expected to know that. Automatically she wrote New Orleans on a scratch pad to remind herself to call and cancel her plane reservation and Harry saved her the effort of saying anything else by literally diving into her office.

"I got tied up," he explained impulsively, then remembered that he hadn't been officially sent for, and went into his act. "Sorry to interrupt you, Ann, but we've got to rework the commercials for Dixie Cups and the first one goes on the air in half an hour."

"*Dixie Cups?*" she asked incredulously. "I haven't—" Then she caught herself being obtuse, stopped short, and said feebly, "Harry, I think you'd better get me some black coffee."

Harry seemed confused. He looked accusingly at Mr. White who replied blandly, "None for me, thanks. I've really got to be going." Then, looking squarely at Ann, Mr. White added with conviction, "But if I were you, young lady, I'd be damned if I'd write Dixie Cup spots or any other spots on a day like this!"

Harry was plainly befuddled. He framed a retort to this impertinent visitor, saw Ann's face grow chalkier, then turned and ran to the coffee machine.

Mr. White picked up his coat and hat, walked over to Ann,

145

patted her hand and said, "Goodbye, Mrs. Long. May I call you Ann? You can call me Stuart."

She didn't realize it, but with this concession from him she definitely was big business.

"Of course," she said. She rose from her chair only to learn that her legs had become sponges that wouldn't support her and sat down again as she said, "Goodbye, Stuart."

Harry placed not one but two cups of coffee on Ann's desk. "Drink 'em both!" he ordered. "Who *was* that bird? When he passed me in the hall just now he looked at me as though I was Simon Legree. Didn't I sound realistic about the spots? I said the first thing that came to my mind."

The hot coffee burned Ann's throat, but she continued to gulp it. She answered Harry by pointing to the check Mr. White had given her.

Harry picked it up, read it, put it down, picked it up again, started to speak, looked at the check, then managed to gasp, "Your book!"

She nodded and smiled weakly. Then she began to feel less numb and her smile broadened as her eyes caught the trademark under the rim of her coffee container.

It said DIXIE CUPS.

14

Two weeks later it was not March, but John, who came in like a lion. A tanned, vigorous lion, ready for his mate. The planeload of Florida passengers, full of sunshine and well-being, emerged into the sunless gloom of LaGuardia and as each brown face appeared at the top of the gangplank it still kept something of the Florida warmth that was so few hours away. But it took only a few breaths of the cold, wet morning air, a few steps toward the airport terminal, a few glances at the winter-pinched faces of the New Yorkers in buttoned overcoats to cut the returnees down to size.

No one could have singled out John Long and said, "He's not a tourist like the rest. He's been in Florida selling *I Want an Enduring Peace*." He looked as brown and rested as the others, he thought, and no wonder. After a once-over-lightly through Tampa, Jacksonville and Tallahassee, he had stretched Miami into a full four days. He'd needed those days not for selling books but for resting and thinking—mostly about Ann. He owed her something that he'd managed to hold back from her since he read her book. He'd built a kind of fence around himself—an invisible fence, to be sure, but one on which he leaned overpolitely to visit with her, careful to keep on his own side, to keep her on hers. As he'd lain on the sand of Miami Beach, ignoring his old sunburn-phobia, he began to tear down that fence, tackling the wrecking job with concentrated thinking. He analyzed the motives that created the fence in the first place. His drinking, his confusion—in fact, all of his tangential behavior started the day he'd read Ann's book. Why? There on the Florida sand he came up with two reasons. One was a simple jealousy of the book as a rival for Ann's time and affection. Like a man adjusting to a baby in the family, John had to accept the book as a part of Ann without resenting the attention she gave it.

The other reason was a subtler one. In her book the first wife reclaimed the husband. This had infuriated John because he didn't love Madge now; he loved Ann. What she had written had pressed a tender place because he probably did have subconscious guilt feelings about leaving Madge. He knew that no matter how much he told the tale against her, nobody is 100 per cent right or wrong in a divorce. Like most second marriages, his had a premise of rationalization. What frightened him was that Ann had given too much importance to these hidden feelings and in so doing had questioned the premise of their own good marriage. He found himself trying to justify his love for Ann when there should be no need for justification. She was the one he loved; there was no one else; why should he have to prove it again every day?

147

But he was through trying to fight the book. He wanted to try to share Ann's happiness in its success instead of resenting it. When she told him in a letter how close she had come to joining him only to cancel out he was ashamed of himself. As the sun baked out his prideful obstinacy it restored a sensible viewpoint. Now he could tell her he was proud of her and mean it. It all boiled down to a simple truth: he needed Ann and one couldn't contain a need behind a fence. His emotional need for her was as strong as his physical need.

When he got to The Estate he decided not to call Ann at the radio station; he'd surprise her. He shaved and showered, preening before the full-length bathroom mirror. He was tanned all over except where his swim trunks had preserved a band of white across his front and bottom and the two-toned effect looked so incongruous he smiled. Soon, very soon, he'd be showing this color scheme to her, he thought, and his private need merged with anticipation, making it difficult for him to get into his shorts. He dressed carefully, choosing a yellow-and-red bow tie above the four-in-hands. It was an April tie, really, but he was of a mind to pre-empt spring.

Prudence had made him trade his Florida topcoat for his winter overcoat, however, and it felt good as he waited for a cab. Although he sniffed the air hopefully, all he could detect was the dry, smoky smell which sometimes presaged a March snowstorm, but nothing —absolutely nothing—could dampen his holiday spirit, nothing lessen his loving mood. He loved New York in spite of the weather, and he loved Ann in spite of the book. No, that was not true. He loved the damned book, too. But mostly Ann, warm, beautiful, soft Ann.

When he got off the elevator at the radio station he was unprepared for Marta's effusive greeting. "Why, John Long! You're so brown and . . . beautiful!"

He couldn't help wondering if effusiveness was an occupational disease with receptionists. "Thank you," he said to her, at the same time questioning the need for gratitude at that damn-fool word "beautiful."

"Is Ann in her office?" he asked. "I want to surprise her."

148

"Yes, she's there," Marta said dramatically, "working away just like she wasn't a millionaire. Isn't it wonderful about her being so famous all of a sudden?"

He tried to smile affably but Marta's stickiness was too much for him. He murmured, "Wonderful," and turned toward Ann's office. When he got there the door was closed and the typewriter inside was singing a long, intense cadenza. He tapped three times. Light little taps.

"Come in," Ann yelled above the continued typing.

He opened the door.

"John!" She rose so quickly she knocked over her chair, and ran to him and kissed him again and again. Finally she stepped back and straightened his bow tie, saying happily, "It's really you, Enoch Arden. You've been gone years and years. Take off your overcoat, darling."

He reddened. "In a minute. It's camouflage."

Now it was her turn to redden. "You're shameless!"

He nodded his head and grinned. "Aren't you going to tell me I'm brown and beautiful? Marta did."

"You are, but I thought you always said you blistered."

"I decided to change all that. Mind over matter. But you should have seen me at the end of the second day. All I needed was a pineapple slice to be ready for the Armour ad."

She put her arms around his neck, got very close to him, kissed him with feeling and then broke away. He threw his overcoat on a chair, perched on a corner of her desk and crossed his long legs. There were so many things he planned to say to her the moment they were together—about the fence coming down, about sharing her good fortune and about how much he loved her. Instead he was able only to muster, "Well—?"

Ann sat down, flipped her finger absentmindedly on the margin-release of her typewriter and said, "Well—?"

"You're rich."

She looked up at him.

"I've been rich a long time. You know the day I got rich. Ten years ago."

"I mean rich in money." He started to tell her what Marta had

149

said about Ann's being a millionaire but decided to skip it. "How much have you got, kid?"

She laughed. "May I be vulgar and count it in public?" He nodded several times. "Well, there's the $20,000 for the Fortune House Prize, plus $90,000 from Royal Pictures—that's just part of the movie rights; there's an escalator clause, whatever that is, and the book club has put up a guarantee of $30,000 more. That's (she pretended to count on her fingers) $140,000."

He swallowed. "It's one helluva lot of moola. Where do you keep it? In your bosom?"

"To tell you the truth, I didn't know where to keep it. All I knew was I didn't want to touch a penny of it until you came home and could count it with me. So I went to the Chase-Manhattan and talked with the one hundred and twenty-fifth vice-president and ended up putting it in a trust. That way, he said, no matter what happens, it's still mine . . . I mean ours. Or rather, *yours*. The money is in trust for John Long by Ann Long, trustee."

"My God! *I'm* a millionaire!"

"Yes, and I love you for your money! Here," Ann handed him some Kleenex which she took from her desk drawer. "You're covered with your trustee's lipstick, so wipe it off. A millionaire shouldn't look smootchy."

Instead of doing so he kissed her on one ear, and murmured into it, "I love being the husband of a celebrity. I love being rich. I love you. But I've been thinking. Money doesn't bring happiness, right? So, let's take all the money and endow a home for worn-out book travelers."

"Fine idea," Ann said. "With hot and cold running bourbon in every room."

"Which reminds me," he said. "Let's go some place for a celebration drink."

"Before lunch?"

"Why not?"

Before lunch. A celebration drink before lunch. A perfectly normal reaction. Still, how many celebration drinks did he need?

"Let me consult my social calendar," she said lightly. "The Upright Roofing Company requests a hundred word statement from me on shingles—roof shingles, that is—and the Orchid House

150

Florists simply insist that I issue a fifty word announcement about their two-flower gardenia corsage for $1.49. However, if you'll be patient for fifteen minutes I'll fulfill these pressing commitments and skip out of here for the rest of the day. Today will be the three-day leave I didn't ask for two weeks ago."

"I'll sit right here and think about you and me," John said.

"Go to hell," she said, flushing.

His good spirits kept him bobbing conversationally like a buoy bouncing on waves. "Maybe my rich wife will introduce me to the one hundred and twenty-fifth vice-president. Maybe he'll spring for the lunch."

Ann laughed. "I'm saving him for dinner at the Four Seasons. Now *shut up* until I finish!"

He shut up as she sailed from Upright Roofing to Orchid House Florists without pausing between modifiers.

On their way out of the building, she said, "Still want that drink?"

He stopped, squeezed her arm and said casually, "I'm suddenly very tired, and I'd like to go home and rest for a while. Aren't you suddenly very tired, too?"

She smiled. "*Very.* But what about lunch?"

But he had already flagged a cab and had the door open for her. He gave the address to the driver, then turned to her with mock seriousness, "They have the best dill pickles in town just around the corner from our house. Shall we stop there first and take our lunch home with us? It might help us to rest better."

"Oh, *let's*" she said wryly, "there's nothing so gratifying, between rests, as a dill pickle."

15

THE spring editorial sales conference of Laverty and Clarke was scheduled to begin at two-thirty the afternoon of Wednesday, March 15th. The Ides of March, John mused, as he stepped into the building elevator; a fitting day for a sales conference, and by the time the elevator door opened on twenty-three he was smiling at the thought of Cecil Laverty in a toga. His reverie ended abruptly with a frontal attack from Jackie.

"Oh, Mr. Long. You're always in such a hurry. Stay a minute."

He tried to fathom what it was about him that set Jackie off this way with no encouragement on his part and thought that it would have been flattering if it weren't just a little depressing.

"It's the talk of the office how your wife's rolling in dough from a book that is not even published yet."

John winced without showing it. *The talk of the office.* His fence-building resentment against the book flared for just an instant, then he caught it and squelched it.

"Wherever she rolls, there roll I," he said flippantly.

He determined not to let Jackie's prattling upset him. Aloud, he said, "Who's the choir leader today?"

"Both Mr. Laverty *and* Mr. Clarke are in there. Stay just a minute more, please. It isn't quite two-thirty, and besides, Mr. Thorgeson hasn't come yet."

"Ransom there?" John asked.

"Course he is. He's Mr. Laverty's shadow. And just between you and I, I think he's odd."

"Why? Because he won't make a pass at you?"

"Uh uh." You could not insult Jackie. "I have my reasons. I run the switchboard around here and I could tell plenty."

"Don't tell it. Write it. Fortune House will buy it all in a minute."

152

Thorg walked in. "Hi, John. Did Ann get my note? I'm really glad for her. She's a genius, that gal."

"I could have told you that a long time ago." John looked at his watch. "Two twenty-nine. They're playing our song," he said pointing to the conference room. "Shall we dance?"

"Oh, yes indeed," Thorg said as they started for the door.

"Mr. Long," Jackie said suddenly and John turned toward her as Thorg walked away. Then, confidentially, she went on, "If you think I'm silly at times it's because I—"

John teetered on the high-rope strung between annoyance and kindness. He started to pat her affectionately on the cheek, changed his mind for fear any sort of encouragement like that might be fatal and said simply, "You're not silly, Jackie. See you later," and walked into the chamber of horrors.

Cecil Laverty sat at what was normally the head of the conference table with Billy Clarke at the foot. John looked hopefully to see if either of Cecil's blind spots was available, but Bob Evans was sitting in one and Jerry Trigg had grabbed the other. John chose a chair next to Billy Clarke which was, he feared, directly in Mr. Laverty's line of near and far vision.

The room was over hot again, already full of smoke, and John tried to analyze why this particular room, which had chairs, tables, carpeting, windows and blinds like a thousand others, filled him with such an overpowering impulse to run amuck.

Billy Clarke took the kickoff, for although he sat at the foot of the conference table, he was the acknowledged head of Laverty and Clarke. Only two people in the room dissented to this: Cecil Laverty, and his shadow, Ransom. Later, John knew, this pair would have their own private gossip session about Long's buttering up Billy Clarke by sitting next to him. Cecil always got a laugh out of Ransom by referring to John as Clarke's "vice-president in charge of everything." In contrast to Cecil's business suit which fit as though it had shrunk two sizes, Billy Clarke was wearing a pair of tan slacks and a burnt-orange sports jacket with patch pockets. The severe effect of his solid brown necktie was balanced by the gay bordered tan-and-brown handkerchief that spouted from the jacket pocket. With his closely cut salt-and-pepper hair and eager,

153

florid face, all he needed was the highball glass to complete the Man-of-Distinction picture.

"Boys," he said pleasantly, "I want to start this meeting on a happy note by passing along a word of thanks from a personal friend of mine—that new star in Laverty and Clarke's crown, Harold Albert. *I Want an Enduring Peace* has already sold one hundred and ten thousand copies in the trade, not counting book clubs, and it should remain America's number one non-fiction best-seller for months to come. Harold said to me only last week, he said, 'Billy, thank your travelers for the fine job they did on the advance sale before publication. They deserve most of the credit for the way my book has caught on.' I'm just telling you what Harold told me. Flowers to the living, and I want to add my own thanks. It's been a source of satisfaction to me to show Harold Albert that Laverty and Clarke can do more for him and his future books than any other publisher."

Billy sat down and Cecil jumped up. "Gentlemen! Mr. Clarke has just paid you a compliment, and that's fine. Now it's up to me to give you a bit of constructive criticism. While you were selling *I Want an Enduring Peace* you were okaying credits for twenty-two thousand copies of *Milk in the Sky*. Now, gentlemen, I know the booksellers get you over a barrel now and then on titles they fail to promote, but whenever you take them off the barrel you put Laverty and Clarke on it in their place. So what are we going to do with twenty-two thousand copies of a book which seems to have slowed down?"

He must have had on his far-sighteds for he pointed straight at John and bellowed. "*You* tell me, Long: what are we going to do with them?"

Some day, John thought to himself, *some day*. He was tempted to tell Cecil what *really* to do with them—and if there were any left over there was always his title-happy wife, Dora, to absorb the surplus. John, himself, with Billy's blessing, had authorized most of the returns for *Milk in the Sky*. The book was a dead pigeon.

He said aloud, "Twenty-two thousand copies aren't too many to have on hand. Booksellers will be reordering that title for years to come."

154

It was so obvious John hadn't meant what he'd just said that Billy Clarke snorted.

"We'll see," Cecil Laverty said, shaking his head doubtfully as though John had been responsible for over-printing the book in the first place. He put both pairs of spectacles in their cases and sat down. His thick lips were clamped together, and John felt sure Cecil practiced the expression in front of a mirror in the belief that it made him look dynamic.

Billy Clarke got up again. "I'd hoped to make an announcement of a new novel by one of America's sure-fire fiction sellers—who is, I might add, a very charming woman. She and her agent are house guests now at my lodge in Maine and they are working out plans to break off with her present publisher so that she can come to Laverty and Clarke. I can't say more now than don't be surprised when you learn we've got a new author who's good for advances of 50,000 copies on every book she writes." He paused. "And she writes one every year."

John could tell from Billy's confident tone that the situation was well in hand. There was quite possibly more involved in this deal than a business proposition, because Billy was never reluctant about using his bachelordom as a business expense. Glancing at Cecil Laverty, John could have sworn that the man was looking his way with a scowl of disapproval. *Now* what? He'd already been blamed for the sour *Milks*—but then, one could never be positive whom Cecil was scowling at. Meanwhile, Ransom had risen and was announcing things to come and although John already knew what the list contained he found himself listening hopefully. Two manuscripts that he had been instrumental in obtaining were postponed to a later list. Ransom was saying, "Our headliner is a long, historical novel by Polly Crabbe. The book will run at least eight hundred pages and, needless to say, it is full of accurate historical detail. Detail is Polly's strong suit. We're going to back it up with everything we've got."

Polly Crabbe! John knew that the travelers around the table were recalling her last novel of which even the larger shops had ordered only fives. Polly was entirely too strong on detail and too weak on story.

"—a biography of Blackstone, the jurist. A collection of maga-

155

zine sketches by Dick Morris, which is tentatively entitled *Short Pieces* . . ."

Thorg Thorgeson interrupted him. "Would you mind repeating the title, sir?"

Ransom stopped and the room became a vacuum. "*Short Pieces*. Mrs. Laverty—"

Thorg continued. "I've been a Dick Morris fan for years. He's bright and clever and a little insane. He deserves a better title."

Ransom looked unhappily at Mr. Laverty, then asked Thorg, "And do you have a better title to suggest?"

"Why, yes I have. I'd call the collection *No Matter How Thin You Slice It*."

Nobody said anything. It had taken guts for Thorg to interrupt, but he was being pinned to the mat by the silence of his associates.

John spoke up. "That's a title with sales appeal! *No Matter How Thin You Slice It* is a book people will buy for the name alone. *Short Pieces* would have to sell for what's inside it."

Cecil chimed in. "If sales would let editorial—"

Jerry Trigg interrupted him to join the insurrection. "There's a title I've been sorta saving up. It would be terrific for a book like that. The name is *Smelling Like Roses*."

Billy Clarke spoke quickly. "Thanks for the suggestions, boys. We'll have a conference with Dick Morris and see what he thinks. Personally, I like both titles better than the one with *Pieces* in it. Too many *Pieces* around here. Let's concentrate on *I Want an Enduring Peace* and call *Short Pieces* something else."

Cecil was furious and he pouted as Ransom continued with the rest of the list. John was attentive to the last juvenile, but it was the same old story. Hundreds of manuscripts tossed into the pool, yet the same kinds always floated to the top: the dull, sparkless ones that pleased Ransom and his editors but did not please the public. Trying to sell them to the booksellers was like trying to peddle rotten eggs to a grocer—you yourself couldn't believe in them so how in hell could you sell them?

"We've tried to give you the best list we know how," Ransom said, exactly as he always said it, and sat down.

It's almost over, John thought, and shifted his legs so that the table speared his kneecaps in a spot that wasn't already sore. But

156

it wasn't all over at all. Cecil Laverty jumped to his feet again and waved both pairs of glasses in the rhythm of a rhumba musician shaking maracas.

"Wait a minute," he cried. "Before we adjourn I'd like to say something which may sound a bit personal to one of you, but which applies equally to you all. It concerns a matter that I discussed with you at our last conference and evidently it didn't sink in then. I refer to what I said about ignoring talent that may be right under your nose."

So this was it, John thought. Cecil *had* been scowling at him!

"I'm sure we all rejoice with Long on his wife's good luck," Cecil said with the cutting edge of his voice. "Her forthcoming novel, *The Heart Being Ready—*"

"HUNGRY," John corrected, biting the word so hard he could hear his teeth chomp together as he said it. *"The Heart Being HUNGRY!"*

Cecil flushed. "Thank you, Long. However, had you been as quick to correct your wife upon her choice of publisher as you are in correcting me on the title, Laverty and Clarke would have a book club selection in May."

John reddened and tried to pass it off. "My wife preferred to be published by a company other than the one I represent. She didn't know she was going to hit the jackpot." As he spoke, he had the feeling he was sounding somehow apologetic for Ann. Was he also sounding kiss-bottomy toward Cecil Laverty?

The man went on: "Mr. Long's negligence in letting this plum escape us is, in my opinion, one of the most unfortunate incidents in the history of Laverty and Company." In his excitement, he had forgotten all about his partner, Billy Clarke, who was at that moment trying to secure his attention so that he could flash him a nix signal, but Cecil was in orbit and nothing could stop him. "We'll be the laughing stock of the publishing business, gentlemen. It's treason. That's what it is: treason!" He put on his far-sighteds and pointed at John, tightening his bulbous lips into thick rubber bands as he drove his point home. "Treason!"

But that was the last word Cecil Laverty said for a long time.

John's chair made a screeching noise as he pushed it back and sprang to his feet. He had a momentary feeling of pride that he

157

was not hysterical. He was angry, yes, but his temper was under control and he was about to do at last what he had so long yearned to do. "Laverty!" he said, and snapped the word off at the end as briskly as he would break a cracker. The "Mr." was ignored, not forgotten.

Every man in the room, Laverty included, was waiting for John's next words, but no words came. He wanted to speak but he couldn't. He wanted to wink at Billy Clarke, but he couldn't even do that. He only turned from the conference table, swooped up his hat and coat, and made the door in three strides.

Outside he brushed past Jackie's desk without looking at her to jab the elevator button savagely.

Jackie spoke to him in a quivering voice bordering on tears. "Are you mad at me, Mr. Long? Did I say something I shouldn't of?"

"No, Jackie," he said, "and I didn't either."

"Huh?" Jackie said.

But the elevator door had already banged shut and he was gone.

Sitting on the bar stool he played the scene back on the tape recorder of his mind and after five martinis this remarkable tape recorder not only reproduced the original conversation, but improved on it. Everything that Cecil Laverty said was still intact, but John Long's role was amplified wonderfully.

"I'll have another," John said to the bartender who nodded. The man belonged to the sloppy school of drink mixers. To make a satisfactory martini he had to pour too much gin and too much vermouth into his glass pitcher, slosh the ingredients around crazily, then waste a good gulp of it down the little holes of the copper drain while transplanting it to the martini glass. He pushed No. 6 toward John and mumbled, "You'll never make it home, buddy, but what th' hell."

John drank half the martini before setting his glass down, then went back to his last word— "Laverty!" He was able to continue now, to play the scene as it should have been played in the first place. "You fat-headed, old twerp, shut up and sit down!" And Laverty sat. "Look here, you stupid shit—" Yes, that was exactly the word, and he could see Billy Clarke gag as he said it. A comforting word, a perfect word, a word men used every day to describe

158

any number of things including the Lavertys of the world. A semantics professor could not choose a better word. "Since you're getting so personal with me, I'll get personal with *you*. I think your last list stank, I think your new list stinks, I think your wife's titles stink, and I think *you* stink! I wouldn't sell another book for you if I got a bonus on every return! I'd live off my wife sooner than take any more of your—"

"I'll have another," he said firmly.

The bartender made a face as though he were in pain as he sloshed No. 7 into life and pushed the glass toward John.

He said, gloomily, "You'll never make it home, buddy, but what th' hell."

It was ten o'clock when he finally got home and when Ann saw him she forgot that she was mad at him for forgetting she'd invited Bill Halcy to dinner.

"John!" she said. "Are you all right?"

"Made it! Made it! Made it! Man at th' bar said I couldn't make it—but I made it!"

Ann moved quickly toward the kitchen. "Bill and I saved you some supper. I'll warm it up."

John wavered impartially from one direction to the other. "Hi, Bill. Big cel'brashun!"

"What's *this* celebration for, Jack?"

John leaned over to him and whispered confidentially, "Beware the Ides of March, Bill. Beware the Ides of March."

"Beware the Ides-plus *one*, old boy. I don't envy you tomorrow's hangover. Ann was sure you'd been run over."

John was under the impression that he was standing still, but he was listing heavily. "Whatcha been doin'?"

"Planning a personal appearance tour for Ann. First part of May. She's going to autograph in the Southern cities before heading for the coast for the Royal Pictures banquet. And guess who gets to go to the coast with her?"

"Me."

"You can come, too. But old Haley goes as a special reward for discovering her."

"Come on, John," Ann coaxed, "eat your dinner."

159

She set the tray of food in front of him.

"Glad somebody discovered 'er. Fix Bill a drink, Ann. He gets a drink for discovre—" He couldn't say it.

Ann made no move to comply. "Bill can have a drink if he wants one but you drink milk!" she said steadily. "What's all this talk about the Ides of March?"

"Beware them," John said. "Beware them *at all costs*." He smiled a crooked smile. "Everythin' happens for the best. Now I c'n go to California with you."

"What?" Ann asked, as though she had not heard him correctly.

"I c'n go with you—if you pay my way."

Ann looked at him. "John," she began, menacingly, "what happened at the sales meeting today?"

"Can't tell. Ladies present."

"Come on, Jack. Tell Bill. What happened? Is everything all right?"

"I don't know if it's aw right with Cecil. But it sure's hell's aw right with me!"

Ann fought to control her curiosity and exasperation. "Tell us about it, darling. We'll just sit here quietly while you tell us everything."

John sat up straight in his chair as though he were ready to make a momentous pronouncement. He waited a full minute before opening his mouth. Then he said solemnly, "Beware the Ides of March!" and passed out.

16

THE living room floor was a small sea of Sunday supplements. John was still in his pajamas and Ann, in a light flannel robe over her gown, was curled up in a chair, her legs tucked under, with several sections of newspapers on her lap. Earlier in the week Mr. White—she couldn't make herself call him Stuart, even mentally—had called to ask if she wanted him to send her the book review sections that publishers get in advance of regular newspaper publication. Ann told him she had made a pact with John that the two of them would savor the reviews alone and that she would wait, thank you.

"Listen to this one," she said now, happily.

" 'No matter how much the reader may disagree with Mrs. Long's premise that a first wife always remains spiritually wed to her husband, he cannot fail to read every word of her brilliant book and wish there were more to read when he is finished.' "

"Who wrote that?" John asked.

"Alice Patton in the *New York Times*. Come over here and get this *Herald Tribune*. It'll bring me luck if you read it."

John took the paper from her and whistled. "Wow. You rate the first inside page. Who's Bruce Sayre?"

"He's a novelist. Go on. What does he say?"

John took a deep breath. "Here goes:

'There are two hearts. The vascular heart and the heart that feels but does not beat. All mortals possess the first, but only a fortunate few are aware of the second. Nor can the one-hearters understand the two-hearters. What is oversentimentality to one group is sensibility to the other.' "

John looked up from the paper. "My God," he said with feeling. "I'd like to write a review of this review. Instead of a book criticism

161

it's a treatise on heart trouble. This man doesn't give a damn what the reader thinks of the *book;* he just wants him to be impressed with the cleverness of his review."

"Simmer down and keep on reading," Ann said. "I still don't know whether Mr. Sayre is going to thumbs-up or thumbs-down me."

John reached for his coffee cup, started reading more of the review, and put the cup back without drinking.

" 'Heart failure is a double tragedy to those with twin hearts. Twice the misery, twice the grief, twice the—' "

"Skip the first half," Ann said. "He has to mention the book *some* place."

"Ah, yes, here it comes. Listen:

'Mrs. Long knows how the human heart works. She knows, too, what the second heart is for. Her story of Mona, Jerry and Norma is a new approach to the eternal triangle. It is an arterial highway connecting both the vascular hearts and the feeling hearts of three intelligent human beings.' "

John groaned. "Did you ever in all your life hear such a bunch of crap?"

"Try the last paragraph," Ann suggested. "Even the windiest reviewer can't begrudge the author the *last* paragraph."

John nodded. "Here it is:

'The Heart Being Hungry introduces a new American talent in the tradition of Ellen Glasgow. In her delineation of character Mrs. Long equals Miss Glasgow at her best. In her sensory detail she improves on the master. Regardless of the kind of heart-person the reader is—' "

John grimaced.

" '—he will find The Heart Being Hungry a powerful study in heartbreak which will bear reading and rereading for years to come.'

Ah, so he likes it. I thought he was going to like his story better than yours."

"Don't be too hard on him," Ann said. "I'm going to write him a thank-you note."

162

"Enclose a purple heart ribbon," John said, as he picked up another paper. "Listen to this one. This old boy gets right into the swing of things:

'Once in a blue moon an extraordinarily moving story comes along which—' "

"Skip that one—I've read it and the book's not that good. Find a mean one instead. Where's *The New Yorker?*"

John picked up *The New Yorker* and turned to the book reviews near the end of the magazine. "I must have the wrong issue. It's not reviewed here."

"Yes it is. You've been spoiled by the up-front reviews. We don't rate the long one. We're after the six page commentary called *Henry James Revisited*. See where it says New Fiction?"

"Oh, yes; here it is. Well, they listed yours first, anyway."

"Read it," Ann commanded, "and weep."

John read it.

" 'The publishers of Mrs. Long's book about a husband who prefers an imperfect first wife to a perfect second one call it "a novel that will live for years." It won't. But the author has a nice way with words which should enable her book to live at least through the current fiction season.' "

John snorted. "If you ask me, this sunuvabitch is damning with faint praise!"

Ann sighed. "Very faint. It's honest, though, and to the point, I think."

"But it doesn't *say* anything," John insisted. "He's laying the foundation for his review of your second one so he can say I *told* you so."

"He'll have a long wait," Ann said. "Me and Margaret Mitchell. There's not going to be a second one."

"That's what all our authors say after their first. Then they get royalty-check-itis and you can't stop 'em."

"No. I mean it," she said quietly. "I told you that I had to get *a* book out of my system—and I got it out. To coin a phrase, that's all she wrote!"

"You really *do* mean it?"

163

"I really do."

Ann started to get up from her chair but John said, "Stay there while I read one more. We can't quit our Sunday Morning Study Club meeting on a sour note." He held up another book section. "Seen this one?"

Ann looked at the paper he was holding and then at him. She loved him like this, intense, completely absorbed, and she couldn't help thinking of the two of them, talking about the book that Sunday morning a hundred years ago when she'd first told him she wanted to write it. She remembered how the conversation had ended then with an unexpected round of spontaneous lovemaking. It would take so little encouragement on her part for a repeat performance now. Maybe after they'd finished the reviews. "That's the *Chicago Tribune,*" she said aloud. "They jumped the publication date and ran their review in last week's paper. It was the first to appear. I could tell the minute the Fortune House people knew about it, because Stuart White called me on the phone to ask if there was anything he could do to make me more comfortable."

John found the review. "Page three," he said, frowning. "The nerve of those Midwesterners."

"Read the first sentence," Ann said, smiling. "It would make a perfect epitaph if it ran on page fifty."

John began the review.

" 'Ann Long's polished first novel, *The Heart Being Hungry,* has already earned for its author the rich Fortune House prize money. This time next year this reviewer hopes her book will have earned for her the Pulitzer Prize for fiction. No novel could be more deserving of it.' "

"Stop!" Ann said. "That's all I want you to read."

"Why?" he argued. "I'd like to go on. It's fun."

"Then read it some place else."

John let the paper fall to the floor, got up, and walked over to her. He said seriously, "You really mean that? I mean you aren't just being coy—and it's true none of these reviews really matters a damn to you?"

Ann shrugged. "It's wonderful that people like the book, but—"

"But what?"

164

"Well, not one of them said what Bess said—that it's real. I'd rather it sounded real than 'brilliant' or 'powerful' or 'polished.'" She lowered her voice. "You haven't told me what *you* think of it. Is it an arterial highway or is it real?"

John was standing near the French doors looking at the first tufts of green in his tiny terrace-garden.

"What do you mean by 'real?'" he asked in a strained voice.

"I mean *true*. Oh, not in the sense that it actually happened, but true in the sense that it could."

John stared at the fast-growing clumps of grass that would soon have to be trimmed. Then he said slowly, "You would ask for the one review that isn't coming to you. I think Bess is wrong and I think you have a sneaking suspicion that she is. It's a swell book and it deserves everything nice that's been said about it, but—"

He paused a few seconds before finishing what he had to say. Her half-mood about the two of them later on was gone, and to her the room and the two of them in it seemed to have grown perceptibly older before he said, "It isn't true. It just isn't true."

Well, she thought, she'd asked for it.

"**D**on't know *why*," *Hazel Watts will tell you, leaning on the why with her Texas drawl*, "but books about the book business just don't sell."

"Why not?" *you ask*.

"Wish I knew. Everything about it from selling to publishing is fascinating to me. Maybe that's the answer. People in the business like it. People on the outside are afraid of it. Anyway, don't ever say on your dust jacket that your novel's about books unless you want to kill it deader'n a doornail."

"But these people in this particular book . . ." *you argue*. "This Ann. She's a lovely and loving girl. Talented, too. She just happens to write a novel that becomes a best-seller. What's wrong with that?"

"I told you."

"And her husband works for a publisher. He could sell shoes but he sells books. Travels some and is a wheel in sales."

"Careful. Got another angle?"

"Well, their trouble comes from John's first wife—"

"Keep talking."

"Ann writes her book to prove her husband's better off with Ann than he was with Madge, but the book runs away from her and—"

"Stop talking books. I told you: books about books don't sell. Call it something else and let the book business just be there."

"Thanks, Hazel. I'll do it. And by the way, there's a bookseller in the story named Hazel Watts, but it's purely coincidental. Common names—Hazel . . . Watts. Coincidence."

"*Wait* a minute—. Why I *never*—. Why, you—"

17

ANN opened her eyes and looked at the shadowed ceiling of the hotel room, then rolled on her side and tried to go to sleep again but she couldn't. She reached for her watch on the bedside table and by squinting her eyes at the dial was able to tell the time in the dim light of the room. Five-thirty. It had been after midnight when she checked into the hotel, yet she was completely awake now. In her own bed at home she often awoke an hour or two before the alarm setting, checked the time, then went back to sleep immediately. This was different. She was in a room in the Peabody Hotel in Memphis, Tennessee and there was a tenseness in her reaction to the strange surroundings that wouldn't let her doze off again.

Although this was only the third hotel room she'd occupied on this fourteen-city autographing tour she'd embarked on, she had already begun to form vivid impressions of hotels. Until now she had known little or nothing about them. The only city hotel remembrance before this trip had been that of the Omaha weekend when she and John had been on their delicious premarital frolic. At night, when John had shot the safety bolt on that hotel room door he'd locked the world out and given them a privacy to luxuriate in. That room was theirs and no one else's. But now, traveling alone, Ann found that the minute she was alone in a hotel room she felt oddly depressed. The room always seemed to be the *same* room; in spite of the framed color prints, the pleasantly nondescript spread, the decorator lamps, there was a neutrality common to them all. This hotel room—any hotel room—to her was a conduit through which flowed a stream of men and women, never the same people, yet somehow always the same people. Bits of the past kept leaking through this conduit into the present and when she walked about the hotel room she was conscious of those who had preceded her.

167

Something of theirs remained, always—a little thing, like powder spilled in a dresser drawer. And what did she look like, the woman who'd spilled it? Was she young? Old? Traveling on business? Caught in an adulterous *cul-de-sac?* And spots on the wall, where someone had spilled or thrown part of a drink. Was he drunk, the man who'd done it, or angry, or was it only an accident?

When she opened the telephone directory to find a number, Ann wondered, too, at the messages scribbled inside. The number of an exchange, followed by the name Helen. You could guess that story but what lay *behind* the call of the person who drew all the triangles-within-triangles on the inside cover of the phone book? Tell me *your* story. The bathroom with its white tiles was incommunicative, yet the handle on the recessed soap dish in the tub had been broken off and patched over. By whom, when, and how long ago? She was acutely conscious of new dust intermingled with old dust in places a vacuum didn't travel. The spread was clean enough, but it had known the person who was here yesterday, and the person the day before, and maybe the person the day before that. The thought could not be dispelled that others' footsteps, phone conversations, love whispers, quarrels, laughter and tears were still with her somehow in this locked room. She was alone, yet not alone, and this was the feeling that kept her wakeful now.

Her watch said five forty-five. She couldn't let herself get out of bed yet, because she wouldn't know what to do with herself, dressed, in this hotel room at such an hour. She bribed herself to stay put by promising to phone room service for coffee and juice in exactly half an hour. But she could not bribe herself not to think about this autographing tour that was responsible for her being awake in this bed in this room at this hour. Whenever she had time to think she thought of nothing else but the tour and she knew already that it was a mistake, but there was no way she could honorably get out of it. When Bill Haley had first outlined the thing it had sounded like fun. He'd told her the truth: that she could sell more books and please the sales manager more if she chose the Eastern circuit, or even the Detroit-Minneapolis-Chicago-St. Louis swing. Most authors of solid best-sellers concentrated their name-signing in the New York and Chicago areas, and she'd had invitations to autograph her book at large stores in both cities, but Bill

168

had laid it on the line: she'd sell a lot more books on a Northern tour, but she could help him most if she toured the South.

While she'd wanted to accommodate Bill Haley, her principal reason for choosing the Southern tour—her reason for autographing in the first place—had been to share with John, all along the way, the cities and bookselling friends he spoke about. She'd wanted to meet them, not just as the author of *The Heart Being Hungry*, but as John Long's wife. Now everything had somehow gone awry. John Long's wife had been forced to leave her husband at loose ends in New York and was, herself, at this moment alone in Memphis, Tennessee trying to keep her own ends intact. She could have put the kibosh on taking the trip alone the night John came home so very drunk from the sales meeting, and she'd started to do so the next day, but by the time she called Bill Haley he had already made long distance calls to a dozen book stores, setting up dates for parties and receiving large orders for her book. She kept hoping John would forgive Cecil Laverty (and vice versa)—that he'd get back into the fold in time to make his usual spring trip. To the day she'd left New York she'd half expected him—and his brief case—to come, too. She had miscalculated, and her miscalculation had backfired. At the last minute Bob Evans had agreed to pinch hit for Laverty and Clarke in the cities that John usually visited. So far every bookseller Ann met had asked, "Where's John?" and she had the uncomfortable feeling that his failure to appear with his new list was somehow tied up, in their minds, with her literary success. In Knoxville a bookseller had asked her point blank if it was true that John had been fired because Fortune House was the publisher of *The Heart Being Hungry* instead of Laverty and Clarke, and Bill hadn't smoothed things over by naively quoting the ridiculous—to him—rumor that John was divorcing Ann because of her choice of a publisher.

There were eleven more cities that she must visit, and while she dreaded each of them as an ordeal, she knew that she was trapped. The booksellers had ordered her book and had started selling it on the strength of her visit. Newspaper, radio and television publicity appointments were already made, social events arranged. To quit now would not only be letting Bill Haley down, but letting down the book people who were John's own friends and customers, and

169

this she could not do. She had, definitely, to keep her head up, her smile straight, and the pen Harry gave her filled with fresh cartridges while making the best of a sorry deal.

There was, however, one gratifying aspect of the trip! She had already found that John was far more than just a seller of books to these people. They respected him, even loved him, and they were genuinely concerned about his absence. She knew now, too, why John always insisted that even a top executive of a publishing firm should leave his ivory tower of a New York office to make frequent selling trips around the country, for it was true that discovering the personal reactions of these people was an essential part of every executive's job. She had even underestimated the profession of traveling. She had believed that John regarded the big push from store to store and town to town as a headache, but now she could see that he actually enjoyed it because these people he sold to were much more than his customers; they were his friends. However, the hardest part of his job, she learned now, was not the selling, but the traveling: the packing and unpacking, the reservations, the planes to catch, the clothes to keep clean. From now on she would have a healthy respect for any man who earned his living on the road.

If Bill were only traveling with her she might at least have someone to complain to, she thought, and it would be a luxury just having somebody along she didn't have to beam at. But Bill was always ahead of her, arranging her calendar of appearances, setting up the autographing parties, checking stock with the booksellers. She might catch up with him briefly in Atlanta where her schedule called for a two-day stopover, but meanwhile, there was Memphis today, then Atlanta, Birmingham, Little Rock, Oklahoma City, Tulsa, New Orleans, Wichita Falls, Fort Worth, Houston, San Antonio, and, finally, Dallas.

She looked at her watch again. Six-fifteen, and she didn't want to do any more thinking. She got up, ordered coffee, put on her robe, and started a letter to John:

My Dearest:

It's barely six a.m. in Memphis and I'm expecting a man to knock on my door—I'll have to pay him, too.

Speaking of money, I'd give every penny of our trust to the

170

one hundred twenty-fifth v-p at Chase-Manhattan if he could somehow transport me from this hotel room into our bed at home by your side. I keep pretending you always stay in this very room when you are here, and knowing you are part of it helps make it bearable, at least. Incidentally, does room 1008 in the Peabody mean anything to you? Say yes, please.

The only thing that sustains me on this tour is the thought that you'll be in Dallas on the 23rd when I get there and will fly to the coast with me. I swear I'd cancel everything and come home this minute if I thought you wouldn't be there. *Promise.* I hear the man with the coffee coming down the hall . . .

The waiter rapped on the door. She asked first, "Yes?" and received the answer, "Room service," then unbolted the night latch, opened the door, and let the man in.

At seven-thirty the telephone rang. "Mrs. Long?"

Ann couldn't make up her mind at first whether the voice was a man's or a woman's, it had such a deep resonance plus a vibrato.

"Yes."

"This is Sally Lee, of Cranshaw's Bookstore."

"Oh yes!" Ann said brightly.

"Did I wake you up?"

"No. I've been awake for a long time."

"There's a feature writer from the paper here with me. Could you meet us in the coffee shop for breakfast and an interview? He wants a story and picture for the afternoon *Press Scimitar.*"

"I'm ready now," Ann said. "All I have to do is seal a letter and I'll meet you in the lobby."

The reporter knew his business and the interview went easily. Even such questions as, "Is your book based on incidents from real life?" didn't bother her too much. Then a photographer arrived and they went to Ann's room for the newspaper picture. (Ann thanked her lucky stars she'd called the housekeeper and asked to have a maid straighten the room. No one but John should see an unmade bed she'd slept in. What sort of complex was that?) After the newspaperman had gone Sally stayed on for a few minutes and kept trying with no success to place her in John's pre-tour briefings. Finally the mystery solved itself when Sally said, "Tell John I send my best

171

—only don't call me Sally. He won't know who you mean. Tell him Doodles sends her love. Isn't that a helluva nickname? Only in Tennessee would anyone brand a girl for life with a name like Doodles."

"Doodles?" Ann said as the pieces fell into place. Then she saw that Sally fitted all John's descriptions of Doodles "*She's tiny, but she has a voice that could muster soldiers or call hogs.*" "*There's a little blonde in Memphis named Doodles—sweet, angelic face, but she's a pistol when a customer—or a traveler—gets out of line.*"

"I've heard a lot of nice things about you," Ann said. She couldn't say Doodles yet.

"Most of the travelers think I'm pretty loud," Sally said. "Don't let my voice startle you. I sound like a bassoon as a compensation for being so small." Then she asked in a more serious tone, "What's the matter with John? Fellow named Evans came through here the other day. Didn't have John's personality."

"It's a long story," Ann said, and then caught the unintentional pun and smiled. "We'll talk about John later, okay? Right now you'd better tell me what you've got lined up for me."

Sally began to call off a timetable of arrivals and departures that sounded vaguely familiar. "At ten-fifteen you're on Geraldine Brown's TV show. You don't have to worry about what to say. You won't get a word in edgewise with Geraldine, but try to plug the autographing party at the bookstore this afternoon if you do get an opening. After her show I'll drive you to the University where you can say a few words to Professor Grosset's class in creative writing; then we'll come back to the hotel where you'll be guest of honor at the Quill Club luncheon. We've got to be in the bookstore by two when the autographing begins." Sally hesitated, biting her lip, "I hate to ask this, but you'd really help us out if you'd come by the store this morning before the TV show and sign some of the advance and mail orders. You'll have a full hour, so do you think you *could?*" Ann nodded, said, of course, and Sally went on, "The store closes at five and I've invited a few people for a cocktail party. We'll be ready for a drink at that point. Then at seven we're having dinner with Mr. and Mrs. Hansford Ball who're giving you a large reception from eight 'til ten, and watch out for Mr. Ball—he's a fanny pincher. I'd suggest you check out and put your bags into the Ball's

172

car when the chauffeur calls for us here, because that way you'll be sure to get to the airport in time to catch your plane for Atlanta."

"Whew." Ann said, smiling. "Wonder what I'll do with all my free time?"

Sally laughed. "It's the custom in the book business for an autographing author to visit other shops and sign the copies they have in stock." Then she said, with exaggerated concern, "My dear, I *wanted* Mrs. Long to come to meet you-all and sign your books but she barely made it to the store in time for the party!" She winked. "Get it? That's one nice thing about this tight schedule."

Ann found herself utterly relaxed with this diminutive firecracker. "I'm glad you're running interference for me, Sally."

"Call me Doodles," Sally said. "I tell you frankly, Ann, that I don't usually like authors, but I knew you'd be nice. John—" She stopped, thinking maybe a man's wife didn't like to be told that her husband discussed her with third parties, and changed the subject. "There's a pill—Allen Hull—who comes through here almost every year with a new book. The standing joke is that an *un*autographed first edition of one of his works is worth a fortune. You're not like him, nor most authors—I-I-I, me-me-me. You're *human*. And I have a feeling you're going to stay that way." She looked at her watch. "We'll have an hour and ten minutes to sign books if we get goin'. Ready for the battle, Annie?"

"Ready, Doodles!" Ann said so heartily that any Southerner would have sworn she was a kissin' cousin!

Geraldine Brown had a funny smell. It had nothing to do with body odor. It was, rather, a borrowed smell, which she assumed from the many people, mostly club women, whom she interviewed daily. Just as she extracted from them the answers she wanted to hear, so did she take on their perfumes, body powders, and gland secretions to make this peculiar aroma.

Geraldine Brown was on the shady side of fifty. After pioneering the first women's forum program in Memphis radio, she'd moved on to television almost ten years ago and pioneered the first woman's page on TV. She had long since stopped listening to what women said, for while they talked she was always thinking of what she could say into the microphone when they finished—or before. She

173

was thin to the point of scrawniness and she manufactured a kind of angular vivacity which kept her constantly on the move, but since the TV camera pinned her down to a sofa or chair the upper part of her torso had to supply all the movement. When her head or elbows weren't bouncing, her walnut-sized breasts were.

Sally and Ann arrived twenty minutes before the broadcast and waited awkwardly while Geraldine memorized a dress-shop commercial. She kept referring to her fact-sheet, closing her eyes, and mumbling phrases aloud. Then finally, pretending just to have discovered her guests, she loped over and greeted them crying, "So *here* you are! Have you been here *long?* I just *spied* you!" Then, grabbing Sally by the shoulders, she said in a long-lost-sister voice, "How are *you*, Doodles-Honey? Good things come in small packages! And this is . . . ?"

Sally introduced Geraldine to Ann.

"Oh, my. You're so *pretty!*" Geraldine bubbled. "Wait 'til the viewers see how very *pretty* you are."

Ann didn't know what to say, but it made no difference. Geraldine was already going on, "*Ann* honey—I *can* call you Ann, can't I?—I'm just goin' to 'fess up and tell you the truth. I haven't had a chance to read your book yet, but your publisher sent me a copy and I'm goin' to read it the first minute I get because everyone says it's *wonderful*. What's the *exact* title?"

Ann was horribly tempted to say *The Sun Also Rises* but she told the truth. "*The Heart Being Hungry.*"

"What does that mean, honey?"

The first question on every interview so far had been, What does the title of your book mean?

"*What does the title of your book mean, Mrs. Long?*"

"*I'm glad you asked me that question. The title comes from a lyric by Edna St. Vincent Millay which begins:*

> *My heart, being hungry, feeds on food*
> *The fat of heart despise . . .*

In other words, the hungry heart welcomes any crumb of affection. Each of the three main characters in my book has a hungry heart, and each satisfies this hunger in a different way . . ."

"I have an idea," Ann said to Geraldine serenely. "Why don't

174

you ask me that very question when we're on the air and I'll answer it then?"

"Grand!" Geraldine cooed. "That's *just grand.* I can see you know all the angles. But why shouldn't you? It said on the poop-sheet I got on you that you're in broadcasting yourself."

Now it was Ann's turn. "Oh no!" she said, "I'm just a broken-down radio continuity writer. I've always envied people like you who can ad lib in front of a camera and sparkle on a moment's notice!"

The director yelled, "Thirty seconds, Geraldine," and Geraldine took Ann's arm and pushed her down onto the sofa, then sat down facing her as Sally suddenly yelled out in her bullying voice, "Don't forget the autographing party at Cranshaw's at two!" Geraldine murdered her with a look for talking so close to air time, but she had to stifle her chagrin in favor of smiling toothily into the camera as she waited for the red signal light to go on. It did, and she began "Hi, out there! It's your friend Geraldine reminding you and you and *you,*" her shoulders acted as pointing sticks, "that it's a *woman's world!* Today I have a real treat for you girls—and you *men, too!* Isn't she *pretty?* Ann Long—author of the new book, *My Heart Is Hungry,* is going to visit with you in your living room through the miracle of TV. This afternoon at two Ann is autographing copies of . . . uh . . . her *book* . . . at Cranshaw's Book Store, and I know you'll want to drop in, say howdy to Doodles Lee, and visit with the author in person!" (Ann thought, that plug is going to cost Cranshaw's a book a month for a year.) "But, before we meet the author do let me tell you girls about the tremendous closeout of all spring dresses at Milady's Dress Shop. I want the camera to catch just a few of these *drastically* reduced creations." As the camera traveled from dress closeup to dress closeup, Geraldine grabbed the fact-sheet and read into her microphone, "Here's a lovely print dress, reduced from $39.95 to $15.00. Here's a Carol Cox original at half price. And here's one of Milady's smartest suits, reduced from $89.95 to $35.00." She looked at Ann as the camera came back to her. "That's a cute suit *you're* wearing, Miss Long . . ."

Ann started to say something but Geraldine had only paused for breath. "Bet you snuck down to Milady's Dress Shop before the broadcast and bought it on sale. Now remember, girls! Whatever

175

else you do today, don't *fail* to go to Milady's *first*. Now! What do you think of Memphis, Ann?"

"Oh, I love it. It's a beautiful city. I want to come back when I can stay longer." This was another stock response that she would repeat, word for word, over an Atlanta station tomorrow. How in hell was she expected to know what she thought of Memphis? She'd arrived after midnight and seen only a hotel room, a coffee shop, a bookstore, a taxi-cab, and a television station.

Geraldine was burbling on. "I know a lot of people visiting with us now are reading your book, Ann. I myself stayed up 'til *three this mornin'* finishing it. Honestly, I just *couldn't* put it down—and though I'm no literary critic, I want everybody to know that Ol' Geraldine considers *The* . . . uh . . . *The Hungry Heart* a masterpiece! Now, tell me, honey. What does your title mean?"

Ann braced herself. "I'm glad you asked me that question. The title comes from . . ."

After the broadcast Sally and Ann took another cab to the University where she spoke to Professor Grosset's creative writing class for thirty minutes. Professor Grosset was sixty-ish, gray-haired, thin-shouldered, soft-voiced, gracious—but Ann was startled to hear him announce in his introduction that her subject would be How to Write A Best-Seller. How all-inclusive can you get? she thought and suddenly remembered a lecture a famous novelist had given to a creative writing class she'd attended at Barnard. He'd made a statement that had stayed with her—fortunately—because this was the moment to use it. She said glibly, "You don't learn how to write a book; only how *not* to write it," and went on from there.

Professor Grosset drove them to the hotel. He was an active member of the Quill Club which was honoring Ann at a luncheon in the Ivory Room of the Peabody Hotel—or was it the French Room, the Green Room, the Southern Room? Anyhow, whatever you called it, it was like all the others, and the menu was typical, too. First, a small glass of tomato juice, diluted on top where the ice had melted, with two crackers on the serving plate; then creamed chicken in timbales, fluorescent green peas, whipped potatoes, a salad plate with shreds of lettuce topped by a glob of pink mayonnaise and, for dessert, a chocolate sundae. Ann couldn't figure out

176

who belonged to the Quill Club, because there obviously was no requirement of having to be published to be eligible for membership. Many of the members weren't writers at all, and the president, on her left, wrote book reviews for the local book page. On her right was Mrs. Hansford Ball, a woman with a stone face and a pouter-pigeon bosom, who, Ann was sure, had never written anything more literary than her signature on a check. However, Mrs. Ball shared top billing at the luncheon because she'd issued a blanket invitation to all Quill Club members to attend the reception for Ann that evening at the Ball mansion.

Ann made a desultory stab at the creamed chicken in its soggy cradle and decided she wasn't hungry. Anyhow this was one way to get back to John, she thought. Eat nothing, don't sleep—and go home a stretcher case.

The President of the Quills was talking to her. "I saw you on TV this morning, Miss Long. Is it Miss Long or Mrs. Long?"

"Mrs." Ann said with a brightness she felt was sickening.

Mrs. Long. Wonder what Mr. Long's doing now? For a month and a half he'd done nothing—nothing at all. Billy Clarke had called him twice and asked him to come to the office but he hadn't gone. She hoped he was at least eating and sleeping properly. She never worried about his being unfaithful—only unsteady—and even the unsteadiness had been a relatively recent thing. When had it started? On their trip to Florida last winter when he'd read the book? Maybe even before that.

"And what does he do?"

"I beg your pardon?"

"Your husband—what does he do?"

"Oh, he—" Ann stopped, shocked that a perverse something within her ached to say, "He drinks."

Instead she lied. "He writes. He's busy doing some research now."

"Oh."

Ann looked at the melted vanilla ice cream bleeding into the chocolate topping and thought, he's probably doing research at the Algonquin Bar this minute—trying to discover the exact number of drinks a human being can hold and still stay on his feet.

"I'll bet he's a great help to you in your work."

177

"Oh yes, he is. A *won*derful help. I couldn't manage without him."

"It's a quarter to two," Sally said. "We've got to leave for the bookstore, Ann. Don't make any elaborate goodbyes. You'll see the whole gang again in just a few minutes at the autographing party. Come on. We only have to run a block and a half."

Any bookseller will tell you that the autographing party, like the old gray mare, ain't what she used to be. In the same breath he'll tell you what a successful party he had for his last author. What he means to convey is that only the complexion of the autographing party has changed. If approached from the proper angle it's still a potent force for selling books.

Twenty years ago, a newspaper announcement saying that a well-known author would autograph books at a certain time in a certain store never failed to pull a crowd of people and sell a stack of books. Television changed that. As Geraldine Brown had pointed out, celebrities made themselves at home in everyman's living room. Viewers were on a first-name basis with the great and the near-great. Most of the people wouldn't walk across the street just to meet a mere book-author, much less plunk down four or five dollars to buy his book.

But even as television annihilated the old-style autographing party it helped create a new kind of thing, the celebrity party. Since celebrity-authors were already living room pals to millions of people, it was merely necessary to get the word out that they were in town and swarms of book buyers materialized. These celebrities, whose books were usually ghosted, were referred to contemptuously as "non-authors" of "non-books." Certainly they were not writers in the pre-television connotation of the word. Literary authors, who belonged to the old-fashioned do-it-yourself school of writing, had to be turned into celebrities before the public bought their books. Both the publicity departments of the New York publishers and the local booksellers did everything they could to make celebrities out of them. Every possible newspaper, radio and television break had to be utilized. Authors were not asked, they were told where they must be and when. Most of the time they were run ragged.

Celebrity-authors were easier to present, but the others, if prop-

178

erly cooperative, had a chance. With a literary author the bookseller had to peg his autographing party onto some group like the Quill Club which acted as sponsor and consumer. Sally Lee had received reservations for thirty-five autographed copies of *The Heart Being Hungry* from Professor Grosset's students at the University, the Quill Club members had reserved more than eighty copies, Mrs. Ball would buy at least twenty copies for her friends. All this represented a lot of hard work. For days before any autographing party Sally and her staff went over lists of names, telephoning them all patiently, asking each one to reserve a copy in advance to be sure of getting a first edition. It was a tedious process, but it was the only way to assure a party's success. The personal-contact advance sales copies started the ball rolling; then the public at large—the newspaper readers, the TV viewers, the radio listeners —kept it rolling.

Ann had one advantage over non-authors: she had no ghost writer, provided you ignored the ghost within herself which had so often overridden her best intentions. Then, too, her processing from author to celebrity had been a thorough one. The publicity people at Fortune House had shot her through the guest-appearance gauntlet on both TV and radio before she started her tour, so she was, in trade parlance, pre-sold. At least seventy-five people had telephoned or written Cranshaw's Book Store for autographed copies of *The Heart Being Hungry* prior to the party.

Add all these things together: the people on the calling lists who said yes, the reservations for the Quill Club and the writing class, the run-of-the-mill book buyers who wanted the book with or without an autograph, plus the people who bought anything if it meant personal contact with a celebrity—and the autographing party was as good as it ever was.

The table where Ann was to sign books held a centerpiece of spring flowers, plus a plastic box with two huge orchids and a card that said, "Best of luck. Bill." The first time she'd found her orchids Ann had been genuinely touched; now she knew they were routine. Bill had written all the cards at the same time, probably weeks ago— an advance man reserved orchids as he did airplane tickets.

The Cranshaw system of selling books at an autographing party

179

was foolproof because not a single copy of *The Heart Being Hungry* was displayed where anyone could pick it up and absent-mindedly forget to pay for it. The customer had to buy his book from one of the staff at the cashier's desk, then get in line to have it signed. This system had been arrived at only after years of trial and error.

Ann's fingers were shaking as she pinned the corsage onto her jacket. She took out the Harry-pen, glanced at the thirty or forty people already waiting, and began her work.

"This one's for me, Miss Long. And this is for my sister-in-law in Toledo. Would you autograph it to her personally?"

"Certainly. What is your sister-in-law's name?"

"Alice. Alice Pollack."

Ann wrote, "For Alice Pollack . . . From the heart . . . Ann Long." This was her super-special one.

"I'm a Quill Club member. Remember? I told you about my children's story—the one about the little turtle who talked backwards?" Ann nodded and beamed. "Say something *really* nice. I spell my name B-e-t-t-e. Bette Edwards."

"Certainly." Ann wrote something *really* nice for B-e-t-t-e Edwards.

Certainly. Certainly. Certainly. Certainly. Certainly.

A woman literally shoved forward a child of fifteen. "This is my daughter Cecilia, Miss Long. Call her CeeCee. She wants to read your book and I'm willing to buy her a copy if you think she isn't too young."

"I . . . uh. . . . Oh, *thank* you, Doodles!" Ann said as Sally handed her a glass of water—and maneuvered CeeCee's mother out of the line for a private conversation.

At four o'clock Ann looked at her flowers. They were still fresh, but she was wilted. She had written steadily for two hours and had used up two ink cartridges. An author on the beam can sign many more than two hundred books in two hours if she doesn't dawdle, but after the first hour corners must be cut. Personal messages are out and so are the *really* nice ones. "From the heart, Ann Long" changes to "Sincerely, Ann Long," and then to "As ever, Ann Long," then, just "Ann Long."

"It could be worse, baby." Sally whispered to Ann at the height of the congestion. "What if your last name was Dostoevski?"

180

Ann collapsed in near hysterics.

Sally's party began promptly at five, as soon as the last customer was discreetly encouraged to leave. A bar materialized on the cashier's desk, and though the choice was restricted, the supply was plentiful: bourbon or Scotch; cola; ginger-ale or water. Sally explained that it was just "a small party for a few people who have been so nice," and Ann thought that a small party differed from a large party only in the number of guests present and the variety of refreshments offered. The per capita consumption of alcohol was the same—and it was considerable. Ann studied the man in shirtsleeves who was acting as bartender. He had called her "Ann" when he fixed her drink and although the soft, courteous voice almost rang a bell she couldn't place him. ("A light one, please," she'd said and he'd poured in a full three ounces.) "Who is he?" Ann said to Sally nodding at him. Sally laughed. "Why, it's Professor Grosset —without his coat and without the Professor." Then she whispered, "He loves to be bartender. Gives him a chance to sneak a few drinks when nobody's lookin'."

Soon, the poor little bookstore, which had had so few moments' peace this whole day, began to bubble again with confusion. This group was different from the autographing crowd, and the laughter was more shrill and less genuine. The smoke was twice as thick and there was a phony gaiety to the party. Where Ann had been queen bee in the afternoon, she now counted far less than anyone else. Here was a collection of people who knew how good they were in their fields and who were not shy about publishing their talents. The reporter and photographer from the paper were here and the reporter handed Ann a copy of the *Press Scimitar*. Her picture, taken that morning was front and center on page one, second section. Then Geraldine Brown announced her arrival by whinnying, *"Dooooooooooodles!"* in a haven't-seen-you-in-forty-years squeal, and Mrs. Hansford Ball dropped in just long enough to speak to the society reporter so she could be listed as one of the guests. Many of the Quill Clubbers were there—and, of course, the Cranshaw sales staff.

Ann saw Sally darting from one end of the store to the other,

181

sticking paper napkins under sweating glasses, then she came over to Ann, who was by herself.

"The sons of bitches," she said in her huskiest tones of contempt. "They don't care if they circle my most expensive art books with their drinks. I was opposed to this party in the bookstore. It was Mr. Cranshaw's idea—and next time I'm go'n let him worry about the guests' drippings."

"You love this store, don't you?" Ann asked.

Sally nodded. "Yes, I really do. The Cranshaws are wonderful to me. Their daughter in Louisville just had her first baby, so that's where they are. They felt terrible leaving the day before the party but I made them go ahead. They'll be tickled with the results."

"Speaking of results," Ann said, "is the author supposed to ask how many?"

Sally grinned. "Never heard of an author who didn't *think* it, so why not *ask*? Including the advance orders you signed this morning we've sold . . ." She counted to herself a moment. "360 copies. Mrs. Ball wants a bunch of the ones you signed for stock, and after all this publicity we'll have a flock of orders tomorrow. I bought 500 books for the party and we'll sell them all and order more within a week. Thanks for signing all that were left. It's twenty times easier to sell an autographed book." She looked at Ann. "You look pooped, dearie."

Ann sighed. "I am. Wonder if I could leave now through the back way? I'd love to sneak a bath before dinner."

"Sure. Wish I could do the same. Don't forget to be ready by quarter to seven. I'll be at your room a few minutes before. Mrs. Ball's chauffeur will pick us up."

Impulsively, Ann took off her corsage and pinned it to Sally's dress. "It's your turn, Doodles. Orchids to you! I'm damned grateful."

She was unprepared for Sally's reaction. The girl was so genuinely moved she kept blinking her eyes, and her voice, not harsh at all, but mellow, half whispered, "I can't wait to tell John what a peach you are, Ann."

Ann asked at the desk if she had any mail and as the clerk gave her a special delivery she saw that it was a letter from Bill, un-

182

doubtedly outlining her agenda for the next two days in Atlanta. Well, she hadn't really expected a letter from John—not really. Perfunctorily, she stepped to the cashier's cage and paid her hotel bill, telling the cashier that she would check out shortly.

She soaked the tiredness out of her body, lingering in the tub for almost a half hour. She wanted to lie down for a few moments' rest but she could not trust herself to stay awake. Instead, she went to the phone and put a collect call in to John. The telephone in their apartment rang ten times before the operator reported no answer, and Ann asked, "Try again in fifteen minutes, will you please?"

Sally arrived as she finished packing, more than a little high. "Thanks for the use of the orchids," she said, handing them to Ann. "Never felt so glamorous in my whole life." Ann split the corsage, got another pin and insisted that Sally wear one of them to the party. "I'm strictly a one-orchid woman," she said as Sally tried to protest, then, mainly to change the subject, she added, "Do you want a cup of coffee or anything before we leave?"

Sally giggled. "I'll bet I smell awful, but don't let it bother you. So will Mrs. Ball."

"You don't mean to say that the regal Mrs. Ball is—?"

"An alcoholic. She never gets blotto, but never gets sober, either. Just stays nicely lubricated all the time, and the more squiffled she gets the more regal she acts."

"Is she so important?" Ann asked dolefully. "Personally, I'd rather sleep till plane time."

"She rules the town, my dear. The account of her reception will run on the society pages of both the morning and evening papers and that's the kind of thing that sells books to people who can't read." (Non-books by non-authors for non-readers, Ann thought!) "She wasn't in the store long enough to get a book today, so I brought along a first edition for you to autograph especially for her. Be sure and remind me not to forget to remind you to sign it for her."

Ann laughed, thinking that Sally herself was nicely lubricated. A bellboy came for the luggage and promptly at 6:45 the doorman called to announce Mrs. Ball's car. They were ready to leave the room when the telephone rang. Ann ran to it. "Wait a minute, Doodles. It must be John. I have a call in to him."

183

"Ann Long?" the operator asked.

"Yes."

"Your New York number still doesn't answer. Should we try again in half an hour?"

"No. Cancel it," Ann said, trying to sound matter-of-fact. "I won't be where I can talk."

"Truer words were never spoken," Sally sighed as they walked to the elevator. "*Nobody* talks at Mrs. Hansford Ball's."

The Balls lived in a castle miles from the hotel. When the chauffeur turned into their private drive Ann nudged Sally, nodded at the huge mansion in its carefully arranged forest backdrop, and whistled.

"You ain't seen nothin' yet," Sally said in a hoarse whisper. And Sally was right: Ann was speechless from the minute Mrs. Ball met them in the foyer. She could not make up her mind which shone more brightly—the cut-glass chandelier or Mrs. Ball's bosom.

The great hall—Ann couldn't think of a better name—was three stories high and straight out of Sir Walter Scott. Crimson carpeting, massive mahogany furniture, chromium smoking stands, and the men's smoking room and women's powder room on opposite sides made Ann think of the lobby of an old-time movie palace.

"So glad you could make it, my dear," Mrs. Ball said in a refined whisper, while Ann secretly guessed that she hadn't really and truly been glad about anything for years and years.

Mr. Ball wandered in from what must have been the library. He was wearing a dinner-coat and black tie and he was shorter and stouter than his wife. He immediately appropriated Ann's arm with a gesture that said plainly, "Everything in this house is mine," and without preliminaries, he began, "Tell me all about your book, young lady. Is it hot?"

"Not really," Ann said, and before he could pounce again Mrs. Ball steered them all into the furniture store that was the living room. Ann got her first whiff of Mrs. Ball's breath then. Sally was right. Their hostess either bathed in whiskey, used it as a mouthwash, or drank it by the tumblerful. She reeked.

"Dry martini?" Mrs. Ball asked Ann, hospitably.

"Don't mind if I do," she said sweetly.

184

"Same for me," echoed Sally.

"I think I'll have just a spot of brandy," Mrs. Ball whispered. The butler already had it poured and waiting—a large spot. Sally was peering at the massive oil paintings that lined the walls of the room when Mr. Ball drifted over to her and began to feel her experimentally as though trying to guess her weight. Mrs. Ball, who had evidently watched him do this sort of thing for years, asked Ann in a dull, blank voice, "What does your husband do, Mrs. Long?"

"He drinks," Ann said casually.

"Oh, how nice," Mrs. Ball said, neither hearing nor caring.

"And what does *your* husband do?"

"Didn't you *know?*" Mrs. Ball came to. "We're in plumbing."

"Plumbing?"

"Yes. Mostly fixtures and fittings."

By some secret signal Ann had not yet fathomed, the butler divined that Mrs. Ball's glass was going to be empty and refilled it as soon as she downed the last of that particular brandy. Ann had floated out of Mr. Ball's reach and now it was Sally's turn to get the feel-treatment. It's a new parlor game we're playing, Ann thought—a combination of post-office and musical chairs. Sally scooted out of reach, so Mr. Ball aimed again at Ann, but just then the butler slipped Mrs. Ball a jigger of brandy, neat (what *was* their signal system?) and turned to the guests to announce dinner.

The reception was played in slow motion. Something about the vast spaces of the rooms made the guests speak softly. Or maybe it was the thick carpeting that muffled their voices into vague sounds. "If ever a gathering needed liquoring up to come alive this one is it," Sally said to Ann. "Look at poor Professor Grosset. His tongue's hanging out for a drink and I don't mean that dreadful sweet lemonade." Ann watched the suffering Professor Grosset. He looked like a man who has just been informed that the governor has refused to sign his last-minute reprieve. It's part of the same pattern, she thought. The Quill Clubbers were here. A few familiar faces from the autographing party. Professor Grosset. Geraldine Brown. No matter how many affairs Ann attended it always boiled down to

185

the same faces at all of them. There were a few more men here, and more of the jewelry was real.

Ann kept looking at her watch to seize the earliest possible moment for escape. At nine-thirty she called Sally aside. "I can't stand any more of this. I'm going to have the chauffeur take me to the airport. Do you want to stay?"

"Hell, no," Sally yawned. "I've been searching for an hour and can't find where she hides her damned brandy."

"Here she comes now," Ann said as Mrs. Ball emerged from the ladies' powder room. From her walk, Ann figured the secret cache must be in there. Either that, or Mrs. Ball had a flask tied around her waist. She was smiling vacuously at the two girls, yet Ann was certain she had no idea who they were.

"This is the loveliest affair I ever remember," Ann lied. "I hate to have to leave, but I must catch the plane to Atlanta. You understand, don't you?"

"Oh, yes," Mrs. Ball said absently. "You must come again soon when you can stay longer."

"I've left a copy of my book by the punch bowl. I autographed it especially for you and your charming husband."

Mrs. Ball nodded slowly, "Make yourselves at home," she said, and floated away.

"Well, I'll be damned," Sally rasped. "Let's get out of here."

"Just a minute," said Ann suddenly. She ran across the foyer to the powder room, disappeared, then reappeared—all within ten seconds.

"That was quick," Sally said.

"I just wanted to inspect those mostly-fixtures-and-fittings," Ann confided. "And it's just as I thought. They're gold, Doodles. *Pure gold.*"

They began running to the car—like children escaping from the wicked witch's castle.

186

18

JOHN's initial impulse when he heard the doorbell was to ignore it. If he rose above the buzzing, refused to recognize it, shut it out of the realm of perception, whoever was out there would go away and quiet would return to his tidy solitary world.

He wasn't even curious as to who was being so persistent. The only person he'd get out of this chair for didn't need to ring because she had a key. He proceeded to use his highball glass to spell her name in the air in large capital letters which disappeared as he outlined them. He took a sip of whiskey, studied his glass reverently and then spelled her name again, only this time he made it the beginning of a message. D-e-a-r A-n-n the letters-which-weren't-letters began, and he thought the rest of it. *Dear Ann: Come home to your foolish one. Dear Ann: I need you. Dear Ann:*—The buzzing had now become a pounding—a man's pounding. A persistent man's. I-know-you're-in-there-John-Long, the pounding said, I-know-damned-well-you're-there, and finally John turned from his preoccupation with the East River to look at the door. He hoped for a quiet moment that whoever it was had gone, but then the pounding resumed—louder, even, if possible.

"Oh, hell," he sighed, and then yelled, "Wait a minute!" without knowing why he yelled it. He put his drink down, started to put on his shoes and decided not to. On his way he stared in the mirror at his whisker-stubble, reminded himself to shave for-sure tomorrow and opened the door.

Billy Clarke, of Laverty and Clarke, Publishers, grinning in triumph, had taken the silk handkerchief from the pocket of his plaid sports coat and was rubbing his pounding-hand with it.

"Y'know," he said as he walked inside, "for just a minute I thought you knew it was the boss out there and didn't want to see him. Was I right?"

187

"You were wrong," John said. "You're one of the few people I'm always glad to see. I'll get you a drink. Irish whiskey okay? I hope so. Scotch is all gone."

Billy Clarke took in everything while John got him the drink. He figured the cost of the apartment, corroborated the rumor he'd heard about the Longs having money of their own, revised upward any price that might grow out of this visit, then determined to have his own way, regardless of amount.

"If I'd known the boss was coming I'd have shaved," John said, handing Billy the drink. "Or at least put on my shoes. My wife's away so I've just been sitting here—"

He didn't go on because it was apparent that Clarke knew he had just been sitting there and what he'd been doing.

"Take off that jacket and necktie," John said. "If this is going to be a battle of wits I'm at a disadvantage in this T-shirt."

Billy tossed his coat on a chair, removed his tie, dropped it carelessly on the floor and then matter-of-factly took off his shoes as John smiled with genuine pleasure. Clarke knew how to make people like him, all right. "Why were you so sure I was here?" John asked. "I paid the doorman to forget where I was."

Billy was enjoying himself now, too. "I paid him more to remember than you paid him to forget."

John laughed as he sank into his chair and placed his legs on the ottoman. He was glad that he'd opened the door, even if he wasn't sure why Billy was here. He knew he would have his answer after two or three drinks. I wish Ann would call, he thought, and ask what I'm doing so I could tell her I'm merely getting tight with Billy Clarke, that's all. More and more now he found it impossible to enjoy a pleasurable experience without Ann to share it with him. Most men lived out certain moments of their lives behind PRIVATE, KEEP OUT signs, and he'd hid behind such signs when he was married to Madge, but now he had to have Ann in on everything that made him happy . . . even when she was miles away he brought her into the room with him by thinking about her.

Billy Clarke was making himself at home. He walked outside to approve the terrace, he went to the bathroom, came back, confessed to using a guest towel, and began fixing his own drinks.

188

"You miss your wife," he said.

"Mind reader," John said softly.

"You must be proud of her success with the book." Billy said. "Doesn't happen often that a first novel hits the jackpot. Ann's got a brilliant career ahead of her."

"Not Ann," John said. "She insists she's never going to write another book."

"She will, though. She won't be able to help it. She has a God-given talent and that you have to use. If you don't you dry up with it." Billy slowly sipped his drink. "How many books has Fortune House got her tied up for? Or is it cricket for me to ask?"

John shrugged. "It's cricket. This one is it. She's not committed to Fortune House or anyone else for any more books, and that's the way she wants it."

Billy fixed himself another drink and walked over to John's chair. He was incongruous in his partly unbuttoned shirt, his lack of necktie, his socks. John studied him for a minute before he said, "Now, I know what you're going to say before you say it. You're going to ask me to come back to work for Laverty and Clarke and you're going to throw in a nice, fat bonus for my talking my wife into writing her next book for *you*, and if I didn't like you, Billy, if I didn't *genuinely* like you, I'd say, 'You make me sick!' "

Billy Clarke's face showed nothing. He turned and walked toward the door that opened on the terrace and kept his back turned to John. "I don't like you when you're cynical, John. In fact, I don't like cynical people at any time. It's easy to be cynical in the publishing business and most people think you've got to be to stand it. But I don't think that. I think it's cynicism—more than any other thing—that has undermined publishing. There's little or no real belief, anywhere, on anyone's part. Editors are cynical about the books they work on, sales managers and travelers about people buying them, and the authors even grow cynical about their own work. It's catching. Until a minute ago I'd thought you chose the book business because you liked it and got a bang out of it, the same as me. You were *never* cynical."

He was still looking away from John but he was talking with intimacy and candor and this was not the fabled Billy Clarke who could turn on irresistible charm to woo another publisher's author.

189

This was—for better or worse—the kind of hard-hitting Billy Clarke book people despised because he was different from them. He was going on. "It's true I inherited money but I made a lot more in a business where people weren't cynical and I moved into publishing because I liked it. I haven't been corrupted yet and maybe I won't be, but that remains to be seen." He turned now and faced John, soberly. "You think I came here to ask you to come back to work so that I could get your wife on our list and that makes *me* sick! Sure, I'd like to have Ann Long on our list. Who wouldn't? But first things first and first I want you—before her or anybody else. You see, the way I look at the publishing world it's only as sick and cynical and defeated as the people who run it and all the time I'm asking myself how can Laverty and Clarke do anything worthwhile with a horse's-ass like Cecil Laverty calling the turn?"

And what about a horse's-ass like Ransom? John thought.

"And a horse's-ass like Ransom," Billy suddenly added.

John nodded. Billy was psychic. No doubt about that.

"So I came here today to ask you to come back and work for *me*. I'm kicking Cecil upstairs to be chairman of the board, with lots of glory and no decisions to make. I'll even try to find a place for Ransom where he can't do us any harm, but I need help—and you're it. You know a lot of the angles; you know selling; you know what bookstore people want and can sell and Cecil doesn't and Ransom doesn't, and neither of 'em wants to know. They are contemptuous of the very thing they ought to be most aware of: who's gonna *buy* their books? They figure out a given sale a book's gotta have to justify the author's advance and the cost of publishing it and they tell the salesmen to go out and make that figure, regardless of what the book's *like*: sell so many to pull them out. That's their cynical way of doing it and when their *Milk in the Sky*s are remaindered at ten cents a throw, they blame everybody but themselves." He walked a few steps closer to John. "You know the editorial end, too, John. It's no accident that every book you've helped put together has made money; and you've done a good job scouting for manuscripts nobody else had sense enough to find. Also, you've been spending more and more time in sales, and you've scored there." He paused. "It's you I want first, John, then you're the one who'll have to want Ann on our side."

190

Billy stooped over, picked up his necktie from the floor. He began tying it and John was surprised to see his hands shaking. He said, "I want you to *work* for me, so take a month or two to think it over. It'll take me that long, anyway, to move those lugheads around. You'll be sales manager—to start with."

John started to say something, couldn't, instinctively put his hand out toward Billy, then pulled it back in mild embarrassment.

Clarke pretended not to have seen him. He had put on his shoes and jacket now and had arranged his silk handkerchief in the pocket the way he liked it, well out. At the door he turned and grinned the way he did when he'd first entered.

"Your wife will write another book, John, and we'll sell the hell out of it —you and me." He was laughing as he closed the door behind him, and it was not cynical laughter.

John automatically started for the bar to fix a fresh drink. Then he suddenly decided against it, and went instead to the writing desk where he began a letter to Ann.

19

THE ringing telephone awakened Ann and she lay in bed for a few seconds trying to figure out where she was and what she was doing here. Then she answered it and heard a man's voice say, "Welcome to Atlanta!"

"Who—who is it?"

Bill stopped disguising his voice. "Why, it's your manager, your press agent, your—"

"My pain in the neck. Bill Haley, what're you *doing* to me? I'm exhausted."

"Relax. You get to rest all day today. That is, until four, when you autograph a few books at a literary tea."

191

"And what of my evening, Simon Legree? Does it belong to me or to the Atlanta equivalent of Mrs. Hansford Ball?"

"It's all yours. Except for a TV broadcast at nine forty-five, just before the news. The big autographing takes place tomorrow morning at ten at the department store. Have you had coffee?"

"No. I'll order for both of us. Give me ten minutes. And do me a favor. See if I have any mail."

"Okay. Ten minutes."

Ann had never seen Bill Haley happier. His round face was dimpled with delight. "Ann, you are a sensation. Your next book is gonna have an advance of fifteen thousand in the South alone."

"*Next* book? Haley, you're in Margaret Mitchell's home town—and when a gal says *no next book* in Atlanta she *means* it. Well, *no next book!*"

"I'll give you a year to change your mind. Here's a letter I picked up for you, from Jack. Airmail special."

She did not try to hide her excitement but if Bill saw her hand trembling he did not let on. She walked over to a chair near the window and began reading, oblivious to the waiter's bringing the breakfast. Bill calmly buttered himself a piece of toast, poured a cup of coffee and began eating.

It was a fairly long letter and John had typed it on the portable at the apartment.

Dearest Ann:

I'm mailing this to the Biltmore in Atlanta and I hope you get it tomorrow. (That's the way you always begin.) How do you like being a traveler? Don't tell me. I can guess. Just remember that the first twenty years are the hardest.

Yesterday I worked in the little garden. You'd be surprised how green the grass is getting already. Sometimes I wish our acreage were two feet longer and two feet wider. Then the gardener wouldn't constantly be scraping his elbows and shins.

In case you're wondering if I'm working, I'm not. But guess who dropped in? Billy Clarke. He really is a swell egg—and does he ever hate Laverty's guts! Billy wants me back with the firm. Said to take it easy for a while and think it over.

Of course there's method in his madness. My wife happens to

192

be one of the most valuable literary properties in the country and the old coot knows he'll never get her signature on an L and C contract unless I'm back on the payroll. He figures that you indirectly got me into my jam and that you can directly get me out. Anyway, Billy Clarke did come to Mohamet for a drink!

To tell the truth, I've been content doing nothing. The days go by . . . go by. . . .

So much for me. Don't let Haley wear you out. He'll try! I've done the same thing to authors. Tell him I envy him the commissions on the books you're selling for him.

Bess drove by for a few minutes yesterday. She's almost finished with Dr. Darnell. I don't know what he's done to her mind, but she sure as hell looks glamorous everywhere else.

Take care of yourself, dear—and don't autograph any *Milk in the Sky* by mistake.

I love you.

John

"Your coffee's getting cold," Bill said quietly.

"Okay. I'm finished."

"What does he say?"

"He says for me not to let you wear me out, and he's holding you personally responsible."

"I'll wire him today you never looked better in your life."

"That's a lie."

"I know it. Eat your toast."

"If you're wondering whether he's working, he isn't."

"Oh."

"He says, 'the days go by, go by.' Wonder what he means by that?"

"That's easy. He means: 'the days go by, go by.'"

And so, finally, Dallas.

Ann had fallen deeper and deeper into the pattern of the tour until she instinctively knew each angle. She could address a ladies' club, be interviewed on a television station, chat amiably with reporters through the closed screen door of her brain. She mastered the winning-smile-with-every-autograph that had been such an effort at first and she learned to say, "How right you are!" at just

193

the right moment to the right person. She learned to be effortlessly surprised when people praised her book. "Come along with me; I need you around for moral support," she would say to them graciously, or, "What a lovely compliment. May I frame your picture and put it on my wall?"

Each city had its Geraldine Browns, its Professor Grossets, its Mrs. Balls, but sometimes the Geraldines were genuine, nice people and sometimes the Mrs. Balls were actually human and sober with hearts as big as the houses they lived in. And Ann remembered especially how nice the man in New Orleans had been—the one who'd interviewed her on his radio program—so nice that she'd enjoyed that radio interview more than any TV show she'd appeared on. *Appeared* spelled the difference between the two media. Television time was so precious one merely paraded before the camera, made a few innocuous remarks and paraded off. Five minutes was a long interview on TV, but this radio interview had taken fifteen and there was a relaxed mood to it that television could not duplicate. They had talked about writing in general, then her own novel in particular; the interviewer knew exactly what to ask, and she somehow had had all the right answers. Afterwards, Ann told him she was glad she worked in "old fashioned radio" instead of in the slicker medium of television, and as she said it, she ached to be back at her desk at WOOZ, near Harry, Irene, Marta and the spot announcements.

Finally there were the Doodles Lees—the bookstore girls who went out of their way to be kind to her. No wonder John liked Susan in Fort Worth and Wanda in Oklahoma City and Peggy in Houston. She liked them, too, because they were understanding, real people, people—not phonies. Nobody impressed them and hot air did not faze them.

"You'll like Hazel Watts best of the lot," John had said to her the night before she left New York and he was right. Ann hadn't expected Hazel to be waiting for her at the Dallas airport at nine o'clock in the morning, but there she was.

"Hello, Ann. I'd recognize you anywhere from that picture on your dust jacket," Hazel said as she walked up, "I've got my car. I'll drive you to your hotel." And then she set the record straight, adding, "I feel like your sister—or mother—or at least a cousin. I

194

know a good deal about you from Johnny and you may as well know he's the apple of my eye."

"It's mutual," Ann replied, hoping she sounded real for a change, because this time she meant it.

When they got to her room and Hazel started to leave, she said, "Don't go yet, please. I'll order us a pot of coffee. I really want you to stay, Hazel."

Hazel sat down. "You're worn out, aren't you?"

"Yes. If there were two autographings left instead of one, I couldn't make it. I'm that tired."

"There's just one person in captivity who *can* do it." Hazel said, nodding positively.

"Do what?"

"Take these long tours in his stride. His name's Allen Hull."

Ann laughed. "Sally Lee told me about him. She says unautographed first editions of his books're priceless."

Hazel chuckled. "*If* you can find one."

The waiter knocked on the door; she got up, opened it, paid the waiter over Ann's objections, poured the coffee, and served Ann's.

"You're not going to budge from this room until time for the party," she said protectively. "I'll tell everybody you were late getting in or that you're sick or something. The papers have been full of you for days and I can tell from the advance orders and calls that we'll be swamped. Six hundred won't be enough, so I've made arrangements with the jobber here to get more when I run out."

"Six hundred!" There was panic in Ann's voice. "Why, when they sold *five* hundred in San Antonio yesterday it seemed like a million. I—"

Hazel reassured her. "It'll be easier than it sounds. I sold a hundred copies before the release date. You're not supposed to, but everybody does and we've sold at least a hundred fifty more since then. I haven't seen anything like it since *Marjorie Morningstar*— which dates *me*. So that's 250. We're holding a hundred mail orders for you to autograph, and that leaves only 250 for the party. So six hundred won't be enough." She paused. "I sure wish Johnny was here to see it all."

"So do I," Ann said softly.

195

"I worry about Johnny. I expect he'd be mad if he knew it, but I worry—just the same."

"So do I," Ann said again. She had written him three times that she was expecting him to meet her here in Dallas and to fly west with her and though he'd never agreed to come, she'd felt a wave of disappointment when he was not at the airport this morning. She still hoped he'd turn up before plane time tomorrow, but she was afraid to mention it to Hazel for fear he wouldn't. However, if she could be sure he'd fly to California direct from New York, she rationalized, it might be better for her, because she looked so whipped at this point, and she could use a few days of rest at Birdie's to pull herself together.

"Is Johnny all right?" Hazel asked, not curiously.

Ann would have liked to say, "No, he's all wrong. He drinks too much, and he's at loose ends, and I'm sick inside, wanting him so much," but she felt strangely that Hazel Watts understood it all without her having to spell it out, so she said, "He made me promise not to sign any *Milk in the Skys* by mistake."

Hazel erupted suddenly.

"*Milk in the Sky!*" she roared. "Oh, my achin' back! *That stinking book* . . . I tell you . . ."

Yes. You could not help liking Hazel Watts. You had to.

The last customer was gone and Hazel had been right. There were only ten books left for autographing and more would have to be ordered tomorrow. Ten from six hundred, and Ann could not have made it if Bill Haley hadn't stood by every moment, helping with people's names, speeding the ones who wanted to visit a while after Ann had signed their books, making private jokes and asides to keep up her drooping spirits. She'd signed the advance orders in Hazel's office before the party started; then, almost from the beginning, omitted even "*Best Wishes*," concentrating on a quick smile and a quick *Ann Long*, book after book.

Hazel, too, seemed exhausted. "Thanks for helping put my daughter through college," she said as Ann was about to leave the store. "I'm not going to say goodbye to you, Ann. I'll be seeing you with Johnny in the fall." And the way Hazel said it, it sounded entirely reasonable to Ann.

196

Bill took her to the hotel and went up to the room with her, and the minute she was inside the door she kicked off her shoes, fell onto the bed, and groaned, "It's finished. The tour's finished, Bill, and so am I."

Bill began to pucker up, and Ann knew he was about to say something solemn. Whenever he took on his solemn expression it was all she could do to keep from laughing. He made a real production of being solemn, right down to the tears in his eyes, but it would be cruel to laugh at him because he so obviously meant each solemn word. He said, "Ann, I'll never be able to tell you how proud I am of you—and how grateful for all you've done for me."

"Stop it, Bill Haley. I've loved it. The only reward I ask is to get to play dead tonight. I don't want to be asked to move a finger."

Bill was plainly disappointed. "All right, but I'd sorta counted on your having dinner with us."

"Please excuse me, Bill. I'll order something to eat up here. I just can not go anywhere where people are tonight." She hesitated, then said, "Who's 'us,' by the way? Hazel?"

"No. Hazel begged off, too." Bill paused, and then, without realizing how transparent he was, asked, "Did you get a chance at all to talk to Hazel's assistant Mabel? Not the little one, no, that's Betty. Mabel—"

Ann nodded. "I know. She was wearing a middy and skirt."

"Ann, there's a real book for you." Bill said with conviction. "Some day, when you're not so tired, I'd like to tell you about Mabel."

Ann looked at him. "She's the 'us,' isn't she, Bill?"

Bill nodded.

"Only not any longer," Ann said. "I mean not 'us' the way she once was."

"How did you know that?" Bill asked guilelessly. "Did Jack say something?"

Ann smiled. "Don't be silly. He wouldn't say anything because —well, because he's a man. Just as I know about Mabel because I'm a woman."

Bill spoke seriously. "Y'see, Ann, Mabel and I used to be . . . Well, it wasn't just something *ordinary*. It was—"

197

"Yes. And then you fell in love with Bess."

He sat down before he answered. "Yes." He sounded like a high school student mooning over his first crush. "I'm going to call Bess on the phone before I meet Mabel."

"For courage, Bill?"

"Yes. I'm not as strong as people think I am," he said, looking away from her, "and that's why I'd hoped you'd come along tonight. Don't misunderstand me, Ann. They don't make 'em any finer than Mabel, but—well, it's going to be hell telling her about Bess."

Ann shook her head. "No it won't. You'll see. Mabel will make it easy for you. I know."

Bill frowned and Ann noticed how grim and un-dimpled he looked. He left his chair with reluctance, shook his head at something he was thinking, and went to the door.

"I'll tell Bess you said hello," he said lamely.

Ann was lonely and the sudden letdown after so many days of sustained pressure and tenseness was a shock. Room service had long since come for the dinner dishes and she had tried to nap, but it was still only nine o'clock. She actually considered dressing and going to a movie, then the thought of people in a crowd deterred her. And yet, being alone didn't seem to help either.

She smiled sardonically at the thought of spending a perfect May evening in Dallas, Texas alone in the Sheraton Hotel. She walked to the closed window, looked down at the street and thought that for all she knew there was a full moon, but even the most active imagination couldn't bring a full moon into this efficiently airconditioned room. *Air-conditioning:* the feeling of staleness and depression came on her full strength. The hint of omnipresent cigar smoke, dust on dust, thoughts that people had left behind all became suddenly so much too much that she began to cry without making any sound. She lay on the bed and cried, remembering the words from John's letter, "The days go by . . . go by . . ."

The telephone rang for a minute before she was aware of it.

"Hello," she said and in a minute John said, from New York, "How are you, dear?"

"Fine. Fine."

"You sound funny. Is anything wrong?"

198

"No—I've . . . I've been crying and now I have hiccups."

"Why are you crying, Ann?" He said it so tenderly she started to cry all over again.

"This is silly of me, John. It's just I'm so tired. I'm all right. Honest, I am."

"I just couldn't come there, Ann. I wanted to but I couldn't. Do you understand?"

"I understand. You can come out west next week, though?"

"Do you really want me to?"

The way he asked it and the way she wanted to tell him how much she needed him made her sob louder. "Yes, darling. *Yes*, I do. *Promise* me you'll come."

"I'm still flotsam and jetsam, honey."

"Come anyway."

"All right. I'll come if you'll stop crying."

She blew her nose. "I've stopped," she said, hiccuped, and added, "Can't stop that, though. Promise me you'll come, for sure."

"Cross my heart."

"And get plenty of rest, darling."

"That's what I called to tell *you*. Rest. Order up a drink. Some-brandy. You need it."

Ann thought of the woman in Memphis—or was it Atlanta? No, *Memphis*. Mrs. Hansford Ball, that was her name. Anyway, she had kept on drinking brandy. Maybe she needed it. She said, "I'll do that, darling."

"How's Hazel?"

"Fine. She misses you. Everybody misses you."

"I'll see you in California. Goodbye, dear."

"Goodbye, John."

Then suddenly, as though she'd forgotten to tell him the most important thing of all she said quickly, "John. Oh John, darling! *I love you!*"

But he was gone. He had already hung up.

199

20

BILL was a noisy sleeper, full of wheezes and snuffles. Ann tabbed him a menace to be reckoned with once flat on his back in his own bed. He was sawing wood now in the reclining chair of the American Airlines Astrojet they'd boarded in Dallas. Bill had told her how much more comfortable the first class seats were, but she guessed he'd sleep as soundly on a park bench. Curious, Ann had asked the man at the ticket counter to name other differences between first class and tourist. "Two-seats-together instead of three, whiskey and champagne free, wider aisles—" and then proof positive: "First class enters in the front; tourist in the tail." Even so, she noticed that most of the passengers had chosen tourist; there were few Bill could disturb in their part of the plane. She smiled as she thought of isolating the snorers into a class of their own.

Of course it was ridiculous, but Ann couldn't shake the outlandish notion that Bill's ex-wives had divorced him on grounds of excessive snoring. Wonder how Bess would react when she learned she'd married a buzz-saw? Or did Bess already know Bill's sleeping habits? It hadn't occurred to Ann until this minute that Bess had slept with Bill. Now that the idea was hatched she couldn't stop dwelling on it. Bess and Bill in bed together. Why not? They—. She forced herself to change her thoughts. One of the by-products of her tiredness was an accentuated sexual inclination. The hotel rooms she'd been in intensified this feeling. The rhythm of the plane made it almost unbearable.

She took a deep breath and turned to watch Bill's sleeping face so peacefully relaxed. In his sleep he had edged over toward her until his head nuzzled her shoulder and his nearness made her think of John. John was such a quiet sleeper; he always went to sleep before she did; sometimes she'd listen to catch his measured breathing, and sometimes his hand would still be on her body when he fell asleep.

200

Ann felt a sudden tremendous surge of desire and thought that trying to put a halter on these obstinate thoughts would have been ludicrous if it wasn't so real.

She motioned to the stewardess and whispered, "Black coffee, please." The stewardess hurried to get it. Probably thinks I'm sick, Ann thought, and maybe in a way I am. She couldn't care less, this flight, about luxury seats, wide aisles and free champagne, because it couldn't be first class for her without John.

"I'll come if you'll stop crying . . . Cross my heart . . . I'll see you in California. Goodbye, dear."

The scalding coffee helped her suppress what her camp counselor used to call "nasty thinking," and forcing herself to remember her mother completed the job. Mother was a surefire moral detergent, all right. In physical appearance, she could have been Grant Wood's model for the woman in American Gothic, and she was just about as cheerful. After "being both father and mother to my daughters" both of them had disappointed her in their marriages. When Birdie eloped with Abe Zelkin Mother gasped, "She's married out of her race. She's committed a crime against nature!" and she had punctuated her outburst with what she herself later diagnosed as "a very slight stroke." Ann, however, considering Birdie and Abe the modern equivalents of Elizabeth and Robert Browning, had done all she could to abet the match.

Abe, a whiz at merchandising, was painfully naive when it came to being a son-in-law to Mother. He closed his eyes to her complaints about his blood lines, his Full-O'-Fashion dresses and his crime-against-nature and invited her to come to California, where she now lived imperially in an expensive apartment in Beverly Hills (Abe was permitted to pay the rent), but she continued to act as though she smelled something unpleasant whenever she went to Birdie's house to visit her tainted grandchildren.

Abe had repaid all favors he owed Ann by getting Mother out of New York just before John's return from Korea. ("To think my daughter could break up a lovely home, a *lovely* home.") When Abe and Birdie had visited New York five years ago Ann reminded Abe that she would be his debtor forever for his mother-in-law sacrifice. They'd had fun together and John genuinely liked his in-laws.

201

For years Birdie had been inviting John and Ann to California, dangling as bait the swimming pool, the gardens, Aunt Ann's room ("That's what the children have always called it") and the weather, but Ann refused to come. She never wanted to go without John, yet knowing Mother, why *should* she throw him to the lions? All this —yet now as the plane neared Los Angeles Ann realized how much she had missed her sister during the years of separation.

She shook Bill by the shoulder. "Wake up, you big dope. We're almost there."

Bill started, recoiled, blinked and closed his eyes in protest, then he opened them again, stretched, and finally grinned. "What time is it?"

"Two o'clock our time. Noon out here."

"I feel wonderful."

"You ought to! You've been sleeping since we left Dallas—half the time on both our chairs. I'm sure everyone thinks you're my son, and I *feel* old enough to be your mother." Ann laughed. "Stop grinning at me. You missed the scenery. Mountains, canyons, deserts—all in technicolor."

"I've seen them all," Bill said. "They give me an inferiority complex." He yawned. "Did you get any sleep, Ma?"

"Me? Sleep's something I've given up. It's so childish."

"No, seriously, Ann. I hope you will get some sleep out here. Lots of it. You have it coming to you."

"You're making me feel older by the minute," Ann said, fastening her seat-belt. "Fix your straps. We're getting ready to land."

Bill adjusted his chair to a sitting angle, fastened his seat belt and said, "If you need anything call me. I'll be at the Town House."

"You told me that earlier. And it's not the Town House any more, it's the Sheraton West."

"Still the Town House to me. Things happened to me in the Town House. Nothing ever happened to me in the Sheraton West, and I doubt that it will. I'll call you Monday about the final plans for the banquet."

"You told me that, too."

"Okay. I won't bother you about anything else for the rest of the week. That leaves you four whole days with nothing planned. Can you stand it?"

202

"Can *you?* What are *you* going to do for four days? Drink the town dry?"

"I am not. I have to see the Royal Pictures people about the banquet; and I want to talk to Bud Johnson, our West Coast man, and I can use some sleep, too. You aren't the only one who's been burning the candle at both ends."

She wanted to tell him what a good job he'd done, to let him know she was aware how hard he'd worked to make the autographing tour a success, but this was not the moment. She'd already spotted Birdie, out of the window of the jet that was taxiing slowly to its ramp and she cried, "There's Birdie. There's my sister Birdie!"

"Where?"

"There—next to that man in the yellow sports shirt. He's Abe, my brother-in-law."

"Your sister doesn't look a thing like you."

"Yes she does. She's heavier, that's all. Birdie always loses weight when I'm around to keep her mind on it. Oh, there's Mother."

"She looks sweet," Bill said quickly.

"And those two children, the ones with the flaming red hair, they must be Lorraine and Raymond. The whole family's turned out!"

"I'm jealous," Bill said. "I love to be met. Hold my hand, Ann. I feel so lonely I think I'm going to cry."

Ann smiled. Bill Haley was joking; however, there was a grain of truth in what he said. She knew the feeling, all right, because she'd been there herself—last night.

"Ann! Ann!" Birdie was hugging and kissing her, and then Abe and the children. Ann walked over to where her mother was standing; Mother offered her cheek and Ann pressed hers to it.

"What a reception," Ann said, trying desperately to throw off her tiredness and appear ebullient. "This is wonderful."

"We're so proud of you," Birdie cried. "Lorraine and Raymond want your autograph."

"I'd know them from their pictures. That hair!" Ann walked over to her niece. "Lorraine, your hair's beautiful. I wish I had it. Wonder where you kids got this red hair?"

"Your father's *mother* had red hair." It was the first thing Ann's

203

mother had said. "They get their hair from the Austin side of the family. Where's your husband?"

Mother. Dear, dear Mother. You have not changed a bit.

Ann let the question go unanswered, introducing Bill. "This is Bill Haley, a friend of ours. Bill knows Bess."

Everyone said hello, and then Birdie asked Bill, "How is Bess? Why doesn't she come to visit us?"

Bill blushed.

Ann laughed. "Why ask *him?* She's a friend of mine, too. Bess is fine."

"Why does it take so long to get your luggage off an airplane?" Bill asked nervously, obviously stunned by such an overdose of family.

"And where is your husband?" Mother asked Ann again, before anyone could answer Bill's question.

"Gee, where *is* John?" Birdie asked. "I was so excited seeing you I forgot about him."

"He's coming out from New York," Ann said casually. "I left from Dallas. He'll be here in a few days. Mother, you look wonderfully well."

"Thanks. You're thin."

"Well, we're going to fix that, starting this minute," Birdie said brightly. "Abe's taking all of us to the Farmers Market for lunch. It's right on the way to Brentwood. Wait 'til you see the Farmers Market, Ann! You'll put it in your next book."

Ann wanted the Farmers Market at the moment about as much as she wanted to write another book. She said, "I'm really not very hungry. They fed us on the plane. Maybe we could go straight home."

"Oh, no, Aunt Ann," Lorraine pleaded. "We want to take you some place special. You'll just love the Farmers Market. They have lots of kinds of food—Mexican, Swedish, Russian—all kinds, and you get to try them all. *Please* come!"

"It's stud, Aunt Ann," Raymond insisted. "Real *stud.*"

Ann put her arms around her niece and nephew and smiled her autograph-smile. "Then of course I'll go. It'll be a party."

"You come too, Bill," Abe said cordially.

204

"I'd love to, but I can't," Bill said. "I have a business appointment this afternoon. I'd better go straight to my hotel."

"Where are you staying? Maybe we can drop you off."

"The Town H—" He caught himself. "I mean the Sheraton West. But I don't want to put you to any trouble. I'll take the airport limousine."

"We'll drive you there," Abe insisted. "It's not out of the way. Besides, we've plenty of time."

"I don't want to crowd you," Bill said.

"You won't. We'll put the luggage in the back and have plenty of room."

Now the bags came and Abe and Bill carried them to the car. Birdie and Ann walked arm in arm, talking a blue streak, and when Ann saw the car she gasped. "What a car! What kind is it?"

"Imperial," Abe said with the proper touch of modesty. "Brand new." He was pleased that she was impressed.

"It's stud." Ann said, and Raymond looked startled.

"Abe likes nice cars," Birdie said, almost apologetically.

"And Birdie likes nice swimming pools," Abe retorted in the same tone of voice.

"They live too high," Mother said. "Everyone lives over their heads out here."

Then she looked at Bill and decided to stop.

There was a great to-do about where everyone would sit, but it wound up with Birdie, Abe and Ann in front, with Mother, Raymond and Bill in back. Lorraine sat on Bill's lap.

"Are you crowded, Bill?" Ann asked over her shoulder.

"Not at all! Lorraine is as light as a feather. Anyhow, I like having a good-looking redhead on my knee."

"You'd have had a nicer ride in the limousine," Ann said, and laughed. "I couldn't have planned it better, though, if I'd deliberately arranged it this way. This is your repayment for some of the tortures you subjected me to on the trip, Buster."

"Don't be silly," Bill said. "This is a pleasure. Why, there I was in that plane wishing sadly there was somebody to meet me . . . and now somebody has."

Ann was tired, sick-tired. She had hoped to go to Birdie's house,

205

take off her clothes, put on her swim suit and unwind. Instead, now that Bill was out of the car, she was being peppered with questions from the front and back seats. This was a worse ordeal than an autographing party because she had to think about what she was saying.

"How's John?" Abe asked.

"Fine. Skinny as ever."

Then, from Mother, "I don't think you two people eat enough. New Yorkers are always in too much of a hurry to fix themselves a decent meal."

From Lorraine. "Aunt Ann, is Rock Hudson *really* going to play the lead in the movie of your book? Will you introduce me to Rock Hudson?"

"Why, Lorraine, *I* don't know Rock Hudson."

"Hedda Hopper mentioned the picture," Lorraine said knowingly. "Rock Hudson and—what's the name of the girl she said, Mother?"

"Elizabeth Taylor," Birdie answered. "I don't know which girl she'll play, though. Which do you think, Ann?"

"I hadn't thought."

"Mother won't let me read your book, Aunt Ann. She said I'm too young."

"Oh, Birdie! Remember how you and I always used to feel when Mother—?" Ann remembered that Mother was with them and then a terrible thought came to her. All the more terrible because she'd never happened to think of it before. "I hope you haven't read it, Mother . . . It's . . . well, it's not your kind of book."

"I certainly have read it," her mother said, "and I think you ought to be ashamed of yourself. Your poor, dead father would turn over in his grave if he knew what his daughter's doing for money."

Abe came to the rescue. "Well, we're here! Here's the Farmers Market! Everybody out!"

Ann winked her thanks at him.

"It's just like being home again," she said.

Mother got out of the car first.

After lunch, they drove Mother to her apartment before going on to Birdie's and Abe's house.

206

"Aren't you going to stay with me—at least till John comes?" Mother asked in a voice which implied that yes would be an imposition and that no would be a cut.

"Why—I—" It hadn't occurred to Ann that she would stay with her mother.

"Let her come to our house for a few days, anyway," Birdie begged. "She can lounge around the swimming pool and take the sun."

"I could use a tan," Ann said. She knew that Mother would capitulate and let her go to Birdie's, but the concession must be Mother's, made in her own way.

Ann dragged herself out of the car and followed her mother into the apartment building, up to the tenth-floor apartment overlooking hills, valleys and a large portion of the city. Ann guessed that Abe paid plenty for Mother's view and thought that it was lucky he could afford it. Then she noticed her father's photograph on the mantel, the same one that had always been on the mantel at home. It gave her a funny feeling to see it again. Whenever she thought of her father she thought of this picture, and seeing it was like seeing him. He never grew older, never smiled and his face still had the same patient expression as though he were listening to Mother's instructions on how to look before the photographer snapped him. She wished she could have known him better. Did Mother ever know him? ("Your poor, dead father's will proved he didn't trust his wife to handle her own money!")

On an impulse, Ann took the picture in her hands and held it close to her as she used to when she was a girl, but her mother, busy getting something, didn't see this.

"I thought you might like to sign my book before anybody else's out here." Mother was holding a copy of The Heart Being Hungry. "It's not the book I'd hoped you'd write, but it's a book, and you did write it."

Ann swallowed. This was too much. The strain of being met, the interminable luncheon, and now this. She could have sat on the floor and wept. "Mother, you don't know what this means to me."

"Write something nice. The lady next door wants to borrow my copy."

Ann wondered how much nearer she could get to the brink of

207

hysteria without tumbling in. She opened her purse, and took out her fountain pen.

"Begin, 'For my dear mother,'" Mother said.

Ann wrote: "For my dear Mother: without whom this book would never have been written. Ann Long." Then she said, "I'll call you tonight, Mother," and fled the room.

"Look, Aunt Ann!" Raymond said. "The lights are in the bottom of the pool. At night they all light up in different colors. It looks real—" He couldn't use the word *stud* now that his aunt had appropriated it. "I'll put the lights on for you tonight," he said importantly.

"I can hardly wait," Ann assured him.

She was lying on a chaise longue beside the swimming pool, in her swim suit at last, hoping to catch the tag-end of the afternoon sun. It was the first peaceful moment she'd had all day. She studied the house. It was like Abe's car: elegant and impressive. Ann's room looked down on an immense flower garden flanked on either side by a row of tall, pointed junipers and she thought that Birdie had understated the grandeur of her house and garden in her letters. This was an estate.

Ann watched Raymond darting about at the far end of the pool. Whenever she saw Birdie's lovely children she thanked God that Abe Zelkin had been persistent in the face of Mother's stone-wall opposition. Birdie herself seemed so thoroughly content that Ann decided to postpone the lecture on diet until she had returned to New York and could deliver it by letter.

Birdie walked over, smiling, to where she lay in the sun. She said, "We're so happy to have you here, Ann. We'd be just as glad even if you weren't famous."

"I'm not famous," Ann said, "but speaking of fame and fortune, I didn't know you were this rich. Abe doesn't strike me as being the kind of person who lives over his head—Mother to the contrary notwithstanding."

"Abe's done very well. There are thirty-nine Full-O'-Fashion shops now." Birdie purposely changed the subject. "Do you think Lorraine will turn out to be a pretty girl?"

"Of course. She's pretty already. How old is she?"

208

"Eleven. Almost twelve. Raymond's nine."

"It doesn't seem possible."

Ann guessed that they were both thinking the same thing, now. *If Mother had had her way.*

Birdie said aloud, "Wasn't Mother typical when she asked you to stay with her?"

"Yes. She didn't really want me to. She just wanted me to say I wouldn't."

Ann decided not to mention the autographed copy.

"I told you your room was waiting for you. We hope you stay a long time. We're never crowded and besides, Abe keeps a room at the Ambassador for such emergencies as store managers when they come to town. They used to end up out here when they couldn't get accommodations; but Abe got tired of that, so he just took a room at the Ambassador by the year. He charges it off his income tax."

"I don't know enough about income taxes," Ann said, "and I've certainly got to start learning."

"Ann—"

Ann knew when Birdie had something on her mind, and there was something on her mind that had nothing to do with income taxes.

"What?"

"You haven't said much about John. Is everything all right with you two? I don't want to pry, but I hope you feel you can talk to me. You were both so much in love when we saw you five years ago."

Ann nodded. "Everything's all right. I love John even more now than I did then, if that's possible."

And that, Ann thought to herself, is the gospel truth.

It was Saturday when Bill Haley called her.

"Willing to talk to me?" he asked. "I'm two days early."

"I couldn't have waited another day," Ann said. "I was going to call you. I've missed you."

"Thanks. You sound normal again. Have you heard from John?"

"Yes. He swears he's leaving the first of the week."

209

"Ann." Pause. "Could I come out there now?"

"Why, sure, Bill. Anything wrong?"

"No." Pause. "Not exactly. I just want to talk to you about something that's come up unexpectedly. I'll be there right away."

"Come ahead."

Ann took off her bathing suit, took a quick shower, and put on a white piqué dress she'd bought yesterday at Magnin's. Birdie got her kicks from going shopping, a kind of sport that Ann never had time to indulge in. Birdie had to visit at least three shops before reaching a decision which usually entailed a return to one of the first two. It had taken the better part of the morning to find this simple dress which Ann, left to herself, could have purchased in less than half an hour. The white of the dress was a perfect foil for her skin after these first few days of sun.

"What a layout," Bill said as soon as he walked inside the house. Ann remembered that circular, oversized bed of Bill's and could understand his being impressed by this display.

She said, "The terrace and swimming pool are out through there."

He started to look outside, but halfway there he jerked his head around to take a second look at Ann. "Hey! You look different! What you been doing to yourself?"

"Stuffing, sun-bathing and sparring with my mother. Could anything be healthier?" She confirmed her original impression of his own appearance. "What have you been doing to yourself? You look awful. Maybe we'd better trade places. You stay here and fight with Mother and I'll move to the Sheraton West." She was disturbed at seeing Bill looking so dissipated and wrung out.

"You can have California," he said venomously.

"What's happened? You sounded on the telephone as though something had gone wrong. Do the Royal Pictures people want their money back?"

"No. They're nuts about the book's movie possibilities. They think they got it cheap, according to the prices best-sellers are bringing these days. The presentation banquet's set for Thursday night at the Ambassador. The leads in the picture ought to be announced

210

then; they may even be there in person. Don't worry—the publicity men will squeeze the occasion dry."

"Hooray! Maybe I'll get to meet a movie star after all. My niece talks about nothing else. She won't be happy until she's touched someone who's touched Rock Hudson. I took Birdie and the children to the studio with me, but Rock was nowhere to be found, so we settled for Jack Lemmon. I love his grin. It's almost as nice as yours."

"You flatter me," Bill said, grinning self-consciously.

"As a matter of fact, everybody was nice to me. Especially one Mr. Hirsch who offered me a job."

"A job?"

"Helping adapt the book for the screen. Fifteen hundred a week."

"Good Lord! That's *money*."

"I've *got* money. I've got $140,000 plus royalties from sales." Ann smiled. "I'll bet I've got more ready cash than Rock Hudson."

"You mean you're not going to take them up on it?"

"I haven't decided. You still haven't told me what's worrying you."

"I'm not worried."

"You're as nervous as a you-know-what in church. For heaven's sake, sit down. You're making *me* nervous."

Bill walked over to a coffee-table with a candy dish on it, picked up a piece of candy, then dropped it back into the dish. He braced himself as a diver does before going off the high board and then he turned and said, "I know this is a lot to ask of you, Ann, but would you be willing to go through just one more autographing?"

Ann was relieved. Without knowing why, she expected something worse. "Is *that* all?"

"Well, not quite. It's Bud Johnson's idea. After all, he *is* the West Coast representative, and a party would boost the book's sales out here."

Ann frowned. "When does Mr. Johnson want to schedule it? I'm not sure how long I'll stay here after the banquet's over."

"Don't call him Mr. Johnson. Everybody calls him Bud. He likes Thursday—the afternoon of the Royal Pictures' banquet. Wednesday's Memorial Day and that's out. Thursday's a natural

211

tie-in to the studio's publicity. But it'll be a rough day for you, and that's why I came out here today. Ads and spot announcements have to be prepared *if* you say you'll do it. I told them that all you'd agreed to was the southern trip and that you were tired and—"

"Who's 'them'?"

"Well—" Bill put out his cigarette and lit another. "The autographing would be at Baker's. They have a large book department with plenty of space for a crowd, and . . ." He fidgeted, plainly thinking about what to say next. "Well, Bud thought he ought to come out here and talk to you, but I figured it would be better for me to come alone because—"

"Oh, Bill, come to the point! Because of *what?*" Ann had never seen him look so miserable. He had a guilty expression, as though he were selling her a bill of goods and knew it. She walked over to him and took hold of his hand, surprised to feel how cold and damp it was. She said, "What *is* it, Bill?"

"Well—." He took a deep breath, then finished his sentence in one quick exhalation. "Madge is the manager of Baker's book department."

"Madge who?"

Bill stared at her, not wanting to repeat the name. "Madge *who?* Madge King. Madge Long. Madge—" He was almost shouting at her. "God-damn-it, *I* don't know what to call her!"

Ann stared at him, her own face expressionless, and he said, "Don't look at me like that, Ann. I *know*, and I told Bud I'd have to talk to you first. He doesn't understand, you see—doesn't know about Madge and Jack. Hell, I don't think he's even read the book."

Ann's lips tightened. "Whose idea was this in the first place? Bud's?"

Bill had the look of a child confessing a major indiscretion. "No, it wasn't. This sounds incredible, but it was Madge's idea. The minute I told her you were in town she wanted the autographing party in her department. I threw cold water on it at first, but then Bud came in and—"

Ann interrupted, "You've seen her? You knew she was in Los Angeles?"

"Yes."

212

"Then why didn't you say something?"

"Why *say* anything? If this hadn't come up you wouldn't have had to know she was here."

"Does John know?"

"I'm not sure."

"Tell me the truth, Bill."

"Well, yes, he does. He doesn't know where she is, though. Just that she's working some place in L.A. That was she who called him Christmas Eve to wish him a Merry Christmas."

"Oh."

"My God, Ann. Don't look like that. If you think for a minute that she's . . . If you let yourself believe . . ." He had a wild look. She was no more than ten feet away from him, yet now he was screaming. "If you think she's still got a hold on Jack you're crazy! She hasn't changed a bit. She's—she's *common!* She's just trash. That's all she is. Trash!"

Ann stood very still.

"Be quiet, Bill. Birdie will be coming down to see what's the matter. Go on outside to the swimming pool and I'll bring you a drink."

He walked onto the terrace and sat down on a glider and in a minute she came with the Scotch. "I didn't bother with the ice. I just put in some water from the tap."

"Swell. Thanks. I need this."

"It seems that Madge has the same effect on all men. You all need it." She wished she hadn't said it.

"I'm sorry I yelled like such a damned fool," Bill said. "It wasn't for your benefit. I was yelling at myself." His face that no longer had its boyish appeal was drawn and sad and he looked as though he might be going to cry. "I've let Bess down, and I hate myself for it. Bess is the nicest thing that ever happened to me, and I've let her down something awful."

"You have not," Ann said. "You wouldn't be admitting these things if you had. And besides, Bess is the one to say if you've let her down—not you."

"Remember Mabel in Dallas? Mabel's fine and good—and yet I told her about things being different with me since I'd met Bess. Then I come out here and meet a dirty *slut—*"

213

"Shut up, Bill. I'm not going to listen to you talk this way."

"You've *got* to listen. In that stubborn, one-track mind of yours you've confused that girl in your book with Madge King. Because that girl changed for the better you think Madge did, too. Well, she hasn't. She's just as rotten, and dirty, and—"

"I don't want to hear it."

"—low. So low. She has a way about her to make you wild for it, and then you feel dirty all over when you—"

"Shut up, Bill! I said I didn't want to hear any more."

"That's why I told Bud I wanted to come out here alone to ask you about the autographing. I thought maybe if you could see for yourself that Madge is still Madge, it might help to set you straight. Oh, hell. I don't know what to do. I just wish that damned banquet was over and I could go home."

Neither of them said anything. The glider squeaked as it rocked to and fro. Ann finished her drink.

"Want another?" she asked.

"Yeah," Bill said. She got it for him. She started to sit down, changed her mind and walked to the pool, had the insane idea to jump in, and backed away in a hurry. She envied people who could obtain even a token release from tension by smoking, pacing, nail-biting, but it was her luck to do it the hard way. She walked quickly toward Bill and stood facing him. "Tell Bud Johnson— and Madge—that I'd love to autograph at Baker's Thursday. Ask them if two o'clock's all right. And tell Bud to ask us all to lunch first."

Bill stared up at her. "Are you serious?"

"It's not exactly my idea of something to joke about."

"Now, Ann, I don't want you to do anything you don't think you ought to."

"That's a strange speech from someone who came here to talk me into it."

"Oh hell," Bill said, "*I* don't know what's happening. I feel like tying this glider around my neck and jumping into the deep end of that pool."

"That would be silly. It's a perfectly good glider even if it does squeak. Anyhow, you'd better be getting back to town. Have you got a car?"

214

"Yes. It's in the driveway."

"Madge's?"

He said it as though she was pulling the answer out of him with pliers. "Yes."

"How many copies of the book does she have on hand?"

"Four or five hundred."

"Tell her to double it. I expect to make her lots of money."

"Stop it, Ann."

"And don't forget to call me about that lunch."

Then her voice lost its intensity and she looked at him kindly. "Bill, it's never too late to face an issue squarely. Don't you forget that."

He kissed her on the cheek and walked quickly toward the car.

She waited just long enough for him to be out of hearing distance and then went to the telephone and dialed long distance. "I'm calling Miss Bess Frankel in New York. Person to person." She gave the number.

She got a break. Bess was home. "Bess. This is Ann."

"I thought you were in California."

"I am."

"Oh!" Bess got excited. "What's the matter?"

"Plenty's the matter. Can you get a plane for Los Angeles right away?"

"I guess I could, but what's wrong? Are you all right?"

"Yes. I'm all right. It's Bill. The poor sap's mixed up and may do something foolish. And he's so in love with you it isn't funny."

"Is it too late, Ann?" Bess asked desperately.

"No. Not if you come out today. He—he's slipped."

"I'll be there. His ex-wife?"

"No. An old friend. Remember, though, you're the one he loves. He thinks he's let you down. I can't tell you all about it now; Bill's your responsibility—and besides, I've got trouble of my own. Just come out to Birdie's house when you get here." She tacked on a question, "How's Dr. Darnell?"

"He finished with me Monday. I'm all through."

"That's just fine. Tell him to save the space for a new customer —a girl with a case history that'll knock his eyes out."

215

"*Are* you all right?" Bess asked again.

"Yes, I'm all right," Ann repeated in a voice which said clearly that she couldn't remember when she had been more all wrong.

21

John called from the airport Thursday morning at ten.

"Birdie? This is John. Let me speak to Ann."

"Hi, John. This is Bess."

"Bess?"

"*Bess*. Bess Frankel. I'm out here."

"Why, Bess, when did you leave New York?"

"Saturday. I tried to call you but you were out. Here's Ann."

"John?"

"Hello, Ann."

She was all-over-goosepimples. Physiologically, his two words had accelerated her pulse, constricted her vocal chords, started her stomach churning, or as the teenagers would say, she was "all shook up."

"Are you there, honey?" he said.

"Sure I'm here. Where the hell are you?"

"I'm the hell at the Los Angeles airport. How do I get to Birdie's place?"

"You . . . no, there's no point in your coming here. I won't be here. There's a luncheon, then an autographing party at two, and tonight's the studio dinner."

"I told you. I should have waited."

"You've waited too long already. Mother's convinced you've ditched me. And this is the only day I've had anything social to do since I've been here. I'm so homesick for you, darling. I was going home tonight—already got my reservation."

216

"Then I'll go right back and meet you at Idlewild."

"You'll do nothing of the kind!" Her mind darted like a bird in a cage. She hadn't included John in her plans for this trying day and she wasn't sure he should get entangled in the luncheon and the autographing party.

"I'm waiting, Baby."

"Take the limousine to the Ambassador Hotel. Abe's driving me downtown as soon as I get dressed. I'll meet you there at eleven-thirty."

"Ambassador?"

"Yes. You need a shave, don't you?"

"How'd you know?"

"I'm clairvoyant. By the time you've had your shave at the barber shop I'll be waiting for you in the lobby near the reservations desk. Don't change your shirt, though. Abe keeps a room at the Ambassador. We'll take your bags up and you can change there."

"I'll have to hurry if I'm going to catch the limousine."

"All right, but wait a minute. There's something important I want to say to you. I always get left with it after you've hung up."

"What's that?"

"I love you, my darling."

"*That's* the way I like to hear my girl talk!"

She saw him first, sitting in one of those fan-backed cane chairs, his face shaved, his shoes shined and looking much too handsome to be left alone in a hotel lobby. She said, "Waiting for someone, mister?" and he jumped to his feet, took her in his arms and kissed her.

"Right here in front of God and the room clerk?" she asked, not caring.

"I don't hear any complaints," he said and stepped back to look her over. "Don't ever leave me again," he said slowly.

"Don't worry, darling. You'll never know how close I came to quitting in the middle of the tour and going home. My, you've got a new suit!"

"Yep. Have to look sharp. Meeting the woman I love today!"

If she was slow with a smile for his compliment it was because

217

she knew a great deal more than he did about whom he was meeting today.

"Abe's parking the car," she said, very fast, "and he'll be here in a minute, but I have a key to his room, so let's get a bellboy to take the bags up. That one there is mine."

It was more than a room. It was a modest suite, with a bedroom and bath opening off the small sitting room. The decor was typically Californian: bright sunlight colors with yellow predominant. It was like an apartment instead of the usual suite. It did not have that transient look.

As soon as the bellboy was gone, John kissed her again. "Feels like a honeymoon," he said.

"It's funny," she said, "but you know, when I'm not with you hotel rooms do terrible things to me. When you're here it's all right."

"Happens to me, too," John said. "It's being alone, and wanting to be with someone that does it. It's worse for me in hotels than in motels. The higher the altitude the lonelier I get." He walked into the bedroom looked around and came back. "You say Abe keeps this place all year 'round? Must cost him plenty."

"His store managers stay here. He's got thirty-nine stores and Birdie says he charges this off his income tax as a company expense."

John came toward her. "Speaking of company, what's Bess doing in L.A.?"

"She got homesick for Bill and, by the way, they won't be at the luncheon. They're splashing around the swimming pool like a couple of kids. You'll see them tonight at the banquet."

"Will I?"

"You *will!* That's why I wouldn't let you go to Brentwood from the airport. I want you right here with me. I brought along my dinner dress and a few necessities, and after the autographing we can have the room to ourselves, then go on to the banquet together."

John shook his head. "It's your party tonight, honey. Include me out. Please."

"A party for me is a party for you," she said firmly. "Make me happy, darling. Say you'll come."

218

"All right, if you put it that way. I'll come."

She kissed him lightly. "Just for that I'll show you what I'm wearing for the movie magnates." She opened her traveling case and lifted out a long white silk brocade dress. "It's the most expensive dress I ever owned. It was $295."

"What!"

"I got it on sale for $140 but the original price-tag was still on it. See?" She held it to herself in the age-old gesture women employ when they want others to imagine the way a dress will look when they get it on. Her hands smoothed the waistline at the approximate place, and she leaned over slightly as she explained, "It's low-cut up here, and has a drape along here. You'll see it tonight."

She was putting her things away when Abe knocked loudly on the door. John opened it; they shook hands amiably and right away there was a good feeling between them all.

"You look the same as ever," John said, observing how little gray there was in Abe's black, wavy hair.

"Five years older," Abe said, smilingly pointing to the first hint of what would some day be a bay-window. He took a key out of his pocket and handed it to John. "Here's your key to the room. Ann already has hers. Later on this afternoon you two'll probably want to—" He stopped, embarrassed, and Ann walked in, just in time to hear what he was trying to say. She kissed him on the cheek. "I nominate you for brother-in-law of the year and you've got to have lunch with us, Abe, so no excuses! We come to California once in a blue moon and you can take this one noon to join us for lunch. *Please.*"

Abe was about to protest his way out when John joined in. "Come along, Abe, and keep me company. I'll need someone to talk to while this one's being lionized."

Ann frowned and then made up Abe's mind for him. "Abe's coming. It's a party. So let's have a drink to celebrate."

"Now? Before lunch?" Abe asked in surprise.

"Now," she answered emphatically. "I need it."

"Okay. I keep a bottle of Scotch in here." Abe opened a small cabinet. "Will running-ice-water do for a mix?"

"Make mine straight with a water chaser," John said.

219

"Mine, too," Ann said. "And make it strong. It's going to be a long, long day."

She waited until Abe had gone for the car before she dared tell John who would be at the luncheon. They were standing near the curb in front of the hotel when she said brightly, "Guess who's having lunch with us?"

"How would I know? I don't even know where we're going."

"To the tea-room of Baker's. *Now* guess."

"You, me, Abe—and Jayne Mansfield."

"Nope. Close, though." She tried to sound flippant. "Madge!"

John looked down at her and instinctively bent over as if to hear better. "Who?"

"*Madge!* Madge King. She's not at Troxell's any more; she's manager of the book department at Baker's."

He turned and took a step away from the street. "I'm not going."

"Why not?" She had her hand on his arm.

"Because. God-damn-it, just because!"

"Listen, John." She had to talk fast because Abe was due any minute. "If I can take this, you ought to be able to, and I've promised Bill to go through with it. Bud Johnson, the West Coast traveler for Fortune House is supposed to be a nice guy and he hasn't the faintest idea of the mess he's caused. He put Bill on the spot—"

"And Bill put *you* on a spot," John interrupted angrily. "No wonder Haley preferred to splash in the pool. He helped arrange the thing and then took a powder—the sonuvabitch."

They were talking very quickly. "Don't blame Bill," Ann said. "He didn't know you were coming in today."

"But he knew what he was letting you in for!"

"Yes, but he gave me a chance to refuse and I told him I'd do it."

"*Why?*"

"Because Madge herself wanted the party. It was her idea. I wasn't going to give her the satisfaction of thinking I was afraid to face her . . . and don't *you* be afraid, either."

"I'm not afraid of Madge. I just don't want to go. I don't want to see her."

"Yes, but surely you *can* take it if I can." She was leaning against

220

him, holding onto his arm now with both hands. To a passerby, she thought, it might have appeared to be a feminine reflex, the woman holding tightly to the man she loved, but to her, holding him here was almost like holding onto her marriage.

"What are you trying to do—*tackle* me?" John said.

"I'm taking no chances."

"Then loosen up. I'm not going to run away."

"You'd better not."

"Oh, God! Why did I ever let my wife write a book?"

"Because you love me, darling. Isn't that reason enough?"

Before he could answer, Abe drove up and opened the front door and Ann pushed John in.

"Now I know why you took that double snifter a minute ago," he mumbled into her ear.

"Wish I'd brought the bottle," she said under her breath.

"You two love-birds stop whispering," Abe said. "I'll bet you're making plans for later today."

"How'd you guess?" Ann said, wincing as John pinched her in vulnerable territory.

As they waited inside the store for Abe they saw the huge photo of Ann hung over the elevators.

"I'd like to have that picture when they're through with it," John said. "It would make a peachy mural for the living room."

"Go to hell," Ann said, reading the words Mezzanine Book Department on the announcement under the picture. She thought, *at least it's not on seven.*

"I feel like Daniel," John said, "only this time the lions are going to win."

A woman rushed up to Ann. "Oh, Mrs. Long! You look just like your picture. What a break for me. I've been keeping my eye on these elevators hoping you'd get here before two. Will you sign mine now?"

"Why, yes. I'd love to."

"Make it Grayce Underwood. Grayce is spelled G-r-a-y-c-e." Ann wrote as Grayce gushed, "I have a collection of autographed copies. I wish you could come to my house to see them."

John looked as though he might throw up.

221

Several people closed in on them, some with books which they shoved at Ann who signed them quickly. A tall woman in a red picture-hat said, "Would you wait here a minute while I run up and buy a copy?" And Ann said, locating Abe, "I'm awfully sorry, we're late for a luncheon. Come to the book department at two and I'll be glad to sign your book there." "But it'll be so *crowded!*" the red picture-hat insisted.

"I *hope* so!" Ann laughed good-naturedly. *Not half so crowded for you, sister, as it will be for me!* She pulled John toward Abe who had a stunned expression on his face, and herded them both ahead of her to the staircase, saying, "We'll walk."

Abe was awed. "My God, you're like a movie star! Except the people have to buy a book before you give them your signature. What a racket. Maybe I should put in book departments in my shops."

As he reached the mezzanine, John collided with a woman who turned obliquely as he was trying to pass her. "Next time you write a book," he said to Ann, "describe someone as being as unpredictable as the way a woman shopper's going to turn in a department store."

"I thought you were opposed to my writing books?"

"I'm more opposed to women shoppers who suddenly change their courses."

"Calm down, we're practically there. I can see the book department from here."

"And I thought Korea was rough," John said as they plowed on through budget dresses, stationery, greeting cards and scrapbooks.

It was more than ten years since Ann had seen Madge, but she was doing the same thing now that she'd been doing then: squeezing a man's arm as she talked to him.

"Damned if she's not still selling *Light from Many Lamps,*" John muttered. "Bet she's telling him she always keeps a copy of it on her bedside table."

This isn't happening, Ann thought, it's a trick of memory. But she did not dare allow him to see her face.

Madge still hadn't noticed them and Ann used her few seconds' advantage to start at the top and work down. Madge still wore her

222

hair short, too short, and it hadn't been red before. Too many tint jobs had made it brittle. But she was not so thin as she used to be and the curves she'd acquired were becoming—damn it. She was wearing a girdle all right, but Ann wasn't certain whether or not she had on a brassiere. She figured Madge's age—thirty and five was thirty-five and nine was forty-four . . .

Madge looked up just as John cleared his throat. He said, "Hello, Madge."

Ann had the same prickly feeling of guilt she'd felt years ago in the other book department. Once more she had the upper hand and instead of following through she wanted to run away.

"How are you, Madge?" John said calmly, putting out his hand.

Madge was absolutely, completely stunned. The easy assurance she'd had a moment ago when talking to the man by her side vanished.

"Hello, Jack," she said weakly, taking a step toward him. "Where did you blow in from?"

"New York City. This is Ann."

The girls smiled and nodded. There was no trace of recognition in Madge's face as she gave Ann a fine-tooth-combed inspection that photographed everything: Italian pumps, silk print dress, black patent bag, white gloves, gold button ear-rings, ears showing. *Wonder what she's like in bed?*

"I'm Bud Johnson," the man by Madge said, shaking hands with John and Ann. There was an awkward pause.

John decided to carry the ball. "This is my brother-in-law, Abe Zelkin. Mr. Johnson and Miss . . . uh . . ."

"King," Madge said.

"We brought Abe in Bill Haley's place," Ann said evenly. "A friend of Bill's came to town and he couldn't make it. He said he'd call you."

"He called."

Another flat silence.

"I didn't know you people knew each other," Bud Johnson said.

"Oh yes—for years and years," Madge said, looking at John and doing some arithmetic of her own. Twenty-three and five is twenty-eight and nine is thirty-seven.

223

"I liked your book, Ann," she said so sweetly that only a woman could tell the icing was sticky.

You would say that in front of him! Aloud, Ann said, "I'm so glad you did. I had no idea when I wrote it, it would ever be a best-seller."

A couple edged nearer the group and the woman said timidly to Madge, "Miss King, I wonder if we could jump the gun and have Mrs. Long sign our copy now?"

"Why, of course," Madge said, and Ann remembered that same courteous warmth in her voice when she had talked to a customer those years ago.

"Mrs. Long, Mr. and Mrs. Pike, two of my best customers. And this is Mr. Long, Mr. Johnson, and Mr.—?"

"Zelkin," Abe said.

Ann shook hands with the couple and wrote a shaky "With Best Wishes."

Other customers started gathering around her now, and she signed a dozen copies in five minutes before she looked up to see where John was. He was perched on the end of a display table, one foot on the floor and the other one swinging lazily, and Madge was talking to him. Her finger tips touched his arm and there was an intent, serious look on her face.

Ann managed to get the "g" on Long, then smiled her phony smile, said to the next-in-line, "I'm sorry. My friends are waiting for me. I'll have to finish autographing after lunch," and walked over to the table where John was. "We'd better eat and get it over with," she said to Madge. "That way I can get an early start."

Abe, who had picked up a copy of Ann's book and was reading from it, said, "Did I hear 'eat'? I second the motion. More than my heart's hungry. I'm hungry all over."

"He's cute," Madge said, laughing, and then she turned to Bud Johnson and said, "I forgot to tell you, Bud, Jack's a big shot with Laverty and Clarke. Sales manager."

How in the hell did she know that? John thought.

Who told her that? Ann thought.

"Well, that takes the cake," Bud Johnson said. "The biggest seller Fortune House has had in ten years turns out to be written by the wife of our competition!"

224

"Do they serve drinks in the tea-room?" John asked suddenly. "No," Madge said. "But I keep a pint in the bottom right hand drawer of my desk. Should I get it, Mr. Zelkin?"

"Call me Abe. Why don't we go someplace else where we can order a drink?"

"I can change it," Madge said, looking at Ann. "You be the judge. What you say goes."

"It's not that important," Ann said, shrugging. "Who needs a drink, anyway?"

Who didn't? she wondered.

They sat at a round table in an inconspicuous corner of the tea-room and the *Los Angeles Times* photographer, whom the store's public relations firm had contacted, complained he had trouble finding them. "You look just like everybody else," he said in a voice which implied authors were supposed to look different. "You'll have to scoot closer to each other at one end of the table so I can get you all in." They scooted close to each other; the man used a second flash bulb ("Let's smile just one more time!"), then wrote down the information for his cut-line: reading from left to right: Ann Long, author; Dwayne Johnson of Fortune House Publishers; Abe Zelkin; Madge King, Manager of Baker's Book Department; and John Long, husband of the author.

After the photographer left they fanned out again and finished their lunch. As they left the tea-room Ann tried to remember what she'd just eaten. She remembered Bud Johnson thanking her with embarrassing profusion for consenting to the autographing and she had the impression that Madge and Abe got along famously. At one point they were telling each other stories, the last lines of which had to be whispered. When she tried to recall something John had said she remembered only that he kept tapping his knife on his plate nervously.

Although it wasn't two o'clock, people were waiting for her in the book department. The lines the salespeople had tried to form suddenly funneled themselves into a polygon which pushed against her, and although Ann could see sales slips in some of the books, she had a feeling of disorganized confusion about this party. But still, even though it was a jumbled system, the old pattern emerged

225

and she knew without thinking what she must say and do. "Miss Long, could you write something nice for my mother? She's eighty-three years old." *Certainly.* "Write anything in mine. Just so it's in your handwriting." *Smile.* "Tell me, Mrs. Long, does your book have a happy ending?" *Did you have to ask me that?* "I'd rather you discover that for yourself!"

She signed books steadily for a full hour, missing Bill's expert blocking. Bud Johnson didn't have Bill's knack for moving people along pleasantly but firmly. She stood up a moment to stretch—but really to look around, and saw with an inward start that Madge and John were missing, but a few minutes later someone placed a tall glass of cola in front of her.

"Brought this from the tea-room for you," John said, leaning over her to set it down, purposely brushing her breast as he did so. Suddenly she felt so much better that she returned to "With Best Wishes" after a series of plain "Ann Long's."

"How do you spell your name?"

"Lipsitz. L-i-p-s-i-t-z. The first name is Melinda."

She worked automatically, reaching for the book, looking up, raising her eyebrows ever so slightly, smiling, looking down, signing the title page, handing the open book to the owner while the ink was drying. Then she would reach for another, look up, raise her eyebrows ever so slightly, smile, look down, sign the title page and hand it over. There was a rhythm to it which restrained even the most anxious book buyer from interrupting. When her fountain pen needed a fresh cartridge she called to John, "I put the box of cartridges in your pocket," and gave him her pen to refill. While waiting for him to give it back, a bird-like creature hopped almost on top of her and chirped, "I reviewed your book for our study club and someone asked me how long it took you to write it. I guessed five years. Was I far wrong?"

John walked up with the pen in time to hear Ann say soberly, "*Six* years. I re-wrote it six times." She calmly accepted the pen, pretending not to notice his double-take.

At four o'clock people were still coming and the store's loudspeaker system was still repeating every ten minutes a recorded announcement of the autographing on the mezzanine. Ann judged there were no more than a hundred copies left now, and she kept

226

signing these spares between personal autographs. When the customers began to bite into that hundred Bud said, "We'll barely have enough left for the telephone and mail orders. I wish we had a couple of hundred more for you to sign for stock."

"May God have mercy on your soul," Ann said wearily. During the next lull she asked John, looking around, "When did Abe leave? I didn't see him go."

"I'm not sure," John said. "He and Madge were going to have a drink in her office about the time you ran out of ink. Guess he left after that."

"No point in your staying here any longer," Ann said. "Take a cab to the hotel and wait for me there. I'll be through soon. Have you got your key to the room?"

John fished in his pocket for it and found it. "Thanks, sweetheart. I swore I'd stick until you released me, but thanks. I'll just look into Madge's office and tell her goodbye."

He's come a long, long way. I'm glad I made him come today. Now I know for sure. Ann thought.

He walked out of Madge's office, and said, "Madge said she'll be with you in a minute. I'll run along now." She smiled goodbye to him, then saw Madge's lipstick smear, and removed one of the "long"s from the distance he'd traveled.

The last customer had been waiting so that she could be the last and as always when an autographing was almost over, Ann found herself weak and trembly. She only heard the woman say quietly, "Mrs. Long, your portrait of Mona was drawn from life, wasn't it?"

"Why, no. All of my characters are fictitious," Ann protested, trying to sound convincing. The woman had an appealing face and Ann thought fleetingly that here was a person she would like to know better—another time, another place.

"That's hard to believe," the woman continued. "Mona is the realest person I've ever read about in a book."

"Thank you," Ann said mechanically, not wanting to encourage her. She autographed the book, handed it over and started to get up from her chair.

"Why, Mrs. Long," the woman said in a surprised voice. "Did

227

you do this on purpose? I thought your first name was Ann. You've written: With Best Wishes—*Norma* Long."

"I'm sorry," Ann said. Many seconds passed before she could continue. "I'll sign another copy for you."

"Oh no! I want this one!" the woman insisted, and there was a knowing smile on her face as she added, "I wouldn't have it any other way."

22

WHEN she returned to the hotel room she found John in his shorts walking around barefoot. He had taken the spread off the bed, folding it neatly and placed it on a chair. "Nudist camp?" she asked.

"I'm a slave," he said, bowing low. "This is all the clothes my mistress gives me."

"What do you give her?"

"I give her not so much really."

"You're just modest."

"Well, I draw her bath. I help her take off her dress when she's too tired to take it off herself." He kissed her and helped her with the dress. "And I have drinks to hand her when she returns from autograph parties."

She took the drink he'd fixed, this time with White Rock and ice; then as he was hanging up her dress she went into the bathroom and found her bath drawn as she liked it: tub half full, water tepid. She took her drink with her into the tub and to keep her company John moved the chair from the writing desk into the bathroom and sat on it with his feet propped onto the tub's side.

"Isn't this cozy?" he asked.

228

Ann smiled at him. "Should I be polite and ask you to join me?" "No thanks. Either I have a tub of my own—or I don't play. The least they could do for unwashed guests is have two tubs—one his, one hers." He studied her a moment. "I've been thinking about something you said in a letter about hotel rooms smacking of sin."

"Why? Do you feel sinful?"

"Very."

"So do I. It's always all over the room, I tell you. And, as you say, it's worse when you're alone. Sin is a commodity, like Kleenex. People bring it with them, and leave behind what they don't use up. There ought to be a sign: *Stop*. Have you forgotten anything? Check your sin."

John laughed. "Don't blame the way I feel on the hotel room." He came to the tub, bent over, and kissed the back of her neck. "Tired?"

"Not so much as I thought I'd be. The drink helps, too. A while longer in this business and I'd be a toper. I thought you were the drinking member of this family, and here you've been a model of temperance."

"Saving my strength for my mistress—after her bath."

She looked down at the soap in her hand, "And what do you do for your mistress after her bath?"

"I do the not-so-much-really."

"John." She pinked around the ears.

"Don't act so prim. I happened to run across the somethings you placed in the medicine chest this morning. I presume it was you. Abe couldn't be *that* thoughtful!"

Ann was tempted to use this moment to tell him something that was on her mind. *"I may be spinning my wheels bringing anything at all, because I'm a full three weeks past due. It's probably a normal reaction from the strain of the tour, but—"* Instead, she said, "Fool," and blushed deeper. "You should be more subtle. Think of people in books—they don't talk like that."

"The hell with people in books," John said. He took her empty glass, and went on into the bedroom to fix fresh drinks. When she came into the bedroom she had a bath towel wrapped around herself.

229

"I couldn't see myself bringing a nightgown when I was only supposed to change my clothes," she explained.

"Who needs a nightgown in the daytime?" John asked, stepping out of his shorts.

She spoke softly. "Does your mistress ever tell you she thinks you're cute?"

"Sometimes. That comes later, though."

"Didn't you just fix new drinks?"

"That comes later, too."

"But—"

"Later!"

He was right. Who needs a nightgown in the daytime?

Ann lay on the bed with the sheet over her and John lay on top of the sheet, naked, his eyes closed.

"Isn't this bliss?" she sighed. "I couldn't move if the house detective walked in. How'll I ever make that banquet? No arms. No legs. No feet."

"Relax," he murmured. "Banquet's a whole hour away. You can be thirty minutes late and still be on time. All you'll miss is what the alcoholics call the Social Hour. Isn't the party here in the hotel?"

"Yes. You're coming, aren't you?"

John rolled over and propped himself up on his elbow. "I did everything you wanted me to do this afternoon. Now please, baby, can we do what I want tonight? I don't want to go. Let me meet you at Birdie's and Abe's when it's over. Bill and Bess can bring you home, and I'll take a cab there with my things. Please don't make me go."

"I won't make you go. See what a nice mistress you have? I'll see you at Birdie's as soon as it's over—and the sooner the better."

He kissed her. "How many copies did you sell all told?"

"About six hundred."

"And what did Madge say to you when you left?"

"She wanted to know what Abe did for a living."

"I mean about the books." He really wanted to know, she could see. "What did she say?"

"She said you look at least twenty years older."

230

"No."

"Yes. I'd be an awful jerk if I made that up."

"Did she thank you for coming?"

"No . . . but then I didn't expect her to. After all, I won and she lost, you know."

"Did she ask why I left early?"

"Yes. I said I didn't know. Now let me ask *you* a question, mister. What did you *two* talk about when you left the department this afternoon?"

"What do you think we talked about?"

"I think she said, 'It's no fun being married to a celebrity, is it?'"

"And what else?"

"She asked you if I'm as good in bed as she is."

"You're a little turned around," John said. "She asked me *that* one first."

"Maybe every first wife wonders if the second is better—just as every second wife wonders if she's as good as the first."

John hesitated. Then he said, half-smiling, "She said a man's always more considerate of his second wife than he is of his first."

"The bitch!" Ann made a face. Then she added reflectively, "She's still an attractive woman, though. I mean that."

John continued to lean on his elbow, and to look directly into her eyes. "Do you think *I* think she's attractive, Ann?"

She waited before answering. "No."

"Don't you want to know what else we talked about?"

"You know I do."

"She asked me if I knew what day today is, and I didn't."

"What day is it?"

"May 31st."

"So?"

"Fifteen years ago today, May 31st, 1947, was the day she and I got married. You mind if I have another drink?"

"No. Fix me another, too."

"Careful. You'll get tight."

"I'd never have thought she was the sentimental type," Ann said after he had handed her the drink.

"She isn't," John said. "She just remembered I used to be."

"How old were you then? Twenty-two?"

231

"Almost twenty-three. She was thirty. I always thought of her as being a lot smarter than I was. I guess she was."

"That's something you'd better never think about me."

"No, I don't. I think we're—equal."

"*That's* the way I like to hear my man talk," Ann said, parroting his expression. "Now kiss me one more time, darling. I've got to start getting ready."

One more time.

The affair was held in the large banquet room of the Ambassador and John was right. At seven-thirty, when Ann arrived, things were barely under way. People congregated near the bar at the drinking end of the room and Ann could tell from the cluster of tables at the dining end that more guests were still due to arrive.

Mr. Hirsch, watching the elevators for her, minimized the shock of stepping into so much noise from so many strangers by greeting her and steering her toward the bar for champagne and on their way he stopped long enough to point out Rock Hudson.

"Does he look like your Jerry?" he asked, and Ann almost said, "Jerry's taller and thinner," but her mental picture of Jerry somehow fused into that of John lying naked on the sheet and she found it impossible to give any answer at all. Mr. Hirsch didn't notice. He called to Rock Hudson and introduced him to Ann. The author and star chatted for a moment, then were interrupted by an exquisite, determined young woman who came over to them and literally dragged Rock Hudson away from Ann. Ann laughed at his boyish grimace and shrug as he let his insistent captor have her way. Ann wished for Lorraine. She'd know the girl's name. Ann needed a spotter. So many of the faces she'd seen, but their names wouldn't come to her.

"And that girl over there—" Ann said to Mr. Hirsch. "I know who she is—but—who *is* she?" He smiled. "Shirley MacLaine. She may well be your Norma."

"And is Elizabeth Taylor really going to play Mona?" she asked. He shook his head. "Don't pay attention to what you read in the papers. Everyone knows more about what's going on than the people involved do. The part isn't cast. I *hear* she is interested in

232

playing Mona, but nothing is definite—except that she was invited tonight and she didn't come."

Ann was enjoying herself now. Her fatigue was gone and she felt more composed, more responsive than she had for weeks. She actually felt smug, because here in the midst of these people who spelled glamour and success to millions she felt herself to be the most loved of all. Had Rock Hudson, for all his charm, helped zip up an evening dress tonight? Had Shirley MacLaine had the back of her neck sprayed with perfume by a tall man who was stark naked?

As the guests began to drift toward the banquet tables, Ann heard Mr. Hirsch say something about publicity pictures, then the photographers cornered Rock Hudson long enough to snap a picture of him and Ann together. Then there was one of Ann and Mr. Hirsch and after that one of Ann, Mr. Hirsch and a Mr. Zufelt, who seemed to be terribly important. The expression on Ann's face in this last picture must have been one of delighted surprise, for she spotted Bill and Bess just as the photographer flashed the picture and she rushed over to them.

"We're late," Bill said. "Couldn't help it." Ann thought she had never seen Bess more beautiful. "I'm going to ask Mr. Hirsch if we can't all sit together," she said.

"It's already arranged," Bill said. "I called Hirsch this morning and asked if I could bring my wife."

"Your *what?*" Ann gasped.

Then Bess held out her ring hand in the traditional gesture, and Ann kissed her, crying, "Bess! I am so glad."

"That's why we're late," Bess said. "We flew to Las Vegas to get married. Oh, Ann, I'm so *happy.*"

"It's sticking out all over you," Ann said laughing. "We'd better go to the table now, we're holding up the works. Later, I'll introduce you to Rock Hudson."

"I've got my Rock Hudson," Bess said, hugging Bill's arm.

"How did it go today?" Bill whispered as they neared the head table.

"We sold a lot of books."

"I don't mean that."

233

She touched his hand. "Bess said it for me, Bill. I've never been happier, either."

She turned to Mr. Hirsch who was holding her chair for her, sat down and looked at a vaguely familiar fruit cocktail.

There was much more champagne during dinner. And there were speeches. Mr. Hirsch had a word, Rock Hudson had a word, Mr. Zufelt had two. Even Bud Johnson had a word. And then Mr. Hirsch was introducing, "That rare phenomenon . . . that combination of beauty and brains . . . the author of *The Heart Being Hungry* . . . Miss Ann Long!"

Still glowing, Ann rose to her feet, thinking she should have been more frightened than she was. She had expected the entire evening to be like a disturbed dream, yet every detail of it was sharp and she felt as aware of this moment as if she were at her typewriter pounding out a radio spot. First of all, she said the thank-you that was expected of her, and then she picked up her champagne glass, knowing exactly what she wanted to say. "I propose a toast to the marriage of my book to your pictures. I hope they are as well mated as two friends of mine who were married today and who are here tonight—Mr. and Mrs. Bill Haley."

Everyone got up to toast the newlyweds. Bess was beaming, Bill was nonplussed. Ann thought they both looked as self-consciously foolish as any marital initiates. She smiled at them, then spoke a private toast to herself: *To Bill's marriage . . . Third time's the charm!*

Bess ran up to her as soon as the banquet was over. "Oh, Ann, I could have just *died!* Why did you do it?" Then she giggled. "I loved it, though."

"For all the tortures, for all the sufferings I ever imposed on you," Bill said, shaking his head dazedly, "you have repaid them all—with interest. Let us get out of here!"

Ann laughed. "I can't go now. Mr. Hirsch and Mr. Zufelt want to talk to me for a few minutes about the screen play."

"And the job?"

"Maybe. You two go on to Birdie's. John is already there. Tell him I won't be long."

Bill nodded. "That'll give us a chance to make the announcement before you steal our thunder."

234

"This is the happiest moment of my life," Bess repeated. "Wait 'till I tell my grandchildren Rock Hudson drank a toast to me on my wedding night!"

"Your grandchildren will think Rock Hudson was another book traveler," Bill said, taking Bess's arm. "See you later, Ann, and make it snappy!"

If Ann had known how soon the conference with Mr. Zufelt and Mr. Hirsch would be over she would have insisted that Bill and Bess wait for her. In a way, though, she was glad they had gone on to Birdie's ahead of her, for even though Bill had been joking about her stealing their thunder, she felt it was better for them to have all the spotlight for their announcement. As soon as Ann arrived Birdie would demand a play-by-play of the banquet.

Mr. Zufelt was surprised when she refused with thanks the chance to stay in Hollywood and work on the screenplay of her book and at first he was almost rude about it, apparently thinking she was holding out for more money. When $500 a week more than Mr. Hirsch had offered brought the same answer from her he acted amazed, and then touched.

"It's really not the money," Ann said. "You offered me too much the first time. The truth is I want to go home, Mr. Hirsch. I'd be unhappy out here and an unhappy writer isn't worth a dime."

"Well, anyway, think it over some more," Mr. Hirsch said, but she knew she had thought the last of it.

It occurred to her that she had forgotten to ask John to take home her things when he took his bags to Birdie's. He'd probably done so. Still, on the chance he had overlooked her dress in the closet and her "somethings" in the medicine chest, she decided to go by the room to make sure. It would be inconvenient not having them at Birdie's. As soon as she left the banquet room she took the elevator to the floor of their room, hurried down the hall, found the key in her evening bag and opened the door, but before she could reach for the light switch she heard a woman's voice from the bedroom: "Don't put on the light."

A hard chill went through her. She knew exactly who it was. She'd have known that voice any place. She'd have known it a

235

week ago, ten years ago. *"Cash or charge?"* She'd never forget the way Madge asked that routine question the day she'd bought *The Big Fisherman* in Troxell's book department. There could be no mistake now. She'd had a refresher course only this afternoon. *"I liked your book, Ann."*

Everything decent in her wound itself into a tight ball inside her stomach. Instinctively, she wanted to turn and run—as far away and quickly as she could. But something held her here—an indecent, compulsive something that urged her to switch on the light.

She stood at the threshold of the dark sitting room. Her eyes could make out dimly now, from the light in the hall behind her, the open bedroom door. She had her finger on the switch. *It's so easy. It takes no effort at all. I just flick this switch with my finger and I can see them. I want to see them. I want to see him with her. I want him always to remember that I saw him with her.*

"For Christ's sake, can't you take the hint?"

"Cash or charge?" . . . *"Cash or charge?"*

Slowly, oh-so-slowly, Ann took her hand from the wall. She turned and started away from the room, leaving the door open. Suddenly, so loud it might have been amplified by a thousand speakers, she heard Madge's laugh. It chased down the hall after her, pursued her all the way down the elevator shaft, through the lobby and out into the street.

She felt doped, drunk, but still her legs took her in the direction of a cab stand. She had no will, no sense of where nor why. The driver saw her coming, reached back and opened the door for her and she made it inside and fell back onto the seat.

"Where to, lady?"

She wanted to sit up, to tell him Birdie's address, but all that she could do was feel the wonderful relief of not having to talk. She rested her head against the cool leather upholstery. She was falling, falling, falling.

"You all right, lady?"

She had to talk, to say something to this man—he must think her drunk—but she did not want to talk and she simply did not care what he thought.

"I'm not drunk," she managed to whisper.

236

"No business of mine, lady. Where to?"

"I'm ill. I'll be all right in a minute. Would you lower this window?"

"Sure. Take it easy."

He got out, and leaning inside to roll down the back window, saw how white she looked. "Should I get a doctor?" he asked.

"No. Brentwood. 37 Canyon Drive."

He started the car; the cool air on her face felt good and she began to swim out of her numbness, to be aware of where she was and where she was going. Then with rationality there came a gradual aching: like a hospital patient who has been unconscious during an operation and then comes out of the anaesthetic to feel pain, she began to hurt. Her head ached and she desperately needed some kind of opiate. "Driver, I'm going to have to have a drink. If you can stop near a bar . . ."

"They won't let me bring a drink outside."

"Then I'll go in with you, and buy you one. Some place small."

"Okay. It's against regulations—but you sure look like you need it."

As he slowed down, looking for a bar, the ugly picture she was trying to black out crawled back into her mind. *John and Madge. Say it!* John and Madge! Madge had had her anniversary celebration after all! Ann remembered something she'd said to John earlier that afternoon. "After all, I won and she lost." She had spoken too soon. Madge had won and she had lost. She'd been right all along—there was an attachment which outlived divorce, and he'd succumbed to the old physical tug. *"Mrs. Long, your portrait of Mona. It was drawn from life, wasn't it?" "Why, no. All of my characters are fictitious."* Mona *had* been drawn from life. Face it. She should have said, "Oh, yes, indeed. Come over here and I'll introduce you to her."

"Here we are, lady. You sure you can make it?"

"Yes."

She had recovered her composure, now. She made it out of the cab on her own and walked into the dirty bar-and-restaurant with the driver.

"Yeah?" the bartender asked, looking suspiciously at the odd-

237

looking woman in the long white dress and then at the shirtsleeved cabdriver.

"A double brandy for me, please," Ann said.

"Make mine bourbon."

"Double?" the bartender asked.

The driver looked at Ann and Ann nodded. "Both double."

She drank all the brandy without stopping, and it burned going down and made her throat feel raw. So different from the White Rock and ice cubes in the drink that afternoon . . .

The driver tried to be friendly. "It's none of my business, lady, but you look like you've had some kind of shock."

"Yes, I have. But I'm better now. Let's go." She put down two bills, and the man tossed off the rest of his drink. They got back into the cab and she began to cry, silently. Because she refused to let herself go, she hurt down deep where the suppressed sobs tried to originate. She was thinking now of everything at once—the past, the present, the future—as they pertained to John. He had never meant to come to the banquet with her, he'd had other plans all along, and he'd tried to throw her off the track by talking of Madge as he did. *Do you think I think she's attractive?*

He *had* thrown her off the track, all right, because she'd believed him, while all the time he had it figured out. *"Let me meet you at Birdie's and Abe's when it's over."* He'd taken it for granted Bill and Bess would take her straight to Birdie's, and *"The sooner the better,"* she'd said.

She had rejected the screenplay work because it meant more to her to be with *him*—to have things exactly the way they used to be. She'd been so sure of herself when she refused, so sure of him, and even as she was turning down the offer, he was up there laughing, playing with Madge in the same hotel. Well, by God! She'd take their job now. She had said she couldn't be happy in California, but after tonight she could be a hell of a lot happier here than in New York.

"Is this the place, Miss?"

"Yes, right here. Just go up the driveway to the door. I'm all right now." She was far from all right, but she was considerably better and she gave the driver a ten dollar bill. "Keep it. And thank you so much."

238

The driver obviously wanted to say something and wondered if he should.

"Cheer up, lady," he said reassuringly as he started to drive off. "Whatever it is, believe me, it ain't worth it."

The front door was open. She could hear voices in the living room, especially Bess's, laughing at something funny and she knew she would have to talk with them for a minute before she could be alone.

"Ann? Is that you?" Birdie called as the screen door slammed.

"Yes." She walked into the room where they were all sitting. Birdie, Mother, Bess, Bill, and John.

John?

She stood there unsteadily, facing the group, stupidly staring at him.

John!

"Did Abe get in touch with you?" asked Birdie. "He had to go into town on business, so he said he'd call you and bring you home in the car."

John . . . Abe.

"We're having the most wonderful honeymoon," Bess cried. "John's giving us a sales talk on Niagara Falls!"

"Are you *here*?" she asked in a pinched voice that could not be hers.

She could see John sensing something was wrong and he came across the room and put his arm around her.

She didn't look at him. Her glazed eyes stared ahead of her. Her neck was bent forward and her shoulders were hunched, as though she were instinctively warding off a blow.

"John," she pleaded, "*John!*"

The gay mood in the room died completely as Bess ran to her. "Why, she's hysterical, she's—"

"I'll get a cold cloth," Birdie said excitedly.

But John was already half supporting, half leading her up the stairs to her room. He made her lie down on the bed and then lay down beside her, holding her to him, repeating softly, "I'm here. I'm here, my darling."

Like the recoil of an overwound spring now she began to sob

239

violently, unable to make any effort to control herself, and he held her, tenderly patting, whispering assurances, soothing her as he would a child until finally she fell asleep, exhausted.

He continued to hold her in his arms for a long time, there in the still room overlooking the garden.

"Does it have a happy ending?"

Booksellers have to be authorities on happy endings. Hardly a day goes by that someone doesn't ask Hazel Watts, "Does it end all right?"

Hazel keeps wondering about that question after the store is closed, sometimes when she's supposed to be asleep. Is there really and truly such a thing as a happy ending? Isn't just being an ending enough to make it sad?

Well, isn't it?

23

THE telephone rang and Hazel Watts answered it. *"The Heart Being Hungry?* Yes, we have *The Heart Being Hungry."* Pause. "$4.50." Another pause. "In *paperback?* Oh no, it isn't *in* paperback. It won't be available in paperback for at least a year." Short pause. "You're *welcome!"* She slammed down the phone with a vengeance. She would have kicked it if it was in a more convenient spot for kicking. "Those damned paperback calls," she said to Mabel. They're getting worse. Anyone who tries to make a go of the book business these days ought to have his head examined."

"You've just got the June jitters," Mabel said. "We're fifteen per cent ahead of '61 and last month was the biggest May we ever had."

"No wonder. We had Ann Long's autographing party. I dread to think of next May. We'll never meet this year's figures."

Mabel laughed. "You're already complaining about next year's business. Be thankful we're doing well now. There'll be something next year. There always is."

Hazel grinned sheepishly.

"I'm ashamed of myself," she admitted. "I've never had it so good. The landlord's paying for the new air-conditioning system. I'm able to send Angel to Europe with the Wellesley Tour. And I've got you around to remind me to count my blessings." She thought for a minute. "But I still wish those paperback phone callers would go to hell."

The phone rang.

"Let me get it," Mabel said, answering the extension phone near the front of the store. She called to Hazel. "It's for you. Long distance from California."

"California? I don't know anybody in California who'd call me long distance." Mabel replaced the extension phone as Hazel picked up the receiver. "Hello."

242

"Is that you, Hazel? This is John Long."

"My God, Johnny. Are you all right?"

"I'm just fine, Hazel. Got a customer?"

"No. Mabel and I're just gabbing."

"Then carry the phone to your office and sit down at your desk. You might as well be comfortable."

She put her hand over the mouthpiece and said to Mabel, "It's Johnny Long. He's lost his mind." She took the telephone into her tiny office, set it on the heap of bills, letters, order sheets, and book review pages which overflowed, cornucopia-like, from the small desk-top. "Okay, Johnny, I'm sitting down. Don't beat around the bush. Tell me what you need and I'll get it to you."

She heard him laugh. "I don't need anything. I was just homesick for the sound of your ole soothin' southern drawl and I happened to open the phone book to the page of long distance rates. It costs only three bucks for three minutes person-to-person from Los Angeles to Dallas."

"I'm not worth a dollar a minute—even if Laverty and Clarke is paying."

"Laverty and Clarke my eye!" John said. "I'm paying, and I consider it a bargain."

She was beginning to settle down. Long distance calls made her nervous and when she placed a call she always told the operator to let her know when the three minutes were up, but John sounded perfectly relaxed, so she relaxed, too. "Sober, Johnny?"

"Absolutely. Sober, happy and back on the beam. Laverty and Clarke paid for the call yesterday—when my boss and I made a deal. I'm going to be his sales manager."

Hazel was loving this. Loving it. She leaned her elbow on the desk and placed her head against the receiver. "Then I'm your first customer, so try to sell me something. Anything. I'll take a hundred. Make it two hundred. I'll even say yes to a sequel to Milk in the Sky."

John was laughing hard and she could see him. Wherever he was sitting, he was perched on his tail-bone with his long legs propped up on a desk or chair or table.

Her voice grew serious. "Does your new title mean no more traveling?"

243

"Are you kidding? A good sales manager's got to keep in touch—and I don't mean by letter. Seeing you and the others is part of the deal."

"How's Ann?"

"She's been sick. Gave me the scare of my life. Passed out from exhaustion."

"I could see it coming," Hazel said. "How is she now?"

"Fine. Still a little weak, but the doctor says she can go home. We're leaving this afternoon." He paused. "Hazel—"

"Yes, Johnny."

"It's all right now. Everything's all right. I kinda thought you'd like to know."

She could tell she was going to cry and she was furious at herself. "I'm glad, Johnny. Real glad." She rapidly pulled five pieces of Kleenex out of the box, one after the other, blew her nose into them and then asked, "Did all hell break loose the way you thought it would?"

"Yes. All hell broke loose—but that's how it had to be."

"You're sweet to call this way," she said softly. "It means a lot. I've been bitchin' 'round all morning—tell Ann they're already wanting her book in paperback—but now I don't feel bitchy any more. You're a good friend, Johnny. Ann's a good friend, too."

"You were her favorite of the whole trip," John said. "And some day she's coming down there with me but first, you and Angel're going to visit us in New York!"

"I just might do that," Hazel sniffed. "I just might meet her in New York when her tour gets back from Europe. *Hey,* this is costing you a fortune!"

"Just one minute more. Never had so much fun for a dollar a minute. Angel—in Europe?"

"Yes. She left Tuesday. She's turning out real nice, Johnny. Pretty and smart, just the way I hoped. Got a half dozen boys on the string."

"And how's Mabel?"

"She's—she's all right."

"Goodbye, Hazel. Be seeing you in a couple of months."

"Goodbye, Johnny. Thanks for calling. Goodbye."

Hazel hung up, pulled out some more tissues, wiped her eyes,

244

blew her nose, carried the phone out of the office to its regular place and said to Mabel, "Johnny sends his love. He'll see us soon." She felt serene, happy, right with the world. At the sound of the telephone, Mabel said, "I'll get it," but Hazel said, "No, *I've* got it." She let it ring two full times, then answered. Her voice was crisp, proprietary—and ready.

Ann sat on the squeaky glider near the pool. There was a breeze, and the sun had not yet become hot. A perfect day, she thought— the kind of June morning that makes Californians insufferable when they try to describe it to strangers. Tomorrow at this time she'd be in New York remembering it—wistfully, maybe, but not really wishing she was still a part of all this.

There was something final about this day. It was more than the end of the autographing tour and the end of her trip. It was really the end of her book. Until the day at Baker's and the night of the banquet she had still been writing it and she hadn't known how it would end. Endings were tricky. They rarely went according to plan and they hardly ever were altogether happy. *"Tell me, Mrs. Long, does your book have a happy ending?"* The ending that satisfies the reader is not always satisfactory for the author but what- ever this visit to California had cost her, it was essential to the real resolution of her book. It had taken all that had happened to prove she wasn't jealous of Madge. She had been jealous of Mona—and now, finally, she was convinced that Mona existed only on paper. Madge King was a real person, all right, but Ann did not envy her. The ending had been bought with distrust, shame and physical shock, so it was at best a bitter-sweet one, but most happy endings are ambivalent, anyway. So many times, the ending that's happy for one person is unhappy for another. She sighed. This feeling of finality was a relief, because she knew now at last how her book really ended. Happy, unhappy, or both—being sure it was finished was a consolation.

Lorraine, who had been swimming and playing in the water, came over to the edge of the pool near Ann.

"Is he really and truly gorgeous, Aunt Ann?"

"Who?"

"Rock Hudson."

245

"Well, I wouldn't call him *gorgeous*. He's very nice-looking. And very polite."

Lorraine mooned. "If I ever had him as close as you did I'd ask him to marry me."

"What if he was already married?"

Lorraine thought for a minute, then turned in exasperation. "Aunt Ann, you can think of the *awfulest things!*"

Abe walked onto the terrace. "Hello, Ann. Feeling better?"

"Good as new. Sit down."

"Don't mind if I do." He sat next to her on the glider. "Lorraine, your mother's in the garden cutting flowers. Go see if she needs any help."

"Okay, Daddy." Lorraine pulled off her swim cap and ran toward the garden, her red hair catching the sun. As soon as she was gone, Abe said, "Poor kid. She's glad to have something to do to keep her busy. Since Raymond's gone to camp she feels left out. She'll go, too, next week, thank goodness."

Ann leaned her head against the back of the glider and pushed her toes to make it rock slowly.

"I've got to get that squeak fixed," Abe said. "It gets on a person's nerves."

"I've become rather attached to it."

Abe looked at the sunlight reflected on the water. "I wish you two weren't leaving today."

"I know you mean that, Abe. I don't have to tell you how much I appreciate all you've done for me—'in sickness and in health!'"

"That's what I want to talk about. I'm the only one who knows why you got so sick all of a sudden."

She had not wanted him to bring this up. She had purposely tried not to think about Abe. Not for a while anyway.

"You must think I'm a pretty big heel," Abe said hesitantly.

"No—"

"Yes, you do. You don't let on but I'll bet anything you've told yourself you'll never stay in this house again."

Ann was surprised at his perspicacity. Only this morning, the last day, she had wondered if she could ever bring herself to come back to Abe's house. Aloud, she said, "Don't be silly, Abe."

"Ann—"

246

"Yes."

"It was the first time I was ever tempted to—" Abe couldn't finish the sentence. "You know what I mean."

He had such a hangdog look Ann hastened to say reassuringly, "I believe you."

She doubted if Abe had any idea how formidable his temptress was.

"I love Birdie. You know that, don't you?"

"Of course."

"I don't want you to think I run around all the time."

"I don't, Abe." She didn't, either.

"If I hadn't gone with you that day I might have stayed on the straight and narrow for life, you know."

Ann thought fleetingly it was unfair of him to intimate that any part of his lapse was her fault for insisting that he come that day—but then wasn't she partly to blame? She had forced the holiday upon him and been secretly happy when he'd risen to Madge's lure, so consciously or unconsciously, she had used him as a decoy to keep Madge away from John. Just because a decoy hadn't been necessary, did she have the right to be surprised that she had let him be used for one? Was the deep peeve she nursed against Abe really a justified one—or was it a transference of her own self-disgust at what she'd thought about John?

"I'm a family man—" Abe was not a talker, and what he was saying now wasn't easy for him.

Suddenly she thought: what did Abe do that I'm not equally guilty of? We both made a mistake and we've both been hurt. He can talk about his mistake to me, but I don't talk about mine to anyone.

"I'm glad you said these things, Abe. I really am."

"You know there's nothing between that woman and me, don't you, Ann?"

He was so contrite that she thought he was going to cry. She had been too hard on Abe.

"Now, let me see," she said. "Weren't you the gentleman who just a week ago was considering book departments as sidelines in his Full-O'-Fashion Shops? 'It's a wonderful business!'" She nudged him.

247

Abe grimaced. "You've got a memory like an elephant," he said, taking her hand and holding it affectionately. "I think I'll stick to costume jewelry."

"What are you two talking about?" Birdie asked, walking to where Ann and Abe sat. Taking it for granted it could be nothing of importance, she began fanning herself with her hand, saying, "It's hot out here in the sunshine." She was wearing a large-flowered print cotton dress; her hair was pinned up, Irish-washerwoman fashion, and her nose mirrored the sun. Birdie was the picture of contentment. *Too much so*, Ann thought.

"I was telling Ann goodbye," Abe said. "She and John will be on their way when I get home tonight, but I'm making her promise they'll come back soon."

"And I'm practically naming the day," Ann said cheerfully. "It's your turn now, though. When're you two coming to New York?"

"Oh, gosh, I'd love to go to New York again," Birdie said dreamily.

"Maybe this fall, then," Abe said, and suddenly something about the idea appealed to him so much that he added, "We'll do it! As soon as school starts we'll go. We'll see the good shows and eat in a different place every night. How does that sound, Birdie?"

"Oh, Abe. Do you really mean it? What about the kids?"

"They're not babies any more. We've got plenty of help. Your mother . . ." He got up, leaving his mother-in-law suspended. "Well, I've got to be going. Goodbye, Ann."

"Aren't you going to kiss me goodbye? or will I have to kiss you?"

He knew he was forgiven. He kissed her and then hesitantly threw her another kiss before going into the house.

Birdie sat down on the glider in the same place where Abe had sat and Ann noticed that the squeak was louder.

"I hate anything that squeaks," Birdie said pettishly.

"You're in a twit today," Ann said. "Calm down."

"It's because you're going. I want you to stay longer."

"Well, you heard what Abe just said. You'll be in New York in four or five months and then we'll have fun together."

Birdie sighed. "I can't make Abe out. Every time I've even sug-

248

gested a trip he changed the subject. Now, all of a sudden *he* suggests we go to New York this fall. Isn't he sweet?"

Ann nodded. "Sometimes I think we all take Abe too much for granted."

"It takes so little to make him happy."

"That's true, but—" She was carefully laying her mine field. "Sometimes men get tired of being taken for granted and do strange things. You know, Birdie, Abe's still a relatively young man, and—"

Birdie looked at her sister. "Ann, you don't *think*—?"

Ann nodded solemnly. "I think it about *all* men, dear!"

"Oh. Well, yes, I *guess* so."

"Sure. A woman has to keep toeing the mark, even with the man she loves." Ann knew she was sounding like an advice columnist. "Now, you take Bess. She's always aware of Bill—always trying to please him. But what if she starts taking him for granted? Starts letting herself go? Do you think she'll be able to hold onto him long?"

Birdie rocked for a moment. Then she asked, solemnly, "Do you think I'm too fat, Ann?"

Ann acted surprised. "Don't ask me questions like that on my last day."

"Why not?"

"Because if I say you're not too fat, I'll be lying to be polite, and if I say you are you'll be angry with me when I leave."

"No. I won't be angry. Tell me the truth. I am—ain't I?"

Ann laughed. "Remember how Mother used to boil over when we said 'ain't'?"

"Mother isn't here now, so, I am, *ain't* I?"

"Yes, you are, Birdie. You're getting a middle-age spread and you're not even middle-aged. It's easy to put it on—but oh, it's murder losing it!"

"I've lost weight before." Birdie said. "I can do it again."

"But your idea of losing weight is to stay on bananas or buttermilk for ten days—and then when the time's up, start eating again and gain it all back. You've got to diet all the time, Birdie."

"When you see me this fall I'm going to be twenty pounds lighter," Birdie said fervently. "Starting today—no bread, no potatoes, no desserts. I'm going to be awful to live with for a while,

249

but the kids will be in camp and Abe'll be gone all day and Mother's been itching to fight with me anyway, so it'll all work out fine."

She rocked earnestly, contemplating her new figure, and the glider squeaked.

Ann walked into the bedroom and found John on the floor, bouncing on the big suitcase, trying to close it. It lacked a full two inches of shutting, even on his downward thrust. By contrast, his own bag was standing nearby, perfectly packed and gracefully slim. "What in *the* hell did you put *in* here?" he asked, accenting the words to coincide with the bounces.

"Let me help," Ann said, sitting on the bag with her back flush to his. "When I say three we'll both bounce together. One . . . two . . . *three!*"

On their mutual bounce there was a definite, rewarding click.

John got to his feet and gave her a hand and when they looked down at the bulging case they both laughed. It had an uncomfortable, forlorn look.

"It's bloated and ridiculous," he said. "Like a woman, nine month's pregnant."

Ann changed the subject. "Think of the excess we'll have to pay. How much do they allow on a plane? I forget."

"Forty pounds," John said. "It's got that many on each side." He spied a belt she had forgotten, folded it quickly and slipped it into the back pocket of his trousers.

"Let's take one last swim," he suggested. "I'm sweaty after that wrestling match."

"I want to talk for a minute," Ann said.

"About what?" He tried to lie down on the chaise longue, overflowing the end of it with his surplus leg length. "I swear this is the most annoying piece of furniture I ever saw," he said, and sitting up straight and looking at her he repeated, "About what?"

"About me." *Is there a delicate way of saying it?* Ann thought, *I'm no good at this,* and went on, "I'm pregnant. Not nine months —just one." She could see John's total, slow surprise and realization as she kept on talking. "I half diagnosed it myself. The doctor confirmed it, and I loved the way he put it: he said I had a classic condition peculiar to women." *Don't just sit there without moving,*

250

she thought, *do something,* and said aloud, "Well, aren't you going to jump up and down or at least let out a war-whoop?"

But John Long did neither and there was nothing classic about his response. He just said softly, "I'm sorry I made that remark about the suitcase."

She walked over to him and looked into his face. "Sure you're not sorry about anything else?"

He looked at her.

"*Sorry?* No. A baby's just what we both need. I was petrified you were going to announce you were pregnant with another book."

She laughed. "You're really glad, aren't you? I can tell."

He held her in his arms. "Yes, I'm really glad. You know what I did this morning? I called Hazel Watts and told her I was going back to work. I didn't know then I was going to have a child to support, and I'm glad I didn't. For a while at least it's nobody's business but our own and we're going to keep it to ourselves."

Ann's mother caught the last words as she walked into the room. "You're going to keep *what* to yourselves?"

"Hello, Mother," Ann said. *Be sweet to her. She's your mother.* "John and I have finished packing and he wants to go for a swim. I'm glad you're here. Please tell him for me that I packed our swim suits on the very bottom of that swollen suitcase."

"No!" John protested. "You see Mother? You have an irresponsible daughter." The minute he said it he wished he hadn't.

"I know it," Mother agreed enthusiastically. "That's why I came over here this morning in a taxi. I had to talk to you both before you left today—about something very personal."

Ann couldn't say anything. *If she announces she's moving back to New York, we're moving to Tahiti,* she thought.

"It's about the money," Mother said. "The money from the movie people. I read about it in the papers. I'm afraid you'll do something foolish with all that money. I'm worried sick about it."

She actually looked worried sick.

"The money's safe, Mother," John said. "It's in the bank and we're not going to touch it."

"I want Ann to promise that," Mother insisted.

Mother's staying in California. We get to keep New York all to ourselves. Promise anything.

251

"I promise," Ann said.

Mother seemed relieved. "I feel a lot better," she said. "Now," she began brusquely where she'd left off earlier, "you're going to keep *what* to yourselves?" She waited. *"What?"*

D o you, dear reader, ever feel "had" when the type suddenly stops and only white space remains? The last word of a book is so hopelessly final. You can't say you've been tricked, exactly, but you do feel more than a little empty. You close the book and you feel like a person walking alone through the airport to the parking lot after waving a plane goodbye.

So let this be the last page and the one before it merely the end of the telling. (The story itself goes on and on, even though we've finished reading. Ann, John, Bess, Bill, Hazel Watts, even Dr. Darnell continue to live chapters you'll never read.)

This really-last-page shan't be about the story nor the people. It will say to the reader what every author wants to say but can't. It may even soften the shock of so much white space.

Thank you.